Chapter 1	1
Chapter 2	9
Chapter 3	15
Chapter 4	25
Chapter 5	35
Chapter 6	41
Chapter 7	45
Chapter 8	53
Chapter 9	61
Chapter 10	71
Chapter 11	75
Chapter 12	79
Chapter 13	85
Chapter 14	89
Chapter 15	95
Chapter 16	101
Chapter 17	111
Chapter 18	117
Chapter 19	127
Chapter 20	131
Chapter 21	135
Chapter 22	139
Chapter 23	143
Chapter 24	153
Chapter 25	161
Chapter 26	165
Chapter 27	173
Chapter 28	179
Chapter 29	189
Chapter 30	195

Chapter 31   205
Chapter 32   213
Chapter 33   219
Chapter 34   229
Chapter 35   241
Chapter 36   249
Chapter 37   259
Chapter 38   269
Chapter 39   279
Chapter 40   289
Chapter 41   295
Chapter 42   307
Chapter 43   313
Chapter 44   321
Chapter 45   327
Chapter 46   333
Chapter 47   339
Chapter 48   345
Chapter 49   355
Chapter 50   359
Chapter 51   369
Chapter 52   375
Chapter 53   381
Chapter 54   387
Chapter 55   399
Chapter 56   405
Chapter 57   409
Chapter 58   423
Epilogue   427

Free Bonus Epilogue   439
About the Author   441
Also by Sylvia Hart   443

One

"It was a dark and stormy night..." Wait, no. Far too cliché. Looking around the parking lot of the Neptune Inn, the cheap motel that I'm staying at tonight, I sigh. It's tricky to write when the weather's like this.

Definitely nothing that's supposed to be romantic. Even though pouring rain is probably my favorite weather, it doesn't lend itself to writing the romance I want to. It makes me crave cuddling up with a book... or a hot guy. You know, if I had one.

I slip my laptop into the brown and teal crocheted bag I picked up at a flea market for under a dollar during college. Bits of yarn have come unraveled; it's just hard letting something unique go. That doesn't mean it's the best laptop bag. Especially when a storm is rolling in and already drizzling. Yarn and water just don't mix when it's supposed to be protecting my computer.

I sling the backpack that holds all my traveling clothes over my back and shove my laptop bag under my shirt. It probably makes me look lumpy and troll-like, but that's never stopped me before.

Raindrops splatter on the pavement as I do my best not to slip while running to the motel office. I can already feel the rivers dripping down my hair by the time I get to the door, sending chills through me. At the same time, I can't help smiling. There's something about cool summer storms that transport me to a scene from a novel.

Inside the office isn't from a book, though. Unless the hero chose this hideout just so no one would look for them here. The steady whir of a box fan spins, and strands of dust hang like streamers in front of it. Constant drips from above fall into an empty paint bucket, and mildew stains ring the ceiling it's coming from.

As the door closes, I expect a bell or beep to sound, but it just clunks loudly, sounding like two pots being banged together.

"Here you go. The keys to the honeymoon suite." A skinny guy wearing a shirt probably two sizes too big slides them across the counter. Sporting an always-in-style porn-stache, he's perfect for this classy place.

The honeymoon suite? But that's the room I reserved. Maybe they have two? I can feel the dismay stirring in my stomach. No chance the Neptune Inn has more than one "suite".

The man standing at the counter nods at Pornstache, and for a moment, I'm yanked out of my current situation as he turns around. He's freaking hot. Not cute guy at the mall, hot. No, this guy is "I get paid to look pretty". And somehow, even though it's pouring outside, he looks as if he just got out of his fancy closet, complete with a personal stylist.

How's it legal for any man to have hair like his? Soft waves that fall almost down to his shoulder as though he wasn't trying, but we all know he probably spent an hour getting it that way. Dark brown with enough highlights and lowlights that I'm not entirely sure whether it's dyed to perfection, or he was just born with perfect hair.

There's nothing unusual about what he's wearing. A nice pair of jeans and button-down shirt. With the sleeves rolled up, showing his hulking arms. Arms that could hold you in place even while you're collapsing…

Get it together, Addison.

He catches me as I'm staring at him and his lip curls up. "Boy or girl or… alien?" he asks and looks down at my stomach.

I follow his gaze. In my stupor, I've twisted the bag so that it's bulging in weird places.

"Robot," I say without a second thought and pull out my laptop bag, which sends the hottest guy in the universe into laughter.

"Is that knitted? Aren't grandmothers supposed to knit hats and sweaters?"

I look down at the brown and teal bag I love so much. And I nope out of this conversation entirely.

Rather than respond to him, I walk to the counter. "I have a room reserved for Addison Adelaide." His eyes go to the damp sweater I'm wearing, which is beginning to cling to me, and he grins.

"Eyes up here, buddy."

The smirk widens, but he says nothing, thankfully. Turning to the computer, he squints for a moment. Then he frowns and looks back at me, and I know that Mr. Sexy definitely took my room.

"Well, it seems like there was some confusion…" he says.

I sigh as I realize that what should have been a simple night is quickly turning into a miserable one. "You gave my reservation away, right?"

With a serious face, he looks at his screen, then back at me.

"We're booked up, but we have a room we can't rent that you could use. If you promise to give the motel a good rating on Yelp, I can hook you up with it for free."

"Why don't you use it? Will I get bed bugs or something?

The clerk just shrugs. "I don't know. An issue about noisy pipes, I think. Does it matter? They filled every room in the county for the annual Snake Tour of America this weekend."

Snake Tour of America? What the hell is that? And how is my luck bad enough to be road tripping to New York during it?

4

"Fine, I'll take it." The clerk, whose name tag reads Jeffrey, gives me a grin and slides a key to me. Not a keycard. An actual key with a huge metal keychain that looks like a trident, complete with sharp points at the ends.

I swipe it off the counter, and he says, "You're in room twenty-seven, and don't forget about that Yelp review. Some assholes complained about the A/C being out and one-starred us. Business has been down because of it."

"Was the air conditioning out?"

Jeffrey raises an eyebrow. "Yeah. Why does that matter?"

I simply don't have words. The middle of summer with no air conditioning sounds unbearable. I simply shake my head and turn to walk out the door. Mr. Sexy's still watching me, and I give him a slight wave as I walk past.

"If the secret torture room doesn't work out for you, I hear that the honeymoon suite has an extra-large king-sized bed. I'd be happy to share with you."

Right. Of course he would. "I think my last resort is sleeping in my car, not your bed."

"I'm in room twenty-five, so it's directly beside yours in case you reconsider."

That won't happen. As I walk out of the office, I notice the rain has died down. I can't stop thinking about the Snake Tour of America. Is that really a thing? Is it big enough to fill up every hotel and motel in the county?

As twenty-seven comes into view, a leaflet is stuck to the entrance about, you guessed it, The Snake Tour of America. I don't have time for that. I need to crawl into bed and pass out, and I pray that nothing else goes wrong.

When I open the door, it looks mostly normal. Dusty, but not a big deal. I set my bags on the table along with the leaflet before locking the door behind me.

A sigh slips out as I peer at the bed. I've been driving for the past twelve hours, coming from Kansas City. If the floor was my only option, I'd take it.

At least when I pull the blanket back, the sheets look clean. Without giving myself a chance to think too hard, I go to my bag and grab my sleep clothes. A pair of comfortable booty shorts and an oversized white Captain Morgan t-shirt I won in some contest while at Kansas State.

My eyes are heavy enough that I'm worried I may pass out before I can even brush my teeth. As soon as the water comes out of the faucet, I decide my teeth don't need to be brushed that badly.

It sounds like an old man is groaning above my head as the water runs red.

What the hell!? Was Mr. Sexy right? Is this the freaking torture room?

Moments go by, and the water turns normal. I see tiny flecks of red in the sink. Looking closer, it all makes sense. It's not blood, as my exhausted brain immediately went to. Bits of rust stick to the sink. I guess that "loud pipes" really means rusty pipes, and I make a mental note not to use the water anymore.

Rather than thinking about it. I head straight to bed, feeling even more exhausted than I was before. Sitting in the parking lot for twenty minutes and trying to begin another book was a mistake, even though I had great ideas during my extended drive. I should've just checked in. Then the honeymoon suite would've been mine instead of this torture room.

I wouldn't be this tired and been unable to shower in the morning.

At least I'm going to get some sleep. That's the important thing. When I lay down in bed, it's surprisingly comfortable. Probably because the bed's older than I am. I just sink into the mattress, and it feels like heaven.

As soon as my head hits the pillow, my eyes close. It takes no time before I'm in the middle of a perfect dream that definitely doesn't star Mr. Sexy dancing in a thong. Absolutely not. Plus, three-minute long dreams don't count.

Because that's how long I'm asleep before the pipes scream and I'm sharing the bed with the ceiling.

Two

It's too bad the woman from the lobby didn't want to take me up on my offer. It's been a long time since I was around anyone who didn't know who I was. Phillip Loughton, heir to the Loughton dynasty.

That's really why I'm here, though. A quick road trip out of the city is exactly what I needed. A chance to see the world from the other side. To experience something different from the sanitized world I've lived in for so long.

When you're the heir to a multi-billion-dollar fortune, you don't do things like climb trees as a kid. Instead, you learn to play piano or sit next to your father at his publishing house, learning all the things that make the machine run.

My brothers lived a different life. Mason made it clear from a young age that he had no interest in the family business. Andrew was interested, but he was always the baby, and no one really expected anything out of him. No, all the weight rested on my shoulders.

Until recently, I welcomed it, for the most part. The responsibility still doesn't bother me. I'm not afraid to run Loughton House Publishing when my father retires. It's that I've lived this life for so long, and I need something new, something to let me find that spark of life again. I don't know if spending time as an average Joe is the answer, but I can't just fade away as just another cog in the machine.

I may be the command center of the machine, but I'm just as much a part of it as any other employee. Probably more so.

That's why I rented a car and just drove. I needed to get out of New York, away from everything I know. I ate at a terrible diner this afternoon halfway between Pittsburgh and Philadelphia. Just like in the movies, I tried a piece of apple pie. It was... not something I'd do again, but at least I can cross that off my list.

Now I'm sitting somewhere west of Pittsburgh at the Neptune Motel, and I'm reconsidering my decision. Even the wallpaper is covered in dust that's probably older than I am.

At least it's something new. Something other than the same boardrooms, the same hotels, the same offices. Truthfully, I feel like I'm having my first real adventure, even if that adventure includes dust that witnessed the moon landing.

Before I can even sit down at the rickety table and have a beer to wind down, I hear a boom and crash, followed by a scream coming from the opposite wall. The one that I share with that woman from the lobby.

I'm on my feet and out the door on instinct alone. The screaming continues and for a split second, I remember the joke I made. The torture room.

But I don't hesitate at all. Leaning my shoulder against the door, I shove as hard as I can, and the door slams open, the doorframe shattering.

The woman is in bed with an enormous piece of the ceiling laying on top of her and water flowing like a water-fall from a broken pipe above her head. I rush to her, and I don't even think she's recognized that I'm in the room with her as she struggles to get the piece of ceiling off her.

Straddling her legs, which stick out from under the drywall that's on top of her, I heave and toss it to the side of the bed. She looks up at me, gives me an odd look and then climbs out of bed. I follow, now completely soaked from head to toe as the water covers the floor and bed.

"I locked the door," she says, more than a little out of breath. It's a good thing that the door was as shitty as the rest of the motel. My gaze goes to the first thing that I notice, and it definitely isn't the drywall mud she's covered in. Her white shirt is completely soaked, sticking to her chest and outlining her breasts. She might as well not even have it on with how transparent it's become.

"I broke it down." God, she's fucking beautiful. Even covered in drywall mud and soaked.

She glances at the door then and sees it barely hanging onto the hinges. "Well, I don't think that I'm giving them a five-star."

I chuckle and meet her gaze. "I don't think there's anything about this place that's worth five stars, but being physically assaulted by the building takes it to a whole new level."

"Facts," she says and shivers. I guess that she's finally coming out of the shock because she looks down and immediately covers up. "Jeez. You could have told me you could see my tits."

I can't help but laugh. "That would have meant that I'd have seen them for at least a few seconds less."

"I'm going to change." Without waiting for an answer, she grabs some clothes off a table and goes to the bathroom. My eyes follow her ass while she stomps away. I'm not entirely sure if I should just leave her alone or if I should stick around. Another look at the door tells me that there's no way in hell that I'm going to leave her alone.

After only a few moments, she's walking back into the room dressed in the same outfit she was wearing earlier. "Just so you know, it's pretty standard practice to let a girl know if her tits are on display and she doesn't know it. Since you literally broke down a door to save me, I'll let it go this time."

"I guess that's fair. My name's Phillip," I say as I put my hand out.

She takes it and says, "Addison." She looks back at the waterfall that we've mostly ignored for the past few minutes and sighs. "I guess I should tell Mr. Jeffrey why he wasn't supposed to rent this room. And maybe that there's currently a small pond in it."

"What are you going to do now that your room has transformed into the motel pool?"

She frowns and shrugs. "I don't know. I guess I'll drive around town and try to find another one. Or maybe just sleep in my car. To think I actually did the smart thing and reserved that room, yet I'm still stuck. How unlucky does a person have to be?"

A grin crosses my lips. "You *could* be very lucky. I have a stupidly oversized bed that you're more than welcome to share with me. It's heart-shaped, so you know it's nice."

Her chin falls, and she glares at me. "Sorry Phil, but I'm not that kind of girl. I make it a point to learn a guy's name at least two hours before I crawl into bed with him, if you know what I mean."

"I'm offended that you'd think that was what I meant after I literally saved your life from an aggressive motel room. Did you notice how the ceiling was groping you?" I say, pretending to be shocked.

Addison smirks, and I continue, "But seriously, you're in a bind, and I have a bed big enough to fit four people. We can even make a little wall out of our luggage. Though, I wouldn't complain if you slept in that other shirt…"

She purses her lips and shakes her head, and it almost looks like she's considering it. "No, I think that I'll go look for another room. I've already had a room attempt to murder me. There's a very good chance that with my current luck, you'll be an axe-murderer, and this whole thing is all just a big setup for an unsolved mystery episode."

I chuckle and turn away from her, but before I get out of the room, I stop. My hand rests on the broken doorframe, and I look back at her. "If you change your mind, you know where I'm staying."

She smiles and nods to me.

I take one last look at Addison before walking back to my room, feeling more than a little bothered by how hopeful I'd been at the prospect of this complete stranger sleeping in my bed. And I had meant what I'd said. No strings attached sleeping.

Well, even if Addison isn't staying with me tonight, at least tonight's been something different. I've had my adventure, but somehow, spending time with her would have been more of an adventure than any freak accident could be.

Three

ADDISON

SON OF A BITCH. JEFFREY THE CLERK HAD BEEN RIGHT. Every single room in the whole town was taken, each of them talking about this ridiculous Snake Tour of America. Now I'm sitting here shivering in my "dry" clothes with the heater on, feeling very much like a nearly drowned mouse.

The storm is only getting worse, and I can barely see through the downpour, so I can't even just get on the highway and drive for another hour. That's why I'm sitting in the freaking Neptune Motel parking lot at ten o'clock trying to convince myself that Phillip is not an axe-murderer.

Because the prospect of sleeping, or other things, in his bed is sounding better and better. "Fuck it," I finally say. If I'm going to die to a serial killer, at least he's hot.

I grab my laptop bag and backpack before sprinting across the pavement to room twenty-five. My heart is pounding out of my chest as I knock a little too quietly. I don't know why I'm hesitant. Other than the whole serial killer possibility, of course.

Then the door opens, and he's only wearing a pair of athletic shorts. Big surprise that he has rippling abs and pecs that look like they're carved from stone. Part of me, the exhausted part, is tempted to reach out and just run my finger across them to see if they're real or just some kind of optical illusion. "Did another room try to murder you?" he asks with only the slightest smile.

I look down at myself and realize that I really am just as wet as I was after the roof caved in on me. "The whole world is trying to murder me tonight…" I mutter, and I guess he hears it because he starts laughing.

"Well, come in out of the rain. I thought for sure that you'd found another place to stay." He turns around and walks toward a cheap table with a chair still pulled out.

I get a look at his back, which is just as ripped as the front, and I decide that I definitely made the right decision coming back here. He offers me a seat and says, "I was about to open a beer. Do you want one?"

God, a beer would be nice. Maybe not as good as the boxed wine and sprite that we had in bulk back in college. Then again, maybe I shouldn't take a drink from a complete stranger. That's mistake number two of too many murder mysteries, and I already flew past mistake one by deciding to sleep with Phillip.

I should just accept that I'm going to end up in a basement somewhere being told to put the lotion on the skin.

"Let me open it," I say, trying to get the best of both worlds.

Phillip gives me a side-eyed glance before going to the mini-fridge, which I'm kind of surprised still works. "Do you think I'm going to roofie you?"

With a shrug, I say. "I have very good kidneys according to my doctor. I'd like to keep them."

He just laughs as he pulls two beers from the fridge. I look at the one he hands me and frown. "I've never even heard of this brand. Are you some kind of beer connoisseur who's going to tell me to sniff it first?"

"Hints of raspberries in coffee," he says with a straight face as he hands me a bottle opener.

I squint and try to imagine a beer with raspberries and coffee flavors. I'm not sure if I hate it or love it. "Are you being serious?"

He snickers and leans back in the chair, the legs lifting into the air just a little, and I'm reminded of my nana yelling at me when I used to do that as a kid. "I don't know. Maybe you should sniff it."

Bringing the beer to his lips, the smile never leaves them as he watches me. Screw it. I pop the cap and put the beer to my nose. Fucking raspberries in coffee, just like he said.

I really can't believe it, and instead of responding to what I'd originally thought was sarcasm, I take a sip. Who buys beer that smells like raspberries and coffee? And what the hell does it actually taste like?

17

Phillip sets his beer down as I stare at him, the flavors washing over my tongue, and I just don't have words. It's thick and frothy and very "beer-y", but at the same time, it's creamy and stout and infused with raspberry coffee— which is a little strange to begin with.

"Not a bad stout, is it?" he asks, and I can hear the beer snob coming out in him. Yet, this time, I can't quite come up with something sarcastic.

"I… Alright, this is definitely better than what I'm used to."

There's an air of confidence to this guy that I'm not accustomed to. He's sitting there without a shirt on, drinking with a complete stranger, and the thing he's worried about is whether I like my beer.

"Are you going to change or sleep in that?" he asks after another sip.

I look down at the soaking wet sweater and cringe. Underneath it is a tank top and bra that are dripping. I want to slap me from yesterday who packed everything except the one outfit and some sleep clothes. "Who cares how much of a troll I look like when I'm moving? I'll just grab some new clothes when I get there…" Idiot.

The sleep clothes are also soaked completely, something Phillip has already seen. That leaves me with the only options being shivering all night or sleeping naked, which definitely isn't happening.

"I don't have any dry clothes, so this is it. Better to be wet in a bed than in the car, right?"

Phillip's lip twitches, and I realize my mistake. "There are definite benefits to being wet in bed…"

"Are you twelve?"

He chuckles and finishes his beer. My eyes follow him as he stands up and walks over to a suitcase made of fancy leather. There's not a single scuff mark on it, and I question what kind of single guy has luggage that nice.

The zipper slides down the side, and he pulls out a silk button-down shirt. "Here. You can wear this if you want." He gives me that questioning look, and for a moment, I hesitate. Staying in a guy's room is weird, but almost understandable in my situation. Drinking his beer is very acceptable, especially when it's raspberry coffee beer. But wearing his clothes? That's a whole new level of uncomfortable. I didn't even wear my ex-boyfriend's clothes.

But it's that or shiver myself to sleep.

"You sure?" I ask.

He nods and comes back to the table. "I'm all out of clean pants, so you'll have to make do with your own on that end. Or, you know, don't wear any. Up to you."

I bite my bottom lip as I take the shirt from him. Another drink of the beer, and it's gone, and Phillip is already heading to the giant heart-shaped bed. I have to hold back a shiver as I see him bend over to pull the blanket back. He may not have another pair of pants, but I might share those with him.

Stop it! Why am I like this? I don't know anything about him other than that he's hot and likes to drink fancy, weird beer. I am about to be a junior editor with Loughton House Publishing, and a professional like that does not act like a feral cat in heat just because a hot guy bends over. Even if he seems to be as much of a gentleman as any girl could hope for.

I shake my head, trying to get a hold of myself, before grabbing the worn backpack. On my way to the bathroom to change, my heart beats a little faster when I notice Phillip watching me from the bed. I shut and lock the bathroom door and try to get my breathing under control. Leaning against the wall and taking slow breaths, I do what I can to ignore how turned on I am.

It may look like the perfect start to a murder mystery, but everything I've seen from Phillip makes me think he's about as dangerous as a teddy bear. Just a quiet guy who's trying to help a girl with the worst luck in the world tonight.

But there *is* something that makes my knees weak when he looks at me like he just did. I don't know why, but when he was watching me, it was like he was seeing through my clothes. I felt so vulnerable to that stare, and for the first time, that vulnerability kicked my libido up to eleven.

Brushing it off, I step away from the wall. It doesn't matter since tomorrow morning we'll part ways and never see each other again after a long night of no hot and heavy touches. No midnight scenes from a steamy romance novel. Just a night of sleeping in wet booty shorts and a random guy's silk shirt in a heart-shaped bed.

My clothes are off in a flash, and I grab a towel from the stack on a shelf to dry myself off. I'm still cold, but at least it feels like I might warm up, eventually. When I wrap myself in Phillip's shirt, it envelopes me. Soft silk against my skin is like the whisper of a caress, and it gives me goosebumps.

And the scent on it is far deeper than I ever expected. Dark and complex, like that beer of his, I can't place what it reminds me of. Something woodsy? Smokey? There's a strength to it, but a gentleness as well.

Don't ask me to explain how a shirt can smell like that. When it's buttoned up, I look at myself in the mirror and am surprised how much I enjoy wearing it. I glance down at the backpack, knowing that I need to get the booty shorts out. They're still soaked, but hopefully they'll dry quickly enough.

Because there's absolutely no way I'm going to crawl into bed without bottoms on. I dig through the soaking wet bag, and when I pull the shorts out, a steady stream of water runs from them onto the linoleum floor.

When I'm done wringing them out, they're still cold and very damp, but it's as good as I can hope for. I feel like most of the night has boiled down to that phrase. *It's as good as I can hope for.*

I'll just pray that when the sun comes up tomorrow, my luck will have changed at least a little.

My teeth grind together as I pull the shorts on. My whole body shivers immediately, and they stick to my legs like a swimsuit, but I finally get them all the way on. I try to pretend like I just got out of a pool, but wearing Phillip's shirt keeps me from ever feeling like that's a reality.

Nope, I'm just a chick in a stranger's shirt and some very damp shorts. When I step out of the bathroom, Phillip's dark eyes are on me immediately. "I think that shirt looks better on you than me," he says, his voice soft and smokey. God, he's sitting up, his head against the rickety head-board, and the blanket is pulled down to his waist. If I didn't know better, he could be naked under that blanket. The more I think about it, the more I wonder which I'd prefer.

"Nice try, Casanova. If your next line is 'It'd look even better on the floor', I will promptly ignore it and steal the covers from you."

He chuckles and shrugs. "Can you blame a guy for telling the truth? I can't remember the last time a more beautiful woman came out of my bathroom wearing my shirt."

"Laying it on pretty thick, don't you think?" Even though I was shivering seconds ago, I can already feel myself warming up.

He just gives a little laugh and lays down on his back before picking up his phone. Somehow, even when his eyes are clearly on his phone, I feel like he's staring at me, and it sends a thrill through me.

"Want me to turn out the lights?" I ask.

He looks up from his phone and glances around the room. "Sure."

I start clicking off the many little switches on the lamps around the room. When I glance back at Phillip, I catch him looking at me, and that warmth inside me turns molten. I wasn't just imagining it. He's been watching me this entire time.

A new kind of shiver runs through me as I climb under the blankets. Turned away from him on my side, I stare at the wall, waiting to see what happens now that I'm in bed.

"Night, Addison."

That's all? My body feels like it's on pins and needles, waiting for his hand to brush my exposed thighs or the small of my back through his shirt. I'm not sure how I'd respond, but the anticipation is killing me.

"Night," I say, and the light next to his side of the bed switches off, leaving us in darkness.

Minutes pass, and nothing happens. No movement. No brushing fingertips.

My eyes stay open as I wait for the inevitable. I'd seen staying with Phillip as the beginning of a murder mystery initially. But now? Well, I can't believe that he's just going to let me go to sleep.

And then I hear him softly snoring next to me. He was telling the truth about no-strings-attached sleeping? Maybe he's gay? But those comments…

My mind races through the possibilities other than the obvious one. That he actually wanted to help a girl who'd stumbled into a series of unfortunate events. It seems so impossible to fathom.

As happens so regularly, I hyper-fixate on a single thought, and it leads me to passing out.

That thought? *What I would do if Phillip ran his hand under my shirt.*

Four

ADDISON

MONDAY MORNING AT A NEW JOB IN A NEW CITY after the most bizarre weekend I've had in a long time is a strange feeling. The movers dropped my stuff off Sunday afternoon about three hours after I got to my new apartment in Brooklyn.

Then, after ordering pizza and picking up a bottle of wine from the convenient store down the street, I passed out. Because guess what? I had to wake up extra early so I could figure out how to get to work, which is not nearly as simple in New York as it is in Kansas City. Subways are a little less intuitive than driving my car to work.

Luckily, I only missed my stop twice on the way this morning. Now, I'm sitting on the bench outside of Loughton House with a coffee and breakfast sandwich, enjoying the warmth of dawn.

My car's sitting in its five-hundred-dollar per month parking spot, and probably won't be used again for quite some time. My crocheted laptop bag is at home, along with the ragged backpack I used to carry my basic essentials on the road trip. Both of them are still drying out in my bathroom.

Being a junior editor at Loughton House means I have to be a professional. There are expectations. And one of those is the dress code. Business casual at a minimum. Business formal when giving presentations.

I feel stiff in the light blue blouse and black slacks, but I want to be taken seriously. This is the beginning of my dream coming true. Even when I was little, I wanted to spend my life around books. Worlds made of words that rival the best daydreams. Characters that make you wish they were your friend or maybe even a boyfriend. Ones that you feel connected to in ways that normal people just don't compare to.

Loughton House is at the very center of that world. There's a very real chance that I'll get to meet some of my favorite authors. Hell, I could even edit some of them eventually. How incredible would it be to help coax an author's vision into something truly wonderful and unforgettable? I may dream of being a world-famous romance author, but the reality is that most people never make it.

I glance down at my phone. A quarter after seven. Still early when I'm supposed to start at eight, but not so early that the doors will be locked. Well, I guess it's time to embrace the beginning of my childhood dreams actually coming true.

Well, shit. That was fast. I'm staring down at my new official work computer that has an unedited manuscript pulled up.

I'd expected to go through some training or orientation. Maybe that's just because I'm used to the college timeline. The first day was just getting familiar with things. I guess that at Loughton House, they just throw you in the fire and see if you can handle the heat.

At least I know what I'm doing here. Just read it, and get it edited to perfection. Turn this unknown author's ideas into something beautiful. How hard can it be?

As I start to read, I hear a giggle from directly behind me, and I turn to look up at a girl wearing the most unusual "business casual" that I've ever seen. A pure white dress with a black corset top over it. White flowers have been embroidered over the corset, pulling the outfit together. Her hair's tied up in a bun, a pencil holding it together, and wispy strands of her blond hair fall over her cheeks.

"You know it's only eight, right?" she asks, leaning against the cubicle wall behind me where another desk is facing the opposite way.

I frown at her. "That's when the workday starts, right? Did I miss something in the non-existent orientation?"

She laughs and sits down on the desk, crossing her legs in the same motion. "You're Addison, right? The new junior editor?"

I nod and turn in my chair. "That's me. Is that your desk, or do you just stop by random people's cubicles in the morning?"

"It's mine, and I make it a habit not to start work before I've had time to get in the right mood. Which means two cups of coffee at a minimum." She hops off the desk as fast as she sat down and crosses the short distance between us. "My name's Sera. Well, it's actually Seraphina because my mother is a nut job, but I go by Sera."

Alright. That's a lot of oversharing from someone I met thirty seconds ago. Trying to stay at least slightly professional, I say, "Nice to meet you, Sera."

I stand up to shake her hand, just like all the YouTube videos told me to. She gets a thoughtful look on her face for a second, which makes me feel more than a little awkward. "Come on. Time for coffee and gossip."

I glance back at the computer screen showing the manuscript that's still on the first page and then back at Sera. I feel like I'm supposed to get to work. That's what James Pritchard, the lead editor-slash-very-serious-boss, told me to do, but Sera doesn't give me a chance to think about it.

She just grabs my hand and pulls me away from the desk toward the break room, ignoring my mumbled objections. She's probably the reason that people have safewords. Maybe I should yell pineapple or red?

A very loud feminine voice says from the doorway we're approaching, "Nope. There's no way I'm seeing Chuckle-Fuck ever again."

What kind of madness did I step into?

"Look Victoria, you don't have to enjoy it, but you have to do it for me. I am living vicariously through your antics, and you have not provided me nearly enough chaos in the past few weeks with the single exception of Chuckle-Fuck."

We step into the break room, and two women are leaning against opposite counters, coffee cups in each of their hands as they smile and turn to see us.

"Who's the new girl?" asks the tall, blonde woman who I now know is Victoria. She's the kind of woman you imagine working in the business world. Every inch of her skirt-suit is perfect. Her nearly platinum hair falls just below her shoulder, with little curls that seem to cling to each other.

Sera drags me to the center of the room and presents me like some kind of debutante. Or maybe a sacrifice. The looks the two women give me don't give me a lot of confidence that it's the first.

"This is my new cubicle-mate, Addison. Junior editor extraordinaire. At least I hope so, since she's in charge of doing the edits on old Jefferson's new attempt at inspiring the nation's youth into revolt."

The second woman sighs. "I can't stand Jefferson's books. How he ever got signed is still beyond me, but they just keep publishing them. My condolences for any excitement you may have because that book will kill it. Then it'll roll your dead excitement into a pit and set it on fire. Or at least that's how I feel every time I open one of his manuscripts."

I grin at the shorter woman who is possibly the very definition of soccer mom. Granted, she's still wearing business casual, but her red hair's a bit of a mess, and unlike Sera and Victoria, she's wearing flats that have a few scuffs. She looks tired in a way that all parents do, even though she's grinning.

"Nice to meet you Addison. I'm Trish, the official office hooker."

I blink at that comment as Sera and Victoria burst out laughing. "That's an… interesting job title," I say.

She gives me a chuckle. "I'm a senior editor, but I specialize in hooks. When other editors know that a section, especially the beginning, needs a little something to draw the reader in, they call me. Hence," she grins and points at herself with both thumbs, "official hooker."

I can't help but laugh alongside the rest of them. "Anyway," Victoria says, turning back to Trish, "there's no way I'm going to see Chuckle-Fuck again. And that's final."

I still don't understand this conversation. Sera stops them and says, "You can't just leave Addison out of the conversation like that." She turns to me and says, "Victoria went out with a hot guy last week." Immediately, Victoria has her phone out and is scrolling through pictures. My eyes follow her movement, but I'm doing my best to pay attention to Sera at the same time.

"They hooked up, and right when he was finishing…" Sera continues.

Trish interrupts. "He chuckles like freaking Seth Rogen." She bends over, puts her hands on the counter and looks behind her—something I wouldn't have imagined happening on my first day at the most famous publishing house in the world. "Just imagine that. Oh, that's it, baby. Harder. Then, instead of grunting, groaning, or moaning, it's just this goofy laughing from behind you."

It's impossible to hold back the laughter. Maybe it's the crassness and hilarity of the moment, but all the stress I've felt for the past three days just evaporates as I laugh. Maybe working at Loughton House won't be as serious as I'd imagined.

Trish continues, "I'm going to write a romcom one day just based on Victoria's terrible and amazing love life. It'll be like the hot chick version of Bridget Jones's Diary."

Victoria just shakes her head. "You know, Addison's first hour here shouldn't involve my terrible love life. She's going to think *I'm* the official office hooker when I'm really just terrible at picking men. How could I have known that this guy would do... that?"

She shows me her phone, and there's a selfie of her and a guy who could have been in a movie. Maybe not as an action hero, but at least the goofy sidekick who's actually cuter than the main character, even if he can't lift a car. Like a Paul Rudd. Great smile, gorgeous eyes, and probably way nicer than the hero.

"Okay, yeah, I don't think I'd run away from him."

She holds her hands out and looks around the room. "See, even the new girl doesn't think I'm crazy. How can I just be that unlucky?"

Trish looks at her for a second, and her lip curls up.

Then, she just slowly starts chuckling, and all of us burst out laughing again.

"You're the worst friends," she says as she slides her phone into her purse and grabs her coffee. "I get no support from any of you."

As she walks out of the room, Trish calls out, "I'll support you and Chuckles forever. Please!"

It's hard not to keep laughing, but I feel like I should go apologize to Victoria. These three seem to have been friends for a long time, and none of them are rushing to tell her sorry.

Sera catches my eye as I glance at the door again and says, "Don't worry about Victoria. She knows that we're all just playing." She glances at Trish with a grin and says, "You should have been here the time that Trish walked into the break room with a giant chocolate stain on the back of her skirt."

Trish's grin turns into a glare. "Three-year-olds are supposed to eat the chocolate, not smear it across Mommy's ass when they give her a hug. It's not fair that I can love someone whose entire purpose is to cause chaos. Absolutely not fair at all."

Sera takes over the conversation then. "Victoria was ruthless. What was it she called you? Oh, right…"

"Good morning," an annoyed and tired man's voice says from behind us, interrupting Sera. A voice I feel like I know, but I can't place.

Trish stiffens immediately, and when Sera glances at the door, the smile fades immediately. I don't want to turn around, don't want to find out who caught us goofing off on my very first morning.

But I have to know, and I slowly turn around. The man standing in the doorway is the last person I'd expect to see here. Hell, he's the last person I'd expect to see anywhere.

Wearing a ten-thousand dollar suit and leaning against the wall, Phillip from the motel that tried to kill me is looking at the three of us like we're children who just got caught trying to make pudding on the kitchen floor.

Until he sees me. "Addison?"

Five

PHILLIP

I DIDN'T THINK I'D EVER SEE ADDISON AGAIN AFTER our bizarre night together. A night that meant more to me than I think anyone would expect. It was the first time I've felt that spark of life. True chaos that made me feel alive in a way that my everyday life just can't.

Even in college, it was so similar to my everyday life. The classes were easy versions of working with my father, which I'd done since I was three. The people knew who I was and everything revolved around my ability to help them either with money or influence. I may have used that to have a bit of fun back then, but the excitement of being a tool to be used goes away quickly enough.

But Addison didn't. Nothing about that night was fake or sanitized. I've dreamed of what might have happened if I hadn't walked out the door before she woke up that next morning.

"Phillip?" she says, just as surprised at seeing me as I am at seeing her.

Seraphina, one of our better cover artists, glances from her to me and back to Addison. "You two know each other?" she asks.

"Yeah," Addison says. "He stole my room at a motel."

I can't help but grin thinking about that night. "You mean you tried to steal mine and failed, right?"

Addison clenches her jaw and glares at me, not saying anything for a moment. Trish, one of our most senior editors with a penchant for hooking readers, steps away from the counter. "Well, time to get back to work."

That's how everyone at Loughton House talks when I get near them. I have a bit of a reputation in the office these days for not putting up with laziness or stupid excuses.

Seraphina gives me a fake smile and walks past me, following Trish. I ignore them both. "You work here?" I whisper.

She nods. "Today's my first day." Gone is the sarcasm and lightness from our chaotic night together. She looks like she's going to treat me exactly the same as the rest of the office does. Short, simple answers to my questions.

"Phillip Loughton," she murmurs, and I see the puzzle pieces click together in her head. "You're the oldest Loughton." It's an accusation, as though being one of four owners of Loughton House is something that I should be ashamed of.

"Well, my father is, but I'm his oldest son." I can't stop staring into her eyes, but it's all the little things about her I'm registering. The stray brown hair that hangs over her left eye that's so reminiscent of the way it hung while she was sleeping in the heart-shaped bed.

How her pale green eyes reveal all her emotions, regardless of what the rest of her does. They're burning bright right now, and I wonder what she's keeping from me.

She presses her lips together—beautiful, kissable lips. "I need to get back to work. It's my first day, and I doubt my boss will be thrilled if I spend too long loitering in the break room."

She tries to push past me, but I step in front of her. "Let me take you to lunch. Wherever you want." It may just be a coincidence that she's working for me, but that night left a mark on me. I've spent so much time trying to find that spark of life that I felt with her on Saturday night. I don't know if it's her or some other piece of that night, but I need to find out.

She shakes her head. "I think I'll pass. I don't think going to eat lunch with my boss's boss's boss is the way to convince people I'm a brilliant editor."

Without waiting for my response, she squeezes between me and the doorway, sliding past me with no trouble, and I turn around to watch her walk away.

But I smile as she walks back to her desk. We're not at a shitty motel anymore. This place is mine, and I don't think that she understands that yet.

Addison is still on my mind as I sit across from a senior editor. This one's name is Jeremy, and he's been with the company for almost five years. There's a grin on his face, pearly white teeth showing, and he has absolutely no idea why he's in my office.

"You're fired," I say quietly, but in the silence of the room, it booms. It's a bit of theatrics that I've perfected over the years. After firing hundreds of people since I was seventeen, I've learned a thing or two about how to do it.

"What?" The look on Jeremy's face goes from excitement to horror in half a second. It's not uncommon.

"You're fired. You can pack up your things after you fill out your paperwork, and then security will escort you outside."

He still looks confused and horrified. He'd expected to receive a promotion. In fact, his promotion is the reason he's here in the first place. It happens regularly. A manager suggests I look over his file to see if he'll be a good fit for a promotion, and in the process, I discover something that I can't ignore.

"But why? What'd I do? The last book I edited received accolades from nearly every major reviewer it was sent to."

I smile grimly, hating the fact that I have to do this. Maybe someone enjoys watching weak links in their teams have their careers destroyed, but I never have. Which is why I assume the responsibility of doing it. But business is business, and the weak links have to go.

"We have a system here, Jeremy. You're not a bad editor, and I'd be happy to give you a recommendation to any other publishing house, but you're not capable of being a lead. In fact, I don't think you'll ever be. Your edits were mostly fine, but there were consistent problems that reviewers mentioned repeatedly."

He sinks even lower, knowing exactly what I'm talking about. "Your dialogue was weak, and it's been weak in nearly every book you've been tasked with editing. You could have asked for someone to run through some of the weak spots with you, but you didn't. You've never asked for help, and turning a draft into a bestseller is a team effort."

Jeremy interrupts, but I put up my hand. "Your last two yearly performance reviews have mentioned your inability to utilize your team. I don't have time to deal with someone who won't change their habits to better benefit the authors and company they work for."

He stares at me blankly as I slide the termination paperwork to him. "Sign the blank at the bottom, and then you can go to your cubicle and collect your things. I'm sorry that it had to come to this, but Loughton House is not in the business of teaching the basics of teamwork."

His hand moves mechanically, pulling the papers and pen to him. He signs it without a word and hands it back to me. I've seen this happen too many times not to know what it is. Shock. He'd expected to get a promotion, and now he has to worry about how he's going to pay his mortgage. How he's going to feed himself or pay for the vacation he promised his girlfriend.

None of those are my problems, but I can't help but take some of that on my shoulders. Anyone who doesn't shouldn't be managing employees. I may have thousands of people under me, but I do my best to make sure that I do what I can for every one of them. The fact that I review all of their files before any of them are promoted or fired is just one facet of that effort.

I tear his carbon copy off and jot down my phone number on the side before sliding it back to him. "Jeremy, if you want a recommendation or some help in finding a new position, let me know. You're a good employee. You're just not a good fit for Loughton House."

Jeremy nods and picks up the pink sheet of paper, his fingers holding it limply as though they don't want to touch the cursed page. He stands up and walks toward the door, but stops halfway there. He turns around, a broken smile on his face. "Thanks," he says. "I'll take you up on that." And then he walks out the door.

I hate this part of my job, but I'm good at it. Like so many other pieces of my life, the only thing that matters is how well I do them. Not how much I enjoy them.

Six

ADDISON

THAT SON OF A BITCH. I STARE INTO THE TINY CLOSET of my apartment that holds two office-appropriate outfits, about ten days of non-office wear, and a single silk button-down shirt. I woke up on Sunday morning after a night filled with dirty dreams about a man I knew only as Phillip.

And he wasn't there when I woke up. The only proof he was real is the shirt I wore that definitely wasn't mine.

I run my fingers over the fabric, remembering the way it felt against my skin. The soft sensuality of wearing a man's shirt. His scent is still on it. My body melts just thinking about it, and I step back, away from the closet, and I close the door, hiding the proof of that moment.

God, why did he leave the next morning? I'd woken up hoping to get his number at the very least. I'd have loved to spend a wild morning with the man that wasn't just hot and funny. He'd gone out of his way to help me without expecting anything in return.

That's not something you find often. After hearing about Victoria's terrible experiences, it just reinforced the thought of the man who might have been perfect.

Now I meet up with him again, and there's no way in hell I could ever do anything with him. He's my boss's boss's boss. He runs the company that is literally my dream job, and I certainly won't be jeopardizing my position there. One night's fantasy versus a lifelong dream becoming real? The right decision is pretty obvious if I look at it like that.

That doesn't mean that it doesn't piss me off, though. I'd have loved to get lunch with him. Or dinner. Maybe at his place. Hell, now I know that he's not just hot and funny and a gentleman. He's also a freaking billionaire.

I kept myself focused on work all day long, but now there's no way I'm thinking about anything else.

Until I get a text from Sera.

SERA WYLDER

Come drink with us. We're at The Drunken Goat, and it's karaoke night.

Oh, that's definitely not what I need to do on a Monday.

Too tired tonight. Rain check for Friday?

Drinks are on Trish tonight. They're on
you on Friday.

I let out an audible sigh. Should I go drinking with people from work on a Monday night? Absolutely not. I'm exhausted and there are so many reasons to just fall into bed.

Looking around my tiny little undecorated apartment leaves me feeling like the responsible answer isn't necessarily the right one. I'm all alone in New York City with no friends or family. I don't even know where to get groceries or how to get them back to my apartment.

Making friends might be more important than hiding from a hangover. Plus, I could just have one drink, and it wouldn't be a big deal...

Fine. Send me an address so I can catch
a cab.

Seven

PHILLIP

"Where were you this weekend? You didn't answer anyone's phone calls."

My father, Russel Loughton, the emperor of Loughton House, sits across from me at the shiny boardroom table. Except we don't have a board of directors. It's just me and my father while Andrew is off in London, heading up the new branch.

I lean back in my chair, the front wheels rising just a little off the ground, a familiar feeling settling over me. We've been in this same position countless times, me in this chair while my father chastises me about something. I look up at the man who built an empire no one could topple based on something he cares so little about.

Books are not Russel Loughton's pastime. Hell, I still don't know if he has one other than chewing my ass and making money.

Standing across the table from me, he's an imposing image. For a man in his sixties, he stands tall, a remnant of a bygone time. I've always thought that he was built with the same stuff as the truly great titans of industry. The Rockefellers, Carnegies, and Vanderbilts. The men who built this country's backbone off the labor of their employees.

White hair covers his head, neatly combed and styled, but without any flair. His suit is a flat charcoal gray, and his shoes shine as though they were brand new. He's not even looking at me, instead facing the wall that constantly shows our most recent releases and quarterly projections.

I was supposed to be his protégé and, more importantly, the heir to his empire. Where Andrew fell into his position in the company because he had nothing else, I've been sitting at my father's side since I could walk. I was the sacrificial lamb for my family, the one who would hold my father's eye every day so that the rest of them could do what they wanted. It was a position I was proud of.

"I wanted to take a break from everything. There weren't any major releases. No interviews or signings. For the first time in months, everything was quiet, so I took the one chance I had to get away from everything. I needed a change of scenery." Little does he know I spent three months making sure that nothing happened this past weekend.

He finally turns to look at me, utter confusion on his face. "Why? I understand taking a vacation, but I tracked your company card expenses, and you ended up in fucking Pennsylvania. If you're trying to hide hookers from me, then that's a little excessive. Just pay cash and don't let them know who you are."

I can't believe he just accused me of driving eight hours to have a party with prostitutes. "Father, I didn't get hookers. I needed to get away from New York. I didn't want to be Phillip Loughton for a few days. For once, I didn't want to have to act a certain way or get treated like I was a Loughton. I just wanted to be normal. Even in some hole in the wall in Pennsylvania."

My father looks disgusted, and I wonder if I should get a trashcan as he puts his hand on his stomach. "Why the hell would you want to be normal even for a minute? I've spent my life trying my damnedest to give you and your brothers a life that the rest of the world could only dream about. What's the fucking point of all of this if you're just going to vacation at some shithole in Pennsylvania?"

I know I should just appease my old man. I should just accept the criticism and tell him I learned my lesson and that he's right. But I've spent my life being criticized, and I'm tired of it. How is it any of his business what I do on my own time? Once again, he's making this about him, and that's bullshit.

"I've spent my life sitting in this boardroom, sleeping in mansions or five-star hotels, and eating food that costs more than most people make in a week because that's what I'm supposed to do. That's what you taught me to do. I've never done anything just because I wanted to. And this weekend, I just wanted to drive a normal car to a normal place and sleep in a normal bed somewhere that no one's even heard of me. I appreciate everything you've done for us, but it shouldn't be some kind of insult to you for me to sleep in a cheap motel."

He turns away from me, and I can hear him sigh. "You couldn't make it a month in the real world, so why even bother thinking about it?"

"Why not? All the employees do. Hell, nearly every person on the planet does. You may not think I can do anything right, but one day you're going to retire, and this place is going to be mine to run as I see fit."

He turns on me then, his hands coming down hard on the boardroom table, and he snarls. "You'll be able to run Loughton House just fine. I've spent your entire life making sure that you will. But you can't even boil water. You may be capable of running a publishing empire, but Phillip, you're as ready for the real world as a six-year-old."

I've always accepted my father's lectures. I've always matched his anger and ferocity with passivity and calmness. It was ingrained in me from the moment I came to this building and sat with him when I was three and my life learning to be his successor began. But something happened this past weekend. Something snapped inside me. I can't just accept things anymore.

I jump to my feet and snarl right back at him. "I'm not a child anymore, and I'll do whatever the hell I want in my free time. Whether you approve or don't, it doesn't really matter."

Father's fuming. No one talks to him like this. No one stands up to the man who has made and broken countless people's careers and futures. I know that if he wanted to, he could cut me out of Loughton House, just like he did with Mason.

But he won't. Like he said, he's spent my entire life, thirty-two years, making sure that someone was here to hand Loughton House to. I may be his oldest son, but his favored child will always be Loughton House. No matter how much I piss him off, as long as I don't endanger his darling business's future, he'll still be depending on me to take care of it.

He glares at me, anger mixing with what I assume is an unexpected emotion—powerlessness. I can't remember a time that he didn't have an answer to a problem, and he definitely sees me as a problem right now. But what's he going to do?

Then something happens that fills me with a sense of dread. He smiles. That's the last thing I'd expected. Here in the silent boardroom, it's like the world takes a breath, holding it so that a pin dropping would sound like an explosion.

My father's whisper destroys that silence like an atomic bomb. And my confidence along with it. "Fine. I can't stop you, and my only real recourse is to yell at you, which obviously does nothing. If you're so damned set on being normal, then quit fucking around with it. Shit or get off the pot, boy.

"Stop being a tourist in their world and go live that life. I'm sure that you'll come crawling back in a week, and I'll be here with the fortune I've built for you. Just to give that statement some teeth, I'll make a deal with you. If you can not only survive, but thrive, as a normal worker bee for a month, I'll stop worrying about your desire to live like a peasant.

"Maybe living like them will give you some perspective. Maybe you'll finally get it out of your system. Then you can come back and focus on what matters instead of this stupid infatuation you've had for so long."

I know this is a trap since he wouldn't be smiling if it weren't, but I can't figure out where I lose in this deal. He's giving me permission to step back for a month. Even when I went to college, I never had time to live outside of Loughton House. I was expected to take care of my coursework and then spend my free time here so that when I graduated, I'd be ready to step in as upper management.

This will be the first time that I'll have any real freedom. A whole month of doing exactly what I've been desperate to try. I'd be an idiot to pass it up.

"Deal." Instinctively, I put my hand out to make the arrangement binding. Just like he taught me from childhood, a handshake is all that's required of a Loughton. Other people may back out of deals, but our name is built on an integrity that the rest of the industry only flirts with.

He takes a long look at my hand, considering whether he's making the right deal with me. Russel Loughton is a confident man, but even he has to admit that I'm the only person who knows a negotiation as well as him. He's taught me to be his equal, and no matter how many times he treats me like a child, he knows that I'm the man that can carry the torch when it comes to Loughton House.

"You're sure about this?" he asks, his smile gone now that it's come to brass tacks.

I nod, feeling no need to say anything. I'm desperate to experience something other than Loughton House. Anything. Even if it's harder than I've ever known.

As he takes my hand and gives it a shake, he says, "From this moment until August 15th, you are no longer the Director of Publishing with Loughton House. Since I'm not a monster, I'll let you continue working here so you don't have to experience genuine desperation. You'll be a junior editor making the typical starting pay."

He pulls his hand back and says, "Give me all your debit and credit cards. I'll set up a new card for this little experiment where your pay will go."

I pull my wallet out. This is exactly what I wanted. How hard can it be, anyway?

As he takes away all of my access to my and my family's fortune, he pulls out a handful of money from his wallet. "Here's five hundred dollars. Make it last. You may need a second job to make ends meet, but that's on you to figure out."

I take the money and slide it into my wallet. "So do I just go home?" I ask as Father turns away from me.

He laughs and doesn't even bother to face me. "What home?"

Eight

ADDISON

THE DRUNKEN GOAT IS A DIVE BAR, BUT IT'S PACKED tonight. Like an outdoor Applebees, it's filled with people that come from all walks of life. A true middle-class bar that probably has more middle-aged soccer moms than drunken college students. Strings of lights hang from trees around the "stage", and a light breeze carries away the scent of spilled beer and cheap wine. It's the kind of place that would be right at home back in Kansas City, and I'm surprised that it's survived this long in Brooklyn.

"Wait, you slept in the same bed as Phillip-The-Frozen-Loughton?" Sera asks as I sip on my third Long Island.

I shrug. "He was a gentleman," I respond, not wanting anyone to think too terribly about the man that I might be both fantasizing about and pissed at.

Trish smirks, and I'm quickly realizing that she's not exactly the most professional friend I could have. "Did you cuddle after he took the hot dog bus to Taco Town?

Or was he just a gentleman because he didn't fire you afterward?"

I nearly spit out the Long Island. "There was no bus to Taco Town. Plus, he didn't know I was going to work for him. It was pure happenstance, and he offered to let me sleep with him after my room literally tried to kill me. Did you miss the part where he saved my life?"

"I wouldn't be surprised if he rented out every room in the city just to make you suffer," Sera says with more than a little venom in her voice. Why do Trish and Sera dislike Phillip so much? I'm just pissed that he's my boss and I can't do anything with him.

"What's wrong with Phillip?" I ask.

Trish laughs. "He's fucking ruthless. Two weeks ago, he cut a lead marketer because he didn't meet his projected numbers. This wasn't just some guy who'd been around for a few months. No, he'd been with Loughton House for ten freaking years."

Sera gives Trish a side-eyed look. "Yeah, but I don't think anybody actually shed tears over Roger getting the boot. He was creepy as fuck. Do you remember the whole dress code 'suggestion'?"

Trish cringes and shivers. "That's true." She turns to me to explain it. "See, the marketing team is basically a combination of advertising and business-to-business sales. They convince companies to endorse and carry books. There's very limited space on bookstore front windows, and the marketing team works to get our books there."

Sera picks up where Trish started. "Yeah, and Roger's grand idea when their success rate fell was to convince that side of his team to show a bit more skin. Specifically, he didn't allow women to wear pantsuits and suggested lower cut tops."

I thought that of all the businesses in the world, the publishing world would be the best for me. It would be filled with people that loved the same things as me. I guess that there are rotten apples in every business.

"How'd he keep his job for that long if he was such a creep?"

Trish glances at Sera who says, "Because he never officially broke a rule. He just made it very obvious that he preferred to work with young women who liked to flirt. They always moved up faster. Everything was documented, and no one could find any actual reason to fault him, but it was impossible to miss."

"So maybe it was just Phillip cleaning house?"

Trish shakes her head. "Phillip doesn't care about anyone, much less who gets promoted. He cares about results, and Roger's results were good for a long time. Then they weren't, so he got fired. That's the problem with Phillip. Not that he fired a creep, but because he let that creep keep his job until he started underperforming."

That doesn't make sense after spending the night with him. He didn't seem like a robot who only cared about numbers. Hell, if he didn't care about people, then why would he go to the effort to help me out? I chew my lip while I try to process it all. "It just doesn't make sense. He seemed like such a good guy, you know?"

Trish grins and sucks down her Cosmo before standing up. "Well, my turn," she says.

Sera and I glance at the screen above the little stage. "Total Eclipse of the Heart" by Bonnie Tyler is showing on it.

That's the thing they didn't tell me before I showed up at the Drunken Goat. It's not only karaoke night. They're requiring me to participate, and my song comes on after Trish's.

"Remember that you have to do the spin," Sera says as Trish walks toward the stage.

She glances back at us with a grin. "Girl, if I don't do the spin, you might want to make sure someone's not impersonating me."

Sera laughs, but I just feel a ball of stress building in my stomach. I'm next, and though I've had my fair share of karaoke nights, today was literally my first at a job I want to be taken seriously at. Now, I'm about to make a fool of myself in front of the first people who were willing to talk to me.

I suck down my Long Island and wave a waitress over to get me another one. Since it seems like there's no way around this, I'm going to need a drink when I'm done. A strong one.

Trish looks completely confident on stage. Fiery red hair brushed back into a ponytail. Wearing a bright red dress that makes her look like she belongs on a stage, the office hooker looks more at home here than she does at work, even though she's been with Loughton House for years.

"Who started this stupid tradition?" I ask as the intro plays from the speakers.

"Oh, this is all Trish. She's been at Loughton House for two or three years longer than me. My first day, she hauled my ass out of the office to this little shithole of a bar. She did the same with Victoria and a few others you haven't met. After she convinced me to do this, I told her we had to convince all the new hires to do it, too."

"But why?" This is ridiculous. And why the hell does it have to be a terrible 80s song? I wasn't even born when this song was popular."

Sera just laughs as Trish belts out the words to "Total Eclipse of the Heart" as though she's auditioning for America's Got Talent or something. I have never, in my entire life, seen someone go so all-out in karaoke. She's moving along the stage like the thirty other people in the bar are paying to see her.

And when it's time for the spin, she does not disappoint. I don't think she even glances at the lyrics. This is a song she knows by heart.

"I'm not doing that," I whisper.

"Me neither," Sera says in agreement. "Nobody else does either, just so you know. This is a Trish thing."

We watch Trish make the most of her moment on the stage. When the closing lines hit, she makes her final spin and collapses to the stage, her flowing dress moving out around her like she knows exactly what she's doing.

The crowd erupts in applause as though they *had* come here to see her perform. Sera and I join in as well, and it's just such a weird thing to do at a karaoke night. When

Trish bows and walks down the steps to come back to the table, it's such a weird vibe.

"How am I supposed to follow that?"

The screen hanging behind the stage changes to Europe's "The Final Countdown" and my stomach tightens.

Sera stands up with a grin on her face. "You aren't going to follow it. We are." She walks between the tables as confident as ever, and I have to hurry to catch up.

"I thought I was doing this song?" I whisper.

She winks as we get on stage and pick up the microphones, not bothering to respond. The familiar electronic beat starts to play and Sera's head nods in rhythm with it.

She's grinning and laughing as we stand in front of the lyric box like there isn't a crowd of people staring up at us. I try not to think about them, and as the first few lyrics start, I do my best to keep from passing out. They say that more people have a fear of public performances than literally dying, and right now, I completely understand.

But Sera doesn't seem bothered by it, and it's hard not to feed on her energy as she belts out the intro. By the time the chorus hits, I'm singing just as loudly as her. When the next set of lyrics appears on the screen, a hand reaches between us to grab a mic, scaring the shit out of me.

I glance behind me and see Trish grinning as she sings along with us. For just a moment, I actually forget about the audience and embrace the energy of being on stage with Sera and Trish. The terrible 80s music just reinforces it as the speaker pumps out electronic beats that almost beg you to forget that you're a terrible singer.

It's chaos, but it's chaos with two people that genuinely want to be happy. That want me to be happy. Nothing at all like what I'm used to. Nothing like the life I left when I came to New York City.

And I love it. As "The Final Countdown" comes to a close, I glance at the two women who were strangers this morning, and I realize that maybe I'm not so alone anymore.

"We're going to have to do this more often," I whisper as we walk down the stairs.

Trish and Sera just grin as we sit down at our table. The song may be over, but as they talk about random topics, I realize that maybe this whole initiation thing makes sense. When I'd shown up here this evening, I'd felt like they were strangers, but after just that one song, it almost feels like they're actually friends now. How the hell does singing a song together do that?

Nine

PHILLIP

I was a billionaire yesterday. Now I'm a three hundred and seventy-two dollar-aire. The five hundred dollars definitely will not last me all week, and that's even if I sleep in the cheapest motel I could find within a cab ride.

That motel in Pennsylvania made this one look like a luxury suite. At least that one wasn't a pay-per-hour motel, complete with very loud, very active neighbors. My father was right in thinking that I was going to struggle, but this is more than I expected. How does anyone afford a roof and food on five hundred dollars for a week? Not to mention cab rides and laundry services. Heaven forbid, I actually wanted to do something other than sit in bed and stare at the wall.

It's absolute madness.

And I'm loving it. From the moment I left Loughton House last night, I've felt free. Free to do whatever I want, however I want. Did I love sleeping in a bed that no one should ever shine a black light on? No. Somehow, that only makes it better, though. I wanted to experience new things, and the daily struggle is just the first of many I can't wait to explore.

None of it compares to what waits for me at the office. As soon as I walk in the door, Travis, the security guard that's been there for the last decade, walks up to me and hands me a note.

"Your father left this for you," he says with a smile.

"Thank you." Glancing down at it, it's just a simple desk assignment in the pre-market group, which is exactly where I'd have expected to work. Those are the groups that work on the editing and covers.

Now that I'm officially a junior editor, it'll be my home. I've always spent most of my time on this floor since it's the one that turns mediocre books into award-winning ones, but now, I'm not in charge of it. I'm just one more worker bee who will spend his days helping someone else to shine more brightly.

And it makes me grin as I ride the elevator to the fourth floor. This is what I've wanted for so long, and it's finally a reality. Okay, maybe not the actual work part, but everything else. Last night, I was stuck trying to figure out where to sleep and how to make things work. But today? Today, I'm going to start this adventure.

Stepping into the cubicle-filled room, I'm reminded of what it used to be. Before the budget cuts four years ago, each of these employees had their own office. Their own little spaces. Then we recognized the need to cut costs and increase the number of books we published, so we brought in more people, took out the offices, and built the cubicle army.

The clicking of keys and mice creates a background noise that almost hides the little snippets of conversation. People notice me and stop talking, moving back to their individual cubicles. I know what I am to the people at Loughton House. They each have team leads and even managers, but everyone knows that I'm the one who sits across from them and tells them they're fired.

That was a request I made a long time ago. Regardless of who it is, I would be the one to review their file personally and decide whether they stay or go, and I would be the one to deliver the bad news. Any other job would be a step backward.

But today, that's not me. I'm not the future CEO of Loughton House. I'm not the Director of Publishing. Not today, and not for the next month.

Today, I'm just Phillip Loughton, a junior editor. The thought is freeing. No more meetings or big questions to answer. No senior marketing execs trying to convince me of anything. I just have to edit a book today. That's it.

I walk between the cubicles and can't help but notice people glancing at me out of the corner of their eyes without turning away from their monitors. Like a cloud of silence surrounds me, people stop talking when they notice me.

For the first time, it bothers me because I'm supposed to be a nobody. I'm supposed to be the guy who rented a shitty motel room in Pennsylvania today, but nobody else got the memo. That's to be expected, I guess. It doesn't mean I have to like it.

I step into my assigned cubicle and move to my desk, one of four in this cubicle. The two women who were already there do their best not to look away from their computers, and I don't bother to look at them. It's not like I'm going to make friends at Loughton House during this experiment.

I take a deep breath and sit down in the chair. It's the worst chair I've ever sat in. Instead of a nice executive office chair like I have in my office, this isn't much better than a plastic seat with a piece of foam for the cushion. Who authorized that budget cut?

Oh well, if a shitty chair is the worst part of my new job, then that sounds like a win in my book.

Opening the new computer, there's a sticky note with my login information. In minutes, I'm pulling up the manuscript that I've been tasked with editing. *Love Beyond Time* is the title, and I sigh. This ought to be good…

"Don't you have an office somewhere?" a voice says, pulling me away from the manuscript before I've even read two lines.

I turn around and see Addison staring at me. I recognize Seraphina as well. She's pretending to be focused on a cover, but I can tell that her attention is on the fact that Addison is talking to me. I guess I should have expected my cubicle-mates to be confused.

All of that runs through my brain in half a second and then is gone because I'm staring at the woman I had wanted to get to know more.

"This is it for now," I say. My eyes move over the thin white blouse she's wearing, and I can't help but imagine the ceiling collapsing so I could get another replay of the night we met.

She looks confused and leans back in the chair, not at all worried about talking to me as though I'm just another guy in the office who moved into her cubicle. "You're the heir to Loughton House, and you don't have an office? What kind of shitshow are you running? You just sit down in a random person's cubicle and work for the day? And are you actually editing a book?"

How do you explain that you're trying out this whole normal human thing for a month? Obviously, you don't.

"I'm taking a step back from my previous role for a month after hearing many complaints about the office environment. Upper management is doing its best to blend employee happiness and lower operating costs." That almost sounds plausible.

It doesn't look like she believes it, though. "Why are you editing a book, then? Don't you have to do important things like, you know, run the company?"

I shake my head, sticking to my story. "No, my father is taking over my duties for the time being. I want to know what it's like to be here on the ground floor. Take, for example, these terrible chairs that are definitely getting replaced. I had no idea how uncomfortable they were."

Seraphina whips around in her seat. I want to ignore her, to focus every bit of my attention on Addison, but I'm stuck in the same cubicle with her for the next month.

"Really? I can walk you through how all the budget…"

I interrupt her. "No. If I'd wanted to hear complaints, I would have put a complaint box outside my office."

She sits there with her mouth open as though she can't believe what I just said. I try to soothe the frustration by turning to her. "I need to see it, and maybe in a week or two, I'll ask around. It's a hard line to walk trying to balance budget needs with the desires of the employees. That's why I'm taking an entire month to gather information about it all. Today is my first day, though, so I just want to do my work and go home like everyone else."

Addison chews her lip, still not believing me. "You're going to be working in our cubicle every day for a month?"

I nod to her, and she sighs. I hear her mutter, "The things a guy will do for a date…" She turns back to her computer and begins reading the manuscript on her screen, making quick, little notes in red pixels.

Seraphina keeps glancing between us, but when she catches me looking at her, she stands up and puts a smile on her face. "Well, if we're going to be working together, I should introduce myself. I'm Sera, and I guess you already know Addison."

I nod to her, taking her hand for a quick shake. "Nice to meet you, Sera. Now, I have to get back to my work. Just like you."

She takes the warning without complaint, and both of us turn back to our screens. Both Addison and Sera put on headphones, but I don't have any, since I typically prefer the quiet of my office over music.

The longer I stare at the manuscript, the harder it is to focus, and my attention wanders. What are the odds that I'd end up in the same cubicle as Addison? It feels like there have been so many coincidences that it's hard to believe it's even possible.

But it happened. Whether there's a naked cherub floating around me with a tiny bow or the stars aligned, I don't know, but I'm quickly realizing that if I don't pursue this, I'm just being an idiot.

I try to remind myself to focus on the manuscript in front of me, but it's harder than I expected. Romance isn't my first choice for books, but I can respect it. It makes up a significant portion of Loughton House's profit, after all. But focusing on the book isn't as easy as focusing on earnings reports and launch strategies. It's slow and steady work rather than big picture thinking. Something I'm not used to.

When Sera breaks the silence in the cubicle after almost an hour, I turn all the way around in my chair. "I'm getting some coffee. Anyone want anything?"

"Coffee would be great," I say, and as Sera gets up, Addison glances at me, nothing but frustration in her eyes.

"I'm going to wait for lunch," Addison says.

Sera looks like she's going to say something, but then she closes her mouth and nods. She throws me a quick smile and walks out of the cubicle.

As soon as she's gone, Addison turns to me and whispers, "This is stupid. I already told you I didn't want to go on a date with you. Why do you have to insist on freaking sitting in my cubicle and acting like you're doing some kind of Secret Boss experiment?"

I shake my head. "I didn't choose this cubicle. Hell, I didn't even choose my project. If I had, it definitely wouldn't be this book. Who the hell would want to read something called *Love Beyond Time*? This really is all just coincidence. No different from the motel."

Addison gapes at me. "You're editing *Love Beyond Time* by freaking Sarah Marshall? I didn't know Loughton House published Sarah Marshall's books. I could actually meet her..."

I arch an eyebrow at her. Should I know who that is? She's obviously not a big name since I work personally with many of them. "That's the title on the file."

Addison just sighs and leans back. "One more reason this is stupid, Phillip." Her words come out nearly silently. They're just loud enough for me to hear when straining, and I don't blame her. The entire office is going to be talking about me working in her cubicle.

"I'm not trying to get a goddamned date, Addison. This has absolutely nothing to do with you."

She snarls and turns back to her computer. "Whatever, boss. I'll just go back to work before you fire me for refusing to accept your terrible lie."

"Why won't you just believe me?"

Addison doesn't even look at me as she slides her headphones over her ears. That's when Sera walks back into the cubicle, a smile on her face. "Here you go," she says, handing me the steaming hot mug of coffee.

I try to smile. I really do, but I'm sure it's closer to a grimace with the frustration I feel. Faking a smile isn't something that I've ever needed to do. "Thank you," I say with at least a little gratitude.

Sera nods and goes back to her desk. I do the same, and as I read more of *Love Beyond Time*, I try to pay a little more attention to it. I'm still not a fan, but I begin to pick out pieces I think might be the cause of Addison's enjoyment.

A sip of coffee makes me think about the espresso machine in my office. Just as quick, I push the thought out of my mind. Junior editors do not have an espresso machine in the break room, and I am a junior editor.

There may be perks to being the heir to a publishing empire, but a monkey with plenty of treats in a cage is still just a monkey in a cage.

Ten

ADDISON

"I can't lend you any." My words hang in the air like drops of rain clinging to the edge of the roof. Waiting for anything to cause them to fall, crashing through the air. This is what so many phone calls with my mom are like. I don't know what it's like for other people, but my mom and I don't exactly have a typical parent child relationship.

Her sigh makes me grit my teeth. "That's fine, sweetheart. It's not like it'll be the first time I've gone without water. I'll just borrow the neighbor's water hose to wash the dishes until I get paid."

I know exactly how many times she's been without water. There's no way I could forget them. The times where I couldn't shower for a week. The times where I had to jump the fence to fill up the water jug in the neighbor's backyard while he was at work so we had something to drink.

It's not that Mom is lazy, or even that she couldn't keep a job. She's just never understood a slow and steady grind. Instead of keeping the one job and moving up the ranks, she'd hear about a different one, and the grass was always greener there.

Which left us with far too many weeks waiting on the hiring process, and no money.

"What happened this time?" I ask, knowing she'll have a very reasonable answer. Maybe I should just let her drink from the neighbor's hose. The internet would tell me that this is a toxic relationship, and I shouldn't keep enabling her. But how do you do that to your own mother?

She starts into the story. "Well, I had that job at the local feed store, but they never let me have full-time hours. It was always thirty-five hours, and those extra five hours really matter, you know? Well, I just couldn't afford…"

I stop her. "How long had you been there, Mom?"

There's a pause. "Almost five months. And I told them I needed full-time when I hired on."

Almost five months. Right. More like just past three months. I sigh. "How much do you need?" I started this conversation by saying I couldn't loan her any money, but I love my mom. No matter how many times she puts herself in a bind and needs help, I can't just ignore her.

"Just like three hundred dollars. I'll stop by the local food bank, and I get paid in a week. The electric company won't shut the power off just for being a week late."

The happiness that had slowly been building inside me drains away. I have enough money to pay her bills, but that'll leave me with no extra from the money I'd saved my senior year. Money I'd earned when I could have been having fun, when I could have been enjoying the college life.

"Fine. I'll send you three hundred and fifty. But Mom, I don't have much left. I can't keep doing this, so you need to just stop changing jobs. Even if the next one you hear about is the job of your dreams, just ignore it. Please. For my sake."

I can hear the excitement in her voice. The sincerity. "Thank you, sweetheart. You're a lifesaver. And I promise that I'm going to stay at Woodson's for a long time. They're the best paying place in town, and they even give Christmas bonuses."

I sigh again, knowing why Woodson's was hiring. The owner doesn't put up with any excuses. Plenty of my friends in high school worked there after they graduated, and nearly all of them got fired after only a few months.

But Mom's always been a hard worker. Maybe she'll keep up, and it really can be a dream job for her. "Okay Mom, I have to go. I'll transfer the money in a few minutes. I love you."

"I love you too, sweetheart," she says as though there's not a problem in the world.

The phone goes dead as I hit end call, and I lean back in the cheap build-it-yourself furniture that I picked up on sale. The legs don't fit together perfectly, and it wobbles, but it's a chair, and I spent six dollars on it.

My new friends at Loughton House wouldn't understand the mismatched furniture in my apartment. Or the crocheted laptop bag sitting in my closet. Or the makeup mirror with a crack in the corner that I bought from a garage sale for a few dollars.

See, when you grow up like I did, you learn to spend as little money as possible because there's always going to be a problem. Whether that's the ancient heater going out or your mother needing a loan that she'll never pay back, it'll always happen. Some people have family or friends they can count on to help them, but not me. I've made it through life knowing that there wasn't anyone to call if I got into a bind. So I save every last penny.

I look around the apartment and sigh again. I won't be hunting for a bookshelf to hold the boxes of used books sitting in the hallway. No, all of that will have to wait another month or two.

It's not like being a junior editor pays well. But I don't have my mother's problems. I understand the idea of sacrificing now to be stable in the future. I'm not afraid to go without so that I can be free of that constant fear.

At least I hope I can.

Eleven

PHILLIP

My phone alarm goes off forty-five minutes before I'm supposed to be in my cubicle. I do my best to stretch a little, but the tables I've pulled together for a makeshift bed aren't stable enough to do much moving. This is not what I'd planned on when I made that deal with my father.

I grab onto the electrical conduit to stable myself as I climb off the "bed". Who knew that my old hiding place in Loughton House would come in so handy? The storage closet is less closet and more dusty, forgotten storage room. Filled with furniture that hasn't been used in decades, the only real purpose for it is being the main hub for the electrical system. There was extra space, so they stuffed old tables and chairs in it, all of which are forgotten about until an electrician needs to fix something.

It turns out that five hundred dollars does not actually buy a room and food for a week in New York City. Part of me wonders what my father expected me to do when I ran out of money. Did he want me to come crawling back in three days when I couldn't get a hot meal? Or did he really want me sleeping on the street?

But it's payday, and I'm ready for an actual bed tonight. Preferably one that I'm not paying for by the hour. This week has been a real eye-opener. Even though sleeping in a storage room isn't the lifestyle of the rich and famous that I'm trying to escape, I could do with a bed. At least that's what the knotted muscles in my back are screaming at me.

I've put a lot of thought into where I'll move for the next three weeks, and the Atrium down the street is the only place that makes sense. I checked the prices on my phone, and it's only two hundred a night for the cheapest room. That should be well within my budget. Their food is excellent, and not that expensive either.

My mouth waters as I think of having seared tuna on a bed of wild rice. Grilled asparagus on the side. A nice glass of Syrah since cheap Cab is terrible.

Good food and a real bed. That's the dream right now. I look at my muddy reflection in the steel panel of the electrical box. I look rough. My shirt's a disgrace with how many wrinkles cover it. My pants have survived a little better. My hair feels like I haven't showered in a week even though it's only been three days. Don't even get me started on how badly I need to shave.

Truthfully, I don't even care. I know I should. My father would be pissed if he saw me coming into the office looking like this. I can't keep the grin off my face. Today's payday. Today is when I get back to doing more than simply surviving.

I do my best to straighten my shirt and put on my tie. I signed up to be normal, and maybe by the end of the day, that's the way I'll feel. Normal. Not homeless and living in a storage room. That's the price of an adventure, though, right? Sometimes, you have to walk through the mud to get to the destination.

And today's destination will have a bed, a decent meal, and a glass of wine.

Twelve

ADDISON

IT'S PAYDAY. MY FIRST PAYCHECK FROM LOUGHTON House. My first grownup paycheck ever. Granted, it barely covers the bills and food, but my budget is just about as perfected as anyone could do. Everything down to the penny is accounted for, and I'll actually have extra.

Maybe I'll take my new friends up on another karaoke night now that I'm building my savings up again. Or I could get that bookshelf. It'd be nice to see the worlds I've spent so much time in getting their fair share of my apartment space rather than relegated to a cardboard box like some kind of trash.

I glance back at Phillip again as he pulls his phone out of his pocket for the twenty-seventh time this morning. I've spent four days with that man in our cubicle, and other than the first day, I haven't said a word to him.

Sera's been a little more vocal around him, but I think it's harder on her to be quiet than it is to blurt things out. I guess that's the difference between an artist and an editor.

But I have been paying attention. It'd be impossible not to. That he's obscenely gorgeous hasn't changed. That jawline hasn't gone away. The intensity of those eyes is still there.

At the same time, he's different. He looks like someone threw a suit on a homeless guy who happens to have the body and face of a model. He looks... hungry? Is that a thing? That first day, he acted like he owned the place. His eyes took everything in like it belonged to him, like we were just borrowing it. But now he just stares blankly.

He hasn't shaved, and the stubble has turned into a short beard. His hair is brushed, but not styled, and the difference between this and the night at the motel is drastic. His clothes are covered in wrinkles. Even the way he moves is wrong, like someone beat him up this morning.

What the hell has happened to him in the past three days?

Now, instead of paying attention to his work, one of the few things that hasn't changed, he's looking at his phone every five minutes.

Finally, it's too much, and I turn all the way around to face him. "What are you doing on your phone? For the guy who expects everyone to sit down and work for eight hours a day, you sure seem distracted."

Sera turns to me, eyes wide like I'm jabbing a bear with a stick. Maybe I am. Maybe I should just ignore the crazy boss and hope he doesn't decide to eat me. But for all the survival instincts I've picked up over the years, the one that never stuck was ignoring things.

He glances at his phone again before turning to me, his chair bumping wildly as he moves it over the rough carpet. "When do we get paid?" he finally asks.

"I got paid before I got up this morning. Why? Worried you won't be able to afford a new house this afternoon?"

He frowns and looks at his phone again. "We don't get a second payment or something?"

I chuckle and shake my head. "Nope. Wait, when did the owner of the company start worrying about his paycheck? I didn't think billionaires even got paychecks. Don't you just have a vault like Scrooge McDuck? On that note, does it hurt diving into a pool filled with gold coins? I've always wondered that."

He glares at me and looks down at his phone again. For a few seconds, Sera and I just watch as he shakes his head back and forth. Finally, he looks up, and it's like all the color's gone from him.

"I can't sleep on tables anymore," he whispers, his gaze not meeting mine or Sera's. He's looking past us like we aren't even there. "How does anyone survive like this?"

Sleeping on tables? What? "Phillip," I say a little louder than normal, and he snaps back. "What's going on, Phillip? Why are you sleeping on tables?"

He shakes his head slowly again, and his mouth opens, but then it closes again. And then I recognize the look on his face. It's the same one I saw on my mother's face so many times as a child.

It's the face you make when you realize you're not going to make it. That the carefully stacked house of cards is about to topple over, and there's absolutely nothing you can do about it. That only happens when you don't have money. But how does the heir to the largest publishing company in the world have money problems?

"You've been sleeping here, haven't you?" I say, just loud enough for him to hear. "I don't know why, but you're out of money. I'd know that face anywhere."

Once again, he opens his mouth and then closes it. I expect him to sit there silently, but the ice holding his emotions back begins to crack, and he nods.

Sera looks like she's in shock. I think for a minute, and just like when I talked to my mom, I know the right answer in this situation. If I were even the least bit intelligent, I would tell him that his problems sound terrible. Then, I'd turn around to do my work. I would ignore the wounded animal caught in the trap and focus on my own problems. Like my mother. Or that my entire future depends on whether I can succeed at this job.

But once again, I'm an idiot.

"Let's get an early lunch," I say and stand up. Sera arches an eyebrow and does the smart thing, turning back to the cover she's working on.

Phillip whispers, "I can't pay."

I chuckle. "I'll loan you a bit of money. Eventually, I bet you'll pay me back."

He doesn't move, his phone cradled in his hands as he stares blankly past me. Instead of waiting for him to hear me, I grab his wrist and pull him up. His body moves instinctively, following my pull, and he comes back to his senses. "It's only eleven," he says. "People take lunch breaks at a quarter to twelve."

The corner of my lip curls up in a half-grin. "Are you going to fire me for buying you lunch?"

That breaks him out of his stupor. At least a little. "No, I guess not."

"Good. Then let's get a sandwich, and you can tell me all about how a billionaire ends up borrowing money for lunch."

Thirteen

PHILLIP

"You are the dumbest man I have ever met," Addison says as she leans forward in the booth, her arms supporting her as she gets closer to me. "You actively went out of your way to *not be rich*. Do you understand how absolutely insane that sounds?"

"Yes. My father said the same thing. But Addison, I've spent my life so focused on Loughton House that I've never actually experienced the world. Everything's so censored, so clean and tidy and fake. Sure, I could take a vacation from my life, maybe go to some island resort somewhere, but that's not real either. That's just a fake world that people escape to. It's no different."

There's no way anyone could understand this over-whelming urge to see the world without the veneer that everyone in my life covers it with. Nothing ever really happens.

I see photos of people working to make a life, of people struggling and fighting and giving it everything they have. I watch movies where people love and sacrifice and make hard decisions.

But I've never understood any of it. The last week has been the hardest struggle of my life. I've worked plenty, don't get me wrong. Hell, I can't think of a point when the majority of my time wasn't spent learning or working on business. It's different, though.

Addison frowns. "You want to be a normal Joe? That's a little bat shit, but I guess rich people do insane things. How are you going to manage that, though? You don't have the money for a deposit, so you'll have to live in a motel. That'll mean you have to get takeout for every meal…"

"I was planning on staying at the Atrium," I interject.

Addison's eyes open wide for a moment and then she laughs. "You realize you're a junior editor, right? Not a manager or even a senior editor. Just a guy straight out of college. There's no freaking way you're going to afford the Atrium."

I don't laugh because nothing about this conversation is funny. "I realized that this morning. How do you survive on that pittance of a wage?"

She just laughs again. Even though I'm beyond frustrated, it's hard not to smile. Her eyes are sparkling and so full of energy.

"I act like I'm poor, Phillip. Because I am. And I guess you are, too. You have to know where your money is going. Every last penny. Just like in business, you need to be a little creative."

She grins for a second. "Have you ever been to a thrift store?"

A thrift store? "I don't think so."

The waitress brings our sandwiches then, and I'm not interested in mine at all.

Addison just keeps grinning. "Well, eat your sandwich so we can get back to work, but then I'm going to take you shopping like us poor folks."

To my father or brothers, I'm sure that statement would have sounded dreadful, but right now, I can't imagine anything I'd rather do. And truthfully, I'm not sure whether it's because I'll be doing something new, which was the entire goal of this month…

Or because I'll be doing it with Addison.

Fourteen

ADDISON

PHILLIP LOUGHTON IS THE WORST THRIFT STORE shopper I have ever met. From the moment we walked into the store, he looked like he was ready to bolt. What's so terrifying about a store that sells used clothes?

"You need a second set of clothes, Phillip. I don't know how you've kept from stinking, but those need to get dry-cleaned. I have a trick for that, too. But your backup clothes don't have to be perfect. You're broke now, so you get to survive without seventeen suits that cost more than cars. You cannot survive, on the other hand, without a second set of clothes."

He glares at me. "These are terrible quality, though. Look at them. The best coat in this whole place was probably bought at Men's Wearhouse."

"Well, Mr. Fancy Pants, you should be happy to get something from Men's Wearhouse right now. You don't get to be quite so choosy when your bed doubles as an eating surface."

Phillip just sighs and starts combing through the racks. I could shop for myself as well, but it's hard not to enjoy watching the man who had the world in the palm of his hand a week ago struggle to find a shirt.

He pulls one out, a ruby button-down that looks pretty good. He checks the tag and frowns before running his hands over the seams. Then he puts the shirt back on the rack, and I stop him.

"What's wrong with it?" I ask.

"It has polyester in it. It has double-stitched seams instead of French seams. I've never heard of the brand. The bottom is probably going to be wrinkled forever, and there's a stain down here." He points at a slight discoloration along the bottom edge.

"Won't that be covered up when you tuck it in?"

"But what's it from, Addison?" He looks like he's about to panic thinking about wearing it. "How do you get a stain there when it's tucked in? That's a definite no."

He puts the shirt back on the rack, and I snatch it up. It's a nice shirt other than the stain. "Here's how you handle it," I say as I go through the rest of the clothes, ignoring his protests. "You are broke, and this shirt is two dollars. We'll wash it, but at least you'll have something to wear. If we find a better one, then we can put this one back. This is how the peasants manage to buy clothes *and* feed ourselves on that 'pittance of a wage'. You said you wanted to find out what it was like to be normal, didn't you?"

Phillip grumbles, but when I turn to him, my eyebrows arched, he slumps his shoulders and sighs. "You're right. I signed up for this. I'll just pretend that someone was eating risotto alla milanese at home."

This time, it's me who is confused, and I guess Phillip notices. "It's a rice and bone broth soup with a lot of saffron," he explains. "Saffron is notorious for *yellow* stains." He glances at the ruby red shirt in my hands. "Like that one. Which is definitely a saffron stain. There is no chance at all that it could be anything else."

I work really hard not to laugh when he keeps staring at it, probably repeating that mantra. I wish that I'd had someone picking out nice clothes like this when I was younger. Instead, I just ended up wearing the same worn-out clothes for years.

He smiles at me and says, "Okay. On to pants. And…" He cringes before saying the next word. "A tie."

This time, the chuckle comes out no matter how hard I try to hold it back. "Just relax like Bruce Lee said. Be formless. Be shapeless. Like water."

He arches an eyebrow. "So you're a thrift store shopping, expert on being poor, junior editor who sleeps in strangers' beds and also happens to be a ninja?"

I pause for a second and shrug. "Pretty much. I also sing terrible karaoke if we're just listing facts about me."

"Noted. I guess we have two things in common then."

I give Phillip a confused look. He grins and says, "I also slept with a stranger in a seedy motel not long ago. Luckily, my stranger was a lot prettier than yours."

The laugh doesn't need to be held back this time. He's good at that. I was just joking before about the Bruce Lee thing, but he's remarkably good at making a bad situation better. For a guy who's probably never been in very many bad situations, he's rolling with the punches pretty well.

I grab his hand and pull him away from the shirt racks. "Come on. Let's get you some pants."

He follows me, but he stops halfway there. "I'm glad we spent that night together." The words are quiet, but it's like the rest of the store has gone silent as I listen to him. "If we hadn't, then I wouldn't be here with you right now. I wouldn't be laughing at your jokes, and I probably wouldn't have even made that deal with my father. Instead, I'd be eating risotto alla milanese and getting saffron stains on my own shirt. This is better, and I don't really know how to explain why."

I smile at him, but I think he's right. I'm annoyed at him interrupting the life I'm building, but it's only because I know he won't stick around. He's the billionaire boss. He's the heartless man that trims the fat at the office. He's untouchable, and even if every moment we spend together makes me like him even more, he'll be gone in three weeks. Back to his mansion. Back to his world, where bad things don't happen.

And I'll still be editing terrible books written by old men. I'll still be shopping at thrift stores and paying my mom's debts and wishing I could find the courage to publish a novel instead of just dreaming about it.

"Me too," I say. "Don't get me wrong, Phillip. I still won't go on a date with you, but you know how to make me smile."

Phillip's lip curls up. "What do you think this is?"

Shit. Quick, come up with something snarky.

"This is charity work. Like working in a soup kitchen, but instead of feeding the poor, I'm convincing a rich guy that it's okay to wear a shirt with a yellow stain on it."

"A saffron stain…" he mutters.

"Right. A saffron stain. Not anything else."

His grin doesn't go away, though. "Fine. Continue your charity work, Addison. I just wanted to tell you I'm glad that you're doing the charity work instead of someone else. That's all."

The only thing he's convinced me of is that a date at the thrift store with a billionaire feels so much better than I imagine being wined and dined would be. Granted, I've never been wined and dined by a billionaire, but something tells me that this is better. I'm learning more about the stranger I slept with right now than I ever would over caviar.

It's just too bad that this is as far as the dates can go. When his little experiment is over, he'll go right back to being the big boss. Everybody knows that dating the boss is a terrible decision, and I've dreamed of this job my entire life.

There's no way I'd bet my dreams on a man that's insane enough to choose to be poor for a month.

Fifteen

PHILLIP

I stare at the subway map with Addison standing next to me, memorizing the routes. I may not know how to survive on a junior editor's salary, but I can memorize anything.

"Are you really going to go back to Loughton House?" she asks. It's hard to hear her over the din of the subway tunnels. Soft footsteps shouldn't be noticeable, but hundreds of them put together, each one of them echoing off the concrete walls, is damn near deafening.

I turn to her, trying to hear her better. "Where else am I supposed to go? Like you said, I don't have a down-payment, and hotels are expensive. Even the cheap one I stayed at the first two nights will burn through my paycheck before next Friday, and I'd like to eat something occasionally."

She chews her lip and slowly shakes her head. "You're such an idiot," she mutters. I can't hear the words, and I know they're not directed at me, but I can read her lips.

"I know I am," I say with a grin. This evening has given me a little more life than I'd had this morning. Even knowing that I'm stuck living in a storage closet for the next three weeks, I don't feel like I'll be crawling back to my father anytime soon.

She just shakes her head more. "I wasn't talking to you. I…" She grits her teeth and says something, but I can't hear it.

"What?" I ask, completely confused about the way she's acting.

"Do you want to sleep on my couch?" she asks, loudly enough for me to hear her.

I'm taken aback. "You want me to live with you?" I say the words slowly and much louder, so there's no mistaking them.

She sighs again, but then she says. "Not particularly. But I have a couch and a shower and a washer and dryer, and I know how to cook so you don't end up starving to death. Mostly, though, you let me sleep in that damn motel bed when we were actual strangers. It wouldn't be right to let you sleep on a freaking table in a storage room after you did that for me."

I don't really know how to respond. If we were doing business, I'd agree that she owed me, but this isn't business.

And I care about how she feels.

That's not something my father would say. It's not something I'd have thought I'd have said, either. At least, not until I met Addison. Now, I think I'd rather sleep on a table in a storage room than make her life more difficult, even if she owes me.

"No. I'll be fine, Addison. I chose to do this experiment, and I'm not down on my luck. There weren't any catastrophes that ended with a roof falling on me and soaking my very white shirt." She glares at me, but I continue, even though my grin gets a little wider. "I basically asked for this, and that means that you're not saddled with taking care of me. Nobody is except me."

She sighs and grabs my hand. Ignoring my objections, she drags me to a different section of the tunnel, completely tuning me out even when the subway I needed to get on stops and the doors open.

When Addison finally stops dragging me across the platform, she turns to me with a fire in her eyes. "Alright, Phillip. Here's how this is going to work. I know how much you get paid. You're going to give me thirty percent for rent and utilities. That way I get something out of it, and there aren't any hard feelings. Then we're going to split the cost of meals. I'll help you survive your experiment, and when you go back to being a billionaire and my boss, you'll pretend like this whole thing never happened. Just like I've been trying to pretend our sex-free one-night-stand never happened. Do you understand?"

"But Addison, that's not something you really want. Not really. You refused to even eat lunch with me before, and now you're trying to force me to live with you? I feel like I'm missing something."

She puts her hands on her hips and gives me one of those "Are you serious?" looks. "I didn't want to go on a date with my boss because that's a recipe for ruining my career. I don't want you to live with me for the same reason, but I can't just watch you be miserable. The same way you didn't want me sleeping in a car in a freaking thunderstorm."

I start to tell her that her staying in my motel room that night had been the highlight of my month, but I stop myself. She wouldn't understand.

"Well, I can't stand seeing you like this, and maybe it won't be that bad, anyway. My apartment gets a little lonely, so it might be nice to have someone around. It's not like you'll take up much space since you only have the two outfits."

I know I should push back harder, to force myself to turn her down. This isn't a single night, this isn't a motel room, and we're definitely not strangers at this point. But I can't. Maybe if I didn't feel so drawn to her or like fate was shoving us together, I might be able to choose the storage room over her offer. But that just isn't the case.

"Okay. I accept the terms," I say and put my hand out to close the deal just like I would in business.

She understands what I'm doing, and takes my hand, but before she shakes, she reminds me. "The last part of the agreement is important, Phillip. Whatever happens, good or bad, cannot change how things work after you go back to being the head honcho at work. My position at Loughton House is the first step of my dream career, so don't let my kindness mess that up."

I nod my head. "I promise."

"Good." She turns as the subway pulls up in front of us, its doors sliding open. "Just so you know, you're going to have to learn to sing karaoke."

"As long as karaoke doesn't count as a date, I'd love to."

She glances at me, one eyebrow raised. "It doesn't."

Sixteen

ADDISON

WHAT THE HELL WAS I THINKING? BUYING PHILLIP lunch was one thing. Showing him how to shop at a thrift store was just like giving a stray cat some food and water. But letting him live with me? This is a terrible idea.

Somehow, I'm struggling to remember why it's so terrible. Especially when he's sitting at my dining room table without a shirt on, wearing nothing but a tiny pair of gym shorts I stole from the guy I dated in college.

"I feel like that night at the motel has really come full circle," he says as he adjusts the shorts as they ride up even higher on his thighs. The washing machine spins loudly as his clothes are washed in the background. And I try not to stare at the rippling muscles that I still feel compelled to touch. *Focus on the food, Addison.*

Except it's Phillip's shoulders that are making my mouth water. Not the food. He picks up his fork and knife and cuts into the chicken.

"I'm sure it's nothing compared to what you're used to," I say, cutting into mine.

He chuckles. "This smells heavenly. Do you know how many days it's been since I had an actual meal? Other than the sandwich at lunch today, I've had nothing but vending machine snacks for three days."

I gape at him. "And you're not dead yet?"

"I was close," he says as he takes the first bite. His face looks like I crawled under the table and started sucking his dick. "Holy shit, Addison. This is the best food I've ever had. Ever."

"It's just a basic chicken breast with some gravy. Don't you normally eat stuff from professional chefs? Things that I couldn't pronounce?"

He chuckles. "Maybe you chose the wrong profession."

"I think it's more likely that your taste buds died in that storage room, along with your dignity."

Phillip just keeps grinning as he eats. My little comments don't seem to bother him at all. "Maybe that's true. At least about the dignity."

At the same time, I can see him warring with himself. His knife cuts are just a little faster as time goes on. The etiquette I assume was drilled into him from birth is slipping as he has his first home cooked meal in a week.

"Well, thank you, regardless. It's been a long time since I cooked for someone who appreciates a good home-cooked meal."

His eyes widen. "There are people that would be disappointed with this? That's crazy."

I don't go into the fact that my mom hates anything that doesn't remind her of fast food. She'd prefer a box of corn dogs to this meal any day of the week. Then there was my boyfriend in college that was used to expensive meals and always wanted to go to a restaurant so he could pretend to be fancy.

Those things don't need to be said, though. I may be sharing my apartment with Phillip, but he's still my boss.

"I don't get close to very many people is all I mean," I say, brushing off the reality of it. "I learned a long time ago that getting close to people is the fastest way to get hurt."

He nods. "My father has said the same thing for a long time. But instead of getting hurt, it's more that they'll take all my money and time and power. Close enough though, right?"

Not at all. But once again, I just let it go. It's hard to remember that the homeless and shirtless guy in front of me is actually the guy who decides who gets fired. The last thing I want to do is let him see any flaws.

Instead of talking, I just pick at the chicken and gravy, and the room goes silent. Just the soft clatter of silverware on cheap dishes. If there'd been a clock on the walls, I'd have been able to hear its soft ticking.

As soon as I finish my plate, I stand up and scrape the extra gravy into the trash and take my dishes to the sink. Phillip is right behind me, his bare feet padding almost silently on the faux hardwood floors.

"Let me get you a pillow and blanket," I say without looking at him. A quiver runs through me as I feel his eyes on me. Just like in that motel, the way he's staring at me has my body going crazy. Did my boss somehow give me a creepy stalker kink?

It's hard not to glance back at him, to see him staring at me. Deep down, I know that if we were to look each other in the face right now, I'd be staring down a very slippery slope.

The night that we slept together still lives rent free in my mind. The way I'd mentally begged him to touch me in the slightest, so I'd have a reason to turn over and do a hell of a lot more than look at him.

He follows me, and when I stop in front of the hall closet, I feel him get closer. Not much. Just a half-step away, and then I smell him. That same dark scent that's on the silk shirt in my closet. I have to take a deep breath to get myself under control.

My body moves instinctively, opening the door and reaching up to the top shelf where the spare blanket and pillows are. I have to stand on my tiptoes to reach it, and then, without saying anything, Phillip reaches over me, his naked chest brushing my back.

He pulls the bedding down, and I'm forced to turn around and look at him. "Thanks," I say, trying to act normal, not at all like I'm having to fight myself not to throw myself at him.

"Just one more perk of having me around, Addison. Maybe you won't hate it as much as you thought. I can even open pickle jars."

He says the words that should be a joke, but with how I'm feeling right now, I'm questioning how I'm ever going to keep the necessary distance between us. I knew this was going to happen, damn it. Even when we were at the subway station, I knew it.

But it's hard to push him away when he's so damned good at making me smile. And the abs don't help at all. "That's cute that you think I need help opening pickle jars."

"I should have known you'd have that under control. The longer I spend with you, the more I'm learning that you're not quite the typical recent college graduate."

The reminder of our age gap helps to build a bit of that resolve. He may be hot and funny, but that doesn't mean that I should act like this. "Come on, boss. Let's get the couch made up for you. I don't want you to miss any creature comforts. I hear that making the owner of your company shiver himself to sleep is bad for my quarterly review."

As I walk past him, he stops me by putting his hand on my shoulder. "Addison," he says softly.

I turn around, the hand on my shoulder radiating a warmth that's almost shocking. "Addison, I promise that I'll uphold the conditions of our roommate agreement. There's nothing you could do that I'd bring to the office. If I don't like something about this little arrangement, I'll just leave and go back to sleeping on tables. Or crawl back to my father if it's really that bad. I doubt either of those will happen, though."

"I know," I say a little too quietly. The way he's touching me, the closeness, it's making my body throb in ways that I've forgotten. "But Phillip, you living with me is weird. It makes me nervous, and I'm sorry, but I tend to get a little sarcastic when I'm nervous."

He chuckles. "That's fine. I just wanted to be clear that the lines are drawn, and I always uphold an agreement."

His hand moves away, and for a moment, our eyes meet, and it's like time slows down. I'd normally be focused on that playful grin or the lines on his shoulders where his muscles come together. Or the little strip of hair that runs between his abs.

I can't turn away, though. Those dark eyes pull me in like pools of shadows, teasing hidden secrets. Maybe it's not just me that has a past they don't want to talk about. Maybe I'm not the only one with scars.

"Let's get my luxury suite set up," he says, taking a step back. "You know, if the Atrium ever wants to upgrade, they could stop by and take some notes. I haven't seen luxury like this since I stayed at Buckingham Palace."

"I offered my interior design advice, but they disagreed with the idea of garage sale sofas," I say as I go back to throwing the old afghan onto the couch. It may not be the warmest blanket in the world with all the little holes in the crochet, but it's one of the few things I have from my childhood. My nana made it when my mom was a kid. I remember sitting at her house and watching Murder She Wrote while she crocheted. And always, I'd be sitting on her couch with that afghan over my legs.

Those were some of the best memories I have of my childhood.

"You know, a week ago I'd have looked down on sleeping on a garage sale sofa, but living in a storage room gave me some perspective. Maybe this experiment isn't as bad an idea as everyone seems to think it is."

I smile at him but try not to get trapped in his gaze. I need to take some time to remind myself that my walls are there for a reason. That Phillip Loughton is the definition of a bad decision, and there's no doubt that he'll be nothing but a weird memory in a month.

Tossing the pillows on top of the afghan, I say, "Maybe. A little perspective never hurt anybody."

He looks at me with a grin. "You know, our night at the Neptune Motel really has come full circle. Except one thing."

"I offered you my couch," I say, but even I can hear my voice cracking a little. Looking at him as he towers over me, wearing shorts that barely cover those muscular thighs and nothing else, I know I'm on the verge of giving into everything that my body wants.

But how am I supposed to convince my vagina that those muscles and that hair are anything but wonderful?

Phillip chuckles and shakes his head. "Oh, sharing a bed? No, I was talking about how you had to sleep in soaking wet bottoms. Jeez, woman. Get your mind out of the gutter."

"Do you… want me to pour water on your crotch, or what?"

As I say it, I glance down at the tight little athletic shorts, and I can't ignore the outline of his cock against them. Or how it's beginning to swell.

Well, now there's no chance that my vagina's going to listen.

"Eyes up here, Addison," he says, his grin getting wider. "I feel like a piece of meat standing here with you ogling me."

"I wasn't ogling. At least not any more than you did when you were staring at my tits in that sleep shirt."

He just laughs. I squint at him, but I finally let it go. "Fine. I'm going to go to bed," I say.

But he stops me. "The full circle thing," he says. "Since I'm not going to sleep in wet shorts, and I won't be jumping into your bed, let me have a beer if you have one. I've never drank 'normal' beer. But it would feel like it'd close the circle up nice and tidy, and I'm a sucker for a nice tight circle." He gives me a grin, and I completely ignore the innuendo.

"Sorry Phillip, the only thing I have to drink is box wine and Sprite. It's not too bad after the first cup, but I don't know if your refined palette could handle it."

"I've gained some perspective, remember? Have a drink with me, and then we can both go to bed. In our own respective sleeping places, of course."

The way he says that makes me wonder if he's saying it to patronize me or just to be clear. "Okay, I'll introduce you to drinking like a college girl on a budget. Watch yourself, though. This magical drink has dropped more than a few panties over the years. Not mine, of course."

I give him a sideways grin, and he chuckles as he follows me into the kitchen where I pull out the box wine and two-liter of Sprite. As I twist the knob and let the white wine flow into a glass, he looks over my shoulder. I shut the tap off and top it with Sprite before handing it to him.

"So, you made bad sparkling wine," he says as I repeat the process for myself. I nod, and when I turn around with my glass, I see him sniffing the wine.

"This is terrible," he admits.

"That's why you add the Sprite."

He grimaces as he puts the glass to his lips, and I just watch him. Expecting him to spit it out like some kind of wine connoisseur, I'm surprised when he swallows it and gets a ponderous look on his face.

"It's still terrible, but very drinkable. If that makes sense. The wine doesn't change, but the soda lets you ignore it, mostly." He stops thinking and asks, "Why didn't you just buy alcohol instead if you were going to attempt to hide it?"

"Box wine is cheaper. Unless we were going to get Everclear, which is a dangerous business for a bunch of girls who are still pretty new at the whole drinking thing. Nobody dies from drinking box wine, but plenty of frat boys get their stomach pumped from liquor."

I take a sip and completely ignore his criticism of the nostalgia-filled flavor that washes over my tongue. "Plus, wine is classy, and Everclear is not."

Phillip laughs. "I think our definitions of classy are a little different," he says.

"Oh, definitely." I get a terrible, but very fun idea. "Phillip, you went to college, right?"

"I did." He says it slowly, as though he's waiting for the real question.

"Well, what was your favorite drinking game…"

Seventeen

"Drinking game?" I ask.

"Yeah, like King's Cup or Smoke and Fire? Games that you play while drinking that are supposed to get you to drink more, or… act a little irresponsibly."

Act irresponsibly? "Like strip poker?"

Addison grins. "Maybe a little less 'let's get naked' and more 'when'd you lose your virginity' if that makes sense. Though, yes, some of them are just excuses to take off clothes."

Does this mean that Addison wants to "act irresponsibly"? Or am I just wishing she was?

"Well, I didn't play any games like that. My college experience was basically just a bunch of work with a few inconsequential relationship moments thrown in for flavor."

She frowns, "That's crazy. College is supposed to be the time when people get to discover themselves. They make terrible decisions so that they can decide what they want from life. Even the Amish know how important that is."

"I doubt my father cares much about Amish philosophy. Plus, I already knew what I was going to do with my life. Unlike most people, my path was laid out in front of me at birth."

She gives me another head shake, and I sip the terrible wine and sprite mixture. "You don't understand. I don't mean that it's a time to figure out your career path. I already knew what I wanted to do when I went to college." She pauses, frowning as she tries to figure out how to word her explanation.

She looks right at me, our gaze locking. "I mean that it's the time for discovering what matters to you. Sure, I knew I wanted to work for a publishing house, but I didn't know why I fell in love with books. I didn't understand love or relationships. Hell, I knew nothing about the world beyond what they taught in school."

"I figured most of that out anyway," I say, though I wish it had been done at some coffee shop at a university instead of alone in an office late at night. I wish I'd had a few more experiences that were both real and didn't matter.

"You know, Addison, sometimes I wonder whether any of that matters. How many people actually do anything with those discoveries? How many people marry someone because they don't hate them, or they got knocked up rather than because they fall head-over-heels in love with them? How many people work in a career because it pays well and they're good at it instead of because it matters to them? You can't tell me that the people working in a factory in Chicago care about those boxes of chocolates they're making."

Addison frowns. "You make life sound so dreary. Like we don't have any choices."

My shrug is how I've felt for as long as I can remember. But today is different. This week has been different. "Maybe I'm wrong, and that's just the way I've felt about things for a long time. Maybe I was wrong the whole time. I mean, you're doing what you want, right? You're working in your dream career, doing something you care about."

Her frown turns thoughtful. "I had to do a lot of things no one expected from me to get here, Phillip. There's a reason I know how to be poor. My childhood wasn't filled with money and niceties. For two years, our car sat in our driveway because we couldn't afford to get the radiator replaced. When I was nine, my mom and I exchanged Christmas cards we drew in the dark instead of presents because the electricity had been turned off and we were dead broke. No one expected me to go to college. And I did it without going into debt.

"I think you're right about some of it, though. A lot of things are easier if you just go down the path that's laid out in front of you. I could have worked in a farming supply store like half the town I grew up in. I could have done the same thing that my mother has, jumping from one job to the next whenever someone's paying a dollar more an hour. But I didn't. There's no television here because I saved my money to move to New York instead of buying one. I have a two-dollar laptop bag instead of a thirty dollar one because I needed those twenty-eight dollars to get here. I made hard choices so I could get what I wanted. And that made all the difference."

I can't help but smile. "Quite the road less traveled story, isn't it? I guess we're both doing that to some degree."

She grins and we both finish our drinks. "Maybe that's the trick to it all," I say. "Just keep your eyes on *your* prize and fuck what everyone else thinks you should do."

With a nod, she stands up. "Well Phillip, it's getting late, and I think I need to get some sleep. I hope you enjoyed the drink that gave me so many unforgettable nights that I barely remember."

I stand up and reply, "Maybe the next time we have them, you can tell me some of the things you do remember."

"Sorry Phillip. You know what they say about college drinking stories."

"That they all involve peeing in awkward places?"

She glares at me, but I can tell it's mostly joking. "No. But also, yes. College stories are meant to be lived. Not talked about with your boss."

114

"You know, that just makes me want to hear about them even more."

"Well, keep dreaming. You've had your drink, and now it's time to go to sleep. I have things to do tomorrow, and you..."

It occurs to me that I don't actually have anything to do tomorrow. Obviously, the first thing that I think of is spending the day with Addison, but like she said, she has things to do. "I'm going to find something brand new to do."

I catch Addison's gaze, and as she smiles, I'm confronted by the very real fact that this has been the best day I can remember. This freedom has a time limit on it, though, and I'm going to live every day to its fullest.

"I'll see you in the morning," I say. When I turn toward the couch, I can feel Addison's eyes follow me. It only makes me want to push her harder, to stop wasting time pretending that we're not both wanting more.

But Addison isn't the kind of woman that would take kindly to being pushed like that. My lip curls up as I begin planning the slow seduction of Addison Adelaide.

Eighteen

PHILLIP

I HAVE NEVER USED A COFFEEMAKER BEFORE. AT LEAST not one like the average American uses. French presses, espresso machines, and even the occasional drip coffee brewer are all options I've used, but Addison doesn't have any of those. She has a… Mr. Coffee.

The apartment is silent as I walk toward the kitchen. I flip on the light and have to blink against the brightness. This shouldn't be that hard. It's not like I haven't ever made coffee before.

There's a brew button, but nothing's in it yet. There's a handle on the top part above the pot, and I try pulling on it. It slides out, and it looks like a massive espresso press, something I have in my office.

I grin as I fill it to the brim just like how I'd make an espresso. Now where's the water go? There's a tank on the back with a lid on it. Since it's not connected to a water line, this must be the water reservoir. I pull the pot out since I don't want it to break, and I put the whole coffeemaker in the sink and turn on the water. The water quickly rises to the top line.

I slide the now full coffeemaker back onto the counter, slide the pot back in, and hit brew. Then I say a silent prayer, hoping I haven't done something catastrophically wrong. I don't know why making a pot of coffee should make me feel like I'm ready to conquer the world, but it does. I know Addison will enjoy a cup of coffee she didn't have to make, but it's more than that. These little things are part of why I walked away from my old life.

They may not be *important* individually, but they're the little things that change everything. I'll be riding the subway today instead of having my driver take me somewhere. The lack of phone calls I'm getting. The couch I slept on. And yes, the Mr. Coffee coffeemaker.

Understanding these little pieces is building the reality of this new life I'm living. I do not feel the same way that I did two weeks ago.

Because the man I was two weeks ago would be worried about the projects I've left behind. Taylor Brooks has a new release on Tuesday, and the reviews should be coming in for us to use in marketing. But... I just don't care. I am not that man. I am a man that uses a Mr. Coffee today. "Fuck it," I whisper.

"Fuck what?" Addison says from down the hall.

I turn to her and can't help but smile. She's wearing a long t-shirt with some kind of band logo on it. It hangs to just above her knees and looks like a bag with how oversized it is.

But for some reason, she looks more beautiful than any woman I've ever seen. In the dim light of a shabby apartment, she seems to glow. Maybe it has something to do with how much we've connected over the past week.

Or maybe she's just fucking beautiful.

"Nothing," I say. "Just thinking about work stuff."

She chuckles as she walks down the hallway. "Did you have nightmares about editing romance? Scared of the steamy scenes?"

"Actually, yes. They were terrifying. Completely vanilla and far too short for my liking."

She blinks as she gets to the table. I'm not totally sure why I said that, but as she raises an eyebrow at me and smirks a little, I'm glad I blurted out the first thing that came to mind.

"Who would have thought that Phillip Loughton, first of his name and Prince of Publishing, has a bit of kink hidden under that cold exterior?"

Maybe seducing Addison will be easier than I expected… "

"I made a pot of coffee," I say, changing the subject. I may want to turn this into something more than being roommates, but I'm not nearly awake enough for this banter. It's not a simple thing to flirt without going too far. Addison's couch was far nicer than the tables in that storage room, and I'd prefer that she didn't kick me out.

Addison just grins and walks into the kitchen. My eyes immediately go to her ass, which is the only real discernible shape under the sleep shirt. Round and perky, I'd love to pull that shirt up and...

Stop that, damn you. There's flirting, and there's being an idiot.

I force my eyes away from her ass to see what she's doing. She stands on her tiptoes to pull two mugs out of the cabinet, her calves tightening, and she glances over at me. "How do you take your coffee?" she asks before rubbing the sleep out of her eyes.

"Black." God, it's hard not to stare as she reaches forward to grab a ceramic jar with a weird purple pineapple on top.

"Disgusting," she says. "But then again, you think chicken and gravy is better than Michelin star chef's food, so your taste buds are obviously in question."

She puts two spoonfuls of sugar into one mug and frowns as she picks up the coffeepot. When she pours the coffee, it... doesn't do what it's supposed to.

Huge chunks of what can only be described as black mud slide out of the pot and into the mug, splashing coffee all over the place, including on Addison. "What the hell?" she exclaims, righting the coffeepot and putting it back. She picks up the mug and looks inside it.

"How many scoops of coffee did you put in there?" she asks with a very confused look on her face.

"Scoops? I just filled that compartment up. Like when you make espresso. I guess that's not how you do it?"

She chuckles. "No. Definitely not," she says as she pulls the compartment out. Then her eyes get even wider, and she lets out a laugh. "You didn't even put a filter in, Phillip. No wonder it's mud."

"A filter?"

"Come here. Yesterday, I taught you how to shop at a thrift store. Now I'm going to teach you to make coffee because an adult cannot adult without coffee. It's a law."

I stand up, and part of me is tempted to be frustrated. Addison is just laughing about it, though. It's in direct opposition to the way my father taught me. There was never anything funny when I made a mistake, even the first time that I did something. It was always anger and frustration.

Addison dumps the coffee pot into the sink, and it's just full of coffee grounds. Completely undrinkable. "Alright. I'm just going to walk you through it, step-by-step. First, you rinse the pot. Then you fill it up."

I watch as she goes through each of the steps, all of them very different from what I'd done. I memorize them. My childhood may not have held a lot of laughter, but I did learn how to learn. It's been a very, very long time since I had to be told something twice.

She pushes the brew button and grins at me. "Thank you for trying. I'm kind of particular about my morning coffee, though, so you might just want to let me make it."

I nod to her, but I know that tomorrow I'll be making another pot of coffee, and it'll be exactly how she did it today. She rinses the mug out, and I grab the roll of paper towels to clean up the mess.

"What's your plan for the day?" I ask when we sit back down at the table.

She eyes me like she's considering not answering that question, or at least not truthfully. It takes a moment, but she finally said, "Well, I was thinking about doing some writing."

Her answer surprises me. I'd thought she'd be exploring the city or spending time with friends or maybe just watching TV. I hadn't pegged her as a writer, though.

"What kind of writing?" At least this is something I know a thing or two about, even if I'm not a writer of anything but reports.

She sighs and leans back in her chair. "Just a book. No big deal, really."

"You're writing a book? That sounds like a big deal to me. What genre? Is it your first? Is that why you started working for Loughton House?"

She holds up her hand. "I will not answer any interrogations until I've had coffee. That's another law. Maybe not for everyone in the world, but in this apartment, all interrogations happen after coffee."

I chuckle. "That's fair. After coffee."

As if the coffee pot is synchronized to our conversation, it beeps, and Addison hops out of her chair and goes to it. This time, it comes out like it's supposed to.

I may have woken up earlier than Addison, but she's right. Coffee comes first. Always. Even in my world, coffee is life, and I'm just glad that I know how to make it now.

She brings the mugs to the table, and I look down at the one she chose for me. "You Make Me Forget Batteries" with an image of a tongue under the words.

I blink in surprise. "I know we haven't had enough coffee for interrogations yet, but please explain this mug."

She giggles. Not a laugh or a chuckle. A giggle like a teenaged girl with an inside joke. "You said you wanted kink, and I assumed…"

"You bought a terrible mug for an unexpected conversation with your boss, who also happens to be your new roommate? I'm going to call bullshit on that one."

Her giggle turns into laughter. "Maybe. Or maybe the only roommates I could stand are the ones that would get a kick out of a mug like that."

"So, you'd have told me to pack my bags if I'd been disgusted by your terrible coffee mug? You know what? Don't answer that. The real question is, why do you *want* this mug?"

She shrugs. "I might have a bit of a collection of thrift store finds…" She turns her mug around and shows me one that says, "Madame Rose's House of Pleasure" with what could only be a riding crop under it.

"I thought about giving you this one, but then I worried you'd think I was into *that* kind of kink. Which I'm not, just so you know." She bites her lip nervously, and for a moment, it looks like her cheeks flush. But then it's gone.

I try very hard to gloss over that comment. Try not to let her realize just how much more I'd like to talk about that specific topic.

But Addison realizes that she's gone into dangerous territory, and she changes the topic. "Okay, I'll talk about my book. Then we won't talk about it again."

I nod to her, mentally shifting gears away from hot kinky sex. Away from fantasizing about the kinds of things I'd like to do to her…

We're talking about her book. But she doesn't want to talk about it in depth. A lot of aspiring and new authors are like this. It's almost like they're ashamed of the fact that they did or are attempting to do something that millions of people dream of.

"I'm writing a romance novel. Well, this is my third romance novel, but the first two don't hit the quality I want, so I'm starting a third, and this is the one I'll be trying to get published. No, I do not want you to read it. No, I do not want you to tell me to send the other two to editors. No, I certainly don't want you to do anything with any of it. It's just a thing I'm doing and want no help or advice about it. That's all."

The room is quiet as I think about what she's said. "You know that I'm probably the best person to help you with it, right?" I finally say.

She smiles at me. "I don't care, and that's not a reasonable decision. It's an emotional one. If I decide that I'm ready to send my book to agents, I will do it when I feel like I want my name attached to it. The first two books are not as good as I want them to be. They were practice pieces, and even this book may end up being a practice piece."

I open my mouth to disagree with her, but she raises her hand. "Nope. That's the conversation. We've had it. Now it's done. No more discussing my book, okay?"

It takes a lot not to push her anymore. I've seen the books that have gone to the printers, and most of them are not masterpieces by any stretch. Plus, it's not like publishing a single romance novel would even really change her life very much. Probably ninety-five percent of romance authors keep their day jobs.

But part of me wonders about whether she could be part of the five percent. It's illogical and the business side of me says I'm being irrational. It doesn't matter though. She doesn't want to talk about it.

"So you're going to write your book today. That's how you want to spend a beautiful Saturday? Holed up in your room?"

Addison glares at me. "Well, I can't write it at work, and I have to spend my evenings teaching you to function, so when else would I write it?"

"That's fair. But I'm finding something to do that does not involve work. This is my first Saturday with no plans in years, and I'm not going to waste it."

She frowns, but then she shrugs. "I hope you have fun on your little adventure." With a grin, she stands up. "Don't go falling into bed with some random woman, since that's what you normally do on Saturday nights."

"That's not true at all!" I say.

She turns around and starts walking back down the hallway. "That's how I met you, isn't it?"

I guess she has a point.

Nineteen

ADDISON

The streetlamps made halos in the misty evening air as Angela stepped out of her bakery, eyes drooping after a long day of cupcake baking. Whoever said that starting a bakery would be fun has obviously never actually baked anything. Sure, looking at a thousand cupcakes is fun, but turning bags of flour and sugar into those cupcakes is damned hard work.

But this particular night is special. Twelve years ago to the day, Angela left New York City with her family, leaving Donovan behind…

I PICK MY PENCIL UP AND TWIRL IT OVER MY FINGERS like a miniature baton, a fidget that I've done since I was a kid. The piece of wood spins so fast that most people can't keep track of it, but I don't even have to think about it. The movement is automatic as I try to decide how Donovan and Angela will reunite.

God, how do these romance authors come up with these stories so quickly? Sure, the first book I wrote was finished in two weeks, but I'd been thinking about that story for years, and it just flowed. This is work, and like Angela's cupcake business, it's a hell of a lot harder than I expected.

I've managed an entire chapter already, and that's a lot more than I've written in a long time. Glancing out the window, I can see that the sun's still low in the sky. It's only been a few hours since Phillip left.

I chew my lip as the pencil spins on my finger. Maybe I shouldn't have written this morning. I've been in New York for a week, and truthfully, the only thing I've done is work and that one night of karaoke. Maybe I should have seen the city. Phillip may know nothing about surviving as one of the bottom ninety-nine percent, but I bet he knows New York better than I do.

He could probably even help me find places to put in my book.

It'd be nice to go to an actual New York bakery to see how Angela's shop could feel. I could see what Central Park is like instead of just what I've read about.

I try not to think about how much I'd probably enjoy just spending time with Phillip. He's still my boss, regardless of where he's sleeping tonight.

Thinking about our not-date at the thrift store makes me smile, though. He was surprisingly fun to shop with, especially for someone who was so against the very idea of wearing another person's clothes.

He's so interesting and different. No one would doubt his ability to run one of the biggest companies in the world. But he can't make coffee? Or use the subway. And doesn't know how to cook.

You'd think he'd been living under a rock his entire life. There's something kind of wonderful about that, though. He's untarnished by the world that's beat so many people down. Little things are still fun with him. Instead of being depressed because he can't buy expensive clothes, he's enjoying the adventure of it all.

I put the pencil on the desk and stand up. One look in the mirror tells me I need to spend some time getting ready, but I think that a day exploring the city could be a welcome change from staring at a computer screen.

Twenty

PHILLIP

THE GRASS IS ALWAYS GREEN HERE. JUST A LITTLE SPOT of life in the middle of Manhattan, not far from my father's townhouse. It's nothing special. There are no marble pillars of grandeur or art exhibits or even a bench.

Just a little patch of green in a world of gray.

I lean against the wall of the neighboring condo building and feel the bumps and ridges of the brick veneer. The ruby red shirt that I bought yesterday with hard-earned money will have a mark or two from me doing this, but I don't care.

My black wingtip dress shoes dig into the grass, breaking the carpet of green for a moment and exposing a bit of brown. I haven't been to this lot in years. Not since I ran away from home one afternoon when I was sixteen.

I'd wanted to go to a movie theater like a normal kid, and my father had ignored my pleas. Instead, I was supposed to go to the office and work on the marketing campaign for some book I'll never remember. All I'd wanted to do was see a movie for once, and his response was that I could see the movie when work was done.

Except the work was never done.

So I'd left. I hadn't gone to the movie like I'd wanted to. Truthfully, I didn't care that much about the movie. What I wanted was freedom. So, I'd come here, just a few blocks away from my father's townhouse, to the only patch of green within walking distance.

It wasn't what I was looking for. I'd only stayed for an hour before realizing there wasn't anything for me here anymore. I couldn't go back to the past just by coming to the place that reminded me of it. *She* wasn't here, and seeing this place again wouldn't bring her back.

This was where my mother had taken my brothers and me when we were young, and she needed to get out of the house. She'd sit in the dirt with us and let us run and yell and be kids. Andrew was still barely crawling then, but Mason and I would chase each other and get dirty. My mother was like that, though. She didn't care about all the things that Father thought were important. She just enjoyed playing with us, and those afternoons were some of the only times that Father let me be a child.

I think that if she'd lived much longer, our lives would have been much different. Maybe father wouldn't have turned out the way he has. Her death hit him harder than the rest of us, and he never dated again.

This was her place. No, that's not true. This was *our* place. The place we went to without my father, with no rules or etiquette. It was freedom from the world we lived in.

I don't know why I came here today, though. I could have done anything, but as soon as I stepped into the subway tunnel this morning, I knew that this was where I wanted to go.

The street's busy today, and even in this little haven of nostalgia, the sound breaks through the memories. People talking on cell phones as they walk. The constant hum of thousands of cars passing. Across the street, a man is yelling something at pedestrians.

I sigh as I rub a bit more of the green away from the dirt, growing the hole I'm mindlessly digging with my shoe. "I don't know what to do now," I whisper. It doesn't make sense to talk to an empty lot, but I need to say the words.

"I stepped away from Father and the life he forced on me. Now I don't know what to do. Where do I go from here?"

For a moment, I hope that there's an answer to my question that's plagued me all the nights I sat in that little storage room. I found freedom, but the craving that I feel isn't sated. I still feel that drive for *something*, but I don't know if it's freedom or even something new anymore. Because that voice in my head is still screaming.

At least when I'm not with Addison…

I sigh, knowing the answer and hating it.

After smoothing the grass back over the hole that I'd begun digging, I push away from the wall. This patch of green isn't what I've been looking for. It's not why I turned away from my fortune and the life that comes along with it.

There's something more to it, something that I crave, and it won't be found in that lot. It won't be found anywhere in my past.

Just like that day I'd run away from home, a place is not what I'm looking for.

Twenty-One

ADDISON

I PICK UP MY PHONE AND AM ABOUT TO TEXT PHILLIP when the door to my apartment opens. I jump, definitely not used to living with anyone. When he walks in, he sees me jump and a smile crosses his face. "All done writing for the day?"

It's like he lights up as soon as he sees me. I don't understand why it happens, but I don't think it's all in my head at this point. There's nothing special about me, but as we've spent more time together, I've seen how he reacts to other people, and it's different.

That first day at Loughton House, I saw him when he didn't know it was me. I saw the coldness in him, that part that Sera and Trish talked about. It didn't look like he'd smiled a single time in his life. But with me?

"Yeah, my brain is mush. I know you just got back, but do you want to play tour guide for me?"

He cocks his head, the smile only getting wider. "Where do you want to go?"

I just shrug. How am I supposed to know where to go in New York? "Dealer's choice. I just want to see the city since my book's set here, and it seems kind of silly to put scenes into it based on internet pictures when I could see them myself."

Phillip chuckles. "I'd agree with that. What kind of places are in your book?"

I frown, not wanting to tell him anything. Everything I say is a step closer to him convincing me to let him read it. "It's a second chance romance novel about a hole-in-the-wall bakery owner."

He nods, hand going to his cheek to scratch at the scruffy beard he's growing. "Cute places. Romantic places. Hmm… Central Park would be the obvious."

"That's what I was thinking, too."

He grins. "If I had my old credit card, I could show you some places that would blow your mind."

"Well, Angela is not a billionaire, and neither is her future husband, so we should probably steer clear of those options. Cheap or free would be optimal."

Phillip seems like he's excited about the whole idea. "I think I can manage. It's not every day I get to escort a beautiful woman on an adventure."

The way he says that so flippantly, like it's the most obvious thing in the world, is probably one of the most honest compliments I've ever had. And it sinks its claws in, each of them taking root as he gives me the same look he did when the pipes burst, and he dug me out from under the wreckage.

I grab my purse and move toward Phillip. "I hope that you're ready for the most romantic afternoon you've ever had," he says.

"What does that even mean?" I counter.

He chuckles. "I thought you were a romance author. Isn't that supposed to be your specialty?"

"Aspiring romance author," I correct.

He doesn't respond to that comment, just smiling as he opens the door. For a moment, it's like time stops. Like I'm being given a choice. I know that if I follow him out this door, things are going to change between the two of us. I've pushed him away several times now. Each time is harder than the last, and he hasn't fought me even the slightest. Instead, he's just... been him.

I take a deep breath and accept the possibility that maybe things will change. Maybe the man I'm standing next to will be a blip of fun in my life, just three weeks of sparks and excitement. Even though I barely know him, I feel like I can trust him to keep what happens right now separate from work when everything goes back to normal.

Plus, who knows exactly what will change?

Twenty-Two

ADDISON

WILDFLOWERS ARE EVERYWHERE AS WE WALK through the trees of Central Park. I didn't understand what Central Park was when I saw pictures of it. I didn't understand the size of it or that there's a freaking lake in the middle of it.

"This place is huge," I say, "and so beautiful. Who'd have thought that all of this was in the middle of Manhattan?"

Phillip smiles as he looks around. "It is pretty. Spring is better, but summer's not too bad." He's quiet as we sit on the bench in the middle of a scene that could have been in any romance novel ever. I'd imagined a thousand pigeons and a walking path around a little pond like in my hometown, but this is enormous and nothing like that.

"Do you come here often?" I ask while he stares off into space. It's odd seeing him in a place like this. Sure, Central Park is in the middle of Manhattan, but it's a different vibe, almost like it's separate from the actual city. And Phillip Loughton belongs in the concrete jungle, not walking around in fields of wildflowers.

He shakes his head. "Nope. When I was young, my mother would take us here occasionally, but not very often. My father didn't want me to waste time in parks. He wanted me at the office doing something 'useful'."

The more time I spend with Phillip, the more I understand why he gave up everything. I'd thought it was insane before, but it feels like he really has spent literally every moment working since he was born. No wonder he wanted some time to do anything else.

"Well, does this fit the characters you're making? Is this where they'd go?"

I look around at the trees that line the path and fill in the spaces between, just enough to blot out the rest of the city, but not enough that you couldn't walk through them. It's like getting lost in the woods only a mile away from the biggest city in the states.

My first instinct is that it could be the perfect place for romance, but after a moment, I shake my head. It's not what Angela would enjoy. She wanted to come to the city, to escape her small-town life. She'd want romance to blossom amidst the buildings and traffic and life there. Not somewhere that would remind her of the forests outside her parents' house in Vermont.

"Probably not," I say with a sigh. I'm still trying to figure out just what kind of scene will prompt their first kiss.

Phillip doesn't seem bothered at all. "Somehow, I had a feeling that it would be wrong. You're basing that book on you, after all, and you're not going to look for love in Central Park."

I squint my eyes at him. "What do you mean?" The real question is how would he know what I was writing other than the tiny little details and hints I've dropped?

He stands up and looks down at me. "You're writing what you know, Addison. Just like most first-time authors. They're the stories you've had in your head forever. Your characters are pieces of yourself. And *you* wouldn't be happy with love being found here."

I don't know what to say. Is it really that easy to tell what I'd write about? And how would he know where I'd be looking for in a romantic scene?

Phillip just chuckles. "Come on. I've got a better spot. It's a short bus ride, and we can talk about how annoyed you are on the ride."

Something's changed in Phillip. I don't know what happened today, but something did. He's been quiet and nervous since Friday, but now, it's like everything's clicked together for him and he's just as confident as he'd been in the office.

I stand up. "Okay, lead the way. I'm intrigued about the spot and even more intrigued about what you think you know about me."

All he does is grin.

.

Twenty-Three

PHILLIP

"WHY WOULD YOU THINK THAT I'M ANGELA?" SHE says, completely confused and frustrated, and it's really hard not to laugh.

We're sitting on the bus as it heads to the Brooklyn Bridge Park, and I feel like this is the closest we've been since we shared a bed. Ever since then, there's always been a distance between us, whether that was physically or emotionally. But now, it's just the two of us, and that gap is closing.

Addison tries to turn more in her seat and her leg brushes against mine. She automatically stops and glances down, but she doesn't pull it away. Instead, she continues her argument. "I don't own a bakery. I'm not bumping into any exes, thank all that's holy. I certainly am not struggling to find time for dating, since dating isn't even on my radar."

It's so hard not to laugh. "Okay, fine. You're not starting your dream career. You're absolutely not spending a bunch of time with a guy you ran into unexpectedly. And you definitely don't struggle to convince yourself to have some fun instead of working constantly."

She glares at me. "I am not Angela," she grumbles and turns in her seat again so she's facing forward.

"You're not an ex, and we aren't dating," she says after a few moments have passed.

"I agree. I didn't say you were Angela. She is a part of you, though. Like any talented author, you're taking your own dreams and putting them into another world where maybe things go a little differently."

She just shakes her head, her jaw clamped shut, and I shrug. I may have plans to woo her, but I'm going to be honest.

Finally, Addison's jaw loosens, and she says, "Maybe you're right. I am starting my dream career, and it's freaking hard. I do feel a little lonely in New York." She turns to look at me, and she smiles. "And maybe I enjoy spending time with a certain guy I ran into unexpectedly."

Well, that was faster than I expected.

She sighs then. "But Phillip, no matter how much I enjoy spending time with you, you're still my boss. And that's not going to change. I am not writing a book based on us."

"Actually…" I say, completely ignoring that last comment, and she pauses. "I'm not your boss. Just a fellow junior editor at Loughton House. I mean, your boss wouldn't be caught dead wearing a shirt with a saffron stain on it."

She can't help but laugh. "Or God forbid he wore something that had touched another human being's skin."

"I'm pretty sure he'd be a lot more concerned about that saffron stain." It's nice to hear Addison laugh. I don't understand why it makes me feel so light, but it does. Everything else in the world may be confusing and stressful, but sitting on a disgusting city bus hearing her laugh makes it all seem unimportant.

The laughter trails off, and she looks alive, but the lightness fades away quickly enough. "That's just temporary, and you know it. In three weeks, you'll be the boss again. Either things will be terrible which affects our work, or things are great which means I'm sleeping with the Prince of Publishing. That obviously affects work."

And for the first time, I become serious. "I already promised that anything that happens between us will not affect what happens at work. Addison, I have *never* broken a promise since I was eight years old."

I know how much fury and frustration I'm showing. How could she know how much a promise means to me? It doesn't matter though. I can't keep my emotions out of my body language when I feel like someone is calling me a liar.

"Okay," she whispers.

I nod to her, and for a moment, tension builds. "Do you have any family?" I ask.

She frowns. "Starting another interrogation?"

"You've had coffee, so it's fair game." I give her a smile to help her get past the seriousness of the previous moment.

"Just my mom. I was an only child, and my sperm donor was nameless. What about you?"

My life is on the record for anyone to read about. Somehow, it's still strange to describe. "There's my father that you've probably heard plenty about. Then there's Andrew who's running the new London branch of Loughton House." I hesitate to even mention Mason.

"What's wrong?" Addison asks.

"There's my other brother, Mason. But we don't talk about him. My father disowned him as soon as he turned eighteen. I haven't heard from him in over ten years, though I suspect Andrew has been in contact with him through the years."

Addison looks shocked. "Your father disowned him? Why? What the hell could he have done that was so bad?"

I chuckle, thinking about the day. "He hit him in the nose."

"Oh."

I shake my head. "Actually, it's not because he hit him. It's because Mason told my father he wasn't going to college. He was leaving, and he wasn't coming back.

"Well, my father has a way of ignoring what you want and forcing you to do what he's decided is best. He's just never been very good at it with Mason. He tried to tell him he was going to cut him off if he didn't go to college and get the degree Father had picked out for him."

I can't help but chuckle again as the memory washes over me. "So Mason told him he could shove his money up his ass. My father said that he was an ungrateful little shit, and he turned around and hit him square in the nose.

Dropped him to the ground. I've never seen my father so pissed and so humiliated in my entire life."

Addison's eyes are wide as she listens. It sounds like some kind of secret family drama, but it really isn't. My brother told plenty of people about it, but truthfully, nobody cares what the owner of a publishing house does.

"Why don't you keep in contact with him?" she asks. "It doesn't seem like you're mad about what he did."

I shrug. "I wouldn't want to be in contact with me if I were him. Where Andrew has always had some separation from my father, that's not the case with me. Until I gave up my fortune, I spent so much time around him it would be impossible to hide talking to Mason. That'd just make everything worse for both of us."

"That's terrible," she says softly. "I wish I had more family. Mine isn't…"

The bus stops suddenly, and I realize where we are. "Time to get off," I say and stand up.

As soon as we step off the bus, we stop and look at the scene in front of us. The sunset is hitting the Brooklyn Bridge at the perfect angle, setting it alight with golds and oranges and making it shine like it's on fire.

"God, it's beautiful," Addison says from beside me.

"I bet Angela could enjoy some romance here," I say as we stand and stare at a view that couldn't be captured by words or a photograph. It's one of those moments that pulls at you and makes you question whether there is any art that can compare to the world we live in.

And as beautiful as the bridge is in the setting sun, I turn away from it to look at Addison. They call this time of day the golden hour. It's when the sun hits everything and makes it glow like it's made of gold. This afternoon, the bridge that Addison is so taken by doesn't compare to the woman standing beside me.

"Angela would love this," she says softly, as though words could ruin the view. She finally breaks away from it and sees me staring at her. "I couldn't do it justice with words, though."

Taking her hand, I give her a grin. I expect her to stiffen at least a little, but she doesn't. Her fingers wrap around mine, entwining themselves in a way that lets me know there is no mistaking that this is more than just two friends holding hands.

"There's a bench," I say and walk to the little copse of trees shading two benches. Addison walks beside me, and it's like all the little things have clicked into place. "Instead of trying to describe what the bridge looks like, explain how it makes you… err, Angela feel."

She frowns as we sit down next to each other leaving no space between us. "I don't know."

"Fine. Tell me how it makes you feel. Tell me all the emotions that it pulls at. What does it remind you of? Just tell me like you were trying to describe the experience to a friend."

She chews her lip and looks back at the bridge. "It makes me feel hopeful. Like the old metal that's normally so dull could be so alive." I nod to her, pushing her to continue. "Maybe it doesn't matter what has happened in the past, and there are times that even a bridge that's seen a hundred and fifty years of hardship can shine brighter than the day it was made."

I smile at her and say, "And maybe a person that's seen twenty-two years of hardship can be just as alive as the day she was made?"

She turns her body toward me, and when her leg presses against mine, she doesn't pull away. "Or a man that's seen thirty... Wait, how old are you?"

I chuckle at how easily her mind is sidetracked, but inside, my body is warming to her touch. "Thirty-two. Only a decade older than you."

She raises an eyebrow. "Thirty-two years old, and you just learned how to make coffee today. I think we need to write that on a calendar and celebrate it like some kind of anniversary."

"I don't think I could forget today," I say, and my body shivers just a little. She's so close. The calculating, business-minded side of me screams to push away from her, to put distance between us. I've lived in that mind for my entire life. Until a week ago, I wouldn't have had a second thought about that decision.

But then I met a beautiful woman who made me feel things that the calculating side didn't understand.

She made me want things that didn't make sense. Why would I risk the perfect situation for my experiment? Why would I make life harder at work than it already is by having a romantic relationship with an employee? Like she's already said, in three weeks, I'll be going back to being her boss.

Yet, none of that matters to me right now. Only the way her hair smells like lilacs with a hint of vanilla. The way her lips are parted just slightly, begging me to crane my neck down and kiss them. The need to feel her skin.

"I guess that's true. You took your first bus today." I grin at her and move just a little closer. Her words grow quieter and trail off as she recognizes the movement. "You definitely won't be able to forget that…" she whispers.

"I don't think that's what I'll remember about today," I whisper back. My body feels like it's reverberating with every heartbeat. And when I bring my hand up to touch her cheek, she leans into it.

"I'm glad you're not my boss," she whispers.

Me too. But instead of saying anything, I lean down and press my lips to hers. My fingers tighten, and the tips dig into the hair at her temple. Her body feels like it melts, but her hand finds my shoulder, and her nails dig in.

It's like something inside me breaks and is remade in that moment. Like my very perception of the world is shifted just a touch.

Addison's eyes had been green a moment before, b now I'm seeing them in exquisite detail. Browns a and whites in a sea of green. A sea that I could

150

"Phillip," she gasps as I move to kiss her neck where her jaw ends, leaning her head back. Her hand moves up the back of my neck to run through my hair, grasping it and pulling me tighter.

"I've wanted to kiss you since that night at the motel," I whisper in her ear.

"I wanted more than that."

So did I. All the walls I've ever had feel like they're crumbling. The strict lessons on etiquette. The necessity of standing apart from the rest of the world. The ability to use logic and ignore emotion.

They're just all… gone. In a kiss.

My lips whisper over her throat, and my hands are desperate to find bare skin to touch. But she pushes away, gasping as she stands up. "We should go home," she gets out between breaths.

That's when I remember that we're on a bench in a popular park. Not in a hidden corner of the world. Not somewhere that I should forget the world.

But damn it, I want to. For a half-second, I almost give into the desires, but then I grin. "Yeah, that'd probably be best. Though I'm not really looking forward to a forty-five minute bus ride right now."

Addison just shakes her head. "We're catching a cab. I'm not ready to be this turned on for forty-five minutes in public."

That's still a thirty-minute ride. And for just a moment, I really wish I had access to my money and my driver. Because we'd be in the back of my limo in two minutes, and then there wouldn't be anything stopping us.

Twenty-Four

ADDISON

HIS HAND RUNS OVER MY THIGH, AND IT MAKES ME shiver. Phillip is the epitome of a terrible decision, but right now, I don't care. The way it felt to kiss him. The way he looks at me as though I'm the most important thing in the room. His touch on my bare skin.

It all just makes me melt. I've been fighting my desires since the moment I met him in that motel lobby, and anyone with any sense would have known that being around him this long was a losing battle.

But how do you push away a man that you can't find any real flaws in? Unless you count him not knowing how to make coffee. And that he lives on my couch.

I can see my apartment building down the street, and as Phillip's hand moves higher up my thigh, his fingers tightening, it takes everything in me not to moan. When I look at him, he's watching me, the same way he watched me in the motel room.

Then his lips move to my neck, his breath hot against my skin, and he whispers, "I've never been this desperate for anyone."

Logical me wants to tell him that's a lie. I'm just some girl. He's a billionaire. He's ten years older than me. There's no way that he wants me more than anyone else he's ever known.

But those eyes tell me I'm wrong.

"Why?" I whisper back.

Without any hesitation, he says, "Because you make me feel more alive than I can remember. Plus, you're fucking gorgeous."

This cab cannot drive any slower. I feel like I'm going to explode before we even get to the apartment. My ex never made me feel anything like this. His words didn't make my body quiver. His kisses didn't make the world feel like it was shattering.

And his touch on my leg definitely did not make me question how I was supposed to keep from begging him to keep going in front of a cab driver.

I put my hand on his thigh, my fingers tightening around the cashmere of his slacks. There's an oddity, a bulge far lower down his thigh than I'd expected, and my eyes open wide as I realize what it is.

The corners of Phillip's lips twist up just the slightest, and he lets out of a soft breath of relief. I know that I'm not mistaken. Normal Addison would pull her hand away and maybe rethink this whole idea, but normal Addison is being held hostage by an absolute slut.

With slutty Addison at the wheel, I smile as I slowly rub his enormous bulge through his pants. He gasps a little, and I catch the cab driver glancing back at us. I should be bothered that a complete stranger can see me fondling my boss's cock, but I'm not.

I doubt anything would bother me at this point. Other than how freaking slow this cab is moving.

Leaning toward Phillip, my lips graze his neck, and I whisper, "I wake up fingering myself after fantasizing about you."

He visibly shivers, but his jaw tightens as though he's trying to resist doing something. And then the car stops.

"That'll be thirty-seven fifty," the cab driver says with a grin, his eyes following my hand on Phillip's thigh.

I take my hand off Phillip to dig in my purse and pull fifty dollars out, quickly handing it to the driver. "Keep the change," I say, and in seconds, I'm standing outside the cab with Phillip. I expect to go straight to the apartment, but he moves in front of me, stopping me in my place.

For all the frantic feelings running through me, when he looks down at me, I feel pinned in place. Instead of dragging me up the stairs and throwing me into bed like I'd seen in my mind's eye, he puts a hand on my cheek, his fingers entwining themselves in my hair.

His thumb presses against my cheek ever so lightly, as though I'm made of porcelain. At the same time, the fingers in my hair tighten, pulling my head backward as he crushes his lips against mine.

I've never experienced the sensations that course through me. His kiss is almost painful. Like a normal kiss couldn't convey the need he has for me. And I know exactly how he feels. I've pushed all my feelings into a dark corner of my mind, but when his lips touched mine at the park, it woke them all up.

Now, I feel a desperation that can only be expressed through touch. A *need* to feel him. All of him. I'd called my temporary madness in the cab slutty Addison, but the reality is that I simply need this man.

I pull him to me, my arm reaching around to his back, and my fingers digging in. "I need to feel you, Phillip," I moan as his lips find the crook of my neck.

"You will," he promises.

Every inch of my body is throbbing, and then his other hand moves under my shirt. Only enough for his thumb and index finger to press against bare skin, and it sends me soaring. They dig into my hip, squeezing me, and it's a teaser of what I'm sure is going to happen as soon as we make it back to my apartment.

Images flash through my mind of what could happen. Me straddling him, those big hands tightened around my waist as he pushes my body to take more of him. Me bent over, him towering behind me with his hands squeezing my ass while he slams into me...

"Please," I beg. "I need you now."

He pulls back, and he's looking at me like I'm someone he's going to devour rather than someone he wants to make love to. It's different, like a man possessed. This morning, I showed him how to make coffee and laughed over ridiculous mugs, and now, he looks like the most dangerous man I've ever met.

Maybe he is dangerous to me. Maybe there's more to the sweet guy who was willing to share a motel room with a complete stranger. But those eyes have never changed. He's always watched me like a predator, and it's always turned me on. From the very first time.

His hand releases my hair, but it doesn't leave me. Instead, his fingers trail down my throat toward my breasts, and as his fingers graze the curves, I gasp. Yet, his breathing is even, completely unfazed by how he's affecting me.

When I glance down at his crotch, there's no mistaking how turned on he is. Hell, it should be illegal for him to be in public with that tent if only because it'd make every woman who passed start drooling.

He finally pulls his hand away from the neckline of my shirt and takes my hand in his. On the surface, it's similar to how he held my hand at the park, but it's completely different. That was soft and sweet. That was innocent.

This is anything but that.

Where I hesitated before, there's none now. I nearly trip over myself trying to get my body to move, but Phillip is there to catch me with a smile on his lips. I see the shadow of the goofy guy I've come to know, but then it's gone. Instead of putting me back on my feet, he turns me around midair, and pulls me to him.

Where there's always been a distance between us, even during these kisses, it's gone. My breasts press against his chest. My legs wrap around his hips, and for the first time, I feel him pressed against me.

And my heart beats through every inch of me. Throbbing like I'm a ticking time bomb.

He stares into my eyes as his hands grip my ass tighter. I feel him walking, but my attention is on his eyes, on his hands, and the desperation to feel what's making that bulge.

When he kisses me this time, it's softer. Not gentle, but not painful, either. His hands don't soften, though, and I wonder if they'll be that insistent after he's ripped my clothes off.

I feel us ascending the stairs. We should be saying things or kissing or anything. But we're not. It's just his hands on my body, my legs wrapped around his waist, and our eyes connecting us in a way that doesn't even make sense.

I'm taking in every inch of his face, memorizing it in perfect detail. The way his lips curve up from that grin he never has at work. How his beard has started to fill out after a week without shaving. His eyes flickering in the moonlight, little sparkles of light in dark pools.

Then I feel the door pressing against my back, and he's kissing me again. Fiery and passionate, his lips dance across the skin of my neck, each touch leaving heat in their wake. I can't help but moan as he gets closer to my collarbone, and when the door swings open to my dark apartment, he carries me straight to the bedroom.

Once again, he surprises me by laying me down gently on my bed. There's one thought in my mind as I look up at him. *How did I ever push this man away?*

The answer's simple. I was an idiot.

Twenty-Five

PHILLIP

GOD, I NEED ADDISON SO MUCH RIGHT NOW. LIKE A moth to the flame, I feel like I'd gladly dance in her light, even if it burned me up in the process. She's laying on her bed, and I'm doing my best to get control of myself.

Instead of ripping the blouse she's wearing apart, I take a breath. "You are the most gorgeous woman I have ever seen," I say. And I mean it. Splayed out and begging me to fuck her, she looks like a goddess. Just as beautiful as she did at the park this afternoon, except this is the version that isn't let out in the sunlight. The side of her that pulls at the part of me the world doesn't want to see.

She doesn't respond, but her breathing hitches slightly, and I can't help myself. My fingers move to the buttons on the cotton blouse, slowly undoing them and revealing the pale skin underneath. Each button that is undone makes me want to rip the rest of them even more.

And when the two sides hang limply over her breasts, her stomach exposed, I give into the desires. Bending at the waist, I put my hands on her wrists, holding them down as I pick up where I'd stopped earlier. My lips press against the exposed curve of her right breast, my teeth grazing the soft skin and leaving goosebumps behind.

My cock is straining against my pants, but anything worth doing is worth doing right, and Addison is certainly worth doing. Plus, I like to see her quiver in my hands. I enjoy the way her body tenses when I touch somewhere new.

"That feels so fucking good," she whispers, as my lips dance across her stomach. I have to let her wrists go to undo her jeans, and her hands move through my hair, her nails lightly scratching my scalp. I undo the button and pull the zipper down. Her scent is intoxicating, and when I finally look back at her, she's staring at me, each breath coming out as a moan or whimper.

Addison wasn't lying when she said she was desperate. "Please don't stop," she whispers in the darkness, and it makes my cock swell even more.

I hook my fingers under the waistband of her jeans, and as soon as I pull, she lifts her ass off the bed so I can get them off. When I slide her panties down her legs, I have to stop for a half-second just to look at her. Just to take a moment to see what I've wanted since the night I met her.

She's squirming on the bed, her skin aching for more, and I know exactly what I want to do. Kneeling on the ground, I pull her ass to the edge. She looks down at me, knowing what I'm about to do, and I can feel her body tensing as I run my hands over her stomach.

Addison may have been the one to say that she was desperate, but I'm going crazy, too. Hell, I've spent nearly as many hours this week thinking about her as I spent working.

I press my lips against her lips while my hands grip her waist. My tongue darts out, tasting her for the first time. Wonderful and sweet. Her scent is everywhere, all-encompassing. I let go.

My tongue finds her slit and slowly teases it, slipping inside for a second before going back to run its length. My hands move over her stomach, my nails grazing her skin.

And I watch her the entire time. I watch her back arch and her breasts press upward. I see her run her hands through her hair and over her skin. She's lost in the sensations, and I don't ever want to stop. I want to feel her come for me. I want to hear her scream my name.

When my tongue finds her clit, her hands move to the back of my head, pulling me harder against her, and her hips begin to buck. Her moans come out like soft whispers. It's hard to breathe with how soaked she is, but I can't imagine pulling away.

"I don't know what you're doing," she mumbles, "but don't stop. Please don't stop."

Her words just make me lick faster. I move my hands down her thighs, and when I press two fingers against her entrance, her eyes open wide. She's so wet that when I push, it's like she swallows them up.

She's like a vise, squeezing my fingers as her eyes open even wider. It only makes me want to be inside her even more.

Addison pulls my head away from her at the same time that she lets out the loudest moan so far. Her body goes taut like raw electricity is coursing through her. She constricts around my fingers as she comes.

A second later, she's panting. I can't help but grin as she looks at me. And that's when I slide my fingers out of her, making her moan and shake.

"That's not fair," she says.

"What are you talking about?" How can anything be "not fair" after that orgasm?

She chuckles and says, "You've got to give a girl a few minutes before you make her come again." Before I can say anything, she's sitting up. She pulls off her shirt and bra and tosses them to the ground before saying, "But while we wait, I have a pretty good idea of what I could do…"

Twenty-Six

My body is still made of liquid lightning as I pull Phillip to his feet. My pussy is still dripping wet, and any other time, I'd feel some kind of embarrassment since I'm the only one that's naked right now.

But I'm going to fix that ASAP, and if Phillip could make me feel that good with just his tongue, I don't know what's waiting for me when I get that cock inside me.

"Now it's my turn," I say as I get down on my knees in front of him. My hands go to his belt, and I have to take a breath as another aftershock runs through me. I've never experienced that strong of an orgasm. Not with a toy and not with a man. I gave Phillip the right mug. He definitely puts the vibrator to shame.

I look up at him and see him panting just a little. I cup his balls through his pants, and his body tenses. Seeing his reaction makes me feel powerful even though I'm on my knees.

A part of me just wants to tease him through his pants, but I know that what comes after is so much better. I fumble through unbuttoning and unzipping him, and then in one movement, I pull his pants and boxers down.

And see a cock that is going to break me.

I can't wait. Never before did I expect to feel like this, but something about Phillip has me wanting him to touch me hard, to fuck me hard, and then to hold me even harder afterward.

I want this. The way he's looked at me tonight shows me that there's more to him than the quiet guy that makes me laugh. There's more behind those eyes than the Prince of Publishing. There's a part of him I'm just meeting.

I run my fingers along the length and smile up at him. He's almost shaking as my tongue flicks over the tip. "God, Addison," he whispers.

And I wrap my lips around the tip at the same time that I wrap my fingers around the shaft. His legs look like they're ready to buckle, and I keep looking up at him as I swallow more of him up.

Somehow, even after being away from all of his fancy cologne, he still smells like that shirt hanging in my closet. Dark and smokey.

I tease him, my hand moving slowly up and down the shaft while my mouth barely moves. My tongue dances over the tip and along the bottom, and Phillip keeps groaning.

"Your mouth is heaven," he moans, and I feel his hands on the back of my head, so similar to how I'd run my hands through his hair. And ground against his face.

Thinking about our roles being reversed makes my body ache. Instead of hoping he'll read my mind, I open my mouth wider and pull my hands away from his cock.

For a moment, Phillip seems to sink, but then I put my hands over his. And push.

His eyes go wide, but he doesn't hesitate to put some pressure on the back of my head, pushing me down on his cock. It slides over my tongue and hits the back of my throat.

My gag reflex kicks in, and my stomach twists while my body tenses. Even when my body rejects his actions, I want more. I don't know what's come over me, but damn it, I want this man to really fuck me. Not just stick his dick in me.

I want to be sore tomorrow from what we do tonight.

So I push his hands down harder, and when the tip hits the back of my throat, I gag again, but I don't release the pressure on his hands.

Tears start running down my cheeks, but I'm wetter than I've ever been. When I finally come up for air, his cock slips out of my mouth, and I smile up at him.

Where he'd been tentative before, he doesn't hesitate now. Doesn't check to see if I'm okay or if I need a break. Even though I'm gasping for air, he just wraps his hand around his cock and guides it into my mouth. With the other hand, he tightens his grip on my hair and thrusts.

It's incredible. Somehow, the back of my throat and my pussy must be connected because the more he fucks my face, the more it throbs. "You're so perfect," he groans as the tip of his cock finally slides just a little into my throat.

He stays there. I'm gagging with tears streaming down my face, and he's looking at me like I'm the most beautiful person in the world. When he finally releases me, I collapse, desperate for air.

Then, he's lifting me into the air and laying me on the bed. When we started this, I'd thought that he was intense, but looking up at him now, I know what the rabbit feels when the wolf stares at her.

And I spread my legs for the wolf. As he undoes his buttons and rips his shirt off, my heart is racing out of control. He kicks off his shoes, drops his pants, and yanks his wallet out of the back pocket. With his other hand, he slowly strokes his cock, my spit providing all the lube he could need. My fingers move to my clit, but it's barely even noticeable at this point. Every other sensation I've had in the last thirty minutes has been so much more intense.

Phillip drops the wallet to the floor as soon as he's dug out a condom. I'll never forget the sound of him tearing the foil wrapper. The only other sound in the room is my finger doing its best to mimic what his tongue had done.

He rolls the condom over his cock without ever actually looking at it. Then he lays down on top of me. His lips find mine at the same time that his cock finds my soaking entrance. In a single thrust, he forces his way inside me.

It hurts a little, but it's like the pain is far away in some corner of my mind that's easily forgotten. Phillip's hand goes to my cheek just like he did when he kissed me hard for the first time. His fingers tighten in my hair as his thumb brushes my cheek.

And his lips find mine. If there was any drug in the world that felt like this, I'd be an addict. How can anything be so all-consuming? So earth-shattering?

His other hand finds my breast and squeezes hard enough that I should pull away, but whatever pain I feel just gets stuffed in the corner. I arch my back to show him just how much I enjoy it.

Phillip thrusts, and I don't know how to react to the sensations. I lose control of my body and instead of bucking my hips, trying to drive him deeper like I did earlier with his fingers, I run my hands over his naked back. I need to feel him. All of him.

And then a dam bursts inside me. When he'd licked my pussy, I'd had an orgasm, but this is more than that. This is explosive. This is a full-body experience, and I didn't even know that was possible.

I scream as my body goes tight, every muscle straining, and Phillip's thrusts only get harder. He pins me down, not letting me escape the pleasure that's too much for my body to handle.

Just as the waves of bliss slow down, he sits up on his knees. His hands go to my hips, and he never lets his cock slip out of me as he repositions himself.

Then he smiles as his fingers tighten their grip. "You're incredible," he says right before he lifts my ass off the bed and holds it in the air as he fucks me like a jackhammer.

I can't help but scream as yet another orgasm rips through me. Everything Phillip does to me drives me higher, yet his touch feels selfish, drawing every bit of pleasure from me. The word ravish is the only one that makes sense.

His cock swells as I constrict around him even while I struggle in his grip. My body shakes, and I can't help but push back. All of it is a blur as I'm consumed by the sensations shattering my awareness of reality. The only thing I'm sure of is that in this moment, I am his, and he is mine in a way that I've never experienced.

He groans out his own release, and for what feels like minutes, but is only the blink of an eye, I'm disappointed that it's over. Even though my body is so sensitive that it doesn't know if I could handle even another minute. Even though my pussy aches and my muscles are exhausted.

Instead of just rolling over like I've come to expect from partners, Phillip leans forward, releasing my hips, and he presses his lips to mine. This kiss is no less passionate than the previous ones. His lips feel just as desperate for me, his breath coming out in soft gasps.

And I breathe him in. His body may be satisfied, but he isn't. "I've dreamed of doing that since the moment I met you," he whispers as his lips move to my neck. His breath tickles my ear just as much as his words tickle my mind and... my heart? His touch and actions were rougher and more demanding than I could have imagined, yet I felt more needed and more desired than ever before.

"Is that what sex is supposed to be like?"

"Yes." Such a simple statement. He says it with complete confidence, as though it was a natural truth like the sun rising in the east or that every cookie could use a little extra vanilla.

"Well, I think I've decided that our arrangement needs some altering," I say through a gasp as he thrusts again. Even though he's gone soft, he's still deep inside me, still sending little lightning bolts through my body with every move.

"Oh yeah? Do I get a say in these changes?"

I grin at him and then my back arches reactively as he thrusts yet again. "Maybe," I say. "But I'm hoping that you'll enthusiastically agree with them."

Phillip's kisses move down my neck to my breasts. "Mmm. I'm all ears. And lips."

He flicks his tongue over my nipple, and it sends a shiver through me. How can I still be this turned on after all that? "I was thinking that maybe…" I let out a moan as he pinches my nipple with his lips. "Maybe we could have a little more intimate roommate agreement."

He looks up, a sparkle in those blue eyes. "Are you asking me to do this to you more often?"

"All the time," I moan.

"I think I can agree with that." He finally sits up, and it's like I can breathe again. "But I have a condition before I can sign such a demanding roommate agreement."

It feels strange to have this conversation with his cock still inside me, even though I was just trying to be sexy. Maybe I'm terrible at dirty talk because this is beginning to feel like an actual negotiation.

"What kind of condition?" I ask cautiously.

Phillip runs his fingers between my breasts and says, "Oh, nothing too difficult. I just want you to teach me to cook. I like the thought of making dinners for you occasionally."

That brings a grin to my lips. A man that wants to give me earth-shattering orgasms *and* cook for me? Yeah, I think I can work that into our roommate agreement. "Deal. But if you keep this up, I'm going to be too sore to walk tomorrow."

"You're turning me on. The thought of a naked woman with a swollen pussy with nothing to do except lie in bed might be a fantasy come true."

His fingers move down my stomach, and just as they're about to touch my lips, I push my knees together in front of him. "Hey now, tomorrow we have a date with my friends at the karaoke bar…"

His eyes go wide, and he rolls off me. "That wasn't part of the roommate agreement at all. I am the worst singer in the world, and those friends of yours are my employees. How can I expect them to respect me?"

I grin at him. "They're not your employees, Junior Editor Extraordinaire. And every new editor has to go through their rite of passage. Singing a terrible 80s song in front of thirty people they don't know. It's a rule."

He sighs. "I didn't know that you were a sadist, Addison. I might not have signed that imaginary roommate agreement if I'd known."

Twenty-Seven

I DON'T KNOW HOW TO RATIONALIZE THE WAY I FEEL about Addison. Being attracted to her makes all the sense in the world. She's gorgeous. A nice round ass. Breasts that beg to be squeezed and held. A smile that can push away any bad mood. Eyes that I can't look away from.

But I don't just want to look at her. I want to be near her. Like being around her makes the storm clouds go away. The simplest things that would be just another task to be completed are enjoyable because I'm standing next to her.

She's wearing an apron right now. That's all. Her cute little ass is sticking out under the tie-string, but I can't reach out to grab it. Instead, I'm stirring a pot of alfredo that she made from scratch, something that I believe might make her a witch. Her knife is damn near invisible as she chops parsley and mushrooms and chicken for our dinner.

"How the hell did you learn to do all of this? Did you take classes in college or something?" I ask as the spoon makes lazy motions through the white sauce. Bits of parmesan cheese are half-melted to the spoon, and I have to scrape them off occasionally.

She doesn't look up as she says, "I got tired of not being able to afford good food, so I learned to cook."

"That's so strange to me. I don't know if I've had to start from square one in learning anything since I can remember. Everything revolved around work, so it was all so connected to other things I already knew."

She stops chopping and looks at me. "You've never picked up a hobby? You've never been intrigued about something and just pursued it? Aren't all rich guys into cigars or whiskey tasting or something? I mean, maybe Daddy Loughton had you drinking Scotch since you could walk like a good billionaire, but I doubt you were puffing on cigars at four years old."

I chuckle at the stereotyping, since it's probably not all that wrong. Except for the fact that my father doesn't drink. "Well, I picked up disc golf at one point when a lot of people were talking about it becoming the new racquetball."

"Disc golf? Where you go to a park and throw frisbees at metal baskets?"

I nod to her, grinning as I think about all the times I threw my disc into the rough just so I could get away from the people I'd gone with. "Yeah, it was a short period of time. My father didn't think it was worth doing, but he couldn't argue that I managed to close a few deals with younger clients because of it. I was never very good, but it was nice to get some time away from the office."

Addison huffs. "Every time you bring up your childhood, I'm traumatized for you, Phillip. You act like it's not a huge deal, but everything you experienced is like the definition of why we have child labor laws. You should have had more time to play."

I know I should have. Every moment I spend with Addison makes me realize that I've missed so much. But the past is the past, and I want to be in the present. Even if the present includes a karaoke bar in an hour.

"Well, I'm playing now. The only thing that would be better is if you weren't wearing that apron and I could see your breasts. Maybe if I could touch them... Squeeze them..."

She gives me a sideways grin as she goes back to chopping. "Yeah. That's not going to happen, Mister. I'm okay wearing nothing but an apron to turn you on, but boiling butter burns on my tits is not worth it."

"A guy has to try," I say as I look down and see that the alfredo sauce is finally becoming a smooth and creamy sauce instead of cream with chunks in it. "I think this is done."

She glances over at the sauce and nods. "Perfect timing." She scoops up everything she was chopping and plops it into the sauce. "Keep stirring. The sauce might stick if you don't."

As she walks past me to the pot of boiling noodles, I reach around and give her ass a quick slap. "Watch it, buddy. Remember that I'm the sadist of the two of us. You might wake up tied to a bed with me in latex."

"Are you Madame Rose after all, and this weird coffee mug collection is just a way to play it off?"

She just shrugs and gives me a grin before draining the noodles with a colander. "I think it's time to eat, and then it's time for your first torture session. Microphone included."

***

I chose to experience new things instead of live the life of a billionaire. I regret that decision right now for more reasons than I'd expected.

Obviously, being a terrible singer at a karaoke bar is not exactly something I'd been excited about. But I've been pretty terrible at quite a few things since joining the normal world. The thing that is making this unbearable is that Victoria, Trish, and Sera are looking at me like I'm about to fire them just for sitting near me.

I'd hoped that Sera wouldn't be so standoffish after spending a week in the same cubicle with her, but this is a very different environment. One that I don't quite understand how anyone is comfortable in.

"Tell me again why I'm required to sing tonight? I think my brain is refusing to accept it."

No one says a word. Each of them, other than Addison, looks like they're going to be sick. Finally, Addison says, "Because you're new, and every new cubicle-mate is required to sing one song here. I had to do it, so you have to do it, too. I didn't make the rules, but I'm not going to let you get out of it."

"Who made the rules?" I ask, and Trish pales. "I'm just curious since I've been calling Addison a sadist since I heard about this." It's supposed to be a little more playful than I guess it came out.

"Trish started it," Sera says softly and glances at her drink, which has been empty since I sat down.

"Yeah, but you don't have to sing anything if you don't want to," Trish adds. "I haven't ever actually forced anyone to sing. It's just a fun team-building thing. That's all."

I sigh. This isn't going anywhere. I didn't go into this with any expectation of making friends or even having the other employees look at me differently, but after getting close to Addison, it eats at me that her friends are terrified of me.

"Let me get the next round of drinks," I say, hoping to liven the mood a little.

"I'm good," Sera says, putting her hand over the empty glass.

"Same," Victoria says.

Trish hesitates and glances at her friends before sighing and saying, "Yeah, I've got work in the morning. Don't want to show up tired."

My stomach sinks as I glance at Addison, who shrugs. Minutes pass as another guy sings "Friends in Low Places". The way she'd talked about her experience singing karaoke, I'd expected it to be a lot of laughing and drinking interspersed with terrifying public singing. It sounded almost enjoyable.

But this is worse than being at a funeral. No stories. No laughter. Just everyone trying not to look at me.

Fuck this. There are plenty of good reasons for them to be afraid of me when I'm the boss at Loughton House, but tonight, I'm just a guy. I'm not wearing a cashmere suit, instead opting for yet another thrift store find from Addison and my shopping trip today.

And instead of being angry, I smile. They still think of me as Phillip Loughton, not Phillip, the guy who slept in a storage cabinet. So, I'll do something that Phillip Loughton wouldn't be caught dead doing.

"Please excuse me for a moment," I say as I stand up.

Addison frowns at me, her expression asking where I'm going, but I just smile at her as I turn around to walk toward the karaoke DJ.

Twenty-Eight

ADDISON

What's Phillip doing? His song is up next, and he's walking away? Is he really fleeing the scene so he doesn't have to sing? Trish may have said he doesn't have to, but I want him to. Once he does, he'll be a part of the group. Just like what happened to me.

And I want him to have friends. Or at least break down some of the mistrust that everyone at the table is feeling. I don't know if this will do it, but it's the only thing I could think of. I had to argue with Sera and Trish for a long time outside that thrift shop this morning to convince them he's different outside the office.

They still don't believe me. Even though Sera's sat in a cubicle with him for a week, and she hasn't been burned alive or even fired yet.

Now he's running away?

My heart sinks. I want my friends. I've lived my whole life basically on my own. It wasn't really possible to have many friends in school with the family life I had. Between always working and being as poor as I was, it just didn't work out.

Now I have three friends that I absolutely love spending time with, even if I barely know them.

But they hate and are terrified of the guy that I'm quickly falling for. After last night, I knew I needed to mend some broken bridges between them. I don't want to distance myself from my friends, but I don't know if it's possible for me to distance myself from Phillip. Not with how he makes me feel.

That's why we're all here. To mend broken bridges and close some gaps so I can have all of them. Maybe that's selfish of me, but truthfully, I don't care. Plus, I know everyone would be happier if they all could just understand that Phillip isn't the guy they're all so afraid of.

I catch Phillip's eye from near the DJ booth, and he's grinning. What the hell is he doing?

When the music for his song comes up, my heart sinks even lower. It's not his song. I decided on Rick Astley's "Never Gonna Give You Up", and instead, Madonna's playing.

Yet, Phillip walks up the stairs as the intro plays. He picks up the microphone just as the beginning lines play. "I made it through the wilderness…" he sings.

I thought he said he was a terrible singer? Low and rumbling, his voice doesn't match the original song's pitch at all, but it fits *him* perfectly. He doesn't just stand in front of the lyric box, either. Actually, he reminds me a hell of a lot more of Trish than of me and Sera…

I glance around the table, and all three women's eyes are wide as they watch their boss strut across the stage, so reminiscent of Madonna in the video.

"Yeah, you made me feel shiny and new," he sings as he turns to us. He looks just as serious as I'd imagine him standing in front of a boardroom of New York's elite. But as he walks down the stairs toward us, the chorus starts…

"Like a virgin…" I didn't know that a man singing this song could turn me into a slutty puddle of goo, but Phillip's done it.

Each step down the stairs terrifies me because I know what he's doing. He's not singing to the audience. He's singing to us. To me.

And holy shit, it's terrifying to have that much attention on me.

"Yeah, your love thawed out what was scared and cold…"

My heart's racing, and I glance at my friends. Every single one of them is damn near panting. It's not just me he's turning on. The audience is as silent as when Trish performed. He's halfway to us and halfway through the song. He's really drawing it out.

God, this man is so freaking hot. I don't know what to do, and I'm sure if it were anyone else, I'd be cringing, but the way he does it, there's absolutely nothing cringeworthy about it.

Phillip Loughton is sex personified.

When he gets to us, instead of turning around or standing still, singing the final chorus to us, he drops to his knees, finishing that last line looking directly up at me.

The crowd is explosive as the music ends, especially the women, and I'm a little surprised that there aren't half-naked women throwing their clothes at him.

"Fuck… That was hot." I turn to see Trish fanning herself as Phillip stands up. "Okay, get your ass back on stage. My song's next, and you're dueting with me." His eyes get wide as he looks at me questioningly. "I mean, if you want to. I… I'd like it if you did because that was awesome."

I just shrug. "Your call," I mouth.

He pauses for a second in the middle of brushing off his pants. He sighs and says, "Fuck it," just loud enough for the microphone to pick it up, and the entire crowd laughs.

Trish jumps out of her chair and hurries to the stage wearing the same red dress she wore the last time. I look around at Victoria and Sera, who are still stunned.

"Did he moonlight as a pro karaoke singer like Trish?" Victoria finally asks.

"I have no freaking idea. All he's said is that he's a terrible singer. I expected him to be as bad as me. Not… that."

Sera just shakes her head. "Yeah, that was a bit of a shock. I mean, he barely says anything at the office, much less be the kind of person who would sing Madonna. And somehow turn me on at the same time?"

I know what she means, but something inside me itches at the thought of Phillip turning anyone else on. Sure, I knew how it made me feel, and I had suspicions about how it was affecting every other female in the room, but Sera telling me I was right bothers me.

It's hard to push the feelings aside, but then Journey's "Don't Stop Believing" pounds out that epic intro, and I find a topic that I can escape into.

"Wait. Trish was a pro karaoke singer? Is that a thing?"

Victoria grins. "Yep. She traveled all over the country competing in karaoke contests and living on the earnings. She literally survived for like five years singing karaoke. Then she met her husband and got knocked up. So, she settled down. I guess the karaoke circuit isn't the best environment to raise a kid."

Insanity. "So that's why she started this whole rite of passage? Just as a reason to go relive her glory days?"

"I think it's more that she knew how much fun it is. And truthfully, when you've got her singing behind you, it's not so terrifying to get up there. After a while, even the shyest person can have fun being the center of attention with her pushing you."

Sera sighs. "But she's met her match with the boss," she says as she points at the stage. Trish is on her knees singing the chorus, and as soon as the transition happens, Phillip walks away from her, belting out the next verse as though they were in a freaking musical.

They even look like they had costumes made for it with him in his business casual, the only thing he currently owns, and her in that fancy red dress. It's a sight.

"Why'd he come with you?" Sera asks suddenly.

I turn to face her, confusion written all over my face. "What do you mean?"

"I get that you and him have some kind of weird motel history, but why'd you come here together? Shouldn't he have a driver taking him places like most people in his tax bracket? And what were you doing with him on a Sunday?"

Oh right. They didn't get the "Our Boss is Homeless" memo.

"He's living with me." I try to say it casually and turn back to see Trish and Phillip singing the final chorus together.

"What?!" It's damn near a shriek from both Sera and Victoria. Victoria continues, "You're sleeping with freaking Phillip Loughton?"

I bite my lip. I don't know how much I'm supposed to say. "He's sleeping on my couch. I guess he's really taking this whole live like an employee thing seriously, so he needed a place to stay, and I could use some help with the rent."

They both just stare at me as Trish and Phillip walk down the stairs, smiles on both of their faces as they come back to the table.

"Holy shit, Phillip. You've got a fucking voice that could melt panties everywhere. If you weren't like the richest person in the world, I'd say you'd missed your calling. Where'd you learn to sing like that?"

He shrugs. "I had a music teacher growing up, and I was left alone most of the time, so I just listened to music all day. I guess I sang along to most of it?"

Trish shakes her head, but Sera and Victoria are still staring at me. She glances at her friends. "What nonsense did Addison say now?" she demands.

Both of them glance at Phillip, and I jump in to save him from feeling like everyone knows that we've slept together. "Phillip is sleeping on my couch." I say it like it's no big deal, even though it definitely is.

Trish cocks her head for a moment and shrugs. "Knowing Addison, I bet it's a terrible couch. You should get him one of those memory foam pads so he doesn't end up with a hunchback or something. He's too pretty to get nicknamed Quasimodo."

Now it's my turn to gape. I guess that singing karaoke with Phillip has officially convinced Trish that he's a living, breathing human that deserves to be mocked. Phillip seems more than happy to hear it. "Don't worry. I do yoga in the morning, so I stave off any possible hunchback problems."

Trish keeps up the conversation as though Phillip isn't the terrifying "cold-as-ice" boss she was talking trash about a week ago. "Smart. Sleeping on couches will kill your back. Trust me on that. Plus, who wants to have to stop in the middle of an hour sex session because their back went out on them? Trust me. It's the worst."

All of us are staring at Trish now, and she finally realizes it. "What? Am I not supposed to support the boss doing yoga or something? For fuck's sake, we're not at the office. We're drinking and singing karaoke. If I'm not allowed to talk about sex, I might as well just go home."

Phillip bursts out laughing. The rest of us are just awestruck at how things have changed. In between bouts of laughter, Phillip says, "It's fine. I don't care."

Who the hell are these people? And how'd it all change in the last fifteen minutes?

"Alright," Trish says. "I'm getting the next round. I guess the boss is broke, so when his month of poverty's over and he's rich again, I expect him to buy the entire night's worth of drinks."

"Done," he says with a grin, and Trish walks toward the bar.

Even though Trish seems to have gotten over her issues with Phillip, Victoria and Sera seem to have reservations still.

It's made even more apparent when Sera broaches a topic I hadn't expected. "Why'd you fire Roger Sanders?" she asks far more seriously than anything else that's been said so far.

That sobers everyone up, including Phillip. He sits up straighter, and I wonder how he's going to answer this. After hearing Sera and Trish talk about that the last time we sang karaoke, I'd like to know as well. I've started falling for Phillip, but I know there's more to him than what he's told me. He's certainly surprised me at every turn.

He clears his throat and smiles seriously at her. The familiar expression he's worn at the office every day washes away the playful one that was there only moments before. "Roger Sanders was fired because of a sexual discrimination report," he says plainly.

"He's been discriminating for years," Sera says. "What changed?"

Phillip is as calm as ever. "There were no reports. Though we suspected things, he had a way of keeping everyone happy. When his group exceeded expectations, which they routinely did, he was very giving of the bonuses. From what I've gathered, most of his team disliked the way he treated his employees, but they enjoyed working for him because of the financial incentives he doled out. All of which were fair and equal. No one reported him because they didn't want him to be fired since he took pay cuts to give his employees more money."

Sera frowns. "How did you miss the fact that every person who got promoted was a hot woman?"

Phillip raises his eyebrow. "I don't know if you're aware, but most of those women were also his top performers. You can say what you want about the sales side of things, but appearances do matter. The discrimination report had nothing to do with promotions, actually. It had to do with him not being willing to give time and help to men, where he was very generous with his time with the women who worked for him. I assume that the reason the discrimination was reported had something to do with their lack of bonuses for two quarters, but maybe Roger just went too far. Tough to tell why exactly someone gave me a chance to do something about it."

He sighs and leans back in his chair. "I shouldn't have said any of that. Maybe my father has it right about not drinking, though I think it's the karaoke that made me forget myself tonight. I'd really prefer it if you didn't repeat any of that since I'd have to deny every word of it. Talking about why someone was terminated is a lawsuit waiting to happen."

Victoria glances at Sera, but it's Trish who speaks up. "That's what I thought the whole time. Fuck Roger. Good job on canning that asshole. Here's the real question, though. At what point do we get scheduled naptime like Google employees?"

Phillip blinks as Trish grins. "If that's what Google does, then you can have naptime when they hire you. Obviously."

She slaps her hand on the table. "Damn. A girl has to try, you know?"

This entire conversation has just been bizarre. Truthfully, the whole night has been super weird. But even Sera seems to lighten up after Phillip explained his reasons.

I try to step in and redirect the conversation. "Okay, we're supposed to remember that Phillip is trying to step away from being the boss. He wants to just be a normal guy, so let's treat him like he's just another new guy."

Sera and Victoria nod to me, but Trish already gave up the hunt for naptime. "I guess that means we can go back to performing."

She grins at everyone else and says, "I'll just go ahead and get us scheduled for Bohemian Rhapsody..."

Twenty-Nine

PHILLIP

"The End." It's done. I sigh as I lean back in my chair. *Love Through Time* has been edited in a week. That's half as long as most books take. Now I send it off to my lead editor, James Pritchard, so he can run through it again and make sure that he's willing to sign off on it.

As I'm sending the email to my boss, someone that I actually promoted to lead editor, a Slack message pops up from my father.

RUSSEL LOUGHTON

Come to my office. We need to discuss some things.

My jaw instinctively tenses, and I can hear my teeth grinding together. My father is the last person I want to see right now. I have a splitting headache from all the drinking last night.

Obviously, this would be the morning my father wants to talk. I don't even know what he'd want to talk about. He agreed to take over for me for an entire month, and it's not like he's interested in what's actually happening to me.

I take a deep breath and hit send on the email before swapping over to my father's message.

PHILLIP LOUGHTON

Fine.

No explanation or questioning. It doesn't matter what I type, he'll just tell me to go talk to him. I glance at Addison, who's staring at me. She mouths, "What's wrong?"

How does she even know that I'm pissed? I just shake my head and stand up. Sera glances up at me as I walk out of the cubicle, but neither of them says a word. I appreciate it because explaining that I get to go have a fight with my father is the last thing I want to do.

I walk the path through the office and take the elevator up to the top floor where my father's office sits. As soon as I step out of the elevator, a shiver runs through me.

My office is right there. The one I've had for more than a decade. Damn near empty except for a single disc golf trophy sitting on a cabinet that I won when I was twenty-three. My diploma hangs on the wall. My desk is empty save for a monitor that I rarely even use.

That was my old life. The one that's waiting for me when this month is over. Empty. Meaningless. Yes, I was good at every piece of that life, and I'm actually kind of terrible at this new one, but I smile and laugh every single day. Even this morning when I woke up with a terrible hangover.

I drank from a coffee mug with two unicorns fucking. I wore a robe I bought at a thrift store for a dollar fifty with a hole over my right butt cheek, which Addison promises to teach me how to fix. I made eggs and toast for us.

More than anything, I laughed and smiled the entire time. I enjoyed being alive today. There was nothing to look forward to except living. No important meetings. No deadlines. No decisions that will impact the company. Nothing except more smiling and laughing with some work thrown in to pay for life.

My father's going to try to take it all away from me. He's going to tell me to give up, to go back to that nearly empty office and buckle down to do more work. To forget the smiles and laughter and be more like him.

My nails dig into my palm as a fist forms. He won't take this away from me. When my month of freedom is over, I will come back to take my place in this office, but things will be different. I will not be the man that did as he was told. I will not be the dutiful son.

Because the dutiful son was a ghost of a man. A haunted cog in a machine that I barely want any part of at this point.

I walk down the hallway, stiff and ready to battle my father. To do what I have to do, even if it involves walking away from the family, just like Mason.

When I get to Russel Loughton's office, I'm surprised because I hear laughter. I don't bother to knock. The door swings open and I see where the laughter came from. My youngest brother, Andrew, is sitting on Father's desk, a grin on his face.

"And I thought I was the crazy brother," he says as he hops off the desk. "But giving up the family fortune for a month is something only you'd do."

I grin as Andrew walks across the room and gives me a hug. It's been months since I've seen him. The only real contact I've had with him is over conference calls.

He steps back and says, "Where the hell did you get this shirt? A dumpster? Is that polyester?"

"I went thrift store shopping yesterday. My nine-hundred dollars a week doesn't go very far."

Andrew's eyes open wide, and he shakes his head. "Fucking Castaway over here. Next, you'll tell me you're rubbing sticks together to make a fire for warmth. Jeez, Dad. You're really letting Phillip live like this?"

My father's lip curls up just a little. Just enough for me to know that he's enjoying this. "He chose this. Not me. He can come back to the fold anytime he wants. Which brings me to why I called you up here, Phillip. I'm going to spend the next two weeks in Beijing to deal with permitting issues for that expansion. London's running well currently, so Andrew will have to manage both the London and New York branches simultaneously. Unless you're ready to be done with this nonsense…"

The words hang in the air, and Andrew's brow arches as he looks at me. I know it'll be a lot of work to manage both branches for Andrew. He's never been one to have responsibility dropped on his shoulders, so he'll probably struggle.

But I've been the one who's carried the load forever. I've been the one who never got a break. This is my time to let someone else take care of things.

"I'm sure he'll manage just fine. I have complete confidence in my little brother."

Father's grin turns into a glare. "You're shirking your responsibilities, Phillip, and you know that."

"No. I'm taking a break." All the frustrations boil inside me. All the realizations I've had since taking a step back come to the surface. "I've spent every moment of my life making sure I took care of my responsibilities. I'm not a machine, Father. I want to do things that make me smile for once instead of worrying about this damned company."

The vein in Father's throat starts to pulse, a clear sign that he's pissed, and I don't care at all. "And just so you're aware," I say, staring straight at the man who's controlled my life since I was born. "When I do come back to run Loughton House, there will be changes. I will delegate, and I *will* have time to do as I wish. I'll continue to run Loughton House to the best of my ability, but I will also enjoy my life alongside running the company."

My father's fuming, and he stands up, more furious than I can remember him. "And what happens if I disapprove of those changes?"

I smile at him, knowing full-well how mad it will make him. Because I've won this, and he simply hasn't realized it. "Then you can either fire me or get the fuck over it."

Without paying even one more second of attention to my father, I turn to Andrew and say, "See you around, little brother."

And I walk out of the office.

Thirty

ADDISON

Angela's body quivers as Donovan runs his fingers over her bare skin. "You're so much more beautiful than I remember," he whispers. His eyes wander over her body like he's taking in a piece of fine art. She's never felt like this, so completely at ease with a man she feels like she barely knows.

Even though he was her first.

"You're pretty beautiful yourself. Though you'd be even more beautiful if you turned off the lights." He grins at her before jumping out of bed and moving toward the light switch. The entire time, Angela can't keep her eyes off his ass. Round and firm, and definitely her favorite place to warm her hands up when they get cold. Even when he complains about her icy fingers.

Maybe that's part of why she enjoys doing it. To see if he cares enough to be uncomfortable for her. Is that her toxic trait? He does laugh every time she does it…

When the lights are off, Donovan crawls into bed next to her and puts his arm under her pillow and wedges himself next to her. His hand goes to her neck, and he cranes down to kiss her. Not hot and heavy like earlier when he was on top of her. Instead, it's soft and sensual. Loving.

Angela doesn't remember ever feeling this way before. This completely at ease…

MY PHONE BUZZES, AND I SIGH AS I LOOK TO SEE who it is. My heart sinks.

"Hey Mom," I say as I click the save button and turn away from the computer. "How's life?"

"Oh Addison, it's going so much better. Thanks again for the loan. I'll repay you as soon as I can." It was a gift. That's the only way I can think of any money I send Mom after all these years because it almost never gets paid back.

I pick up my pencil and begin spinning it over my fingers, turning it into a blur like normal. "Is the job with Woodson's going well? You're getting along well with everybody?"

"Absolutely. Woodson himself is a little crotchety, but that's the way it is with old men who have had to deal with a bunch of teenagers working for them for as long as he has. Do you have any idea how lazy some of them are? I caught one girl just sitting in the warehouse scrolling through her phone while she was clocked in. Can you believe that?"

"I sure can, Mom. I hope you're not picking up bad habits working with teenagers. If you start texting me in the middle of the day, I'm going to call you out on it."

She huffs. "I've never lost my job before, sweetheart. You know that, and I won't be losing this one so I can text you pictures of cats. Or whatever these kids are doing."

It's almost comical because I know how much she'd enjoy all the short videos on Instagram. "I'm glad it's all working out for you, Mom. Just remember that I'm basically out of money. Living in New York is expensive, and my entry-level job doesn't pay that well."

"I'm completely happy here. Don't worry about me at all. Now tell me what it's like living in New York. Have you made any friends? Met any boys? Did you get lost on the subways?"

I grin, but hearing my mom after spending so much time with Phillip makes me realize just how different our childhoods were. Where he never had to worry about where his next meal was coming from or whether he'd be able to shower, he never had a loving relationship with his parents. Or at least his dad. I still don't know anything about his mom.

"I've made some friends, and we've gone to a karaoke bar twice now. They're hilarious, and I think you'd like them."

Mom laughs, and I can imagine her sitting in her easy chair with the TV tray next to her. The old brown shag carpet that's been in the living room for my entire life. The TV is probably on even though she isn't watching it, the volume turned way down.

"What about boys? I know that those fancy offices are as slutty as frat houses. I've seen the movies, so you can't even deny it."

"Mom, I've been here for like two weeks. No, I have not gone on dates with slutty office guys. Jeez. I have priorities." Inside I'm cringing. Not only have I gone on dates with a hot office guy, but he's currently laying on my couch watching Netflix on his work laptop. Without any clothes on.

"Well, you've got to get out there. I know you have your priorities, but sometimes, you've just got to live a little. Just remember to use protection. You don't want to get knocked up and end up…"

Sigh. "I've been on the pill since I was fifteen years old, and you know that. I do not need a sperm donor anytime soon."

"It's my job to remind you. I love you, Addy."

"I know you do, Mom. But hey, I've got to go. Trying to finish a chapter in my book."

She's quick to respond. "When are you going to let me read it? You don't have to be afraid of dear old Mom getting prudish about a steamy scene or two. You know…"

"Bye Mom. I love you, and I'll talk to you later."

"Okay. I love you too."

With a sigh, I hang up the phone. I love my mom, but she's a little much sometimes. At least things are going better for her now.

But as usual, I can't write after talking to her. I've got to get up and do something before I can finish the last five hundred words or so of this chapter. When I walk out of my room, Phillip is sitting at the dining room table, still totally naked.

"Get tired of Gossip Girl?" I ask with a grin.

He shakes his head. "You and your mom have such a pleasant relationship," he says as he slowly spins a coffee mug on the table. The one he drank out of the first day, "You make me forget batteries".

"Yeah, other than that she'd probably be homeless at this point if she couldn't borrow money from me."

He shrugs. "Money comes and money goes. Having someone like that in your corner isn't something that happens to everyone." He looks up at me and gives me a broken smile. It only reminds me again of how fucked up his relationship with his dad is.

"That's true," I say. "But don't you have a brother you're kind of close with? Why don't you call him just to chat? I know that's not really your family's thing, but it *could* be. And if you want a relationship like that, you've got to do some of the reaching, you know?"

He nods and chews his lip. Then he looks up at me with a grin. "What do poor people do together? Like, if you wanted to invite people over, but wanted to do something as well so no one's just staring at each other, what would that entail?"

"A lot of people just sit around and talk. In college, we used to play board games sometimes. Drinking games were definitely an option, though I don't know how excited I'd be to end up making an ass of myself around anyone these days. Why? Is there someone you'd like to invite over?"

He leans back, his arms behind his head, and the chair leans back just a little along with him. I can hear my Nana in my head yelling at me when I used to do the same thing. *You're gonna crack your head open doing that. And I just mopped, so you'd better not get blood all over the tiles.*

"My brother is in town for the next two weeks, and I thought it'd be fun to do something. And maybe give him a chance to meet my 'roommate'."

He uses air quotes, and a part of me wonders just what he thinks of us. Sure, we're sleeping together, but there's really nothing that will keep us together after his self-imposed poverty is over. We're just too different. Plus, he'll be the boss with far too many responsibilities to spend any time with me.

"Maybe," he says as he spins the mug again, his finger pressing against the handle as his hands twirl it from above. The ceramic slides against the cheap veneer of my table with a scratching sound. "Maybe we could have a game night. Do you think any of your friends would want to play... something? We could make it a lot less intense with more normal people. It's hard for me to keep from going back to the way I used to be around my family."

I nod. I understand what he means by that. Every time I talk to Mom, I feel like I did when I was thirteen. That strange combination of looking up to her and being pissed at her for needing help from me. I don't know why I can't act the same as I normally do when I'm around my mom.

"That sounds like fun. We'd need to find some good group games, though. Ones that no one's actually good at. Maybe Pictionary?"

Phillip shakes his head. "Sera's a graphic designer, and half her portfolio is illustrations. Andrew minored in art at Stanford. I'll figure something out that we can all be terrible at together."

He smiles at me, but it's got a hint of sadness to it. I want to ask him what's wrong, but it feels like I'd be prying.

I don't have time to think too much about it because he lets the legs of his chair hit the floor as he stands up with a grin on his face. He walks around the table and says, "But that's enough about that. If you're done writing, maybe it's time to have a little fun..."

He steps toward me, his cock nearly at eye level, and I look up at him, knowing exactly what he's thinking. He runs his hand through my hair, his fingers tightening just enough that I feel the pressure, and I reach for his balls.

I can't stop grinning as he groans, but as my nails caress them, I say, "You're going to have to wait until I finish this chapter up." I can feel his heart beating through his balls, and part of me wishes I was about to write the next five hundred words of a steamy scene instead of pillow talk.

Phillip groans again, this time in dismay, as I pull my hand away. "For the next thirty minutes, I'm going to sit at my desk and get some work done, but if you can leave me alone, I'm all yours afterward."

His lip curls up, and he says, "The real question is what you mean by 'leave you alone'. Does that mean you don't want me to talk to you? Or does it mean that you don't want me to pretend to be your naked secretary sitting under your desk while you do your work…"

That actually makes me blush. Thinking about Phillip crawling under my desk is hot, but I don't know if I could think about anything while he's down there.

Then he keeps talking, and I blush even more. "Of course, if I did that for you, when I go back to being Director of Publishing, you'll have to return the favor. I can't wait to have an over-the-phone meeting with your lips wrapped around my cock."

Fuck me. For some reason it hadn't occurred to me that when he goes back to his old position, he might want to do things at the office. I can't imagine how hot that'd be.

I open my mouth and try to tell him I need to get my words written, but then his cock swells. Instead of saying anything, I give up on the idea of getting work done. I don't know if this book will ever get written with how easily I get distracted by him.

My mouth stays open just a little too long, and Phillip puts a little pressure on the back of my head. I don't need much coaxing, though, and without further suggestion, his cock is in my mouth, and my tongue is dancing over the tip.

"If thinking about getting fucked in the office turned you on that much, maybe we need to explore some other options as well," he whispers.

Other options? What does that even mean? And yes, please? To emphasize how much I like that idea, I push myself down on him, letting his cock touch the back of my throat.

"Oh yes, we'll definitely have to try some other things," he moans. "But first, I'm going to get you into bed. I can't have you getting this worked up without some relief."

He pulls away from me, and I can't help but smile at him. Who would have believed that I'd have found a man who could turn me on this much and, at the same time, keep me grinning like an idiot almost constantly? It almost seems like Phillip is a guy out of a fantasy.

Except that he's right here in my apartment, about to blow my mind with that magic cock once again.

In the back of my mind, a tiny voice is screaming, though. After all these years of catastrophe following every good moment, I know that the other shoe is going to fall at some point.

But right now, I'm lost in a man named Phillip Loughton, and that little voice can't be heard over the moaning of my very hungry vagina.

Thirty-One

PHILLIP

THE OFFICE THRUMS WITH LIFE THESE DAYS. Now that people understand that I'm not acting like their boss anymore, they're louder, and I can even hear laughter. A part of me questions if the productivity is still as high as it normally is, but I don't dwell on it very much.

It's Thursday of my second week as a junior editor, and I'm used to the schedule now. Thirty minutes of chatting in the break room over coffee with Victoria, Trish, Sera, and, of course, Addison. I have a feeling that the stories and jokes were a little more off-color before I joined their group, but that's okay. Eventually, I will be in charge of disciplining again, so maybe it's best that there's still some separation between us.

Trish sighs and stands up away from the cabinet she's been leaning on, the sign that it's time for everyone to get back to work. Before they walk away, though, Addison stops them.

"Hey, are any of you free tomorrow night? I'm going to have a game night at my place at six-ish if you want to come."

Sera grins. "Oh, definitely count me in. I was just trying to figure out what to do with my Friday night."

Victoria shakes her head. "Not me. I've got a date." She immediately turns to Trish, whose eyes are lit up like she's about to explode with excitement. "And no, it's not Chuckle Fuck."

It's like someone took Trish's happiness and hit it with a sledgehammer. I have never seen someone go from ecstatic to depressed in a single sentence before. "Who's Chuckle Fuck?" I ask. Then I realize just how ridiculous that sentence sounds.

"I'll explain him later," Addison says.

Trish ignores Addison and tries to explain the mystery man. "A majestic creature whose only purpose in life is to create hilarious stories that have no competition. No one in the history of men is more perfect for Victoria, and she's thrown him away like last night's Chinese food takeout."

She must have been extremely invested in this guy. Sera tries to lighten the mood by saying, "Well, make sure you take a picture of the guy, and we'll be ready for story time on Monday."

Trish sighs dramatically and shakes her head. "Who-ever he is, he'll never compete with Chuckle Fuck." Then she turns to Addison and says, "You good with me bringing my guy? Friday is our date night, so the hubs and I are a package deal."

"Sure," Addison says. "The more the merrier. I might have to break out the folding chairs, though."

Trish nods to her. "Excellent. We'll bring some board games the kids haven't eaten the pieces to. Just so you're aware, if your kid ever eats the car from Monopoly, the ER will send you home and tell you to watch his poops until you fish it out. You can thank me later for that nugget of parenting gold."

Then she walks out. I don't really understand how this group of friends work. They're all at such different points in their lives. Trish is happily married with kids. Victoria is actively dating. Addison is just trying to figure out her new life. And Sera... Well, I don't know anything about Sera's life outside of work, and Addison doesn't seem to, either.

Addison's friends go back to their cubicle as Addison finishes the last bit of her coffee, but before she can walk away, I pin her against the cabinets. She looks at me with shock in her eyes before glancing toward the doorway.

"You can't do this here. What if someone saw? You're not just some employee."

She's right, and this is not something I'd have done before. At the same time, after spending so much time with Addison, I'm thinking that maybe making bad decisions isn't always such a terrible idea. Maybe Victoria's terrible stories are better than choosing a boring guy and making all the right decisions. Maybe going to college and getting a good job as an editor isn't as important as spending five years being a pro karaoke singer.

And maybe kissing the woman that I've become infatuated with in the breakroom is a smarter decision than hiding what I want while we're at work.

When I try to lean in for the kiss, Addison slides away from me, though. "Not here. Not like this, Phillip. I can't let anyone see that at work. I… I want to, but I can't. Not where people from work could catch us."

A part of me is disappointed, but the other part, the part that's growing more and more fearless every day, just sees it as another opening. I lean in and whisper to her, "Then I guess I'll have to play with you somewhere that *work* people can't catch us…"

She hears the emphasis on work, and her eyes go wide. Her fingers do that thing where she pulls at her blouse. I let the words hang in the air for a second and give her a moment to let the thoughts sink in.

"Maybe I'd let you," she whispers back. "Maybe I'd even like it. But not here where my coworkers can see."

I grin and take a step back. "I can work with that," I say before walking past her. She's left breathing hard, and I'm enjoying the fact that she'll wonder where I went when she gets back to the cubicle.

I have to call Andrew to see if he even wants to do a game night tomorrow. Stepping into the hallway to make the call, I know there's nothing to be nervous about, but I'm still hesitant. In thousands of business calls, I've never been this worried. He's my brother, and I should feel more at ease with him than anyone else.

But I'm not.

There was always that separation between us. Even more than between me and Addison's friends. I was almost an extension of my father, and that meant that I wasn't fun. I wasn't someone you played with. Everyone knew I was an adult in a child's body, and that's how they treated me.

It's important to brush our history aside. I told Father that things were going to change when I came back to work for him, but I wasn't only talking about business. Whether or not I work at Loughton House, I'm going to be a human, not just a cog in a machine. Part of that is building the ties I should already have with my brothers. Both of them.

I push the call button, and almost instantly, Andrew picks up. "Phillip! What's going on? Is everything alright?" Of course, he thinks something's wrong. I don't have business to talk about, so why else would I call him?

"Everything's fine. I was just wondering what you were doing tomorrow evening."

There's a pause, and in my mind, I can see him frowning. He's confused since he can't see where the puzzle pieces connect, so I put them together for him. "A few people that I'm working with are having a game night, and I wanted to see if you were interested in joining."

Immediately, he laughs. "Games? Like board games? With employees? Phillip, this is perfect. Dad would have a heart attack if he heard about this. I had some stuff planned for tomorrow night, but I'll definitely cancel. I can't imagine a better Friday night. Do I... need to bring something?"

I pause. I'd kind of expected that reaction. Thinking back to a month ago, I wouldn't have been caught dead playing board games with employees either. But things have changed a lot for me since then.

"Don't worry about bringing anything. I'll text you the address and information."

"Sounds good," he says, but then he pauses. "Man, what's going on with you? Sure, you needed a break after being Dad's puppet for the past twenty years, but you're kind of going off the deep end. Why not just tell him you needed a break instead of living without money? Now you're having a game night? Maybe you need to schedule an appointment with a shrink or something."

I grin even though he can't see it. "Everything's fine. In fact, I don't think I've been happier in my life. I'm broke, but I don't care. And truthfully, after everything that's happened in my life, I think I needed something pretty crazy."

"I guess that's true. I just worry about you. People crack under pressure, and Dad's been squeezing you since birth. I don't think anyone could have made it through everything without losing it a little."

Maybe he's right, and I have cracked. But maybe it's not so much a crack as change. "Who knows? The only thing I'm sure of is that I'm excited to play stupid board games with people who have absolutely no ulterior motives. They just want to play, and I am absolutely ready for that."

Andrew lets out a little laugh, and it's almost like he gets it. "Well, if that's what you want to do, then I'll be there. I'm glad you called me, Phillip. It's been too long since we've spent any time together outside of work."

"It has. And on that note, I have to get back to work. I don't know if my boss, James Pritchard, has the balls to write me up for making phone calls before I've even turned on my computer, but I sure as hell deserve one."

"So typical. Even working for pennies, you've got your nose to the grindstone. Well, let me know if anything changes for game night. I'll talk to you later."

"See you then," I say and hang up. I lean against the wall and take a deep breath. I don't know why, but that call terrified me. Maybe it's because I really wanted Andrew to come, to spend time with me doing something stupid instead of something "important". I'm jealous of the way he and Mason have always had a friendship, and I want that in my life.

Steeling my jaw, I smile. I'm going to build these friendships regardless of what Father wants. One day, this company is going to be mine, but I won't let it own me. I won't give up the things that make me smile. And having my brother be more than a coworker is one of those things.

Thirty-Two

ADDISON

We step off the subway after one of the strangest days I can remember. Other than the day that Phillip came home with me, of course. Come to think of it, the day wasn't that strange other than how Phillip was acting.

He tried to do *something* with me in the breakroom. Then he stayed away from the cubicle for almost twenty minutes afterward. And *then*, he took a long lunch. I don't even understand what he was doing since he wasn't eating with me.

There's something going on, and I don't know how to feel. He just kept grinning at me like an idiot, which only made me nervous. Now he was touching me the entire ride home. His hand was on my thigh or lower back almost constantly. It was just so bizarre.

As soon as our feet touch solid ground, he pulls me to him. His hands are on my hips, and right there, in the midst of the people exiting the subway, he kisses me. My instincts are to move away from the tide of people that brush past us, to escape the crowd so they don't trample me.

Surprisingly, not a single one of them touches me. Phillip feels desperate as he crushes me with his lips, and even though my instincts are to move, I get lost in the kiss. There's something about the way his fingers dig into my skin that makes me want to forget about anything else. The way his lips crave me as though he were a drowning man, and my breath is the only air he could get.

"I've been wanting to do that since this morning," he whispers to me, and that's when I notice his body keeps shifting and moving as people bump and push past him. He stands straight through it all, a shield against the masses, and he doesn't even seem to notice them.

"Come on," I say, pulling him away from the subway, and catch dirty glances from several of the passengers who've bumped into Phillip. When we're away from the mobs, I ask him, "Why didn't you kiss me before then?"

He grins. "Because someone could have seen, and you were very adamant that you didn't want anyone from the office to know. I know how to work within an agreement."

"You've been waiting all day to kiss me? Does that have some connection to your exceptionally long lunch, too?"

His grin only widens, and I see his grip tighten on his laptop bag. "Not directly, but kind of. It definitely has something to do with you."

"Wait, are we keeping secrets now? Is this some kind of surprise where I'm going to walk into a room full of balloons or something?"

And Phillip just shrugs. What an asshole.

"Just so you're aware, I am not a fan of surprises. If people jump out and try to surprise me, they will most likely be hit repeatedly on instinct and reflex alone."

He takes my hand just like he did at the park, and somehow, even after fucking like rabbits for the past few days, this is what makes me melt. As he leads me out of the subway, he says, "This has nothing to do with scaring you or surprising you quite like that. I think you'll enjoy it. At least I hope you do."

Phillip's so calm as he talks about it. He has no idea how scary surprises are to me. In my world, surprises are things like a water leak that ends with having an outrageous repair bill. Or when you find out your property taxes are going up. Fun stuff.

"I made a phone call at lunch and went shopping," he says. "And no, I didn't buy you anything, but I think you'll enjoy the date I've planned."

I turn my head so fast, I nearly get whiplash. "Date? I thought we had an understanding. We're just roommates."

He chuckles. "Roommates that share a bed and make out on subway platforms. Fine. Not a date date. A sex date. Is that better?"

I squint at him. "What? There's no such thing as a sex date."

"Maybe not in Addison's world. But for once, I'm going to show you a thing or two about what I could have had if I'd been more like my brother."

"I don't even know what that's supposed to mean. Is your brother a man whore or something?"

Phillip grins and sighs. "No, he spends money to impress people. He helps them do things that normal people aren't able to do."

I don't know how I feel about all of this. Our little dynamic made sense. I teach Phillip how to do things like make coffee, and we have awesome sex. And maybe he gives me inspiration for my book. Just a little.

"You're serious about wanting to do this? You really want to dip your toes into the billionaire world again while you're specifically on vacation away from it?"

He nods. "I want to let you experience something new. Not just me. You've made the past week better than any I can remember, and I want to return the favor."

Should I tell him that since he moved in, I've been happier than I can remember? I don't know. We have an agreement. We're just roommates that share a bed. But he really has been pretty amazing.

I don't want to admit it, even to myself, but I'm really falling for Phillip Loughton. Even though I know all the reasons I shouldn't. There are some people that you can't turn away from.

"Okay, I'll go on your weird billionaire sex date, Phillip. Just remember that we're both broke, and I refuse to dine and dash. I will force you to wash dishes all night if you can't afford dinner we order."

He has to stop walking, leaning against a streetlight, as he starts laughing. I don't know if it's laughing or actually cackling. "Oh no, we won't be eating on this date. Well, you won't be."

"Damn it, Phillip. Now I don't even know what to wear. Just freaking tell me."

He grins and opens his laptop bag. Then he does something I definitely did not expect. He pulls out a pair of board shorts. With cookie monster on the front of them. "You're going to wear a swimsuit."

Thirty-Three

PHILLIP

ADDISON'S CONFUSED, AND I UNDERSTAND WHY. A billionaire sex date? In a swimsuit? That's just not exactly what most people would expect, but I know a guy with a very unique swimming pool.

And he owes me a favor. See, the thing about being rich is that money is only one type of currency that's exchanged. Sure, it's the thing that's written down and tracked by the government, but the real deals happen because of the more dangerous currency: favors.

I may not have access to money right now, but I still have a bank account full of favors in the world of the rich and famous, and I've never cashed in any of them. I never even thought about it since I didn't really have a reason before. What could I possibly need from a multi-platinum rock star in my previous life? They didn't influence readers or book buyers.

But they do have really extravagant pools.

"Don't let yourself get all twisted up over the details, Addison. Just go with it. I put a lot of thought into this, so for once, just trust me."

I can see her hesitancy, but she sighs and says, "Fine. Take me swimming on a roommate adventure. Not a sex date because that feels weird and creepy."

"Weird and creepy? I feel like you should have a mug that says something similar."

Her hesitancy seems to fall away as she grins at me. "Maybe I should. Then it could be your cup. How about 'You're weird and creepy. And I like it.'?"

I grab her hand again as we laugh, and I see her eyes soften at my touch. I never thought I'd enjoy touching her quite this much. She seems to feel the same.

"Come on. Let's go pick up your swimsuit so we can go on our 'roommate adventure' together. I can't wait for you to see where we're going."

"No. This is not real. You put LSD in my drink, and I'm tripping balls right now."

We're standing on the glass rooftop of a skyscraper. Hundreds of feet above the city, it's like we're completely separate from the rest of the world. And the scene below our feet is even more otherworldly.

The Olympic-size pool is directly in front of us, with water glowing purple in the fading sunlight. The pool itself isn't all that special except that it also has a glass bottom.

What's below it is nearly impossible, though. An aquarium that fills most of the floor below us with water that glows blue. Jellyfish float under our feet. Lionfish prowl the plants, looking for prey that will never be there. Angelfish swim through the throngs of sea life, their wispy white fins almost glowing in the blue light.

It's not something you could find anywhere else in the world and probably should be impossible. Except that this building was designed with this rooftop in mind. That's what happens when you're one of the richest people in the world. People design skyscrapers around your craziness.

"You're not on drugs. I've been here before, and it was just as crazy then as it is now. Yes, those fish are alive."

Addison just stares in awe at everything under her feet. "How the hell did you manage this? You're just as broke as me."

I chuckle and say, "I may not have any money, but that doesn't change that I'm a billionaire. The guy who owns this penthouse doesn't know that anything's changed. He just jumped at the chance to repay a debt to me."

Addison walks to the edge of the pool and shakes her head. "There aren't any fish in the pool?"

"Nope. There's a very thick piece of glass separating the pool from the aquarium."

She shivers as I put my hand on her lower back. When she looks up at me, she's got this strange mix of excitement and terror in her eyes. "Alright, so where do we change?"

I grin, and without saying a word, I turn her toward me. Her bottom lip quivers as I move my fingers to the buttons on her blouse. The cornflower blue satin shimmers in the light from the aquarium.

"No one's here." The first button comes undone, and my fingers move to the next one. "The door to the penthouse is locked." Her white bra comes into view as the next button comes loose.

"But what about the other buildings?" she whispers as I undo the rest. "They'll see us."

I grin and pull the blouse open. "So let them see. No one knows who you are, and no one cares who I am. I doubt anyone from work can see us."

Addison shivers as I run my fingers between her breasts. "You can always say no," I whisper, leaning in and letting my lips tickle her neck. I say that, but my hands are already moving to her skirt, slowly pulling it down.

She doesn't stop me. "I'm nervous," she whispers back.

"Then just trust me, Addison. Sometimes you need someone to guide you when you're doing something crazy. Like getting naked on a rooftop and swimming with fish."

She grins. "Or trying to work a coffeemaker."

"That too," I say at the same time that her skirt falls to the glass below us. She shivers, and the air is still warm.

"Well, are you going to take off any of your clothes? Or is this just a prank where everyone from the office is going to jump out and I'll have to move back to Kansas City so I never have to see them again?"

I take a step back and slowly undo my tie. God, she looks so beautiful tonight. The blue and purple lights make her seem almost alien. Like she belongs in this bizarre place where fish swim hundreds of feet above the ground.

The tie hits the ground, and I pull the ruby red shirt out from my pants. For the first time, I don't pay any attention to the stain as my fingers can't move fast enough. I can't pay attention to anything but her, and like Addison said earlier, I'm sure I'm being creepy just staring at her in her underwear. How could any straight man do anything different?

As soon as my shirt's on the glass, I kick off my shoes and yank my socks off. Addison's watching me just as much as I was watching her. She giggles as I hop around for a minute trying to get the damn sock off.

"You know, I thought we were going to wear swimsuits," she says.

"You could if you want to, and I guess this would actually be a roommate adventure then. But I didn't ask you to go on a roommate adventure. Those were your words."

She bites her lip as I move my hands to my pants. "If that's the case, I'll go downstairs and change. But I've never gone skinny dipping before, much less on a rooftop pool with angelfish underneath me."

It only takes a second for her to stop me. "No. I want to do this." It sounds like she's talking herself up to it.

I didn't walk away from my fortune to sit around Addison's apartment playing house. I wanted to do things I'd never done before. The goal was to experience as much as I could in a single month. Like I just told Addison, I'd never gone skinny dipping before, and there's nobody else in the world that I'd rather do it with for the first time.

She grins. "This is freaking insane, Phillip. Then again, everything with you is at least slightly insane, and I'm here for it." She reaches around and undoes her bra, letting it fall to her feet, and just as quick, she pulls her panties to the floor. When she stands up, I'm just staring at her, a grin on my face.

And I yell, "Surprise!" and turn toward the door as though people are about to barge onto the rooftop.

She shrieks and covers up, fully expecting that exact thing to happen. Except it doesn't, and I just start laughing. It takes her a second, but she finally stands back up, exposing herself at least a little. If dirty looks could burn people, I'd be a heap of ash with the way she's looking at me.

"You're such an asshole," she whisper-yells at me. I don't respond. Instead, I just walk up to her and run my hand through her hair. For a moment, she thinks about pulling away, but I don't let her and as my grip tightens, I pull her head back.

And I kiss her. I kiss her like we're the only two people in the world. She kisses me back with all the fire she'd had in her eyes a moment ago. I may have pissed her off, but she's just as happy to burn me with her lips as with her eyes.

"You're still an asshole," she whispers, but she's not mad anymore.

"It was funny," I say as I let go of her hair and take a step back. "But I won't ever embarrass you. I promise."

"I almost trust you, but I need reassurance. Drop those pants, Mister. If I'm going to die from shame, you will too."

I grin, but in a second, my pants and boxers are on the glass, and she's grinning alongside me. Taking her hand in mine, I pull her toward the pool. We didn't come here to be naked on a rooftop.

The water's warm as we walk down the steps together. It's unnerving looking down and seeing all the fish through the crystal-clear water. I give her a smile and push off into the water. I keep my eyes open as I swim down to the bottom to look at the fish.

The entire time, I'm acutely aware of how different it is to swim without clothes on. Everything floats strangely, and as the water goes by, it tickles.

As I'm looking through the glass that separates me from the fish below, I get a shock as I feel something tug on my cock. My first thought is that I was wrong and there are fish in the pool, too. Terrified that a fish is biting my dick, I whip my head around only to see Addison behind me, bubbles streaming from her mouth as she laughs.

It makes me grin, and I reach out to tickle her, but she kicks backward, floating out of reach. I'm running out of air and head to the surface instead of chasing Addison.

She surfaces only seconds later. "You shouldn't scare a guy like that. I thought a fish was trying to swallow my dick."

She laughs again, but not before she says, "Oh, did it make you think about asking the fish to be your roommate, too?"

Now it's my turn to glare. "You're hilarious. It didn't occur to me since I assumed you weren't looking for any more dick swallowing roommates. Was I wrong?"

She grins but doesn't respond. "Let's go look at the fish," she says and swims down again.

I follow behind her, my eyes on her body as she kicks, mesmerized by the way her body moves in the water. She goes right to the bottom of the pool to watch the fish below us, and I end up right next to her. She points out several beautifully colored fish, and then we have to surface again.

We repeat the motions, going to different areas of the pool each time, and her smile grows. I was nervous about this date idea, but now I'm having a blast, and she is, too.

And then she swims toward the stairs, and I follow her. She sighs as she sits down. "I don't know how I feel about the whole skinny-dipping thing, but this place is incredible."

"It is," I agree. Silence begins to build as she looks over the side of the building at the city that spreads out in front of us. Skyscrapers rise around us, some stopping below and others climbing far higher.

"Why didn't you do things like this before? Why didn't you spend your nights playing in places that only the elite are allowed?"

I shrug. "What was the point? Sure, I could have come

here before, but I didn't have anyone then. It would have been pretty, but would it have been worth asking for the favor? Probably not."

She doesn't even look at me as she talks. "You could have dated some celebrity. Or a model or basically anybody."

I shrug again, but I don't turn to her. "But then they'd be with me for the money. They wouldn't give a shit about me. Only the bank account."

"There are plenty of men in the world that would be happy to use that money to have all the fun they could imagine."

This time, I turn and look at her. My fingers move to her chin, gripping just hard enough that she can't ignore me as I turn her face to look at me. "I'm not that guy, Addison. I've dated people before, but it always boiled down to the same problems. The same issues cropped up every single time. Why wasn't I spending more money on them? Why wouldn't I take time off work to take them traveling? Why wouldn't I do things for them? And remember, most of these 'relationships' lasted all of a few months."

Addison pushes my hand away. "I'd expect you to do things for me if we dated. I'd expect you to spend some of your money on me. Just like I'd do things for you, and I'd spend my money on you. That's what happens when you date someone."

I shake my head. "You don't understand. I know what a relationship is supposed to be, and these weren't that. I felt like the entire thing was a transaction. I give them money and they spend time with me. That's not what I want."

She frowns. "That's fair," she says as she stands up and looks down at me. I stare up at her, enjoying the sight. Water runs in rivers down her naked body, curving along her skin in chaotic lines. And all of her glows purple from the reflected lights below us.

"You're beautiful, Addison. I don't think I've told you that today."

She grins and for a second, her fingers do a weird little dancing motion. "Well, handsome, you said you'd take me on a sex date, but I'm not going to fuck you at some random rich guy's house. You're going to have to figure out something else to get into my pants."

I can't help but grin. "Why would I want in your pants? They're on the ground over there."

She straddles me, still standing up, and I can feel my cock swelling. Fuck. "Here in a few seconds, they won't be. So, you'd better start thinking because it'd be creepy, not to mention extremely uncomfortable, to do anything here."

She takes another step, this time away from me, and I'm left feeling very desperate to do exactly what she suggested. "I have an idea," I say, and she turns around, her eyebrows arched in question.

"I know a guy…"

Thirty-Four

ADDISON

My body is going crazy as Phillip leads me to yet another acquaintance of his. Skinny dipping was not on my list of normal roommate adventures, but I'm beginning to think that my list of adventures may be missing some important items.

There's something sensual about naked swimming. The way the water flows over your body. It's obviously something I've never done before, but it felt so natural.

But having sex at some random guy's house just isn't a line I'm ready to cross. Even on a billionaire sex date, whatever that was supposed to mean.

That doesn't change the way I'm feeling. I don't know if I'm going to make it to the next insane destination. It's taking everything in me not to just grind against him and convince him to go home.

"Fuck it," I mutter and grab Phillip's hand as we pass an alley. I drag him into the shadows between the two brownstones. Dirty brick walls rise high into the air on either side of us, and though the street only a few feet away is brightly lit, it's nearly pitch black here.

"What are you doing?" he whispers, but I shut him up with a kiss. It's strange being the one to initiate things. To push Phillip to do something he wasn't expecting to.

My heart is racing as I run my hand down his pants and feel his cock swelling. "You wanted a sex date, but I'm not fucking you on some guy's roof, and I'm not fucking you in another guy's club or wherever else you were bringing me. I'm not even going to fuck you in a back alley."

"Then what are you doing?" he whispers and follows it up with a groan as I squeeze his shaft.

"I'm telling you I'm ready to be done with this date in a very dramatic way. If you're not inside of me soon, I'm going to go home by myself so I can get some relief. I think we'd both enjoy going home together."

Phillip's hand seems like it comes out of nowhere and pulls my head back by my hair. His lips latch onto my neck, kissing me hard enough that he probably leaves a bruise.

"Maybe I wanted you to get that turned on," he whispers before nibbling on my ear and sending tingles through me. I squeeze his cock and slowly stroke it.

Then I pull my hand away and take a step backward. "Well, you're about to ruin in. Take me home, Phillip. I want you to do dirty things to me."

I've never wanted to be rich more than I did twenty minutes ago. When I pulled Phillip into that alley, I didn't want to go home. I wanted to take a cab to the nearest hotel and ride him until we both collapsed from exhaustion.

Instead, we had a twenty-minute cab ride back home. As soon as I paid the driver, I'm dragging my "roommate" upstairs. I don't have it in me to make out in the parking lot like we did the last time we got worked up outside of the apartment.

I drop the keys because of my shaking hands, and when I bend over to pick them up, Phillip's hand runs between my legs, making my body quiver even more. "You're soaked," he whispers. Jeez, can he really tell how wet I am through my freaking pants and underwear?

"I'm pretty positive that you built a freaking fountain between my legs that just stays wet all the damn time. At least when I'm around you."

He grins, but the key is already turning in the door, and I pull him in behind me. I toss the keys and my stuff onto the couch as I hurry through the apartment. I don't know what Phillip's thinking about, but I've got a one-track mind right now. My clothes come off as I walk, each step shedding another piece of clothing.

When I turn around once I'm in the bedroom, Phillip is still completely clothed with a grin on his face. "What the hell are you doing?" I ask. "Why aren't you naked?"

His grin only widens as he puts his hands on my waist and lifts me into the air. It's not the first time he's done this, but like every time, my instincts kick in, and I have to grab his shoulders as I tense. He has me, though, and when he lays me down on the bed, I feel like I can finally breathe again.

"Faster isn't always better," he whispers.

"Sure feels like it is right now," I huff in response. "Maybe you're just not as turned on as I am."

He presses his crotch to me, and I stand corrected by the fact he could probably fuck me even with his pants on right now. "Oh. Maybe you are," I whisper.

His breath tickles my neck as his hands trace my curves, fingers digging in occasionally and making me gasp. "I didn't go to all this trouble just to fuck you for five minutes. I hope you're ready to beg me to stop."

Beg him to stop? Why would I ever want that? "I think you may overestimate your skills. I…" He takes a nipple between his lips and flicks his tongue. My words disappear as I gasp.

He looks at me the entire time that he kisses down to my stomach. His hands move to my inner thighs, and he pushes my legs apart. His fingers tighten and his nails dig into the sensitive skin. Then he kisses between my legs, his lips pressing against mine, hard and passionate.

He watches me as he does it, though, and just like from the very first night with him, it's the watching that is the real turn on. His tongue finds my clit, and it's wonderful and overwhelming, but more than anything, I feel vulnerable with him like this.

He's clothed and I'm naked. He's in control and I'm losing it. I feel like I'm just a toy for him to play with, except that I'm the one who was basically begging him to do this to me. However hard that is to wrap my mind around, it's the truth.

The worst part? I wish he were naked so I could get a hold of his cock. I don't know whether I'd rather stroke it or suck it, but something about touching his cock while he plays with me like this gives me some of the power back. That's probably not going to happen right now.

"You taste so fucking good," he says as he picks his head up to breathe. How does he make me feel like I want to blush like this? I mean, we just went skinny dipping together, and I was the one putting my hand down his pants in a back alley. But those words are what redden my cheeks?

He runs his fingers along my lips, his touch lighter than a feather, and then he brings his glistening finger to his lips and smiles as he tastes me again. "I think I could drink you dry, Addison. Maybe I'll do just that," he growls as he puts his face between my legs again.

Instead of focusing on my clit, he shoves his tongue deep inside me, something he's never done before, and when he makes circles along my entrance, it's just too much. I try to push away, but his hands hold me still, like vises.

"It's too much," I whisper right before I moan. Lightning shoots through me, making my body jerk, but Phillip just keeps licking. There's that feeling in the pit of my stomach again, that feeling like I'm going to burst, except that this time, I don't have any control over it.

I can't push his face harder or scoot back a little when it gets too much. No, he's in control, and I feel myself let go. The lightning still rushes through me, and my body still quakes and shivers, but I don't struggle in his grasp.

The feeling just keeps building while he watches me. His tongue flicks back to my clit, this time pressing harder and more insistent. "God Phillip, it feels so good," I moan. "How do you make me feel like this?"

He doesn't respond. His tongue is far too busy driving me freaking crazy. His fingers dig in harder, but then they let go. For a half-second, my body tries to scoot away, but his hands find my breasts and begin mauling them. It's too much, and the pressure building inside me explodes outward in a deep moan and full-body trembles.

I expect Phillip to stop, but he doesn't. His tongue just moves faster, more insistently, and what I'd thought would be a great orgasm transforms into something else. Something almost unpleasant, and I realize he was right to say what he did earlier.

"Please stop," I whisper between moans. And he does. My body is a traitorous bitch, though, and even when I can't handle the sensations, it wants more and grinds against the empty air. Phillip may not be licking me, but his hands on my breasts keep me expecting more.

He sits up, a grin on his face. "Just stop altogether?"

I'm still grinding, and I know what my body wants. "I need your cock, not your tongue. Please?"

"As you request," he says almost formally and stands up. This time, it's me watching like a wolf eyeing a rabbit. I remember the first time that he stripped in front of me, and this is not like that. The clothes come off smoothly, as though he'd moonlighted as a stripper in a past life or something.

When his cock finally comes to view, my mouth waters. That's what brings me all the pleasure in the world. But what if he does the same thing with that? What if he fucks me until I'm begging him to stop?

He reaches into the dresser drawer as he strokes his cock in front of me. He pulls out a condom from the box we bought and grins down at me. Seeing him move his hand over his cock only makes me want it more. I don't care if he tortures me with it. I can't imagine ever telling him to stop.

"Flip over," he commands. For the first time, I see that part of him that could demand obedience in the office blend with the Phillip I've gotten to know over the past two weeks.

I'm on my hands and knees in a heartbeat, my pussy dripping with need, and when I look behind me, he's got the condom on and looking at me with hungry eyes.

He runs his finger over my slit as he kneels behind me. "Such a pretty little pussy. So slick and ready for me." He's not even talking to me. He's just commenting and letting me hear him.

When he lines up with my entrance, my body tries to relax, but I'm too needy for him. I know the pleasure that's waiting, and his tongue between my legs pales in comparison.

Instead of just thrusting, though, he slaps my ass. I jerk, surprised by the action and the sting that's turning my skin red. He thrusts and with his other hand, he grips my hip while he slaps my ass again. Every time he fucks me, it feels like he's splitting me in two, but this spanking thing is new.

And I fucking love it.

My arms are shaking as I look back at Phillip, but just like earlier, he's looking between my legs. "Have you ever begged for someone to come, Addison?" he growls.

I quiver as his left hand grips my ass and he slams into me. I'd have fallen forward, but the hand on my hip holds me in place as he treats me like his little fuck doll even more. "No," I moan.

The hand on my ass slides across my skin to my hair, and he balls his fist in it before pulling it tight. My head is pulled back, and I'm forced to look at the wall instead of Phillip as he begins to really fuck me.

"It hurts. Please don't stop." The words tumble out of me with no control or filter. As soon as they're out, I barely know I've said them.

My fingers tighten in the comforter as his cock finally stretches me out enough that his balls are slapping my clit. My insanely sensitive clit. I'm still riding the aftershocks of that orgasm, and now each thrust is sending that liquid lightning through me.

And I can't see Phillip. Nothing except a shadow on the wall out of the corner of my eyes. I can't take my eyes off it. My body is experiencing things that I barely comprehend now that I can't see the man who's doing it.

The shadow on the wall is the only difference between this and wearing a blindfold.

I know he's still watching me, though. I know he's watching my ass shake as he slaps it. He's listening to me moan when he slams into me. It all goes back to being a plaything for him.

"I bet you'll enjoy me doing this same thing over my desk when I'm back in my old position, won't you?" he whispers in my ear. "Your tits pressed against the desk. Your panties around your ankles. My cock so deep inside you that you wonder why you can't taste it yet. I bet you'll be so ashamed walking down the hall with my handprint throbbing on that pretty little ass, won't you?"

I come for him. Where his cock and balls have pushed me to the edge, it's his words that shove me off the cliff. With a scream, my body quakes and my hands ball in the comforter. "That's a good girl, Addison. Scream for me. Show me just how much you love my cock."

Each thrust takes me higher, and I don't even realize that Phillip is panting behind me. His grip is so tight that there's no doubt I'll have little fingerprint bruises on my hip.

Before this orgasm has even finished, I feel the next one building. It's absolutely too much, and even with how much it hurts, I turn my head to look at Phillip. The look in his eyes is wild, nothing like ever before. He's pouring sweat. Every muscle in his body is straining.

"Please come," I groan. It's like he'd been waiting for that specific phrase this whole time because he lets go of my hair and pistons in and out of me as fast as he can. I collapse in front of him as the orgasm that had been building rolls through me. He doesn't let that stop him, though.

His hands squeeze my ass, and with a sound that resembles a roar, I feel him finally let go. I've never felt him like this, and when he loosens his grip, I turn over, almost nervous about what I'll see.

There he is, back to the man I've felt myself falling for. Sweet and a little goofy. Intense, but only in the best ways. "That was…" he whispers.

"Incredible? Insane? Perfect?" I finish.

He doesn't answer for a minute, but then he asks, "Are you okay? Did I hurt you?" He glances at my hips and my eyes follow his gaze. Just like I thought, there are little purple bruises already appearing.

"Love marks," I say. "Though, I might have to get you to check if there's a hole in my vagina because I could swear that monster was somewhere in my chest by the end."

He chuckles in between heavy breaths. "Addison, I meant for it to be intense, but I didn't mean to get quite so carried away."

Without warning, I reach across the bed and grab his balls lightly enough not to hurt them, but quickly enough to scare him. He stops moving, a look of panic in his eyes. "Good. I've got your attention now," I say with a grin. "That was fucking wonderful fucking. I would like to do it again regularly. I do not care about a few little bruises, just like I don't mind that my pussy is going to ache for the next three days because of it. Are we clear?"

Phillip just blinks, and I tug a little on his balls. "Very clear. You liked it a lot." His words tumble out as though he thinks I'm actually going to hurt him.

I grin and let go of his balls. "I wouldn't hurt you. You know that, right?" I ask.

"Yeah. But I didn't want to test you, Addison. You're kind of a hellcat when you get worked up."

Probably for the best. Though, I can't think of another time in my life when I felt this confident. I certainly never acted this way around my exes. That's when it occurs to me. "You're the only one that makes me get like that. Did you know that?"

He chuckles. "You're the only one who's ever gotten me that worked up, too. Maybe we fit better than either of us ever expected. Which is more than a little strange since we're so different in so many ways."

But are we? Sure, he's a billionaire regardless of what's in his wallet right now, which tonight proved, and I'm a broke chick trying to find my way in a brand new world. But does that even matter? Does it matter that he's my boss?

I thought it mattered only a couple weeks ago, but now I'm not so sure. Everything that we've done together has been ridiculous and insane, but I wouldn't change a single moment of it.

"I think we more than fit," I say. Phillip smiles at me but doesn't say anything else. It's probably for the best. Trying to understand things like the butterflies in my stomach is not a good way to spend my post-orgasmic bliss.

There is one thing that's bothering me, though. I'm not so sure I like our roommate agreement. I think I might actually want something more…

Thirty-Five

PHILLIP

"Fuck. Fuck. Fuck." The words come out, and I barely register them. I should have used tongs like Addison suggested.

Stuffed mushrooms are the hors d'oeuvres, or snack food as Addison calls them, we settled on for the party. Along with chips, dip, and a charcuterie board comprised of pressed meat and cheddar cheese. Addison had suggested getting a can of cheese wiz, something I'd never even heard of before, but I assured her that no cheese should ever come from an aerosol can.

But I'm cooking the stuffed mushrooms. This isn't something I'd have done when I took a limo to work, and now I'm reconsidering my skills, since the tip of every one of my fingers is at least a little burned. But judging from the face Addison gave me when she tried one, I didn't screw them up too badly.

I have to turn each of them over while they're still boiling lava hot and drain the grease from them. It seems that cheddar cheese turns into a puddle of oil in the oven.

I suggested parmesan, but the only one that fit her budget for the night didn't have to be refrigerated, which means I'm sticking it in the same "not edible" category as cheese wiz.

"Have you talked to your brother?" Addison asks as she puts the little slices of cheddar and ham on a plate.

I nod to her as I go to the sink to run my fingertips under cold water. "Yeah, he said he wouldn't miss it for the world."

"Good. Sera and Trish are on their way, and Trish says her husband's very excited since he doesn't do a lot of social stuff. It almost scares me, you know? Trish is a little 'extra' on good days, and I'm struggling to imagine the person she would fall for."

I grin at her. Trish is probably insane, but I'm realizing that insanity doesn't bother me as much as it might have in the past.

Though, I don't think I could live in the same house as her, so whoever she married has to be a bit off as well. It just makes the prospect of tonight even better.

There's a knock at the door, and Addison hops up, nearly knocking off the tray of meat and cheese in the process. I don't understand why she's so nervous. It's almost like she's never had people visit her before.

She opens the door, and I hear Sera's voice. And Andrew's. They must have shown up at the same time.

"You must be Andrew," Addison says. "I'm Addison. Phillip's roommate."

"You mean savior?" he says, and I can hear the grin in his voice. "He told me how you basically dragged him out of a storage closet and forced him to sleep on your couch."

"I don't know if that's how I'd describe it…"

I'm doing my best to get these damned mushrooms off the tray and onto the serving dish so I can actually see my brother when Trish's voice joins the party. "Holy shit, Andrew-fucking-Loughton showing up to my date night."

I get the last mushroom onto the serving tray and walk into the living room to see everyone grinning except my brother, who looks a little concerned. "I'm sorry. I don't think I've met you before."

Trish moves to introduce herself, and I catch sight of the only person I haven't met yet. He looks completely normal. We'd both been nervous about who would marry Trish, but this guy looks like he'd fit in just about anywhere.

"I'm Trish, Loughton House's official hooker." Andrew blinks, confusion written all over his face, and he glances at me with a "What the fuck did she just say?" look.

I chuckle. "She's the person who gets called when the first chapter needs some work."

"Oh!" Relief washes over him as he recognizes what she meant. "You write hooks. Okay. For a minute, I thought my brother had truly lost his mind."

That's when we begin to find out that Trish may be the more normal of the two of them. Her husband steps behind her and wraps his arms around her stomach in an embrace which feels far too intimate for the occasion. I don't even know his name…

"Trish may be a hooker, but I'm her only John," he says, and everyone except Sera looks a little bothered by the pre-introduction PDA.

Trish grins back at her husband and says, "Everybody, this is my husband, John. Don't mind the terrible joke. He is a dad after all, so it's legal."

Sera breaks the tension. She obviously already knows John, and isn't bothered by his terrible dad joke. Or the PDA. "Okay, now that everybody's met, what are we drinking and what are we playing?"

Addison says, "We've got two options for drinks. Andrew was gracious enough to bring a…" She looks down at the bottle and makes a face. "Chateau… Okay, I'm not even going to try to pronounce this. It's French. Or Italian. European wine. Andrew brought European wine."

He chuckles. "Chateau Cos d'Estournel. It's a cab from France."

"And I made three gallons of sprite and box wine. So if you hate wine, you'd better have brought something else."

"Excellent. Who doesn't like to remember the college years?" Sera says with a grin. "And what do we have for games?"

"Monopoly," I say. Immediately, Sera boos me. "What's wrong with Monopoly?"

"We're here to laugh and make fun of each other, not pay rent. Next."

Trish nods. "Yeah, I'm vetoing Monopoly. You and your brother would end up writing contracts and getting lawyers involved. I suggest poker."

"And if we get drunk enough, we can play strip poker," Sera says in agreement.

I feel like we're losing control of this. I didn't sign up to play strip poker with anyone. "Maybe we dodge the sexual harassment suit," Andrew says before I can. "A simple game of charades, maybe? I'm sure there'll be plenty of chances for laughs then."

Everyone glances around the room, seeing if anyone disagrees with that suggestion, and we all kind of shrug with acceptance.

"Well, if it gets boring watching my bosses act like elephants, we can always get the cards out. I wouldn't mind playing some high stakes poker with the boss."

Finally, I jump in. "Are you sure we'd be that easy to beat?"

"With my eyes closed, Madonna. I may have traveled the country as a karaoke singer, but I paid for food with poker winnings from guys who take gambling a lot more seriously than the two of you."

I chuckle. "Maybe we'll have to play another time."

Trish winks at me, and we all go into the dining room to make drinks. Andrew's bottle of wine never gets opened, surprisingly. I know the brand. It was our go to "cheap wine". Now it's a week's worth of groceries. I can't help but grin at the tiny differences in my life.

Andrew falls to the back of the line and whispers, "I understand why you did this now."

My eyebrows arch. "What do you mean?"

"It's because of her, isn't it? The one you're living with."

For a second, my jaw clenches. "I didn't know that I'd be living with her when I stepped away from my position at Loughton House. I slept on tables in a storage room for almost a week."

Andrew just grins. "I didn't mean that you did it to live with her. But she's the one that made you want to step aside, isn't she?"

He's always been clever, but I'm surprised at him figuring it out, mostly because I hadn't quite put those pieces together myself. It had been very coincidental, but thinking about that night at the motel, that's when things changed. That's when I realized I needed a change.

It wasn't the motel or the weird night, though. It was Addison. "Yeah. She doesn't know it, though."

Addison and her friends are laughing as they make drinks, and I can't help but smile.

"It's not like you to get wrapped up in a girl, Phillip. What's so different about her?"

I shrug. How do I put into words the way she makes me feel? How do I explain the way I wake up smiling just because she's in the same room as me? It doesn't make sense. Hell, nothing in my life really makes sense anymore.

"She makes me realize that there's more to life than business. At the same time, I'm considering going back to my old job early."

Andrew looks at me with surprise all over his face. "You aren't struggling. Dad thinks you're living in some homeless shelter or something, but you're not. You're just living a worker bee life, and there's nothing wrong with that. Why would you want to go back to the way things were before?"

"Because they won't be that way anymore. Plus, Addison gives me a reason to have extra money."

Andrew glances at Addison and shrugs. "Okay, that makes sense. Dad's going to kill you. Or her maybe. You know that, don't you?"

"No, he won't." I say it with complete confidence. "We all know that I'm the only one he's prepared to give Loughton House to, and I swear on everything that's holy that I will walk away just like Mason if he tries to push us apart."

Andrew cocks his head just a little. "You know that nobody ever gets Dad by the short and curlies. Nobody forces him to do anything."

"He taught me everything he knows, Andrew. I am Father without having to struggle to figure anything out, and I've spent the last decade doing things better than him. It's why he doesn't even look over what I've done anymore. He's not as good as me. Not at business and not at controlling a situation. And I have nothing to lose by walking away, but he does."

Andrew's eyes widen a little, and then he shakes it off. "Alright, brother. It's your call." His eyes move to Sera, who's watching him out of the corner of her eyes. "How do you know her?"

"She's one of Addison's friends. Why?"

Andrew shrugs. "No reason. Just wondering."

I frown, knowing exactly why he'd be looking at Sera that way. "Don't fuck things up for me, Andrew," I caution. He just grins at me and walks into the kitchen.

Son of a bitch.

Thirty-Six

ADDISON

CHARADES ISN'T WHAT I'D EXPECTED WHEN I DECIDED to have a game night. I'd thought we'd play something like Trivial Pursuit or even Monopoly, but looking at the people in the room, it does kind of make more sense. There's just too big of a distance between the Loughtons and the rest of us. I mean, Phillip didn't know how to use a coffee pot. How would anyone expect him to know about pop culture?

And Andrew is a mystery. Nobody except Phillip knows anything about him. I guess Trish knows who he is, and maybe Sera does, too.

"We'll just split into obvious teams," Trish says.

"Obvious teams? Boys versus girls?" Andrew's sitting in a folding chair that might have been borrowed from a friend and never returned.

"Couples," John says as he pats Trish's leg and grins. "Then we get the drama when one couple is terrible together."

Everyone glances at Phillip and me. We're not sitting next to each other, and we're definitely not acting like a couple. So why is everyone acting like we are?

"So me and John," Trish says. "Phillip and Addison. And Sera and Andrew. Good luck, you two."

Andrew glances at Sera, and she shrugs. "That works," he says and drags his folding chair over to the ottoman she's sitting on. I make a note to buy more furniture or at least folding chairs if I'm going to have people over. Though, it's all new to me since this is literally the first time I've had anyone at my place. Even in college, the only person who ever came over was my boyfriend. I don't like my space invaded.

These people are different, though. Other than Andrew and John, I feel closer to most of the people in this room than I have to anyone else in a very long time.

Phillip gets up and sits next to me, a grin on his face as he whispers, "Just so you know, I'm very competitive, and I really want to beat Andrew at this."

I just grin back at him. I can be competitive, but I don't know the vibe tonight. Is it just a reason to laugh and drink or are we going to have an intense game?

A stack of notecards sits on the coffee table. Each of them has a word handwritten on it, and without asking anyone, Andrew stands up and grabs the top card.

Sera sits up straighter on the ottoman. John and Trish cuddle up next to each other on the couch. I set a timer on my phone for three minutes, and I say, "Ready, set, go!"

And Andrew sets the mood for the night. Barely holding back laughter, he turns around, puts his hands on his knees, and begins shaking his ass.

See, we didn't have an actual charades game. Each of us came up with a word for each of our thirty notecards. This is going to be a very chaotic night.

"Twerking!" she shouts.

And it's over. "Twerk was the answer," he says as he drops the card on the coffee table and goes back to sit next to Sera. He gives a little grin to Phillip, and I feel like I'm understanding what vibe we're going for. Competitive chaos.

"Trish, that's ridiculous," Sera says. "Next, someone's going to get stripper."

Trish is laughing. "Wasn't me. I'm not going to twerk in front of my bosses."

And then I see Sera grinning… And blushing? Maybe it's the lighting, but I could swear that she almost looks a little embarrassed.

I put a mark down beside Sera and Andrew's names. "You or me?" I ask Phillip, and he gets up, not at all worried about making a fool of himself. Truthfully, how could anyone be embarrassed of charades after his Madonna performance?

Phillip picks up a card, and I watch him carefully as his face sinks. What could it be on the card?

He's just shaking his head as I set the timer for three minutes again. "Ready, set, go?" I say without as much gusto as I'd had the last time.

Everyone's watching as he sighs. "Old man yelling at clouds." He glares at me and shakes his head while Sera and Andrew laugh. He stops for a minute before running into the kitchen and… comes back with a broom? What?

He stands still for a moment, and I hear him mutter, "I've had. The time of my life…" And Andrew looks like he's about to yell something, but Phillip goes quiet.

Then he starts… dancing? Is that what you'd call it? He holds the broom like he's doing a waltz, but it's too close? Like a slutty waltz? He's shaking his hips and twirling the broom around like it's a princess, but it's far too slow to be anything I'm familiar with.

"Dancing?" I ask, very unsure of myself. "Old dancing? Retirement home?"

He ignores me as he walks across the room away from me. What the hell is he doing?

Then he turns around and stops like he's looking straight at me for a few seconds. Gripping the broom in both hands, he lifts it high into the air until it's parallel to the ground. There's a big grin on his face as he stares up at it.

Is that supposed to be a person? The time is running out, and I don't have any idea.

"Ice skating? Gymnastics? Ballet?" Nearly everyone in the room is laughing their asses off, but Trish is loudest, barely staying in her seat.

He slowly spins as he looks up at the broom, a smile on his face.

The timer goes off, and Trish practically screams, "It's Dirty Dancing. Oh my God, Phillip that was perfect."

"What's Dirty Dancing?" I ask. "Like the old movie?"

Phillip asks, "You haven't seen Dirty Dancing?" It's like everyone in the room is completely shocked I haven't seen it.

"It was made like twenty years before I was born. Why would I have watched it?"

Phillip sits down next to me. "If you haven't seen Dirty Dancing, we'll have to put it on the to-watch list. I've seen it dozens of times."

Andrew joins the conversation. "That was Mom's favorite, right?"

Phillip grins and nods.

"Yes, everyone has to watch it," Trish says. "Everyone. But now it's our turn."

So that's who wrote that card. I don't argue, and the group mostly calms down. John stands up almost solemnly and grabs a card. When he grins, I don't know what to expect. Maybe we should have gone out and bought a copy of the actual charades game so we didn't have such chaotic words.

He stands in front of everyone, the widest grin I could imagine on his face, and I set the timer. As soon as I say go, he hooks his fingers over his ears, making them look like they've got tips on them. I don't have any idea what that could mean, but Trish does.

"Elf." She says it like it's a sure thing, and he nods to her, his grin somehow widening even more. Who the hell would instantly go to elf? And who put that card in the stack? But he's not done.

He put his hands on his hips and starts walking, swaying them, but he only takes two steps before stopping. Trish doesn't say anything, just watching him as he suddenly looks like he's pulling something out of both pockets at the same time.

"Sexy elf rogue in black leather." She stands up before he's even confirmed it and walks toward the snack tray, completely confident in her answer.

"Yep. I knew you'd get it." What? How could anyone get that? Much less gotten it immediately. I glance at the rest of the group, who are all looking a little dumbfounded as we all think the same thing.

He sits back down and watches Trish getting food, but nobody moves until Andrew says, "Okay, who wrote that card? Because that's nuts."

John turns to him. "Oh, that was my card. I mean, Trish hadn't seen it, so it was fair game."

"Then how the hell did you guess 'in black leather'? I kind of understand elf. Same with sexy. And *maybe* rogue. But 'black leather'?"

Trish is laughing as she walks back into the living room with a tray of snacks. "Oh, as soon as I got elf, I knew it was John's, and he always thinks of sexy rogues in black leather. I wasn't sure if he'd written it on the card, but it doesn't hurt to say extra words."

He wraps his arm around her. "It was on there. You know me so well."

I can't help myself. "How do you know what he thinks a sexy elf looks like?"

Trish grins and glances at John before turning back to me. "Well, I might have a sexy elf outfit in my closet.

Made of black leather…" What? I knew Trish was chaos in a soccer mom's body, but that's not something I'd expected. She continues, "But in our Dungeons and Dragons game, I play an elf rogue who definitely wears black armor while slaying dragons."

"I didn't know that you played Dungeons and Dragons," Sera says. "That seems… surprising."

Trish shrugs. "Is it? Really?"

"She plays because it's my hobby, and I needed another player one night. The same way that I watch the kids whenever she wants to have an impromptu karaoke night." John pulls her close to him. What I originally saw as inappropriate PDA, I'm beginning to realize is something totally different. Love that neither one of them has any desire to hold in.

"Look, it's a lot of fun. Maybe I wouldn't play with just anybody, but if my husband can put up with all of my antics, I can pretend to be a murdering elf who wears leather pants for him. Why wouldn't I play a game when it makes him happy?"

The way she says it, I feel like it's one of those universal truths that's so simple, that should be in the "How to Win at Relationships" handbook. Why wouldn't she play a game that made her husband grin and maybe have a few fantasies about her? Why wouldn't he watch the kids when she just needs to get out and put on a show for a bunch of people at a bar so she doesn't go crazy?

I glance at Phillip, and I see the wheels turning in his head as well. Maybe he's realizing the same things as I am.

Why don't more people set aside their expectations to make their partners happy? Obviously, no two people have exactly the same hobbies, but why wouldn't you join in if it makes the other person happy? Or do what you can to support them?

Instinctively, my thoughts go to Phillip, and whether I'm supporting the things he enjoys enough. *But we're not partners. We're just roommates.* And that voice inside me that loves to call me out is saying, "Roommates. Right…"

"Well, good for you," Andrew says. "I don't understand it at all, and I really can't imagine dressing up as a leather-clad elf, but if that's what tickles your pickle, that's all that really matters."

Sera grins at him. "You can't tell me you've never roleplayed with a girl."

He huffs. "Sure. She's the sexy maid who's terrible at her job but doesn't want to lose it, so she agrees to get a spanking when she messes up. More short skirts and less pointy ears."

"You mean you prefer to do nothing and let your friend do the roleplaying. Makes sense."

The smirk is unmistakable. "Well Sera, just so you're aware, I do plenty. For hours. I just let her do the dressing up."

The tension between them is bizarre. It's almost like they know each other from somewhere else. Sera's worked for Loughton House for a lot longer than me, so maybe Andrew had been more involved back then.

"Right. Hours. I've always known that men get confused about the difference between three and eight inches, but confusing two minutes and hours is a new one."

The smirk shifts into a glare. The rest of us kind of just stare at them. Then Sera stands up, everything about her exuding an anger I've never seen before, and grabs a card off the stack. She makes Phillip look like he'd just won the lottery when he looked at his card.

"Nope. I'm not doing this one." She tosses the card to me, and I frown. "I'll do a different one, or we can say that we lost this one, but I'm not doing it. At least not with *him*."

I glance down at the card. *Tell Santa what you want for Christmas.* "How about we take a break? Maybe get some food and pick a different game?"

John and Trish glance at Sera, who's looking pissed and nod. "That sounds good."

Sera and Andrew keep a wide distance between them as they make their way to the dining room to make plates, and as Phillip tries to go with them, I stop him.

"Is there something I should know about them?" I whisper.

He shrugs. "Not that I know of. I didn't think they'd ever met."

Phillip is definitely wrong on that account. Those two have a history, and I can't imagine it has anything to do with work. "Maybe we shouldn't invite them to the same events anymore," I whisper back.

He frowns and nods before walking toward the dining room to get some food for himself. Who knew that I'd learn so much about my friends from a simple game of charades?

And who knew that I'd come to realize things about myself as well? Like how I can't help but think about Phillip as my partner.

I don't know how I could have been so naive to think our roommate agreement could work out. I am a romance author, after all. All I can do is hope that we can make things stick even after he goes back to being my boss.

Thirty-Seven

PHILLIP

"LET ME READ IT. PLEASE." ADDISON IS WEARING MY favorite pajamas on our last lazy Saturday morning while she leans back on the couch, her legs over my knees. Just the button-up shirt I left with her on that fateful night at the motel. She's started wearing it around the apartment on lazy weekend mornings. I can't help but think how beautiful she looks.

She throws her hands up. "I can't let you read anything! It's not done, and I haven't even started touching edits. You'll go all publisher-slash-editor on me and rip me apart."

I run my fingers over the bare skin of her inner thigh and grin. "I only tear you apart in bed, Addison."

She doesn't let out the little moan I'm used to hearing when I touch her like this. This is a more serious topic than I'd thought. "You know what I mean. That's my baby, and if you rip it apart, it's like you're telling me I'm stupid or my story is stupid. Plus, you don't even like romance!"

I push her legs apart just a little, and I get a glimpse of what's between them. It makes my cock swell, but this is a serious topic for me too, so I push those thoughts away. There'll be plenty of time for that after.

"I have edited two different romances since becoming a junior editor, and James Pritchard hasn't had a problem with any of it. I may not choose romance as my first choice, but it's grown on me. Anything you write is officially my favorite genre, though."

She frowns and shakes her head. "No, Phillip. I already said I didn't want to talk about my book with you. I don't want to mix business and pleasure, and there's no way you can read it without critiquing it. Please don't push this."

"Fine." I don't want to let it go, but I've learned to recognize when Addison has drawn the line on a conversation. "Will you let me read it when you've finished it?"

She chews her lip, not sure whether she wants to give in and push this conversation to a later date. I've come to understand a lot of things about the beautiful woman with her legs across my knees. One of them is that she doesn't like to tackle problems that she can push into the future.

"I don't think I'll want you to read it then either," she says.

"Well, when you publish it, I'm going to read it for sure." I take one of her feet in my hands and begin to massage it. "And don't you dare tell me you aren't getting it published. You're in a relationship with the Director of Publishing for the largest publisher in New York."

Something snaps in Addison, and she pulls her feet away from me. "No." She twists on the couch so she's sitting on her knees. Not a single inch of her body is relaxed anymore. I don't really understand what changed, but I'm sure she'll tell me.

"No, Phillip. You will not push my book through and get it published just because we're sleeping together. That *will not* happen. Either I'm good enough, or I'm not, and if I smell even one touch of your influence on its success, I will turn down any offer and stop talking to you completely. Do you understand?"

Why's she being like this? Half of getting a publishing deal is luck, so why not take that out of the equation? It's not like I can influence the reviews she received, so in the end, her success or failure will come down to her book. Not me. I may be able to push a single book through, but I can't turn her into a professional author. That'd take multiple books, all of them being successful.

"Why not? Why not let me take luck out of the equation?"

She snarls and stands up. "Haven't you learned anything about me? I don't want your help to succeed. I don't want anyone's help. My entire life, I've done it all alone, and I'm stronger because of it. I will not be my mother, asking for help from anyone she knows. I'm not some charity case."

What? I stand up and move to her, my arms wrapping around her body and pulling her to me. She struggles a little, but I hold her tight. "You're not a charity case, Addison. You're the most amazing person I know, and I want people to see how wonderful you are. That's all. I don't want some miserable woman sitting at some desk in Loughton House deciding what happens to your book."

She sighs but doesn't back down. "I don't care," she says, her voice softening. "If that's who decides everyone else's future, then I want her to decide mine, too. I just want what I deserve. Not what someone gives me."

I take a deep breath and let it out before letting her go. "Fine. I'll make you a deal. I won't have any part in your book getting published. None. I will let you query agents and do the whole thing.

"But I won't let you do it on your own. I will help you pick agents to submit to. Ones I know are good. I will help you with your query letters and make sure that you don't get lost in the slush pile."

Addison gets a thoughtful look on her face and almost interrupts, but I don't let her. "Look. This isn't charity any more than you showing me how to buy clothes at a thrift store is charity. It's someone with skills teaching you. I won't write your query letters, but I'll help you make them better than anyone else."

She slowly nods. "I think I can handle that. That's teaching a man to fish, not giving him a handout."

"Good. You really should let me help you work on the editing, though. You've done so much for me over the last month, and this is how I can repay you."

A frown etches itself into her expression, and I want to jump in and try to reassure her it's better this way. She's faster than me, though. "I don't want you to read it."

"But…" she stops me by raising her hand.

"I don't want anyone to read it because I'm terrified it's awful." She takes a deep breath and looks down. "But someone has to read it. You know this industry better than probably any other person in the world, and you're a damn fine editor too. I'd be a fool to turn you down."

"Thank you," I say.

She's not done, though. "Phillip, I'm fragile when it comes to my writing. I can roll with the punches in real life perfectly fine, but I don't know how to take criticism about my writing. That's why no one's ever read them. I trust your opinion, but I don't know how to separate myself from them. I know it's a terrible trait for an author."

"It's also one of the most common," I tell her and take her hand in mine, squeezing it tightly. "Don't worry, Addison. I'll be gentle."

She grins and squeezes my hand back. "Thank you. I'll let you read it when I'm finished, okay?"

With a nod, I pull her in for a hug. I've never been someone that enjoyed hugs, but the more time I've spent with Addison, the more I've begun to understand them. And enjoy them.

She looks up at me and says, "What are we going to do when things go back to the way they were before?"

I give her a crooked smile. "That's entirely up to you. You can stay here, and I'll even ride the subway to come spend most nights with you. Or…"

I leave the words hanging, letting her realize what I've been thinking about for so long. "Or I move in with you?" she asks.

I nod to her. "You can keep your apartment, so you don't feel any pressure. See how you enjoy being my roommate instead of the other way around."

"That'd be very strange," she says. "You'd have to teach me how to use your fancy coffee maker."

I chuckle, thinking about that morning not so long ago. "I have very strict roommate requirements, though."

She frowns. "What?"

"You'd have to officially date me. And you'd have to occasionally wear my shirts around without any bottoms. I think you gave me a fetish that night at the motel."

She pushes away from me, a grin on her face. "Guess I'll be staying here then," she says as she turns around and walks toward the bedroom door, the shirt barely covering her perky ass and making me want to ravage her.

"You really won't make this official? We both know that we're not just roommates. Hell, even your friends call us a couple. Whether or not you want to say the words, that's what we're doing."

She walks into the bedroom and shouts, "That's not what I have a problem with!"

I go into the bedroom, so I don't have to shout and see her standing by the closet.

God, she looks fucking hot wearing my shirt. I wasn't joking when I said she gave me a fetish. It's enormous on her, going almost all the way to her knees, but there's something about knowing she's wearing my clothes that turns me on.

She crosses her arms and says, "I've been fantasizing about wearing your shirts for so long that I had assumed that's what I'd walk around in all the time if I lived with you."

"So, what's the problem?" I feel very dumb right now.

"Well, you said occasionally, and I think I'd go crazy if I had access to your closet every day and didn't get to just put one on any time I wanted."

"You little shit," I mutter and cross the room to wrap my arms around Addison. "So, you're moving in?" I whisper.

She gives me a peck on the lips and grins. "Of course. I don't want to be away from you any more than I have to. If you're moving back into your old place, I want to go too. Plus, I'm pretty desperate to redecorate your fancy house in thrift store mugs. I bet your family would die of shock if I did that."

I feel my jaw tense ever so slightly at the thought of my family. Namely, my father. He's been back in town for a week, and I haven't heard a word from him. I'll see him Monday, though, and I'll have to tell him that Addison is moving in with me.

The fight is going to be intense, but it's worth it. Hell, anything's worth it to keep Addison in my life.

"You can decorate my house however you like because that's what a man does for a woman he loves."

Her head moves so fast I have a hard time not worrying about her getting whiplash. "Did you mean to say that?" she whispers.

"That I love you? Absolutely. That you can decorate my house however you want? I'm kind of rethinking that already."

In the movies, there's always this pause when someone says those magic words to their partner for the first time. I guess Addison doesn't understand the way these things are supposed to work because she instantly retaliates.

"Well, that's stupid," she says with a nearly straight face.

"You think me loving you is stupid?"

She shakes her head and rolls her eyes. "No Phillip. I've been hoping you'd say that for at least a week now. Ever since the game of charades. I meant letting me decorate your house. That's obviously a terrible idea."

"What about charades made you want me to tell you I love you? Seems like an odd time to realize your undying love."

She gives me a sideways grin. "Watching you act out that scene from Dirty Dancing made me realize how truly wonderful you are. And how much I love you, too."

I don't get it, but maybe I shouldn't try to understand. This may be one of those traps women lay for men's brains where their explanations only make things more confusing. On second thought, I'm sure that I should not ask for an explanation.

"Well, as long as you love me, I guess it doesn't matter what made you come to the conclusion."

She gives me a wink and pulls away. "Now that everything's settled, you get to help me get boxes so I can start packing my things."

I can't stop thinking about her moving in with me. Or about what that means. When I moved in with Addison, I didn't plan on this. I didn't plan on anything that's happened, and I definitely didn't plan to fall in love with her.

Looking back, though, it would have been impossible to keep my distance. She's been a shining light in a world of darkness, and I can't just walk away at the end of the month.

Now I know that there's no way in hell that I'll let anything take her away from me. Not Loughton House. Not even my father.

Thirty-Eight

ADDISON

"HE'S BACK IN HIS OFFICE TODAY? HOLY SHIT. YOU'VE gotta find a reason to spend the afternoon under his desk like a filthy little whore. That's the dream, right?"

I can't believe Trish actually said that, and I'm pretty sure my expression tells her exactly how I feel about it.

"What? I'd wear a tiny little skirt without panties if my guy was the Director. And I definitely would be suck... Oh, hey boss."

James Pritchard frowns as he walks into the break room. "Kind of late to be chatting over coffee, don't you think?"

We nod to him, and as we walk past him, he says, "Addison, Phillip Loughton wants to talk to you in his office. Do you know where it is?"

Butterflies explode in my stomach, and Trish turns back toward me, silently laughing. "I don't have any idea where it is."

James Pritchard gives me directions to the office on the top floor, a floor devoted to the absolute pinnacle of the publishing world. They're the men and women who make and break careers. The ones who make the shifts in the types of books that are published.

And my boyfriend is up there asking for me to come talk to him. Before he made the insane decision to give up all his money for a month, he'd never have done that. I'm not worth his time. Unless he was going to fire me or promote me, of course.

James Pritchard frowns as I nod and walk toward the elevator. I'm sure he's wondering if there's something going on between us, even though we've been strictly professional at work. The only other options would be that I was on the chopping block or up for a promotion, neither of which makes sense after working for Loughton House for only a month.

It only makes me realize how quickly my life has gone from simple to absolute madness, and it all boils down to the man waiting for me at the top of the world. A man that I can't think of as just my roommate anymore.

Not when I'm moving into his multi-million-dollar home tonight.

Not when I'm going to do very dirty things with him in *his* bed.

Not when I'm absolutely head-over-heels in love with him.

I knock on the closed door, and I hear Phillip's gruff voice call out, "Come in." It feels bizarre to go into his office when his blinds are closed. I feel like a teenager sneaking around after my mom's gone to bed.

I slip inside the room, and I'm shocked at the size of it. I share a cubicle that's barely large enough for us all to sit in, and Phillip's office is about ten times as large as that.

His desk is massive, completely unused. An entire wall is devoted to a white board with multitudes of names on it, each of which has notes under it, many of which include the names of cities. The wall behind him is a single massive window that peers out onto the city below us.

"Lock the door," he says as he gets up from his desk. All the playfulness that I'm used to seems to be gone, and he's back to being the Phillip "Ice Cold" Loughton.

I turn the lock and when I look back at Phillip, he's just staring at me. "I'm sorry for bothering you," he says as he sits down on the desk.

"Why? I'd always wondered what your office would be like. Jeez Phillip, I guess you really are important with an office like this." I give him a grin as I cross the room to wrap my arms around him.

God, it feels good to touch him. When we were both working in the cubicle, I didn't feel the same distance between us. We were there together, destroying books and rebuilding them. Each of us had our own projects, but we were doing the same things. We had our own minor triumphs and troubles, but there was no distance between us.

Sure, we haven't made anything official, but by the end of last week, I knew how I felt about Phillip Loughton, and I was pretty sure he did too.

But now, there's so much distance, and all I want to do is pull up a chair next to him. He could teach me to run Loughton House, and we could do it all together.

That's just a crazy dream, though. Even if we got married, I'd never sit next to him and run Loughton House. He's spent his entire life preparing for it, and I haven't.

"I missed you," he whispers as he kisses my forehead.

I love the way he touches me, especially the little kisses. "We've only been at work for two hours. I'm already going crazy being this far away from you."

He chuckles. "Well, you could always give up editing and become my secretary."

The conversation with Trish flashes through my mind. "I bet you'd have me wearing a slutty little outfit, too. And bending over to get the paper you keep dropping?"

"Absolutely not. I'd buy you a cute little cushion, and you could just sit under my desk."

My hand rubs his crotch, and I arch my eyebrow. "I bet you'd struggle to get any work done that way. Could you imagine if your father walked in?"

And there's a knock on the door. My heart sinks. What am I supposed to do? We were supposed to keep things professional at work. Now he's been at work for two hours, and already I'm in his office.

"Open the damn door," a voice says from the other side, and I instantly know who it is even though I've never met the man. There's only one man who would have the audacity to talk to Phillip like that.

It's Russel Loughton, Phillip's father. The only person in the world that makes Phillip look and feel like that.

Phillip takes a breath and says, "Just a second."

He turns to me and whispers, "Don't try to help me. Let me talk, okay?"

I nod to him, not wanting any part of getting between him and his father. Phillip opens the door, and Russel walks in. I'm immediately surprised by him. He's definitely older, but he doesn't act like it. There are lines on his face, and his hair is graying, but he doesn't slouch at all, and there's no lack of poise.

Russel Loughton is a man that looks like he should be a billionaire. The suit doesn't even matter. Giving him a single glance, you know that you're nothing to him. He glances at me for half a second before turning back to Phillip. "Addison Adelaide. The woman you've been living with for the past month?"

Phillip nods. "You're here to return my cards, I assume?"

"I don't know if you deserve them after the stress you've put on the family and the company."

Phillip doesn't let him walk over him. "You agreed to the deal, so if anyone's put people under undue stress, it's you. You're the owner, after all. Actually, you suggested it. Maybe we should take away your access to the bank account if the decision was that bad."

Russel Loughton is the most powerful man in the publishing world. Every other major publishing house is a publicly traded company, but Loughton House is owned by him. One man. His sons are prominent figures, but at the end of the day, it all comes down to him.

"Don't be stupid, Phillip. I knew what I was getting into. What I didn't know was that you'd find some woman to take you in like a stray puppy. I hope you've enjoyed your time together because it's time to get things back in line. I need you to start off by taking a trip to LA to talk with a start-up agency."

Phillip chuckles and shakes his head. "Sorry. That's not going to happen."

Russel cocks his head, visibly surprised at his son's response. I try my absolute best not to move a muscle. "What are you saying?" Russel says very slowly.

"I'm saying that I'm not going to LA today. I need to figure out what all has happened while I've been gone. You can go to LA or send someone else, but I'm not going."

Watching them have this discussion is like watching two wolves growl at each other, and I'm not sure which one is going to back down. I'm sure that Phillip knew this kind of thing would happen after pushing away from his father, but did it have to happen two hours after he got back to work? More importantly, did it have to happen with me in the room? I feel like I'm going to end up a casualty in whatever fight happens.

"You can do all of that on the flight. Talk to the agency reps and then hop on the plane to be back here by the morning."

Phillip just shakes his head. "I don't understand what you're confused about, Father. I told you what I'm doing, and that's what is going to happen."

The comment seems straightforward. It's probably a little too aggressive, but there's no part of it that could be misunderstood. For some reason, Russel seems extremely confused. "Why aren't you going to LA? This isn't a new expectation."

The words come out slowly, more a mutter than an actual question. Then it's like a light clicks on in his head. And he turns back to me. "You're why. You're the reason all of this happened, aren't you? When I found out that my son was living with some woman, I thought he'd promised you a raise when he was done with his little mid-life crisis. Now I'm wondering if it's something else."

I don't know what to say. I've always thought that Phillip's stare was so intense, but it was hot. When Russel looks at me, it's like I'm frozen. I don't know if it's fear or something else, but I don't know what to do or say.

And for the first time, I see Phillip become the man who the rest of the world sees. "Leave her out of it, Father," he growls. The wolf imagery fits even better as he takes two steps toward Russel.

I feel like I can move again as his gaze moves away from me, and I step back even further. Russel says, "I'll talk to any employee I want, boy. This is my company, after all."

And Phillip smiles at him. "Don't push me. I've done everything you've said for my entire life, learned every lesson you've ever taught, and truthfully, we both know that I'm better at running this company than you."

There's a pause as Russel stares his son down, both of them refusing to drop the argument. "Why shouldn't I push you? Why shouldn't I demand whatever I want from you? You owe everything to me."

Phillip smiles at him, and Russel's posture shifts just a little. Not enough to be noticeable to most people, but I've spent damn near every moment of every day for a month with Phillip, and it's the same thing that Phillip does.

"Father, I don't need you, and I don't need this company. Mason stepped away, and he's done just fine. I thought I needed you before my little 'mid-life crisis', but now I know I can manage just fine. Plus, I bet that Murray Press would hire me in a heartbeat. You need me, though. Andrew can't run Loughton House, and you're getting old. It won't be long before the cracks appear, and you're just not as good as you once were."

A silent tremble runs through Russel, and I can see the rage in his eyes. "I can't believe you'd suggest working for Murray Press."

Phillip shrugs and turns his back on his father. "You're the one who won't listen. You're the one who refuses to allow me the few things I've asked for. Privacy. My own decisions. The respect from you that I deserve. I would prefer to run Loughton House for the rest of my life, but I won't do it the same way that I've done it for all these years. I won't give up my life to run your company, Father. And if it's between giving up the company or giving up my life, I will gladly walk out the door."

He sits down at his desk as Russel stares at him. "Now, I have things to do. If you'd like me to go to LA, I can make it there on Friday afternoon. Please send me the information on this new agency you'd like to work with."

Russel glares at his son for a few more moments and turns to walk away. Before he gets to the door, though, Phillip stops him. "And if you do literally anything to Addison Adelaide. I swear I will work for our biggest competitor and spend the rest of my life working to destroy Loughton House."

The only response Russel gives is standing just a little taller as he walks out the door, slamming it behind him.

Thirty-Nine

ADDISON

I IMMEDIATELY GO TO PHILLIP, WHO SINKS IN HIS chair. "Holy shit, Phillip. That was intense."

"He's not finished," Phillip says as he looks up at me, a sad smile on his face, "but I can't go back to the way things were before. I have a lot of leverage, but my father doesn't handle being pushed around very well. A lot of bad things could happen."

"Were you telling the truth about being willing to work for Murray Press?"

Phillip shrugs. "If my father cuts me out of Loughton House, why shouldn't I? It's not like he'd be showing me any loyalty."

That's crazy. Phillip's entire life has been centered around this company. I can't think of anyone who's worked harder to be the best in an industry than him, and Russel would be an idiot to send him to work for his competition. Then again, I saw the hate in Russel's eyes. The way he realized how little power he had right then.

"Do you think he'll cut you out?" The thought of Loughton House not having Phillip at the helm is kind of terrifying, actually.

He just shrugs. "I was telling the truth," he says with a sigh. "I won't ever give up my life for a company again. That's not a sacrifice I'm willing to make. There have been so many years that I've missed out on, and I won't let anyone take that away from me."

With a grin, he turns his chair and pulls me into his lap. "And I won't let anyone take me away from you. You need to understand that."

I heard him stand up to his father when it came to me. I know what he's prepared to do to protect me. Thinking about it is a little scary, but it's also crazy sexy.

"I'm so used to you being my goofy roommate, sometimes I forget that you're this big, powerful guy. It's a little easier to remember now that you're wearing that suit instead of the 'saffron stained' one. That conversation was so different from anything I've seen before, though."

He wraps his arms around me and says, "I don't enjoy having to fight like that, Addison, but in this business, and especially with my father, sometimes it comes down to using leverage on them. Otherwise, they'll run you over."

"Well, it was fucking hot. Just so you know. You were in super alpha male mode, and I'm kind of wondering when you're going to bend me over and take out your aggressions on me."

He arches an eyebrow and grins. "Oh, is that so? I thought you were against the idea of being my sexy little secretary."

"There's a difference between living under your desk and getting ravaged by the alpha male boss." I can already feel his cock swelling under my ass, and I know that there's a very good chance that he's going to take me up on my offer.

He takes a deep breath and lets it out slowly. "I can't. Damn it, I want to, but I have an insane amount of work to catch up on. Plus, I don't even have any condoms."

I run my fingers over his silk shirt and move closer to his ear. Leaning in, I whisper, "You don't need a condom. I've been on the pill since I found out how babies are made. How hot would it be knowing that I'm going to walk out of your office full of your come?"

For just the briefest of moments, he hesitates, and then he's lifting me off his lap. "Lift your skirt and bend over the desk," he whispers. "I'm going to go lock the door, and you're going to be very quiet."

I'd thought that him arguing with his father had been hot, but this is something else. He may have been rough and dominant in the bedroom before, but this isn't in the bedroom. This is right here in his office.

I do as he says, and I watch as he walks to the door, not hurrying at all. I feel almost nervous. Not because someone's going to walk in on us, but because this is the first time we're going to do something outside of *my* space. This is his domain, and he already feels different.

He's smirking as he walks around the desk. "Those panties are lovely, but they're going to have to go." He runs his hand over the black lace, and then cups my pussy, pressing hard against it. Fuck. I'd known I was wet before, but I'm pretty sure that I'd leave a puddle in any chairs I sat in right now.

I look behind me, and Phillip isn't paying attention to my face. His eyes are locked between my legs. Not in the dark of a bedroom or even in the living room, like the time we were watching a movie.

No, this is the bright light of day in the office, and he's admiring it. "I think you're going to have to get used to eating lunch with me," he says. "Or rather, you eating lunch while I eat you."

The thought of that makes me shiver. Could I fuck my boyfriend, the boss everyone fears, every day at the office? Could I walk around, swollen and soaking, after having been used like a sex toy every day?

The logical part of my brain says that's insanity. But, like so many times since I met Phillip, that part is locked away.

"If you're going to treat me like your personal office whore, I hope I get more than your tongue," I say.

He grabs my ass hard enough that I have to muffle the moan. "You'd better stay quiet," he whispers. "Otherwise, people might hear your screams and think that I was doing something you don't want. Could you imagine having to explain that it was your idea to begin with? That your soaking pussy needed to be fucked hard enough that it made you scream?"

I bite my tongue as he slips two fingers inside me. Fuck. I don't even know how to be quiet. Especially not when he's like this.

He pulls his fingers out of me, and I feel confused. On the one hand, I feel like I can breathe again, but on the other, I feel empty and desperate to be filled again. "You taste so fucking good," he whispers. "It's too bad I don't have time to savor you. Tomorrow, I'm setting aside at least an hour. An hour of you trying not to scream. Of you coming over and over again. Silently."

Oh no. I can't do that. I can't handle being quiet like that. Turning my head, I look at Phillip, and I'm surprised at the fact that he's not wearing pants anymore. How did he take off his pants without me knowing?

Maybe it's because my heart is beating so fast and loudly that it's a drumbeat in my ears.

His cock is standing at full attention, and just like every time, I wonder how it fits. This time, there's not the sheen of slippery latex over it, though. "I've fantasized about feeling your little pussy pressing against my cock for so long. Nothing between us except your wetness."

I'm panting now, desperate for him. I stand on my tiptoes as he lines himself up with my entrance. The tip presses against me, and that's when the electricity starts coursing through my veins.

Instead of gripping my hips like he does so often, he wraps his hand around the back of my neck and forces me to the desk. My face is turned so that I'm watching him as he slowly pushes inside me. His expression doesn't soften even as his body seems to relax.

I'd assumed he'd fuck me hard and fast with how much I've teased him, but he's savoring it. From the very first time, I've fallen further and further down the rabbit hole of roughness. Maybe someone somewhere would consider this degrading and rough, but it's not. It's sensual. It's loving. It's kind.

The edge of the desk bites against my thighs as his legs press against mine, his cock stretching me to my limits. The cold wood under me has goosebumps running across my skin.

And I feel absolutely, unquestioningly loved. Nothing about us makes sense, from our backgrounds to our personalities to our sex, and this is just one more example. I know he feels wonderful, and that he knows I feel even better.

The moans that slip from my lips are expressions of that love. When he slaps my ass and leaves my skin stinging, I want to thank him.

"This is what you wanted, isn't it?" he whispers.

"Yes." I'm too lost in the sensations of him inside me to have words beyond that. How did I go this long without letting him know we didn't need condoms? How did I miss so many instances where we could feel like this?

Phillip releases my neck and runs his hand through my hair. There's no way to describe the sensations that run from my scalp through my body to my core. Electricity? Pleasure? Magic? When his fingers tighten, I have to bite my lip to keep from moaning too loudly.

"God, your body is something special, Addison. I can't get enough of you. Fucking you isn't good enough. I want to consume you, to make you a part of me that I could never lose."

"Then do it," I whisper. "I'm yours, Phillip."

His body goes taut again at my words, and his hand tightens even more in my hair. He grips my ass so hard I'm sure that I'll have bruises. And he fucks me like never before.

My hips are pinned between the massive desk and his muscular legs. When he slams into me hard enough to shake the desk, I can't move. I can't scream. I can't do anything except watch him. My entire world fades except for his face and that wonderful mix of pain and ecstasy that's throbbing between my legs.

A scratching sound irritates the back of my mind while I do my best not to moan. I don't even know how I can hear something other than my body being slammed against the edge of the desk. Well, that and the growls coming from Phillip.

Somehow, I feel the pressure building in me. The feeling I've become so used to when Phillip has his hands around me and his cock inside me. My moans become pants as I give into the sensations even more.

He lets go of my hair, and both of his hands move to my waist. Fingers run under the waistband of the skirt and dig into my stomach. I barely know what's happening, though. My eyes are on Phillip's and his are on mine.

"I love you," he whispers.

"Always," I whisper back.

And he lets out the deepest groan I've ever heard. I can *feel* him coming. Strange sensations that I've never had.

The dam inside me breaks. I can't breathe. I can't think. I can't do anything except succumb to the quaking and quivering orgasm that rushes through me. Every muscle in my body is drawn tight enough that at another time, I might be afraid they'd snap.

Phillip's groan turns into a moan as my walls squeezes him, and I can feel his hands shaking as he releases me. "Addison," he whispers in my ear as he bends over me. I can't respond. The air rushes into me as I take ragged breaths.

When he steps back, my legs nearly give out on me. Still, I don't turn away from him. His cock is dripping with the evidence of what we've done. "I love you," I finally say.

"You're so perfect," he says.

I try to push myself off the desk, and it takes a little help from Phillip to get me standing again. "I don't know if I can handle that every day," I say as my legs threaten to give out.

He chuckles and pulls a box of tissues out of his desk drawer to clean himself off before holding the box out to me. I consider taking a few as well, but then I grin and grab my panties. There's a confused look on his face, and I say, "You're going to have to think about me walking around with your come inside me. I wonder how much work you'll actually get done with that thought on your mind."

Phillip grins, but I can see his breathing pick up. I pull on the panties, more than a little nervous at how dirty I feel, but something about this feels right in a way that other options don't.

"I don't know how I was lucky enough to convince you to fall in love with me," he says through the grin.

"Well, it wasn't your coffee making or cooking, that's for sure." I try to straighten my skirt out and question just how obvious it'll be that I just fucked my boss at nine o'clock in the morning.

"Must have been my hair, then." He runs his hands through his hair and gives me a grin like some kind of cheesy 80s heartthrob.

I lean in and kiss him. A passionate kiss that pushes away the need to keep up the banter. Long and slow, the kind that leaves your lips wondering if they'll ever stop throbbing.

When I pull back, I give his cock just the slightest pat and say, "It was definitely the hair. But now we both have to go back to work."

"I guess," he mutters, still pants-less.

"We do," I affirm. "Plus, if I stay much longer, you'll have me laying on your desk, legs spread, and there's no way that I'd be able to be quiet for another round. I'm already too sore to keep from screaming."

He chuckles, but he says, "I love you, Addison. Have fun editing something."

"I will. And don't get into any more fights with your dad. I want you in a good mood tonight since I'm moving in."

He nods, and I turn around to walk away. I know he's watching me walk away, and when I get to the door, I flip my skirt up to show him my lace panties again. I can hear his feet moving as he rushes toward me, but I'm too fast, and I slip outside his office before he can get to me.

I take a deep breath as soon as I'm in the hall. It's like I'm finally back in the real world again. A world where this hallway is full of dangerous men who could crush my dreams with a single word.

Phillip is both the reason they might and the only reason they don't. I know that no one in his world would approve of me. I know that I'm the enemy in their eyes, a gold-digger that got her hooks into a billionaire.

But I'm not, and Phillip knows that. Hell, I'm the one who tried to push him away from the very beginning. I don't even really understand what it'd be like to have access to more money than I make as a junior editor.

Tonight, I guess I'll find out. Part of me is terrified, but the other part can't wait. For now, though, I'm just going to get through the day without going crazy.

Forty

PHILLIP

I'VE DREADED THIS FOR SO LONG. THE DAY I HAVE TO leave the bliss and wonder of spending my days doing simple, stress-free work and my nights with Addison. As I look out at the city under my office, I don't feel that dread. In fact, I'm ready for this melding of two lives.

There were so many wonderful pieces of my life as a junior editor. The laughing at the breakfast table. All the new experiences. And, of course, Addison.

But I felt helpless there. I didn't have the tools I was so used to having. Waiting for buses or subways. The struggle to have fun with her without breaking our budgets. More than anything, the looming end of that month.

Today, I get to bring the good from that life into my world, where I have answers for everything. There are sacrifices I have to make to do that, but they're nothing compared to going back to the nothingness I had before I met Addison.

And no matter how much I try to pretend like I don't care, I've missed being at the heart of Loughton House.

I've spent every day of my life working for this place, and it's a part of me just as much as I'm a part of it. I'd leave if it came down to choosing Addison or it, but the loss would hurt.

Taking a deep breath, I turn away from the window and look at my desk that's never changed for more than a decade. Simple, unmarked cherry wood that I've sat behind every day. A symbol of my solitude if I want to get metaphysical about it.

And right where I rest my hand during meetings, there are deep scratches that weren't there this morning. Scratches that Addison made while I fucked her raw for the first time. I'll touch those scratches and remember that moment every day.

I can't help smiling at that knowledge. But it's time to go, to embrace the change that both of us have dreaded for a month.

I stand up and walk down to meet the girl I love. A limo is waiting outside to take us home. I can't wait to let her have fun redecorating it. We'd joked about that earlier, but there's no doubt she'll do just that since my home is as empty as my life was before her.

Addison is standing nervously by the break room, waiting like she said she'd be. I give her a smile as I walk toward her, and I can tell she's not sure what to do. When we first met, there wasn't an ounce of nervousness in her. She'd been fast with a sassy comment at every turn. Hell, even when I'd started working in her cubicle, she hadn't been afraid. The rest of the office would have kept their heads down and tried not to draw my attention, but Addison hadn't.

Now, she's standing there like a girl on her first day at a new school. I guess that it's understandable, but I hate it. I want her to be excited, to be ready for all the new opportunities.

"Ready to go?" I ask when I get close.

"Yeah." She pauses and continues, "Us leaving together like this is weird. I mean, when you were wearing stained shirts and pretending to be like the rest of us peasants, it was easy to forget that you're the big boss. Now, it's different. It almost feels inappropriate."

"What we did this morning was inappropriate," I say with a grin. "This is fine as long as I don't touch your career, something we both agreed to. Plus, as soon as you publish your novel, I'll have to find another junior editor."

That ought to bring out the fierceness in her. She always gets pissy when I mention her novel being published.

"Just forget about the damn novel," she snarls. "I'm stuck on the dark night, and I think I'm ready to give the whole thing up."

I just chuckle. Addison still hasn't let me read anything, and she's barely told me anything about it. "I'm sure you'll get it figured out. You're probably just letting all the changes in your life mess with you. Let's get you settled in, and then you can tell me all about your struggles over fancy beer."

She cocks her head. "You have some more of that weird stuff you had at the motel? The raspberries in coffee kind?"

"All that you can drink."

With a deep breath, she puts her hand in mine and says, "Alright boss, show me to my new mansion. I hope you remembered to cage the tigers and sent the strippers home."

"Absolutely. The tigers were sent home and the strippers are in their cages."

She chuckles, and in the middle of walking out of the room, I stop. She gives me a confused look, and I run my fingers over her cheek. "It's going to be fine, Addison. I promise."

There's a brief pause, but then she nods. I have some idea of what she's going through. The fear of a new place, of not knowing anything about a new life. Not that long ago, I went through these same emotions in reverse.

But I didn't have Addison with me when I left my life behind. I'd blindly jumped, and luckily, she'd appeared to catch me. The image in my head of that metaphor is more than a little comical, but the reality wasn't funny at all.

She has me, though. She doesn't have to worry about walking into a new world all alone.

I give her hand a squeeze, and she smiles. "Jeez, get a room. I'd feel more comfortable if you were slapping her ass and pulling her hair."

We both whirl around to see Trish leaning against a cubicle wall with a grin on her face. "Shut up," Addison says with a laugh. "You can't talk to your boss like that."

It's Sera's turn to pipe up. "It's okay. We're safe since I have blackmail material. I have his entire performance of *Like a Virgin* recorded, and I'm not afraid to send it to Andrew."

"You'd better not," I say. "He wouldn't ever let me live that down."

They both just start laughing. I should be pissed. But truthfully, I don't know if there's anything that could piss me off right now.

I shake my head and take Addison's hand, pulling her to the front of Loughton House, where the limo's waiting for me. Addison seems less nervous, but as soon as I open the door to the car for her, she tenses.

"I love you, Addison. Let's go home."

And she smiles. "Yes. Let's go home."

Forty-One

ADDISON

"You have so many freaking cabinets!" I've never seen anything like this before. Sure, I'd known that he lived in a big house, but this is madness. Four thousand square feet in the middle of Manhattan is bonkers. "And they're all empty. What did you even do with a kitchen, anyway?"

He just grins as he leans against the counter while I explore his house. "You can't buy a big house without a kitchen, Addison. They don't come that way. Plus, I occasionally have a chef come cook for me when I'm spending a lot of time working from home."

I gawk at him. A chef comes to his house to cook? "Okay, we are not the same. Wait. Could you get one to come and give me lessons on bread-making? I've always wanted to learn… You know what, don't answer that. I'm just going to assume that you can do anything you want. Well, I don't have to worry about having enough space to keep my coffee mugs, right?"

I walk away from the pristine kitchen into the living room. It's enormous. Three story tall ceiling with the rest of the house built around it. A massive crystal chandelier hangs from the roof, and there's a fireplace that you could probably cook a whole cow in. I feel far too much like we're on a movie set right now.

Maybe that's the problem. It's so pretty, but almost like it's a pretend house. Like no one's lazed on the double-length couch—which is a very confusing piece of furniture for my brain.

"Do you have parties? Or just live here? Why would you want a house this big if you aren't going to use any of the space?"

Phillip steps behind me and wraps his arms around my waist. "I don't know," he says into my ear. "Maybe it's all so that you'd have four thousand square feet to fill with kinky mugs and mismatched furniture when you moved in? Maybe I was compelled because deep down I already knew that a crazy lady was going to need all this space."

I huff. "I'm not crazy. You're the crazy one to buy all of this without any reason. I just…" I turn around in his arms. "When I was in third grade, my shoes wore out to where the bottoms came off. Like all the way off. I got grass stains on my feet when I played at a park. My feet were freaking green. I didn't get another pair of shoes for three weeks, Phillip. And that's because one of my teachers bought them for me."

I expect him to stop me, to tell me I don't have to worry about that anymore or something. But he doesn't. He just listens. "I've spent my entire life chained down by being poor. Literally, every problem in life could have been fixed with just a little more money. And you… You have so much. More than I could ever even imagine. Rich is wrecking a car and then buying a new one the next day. This is… something different. I didn't understand…"

He smiles at me. "It's definitely different, Addison. But you don't have to spend money if you don't want to. You can, of course, but if you want to keep riding the subway to work and buying clothes at thrift stores, then that's fine with me. The money won't go away if we don't use it."

I have to take a step back as I shake my head. "No Phillip, you don't understand at all. Why would I want to buy clothes at a thrift store? I mean, I'm probably never going to understand buying thousand dollar dresses, but I don't even know *how* to spend money like this. How do you get a chef to come cook for you? Is that just something you google?

"We're supposed to be dating or something. I mean, I'm living with you as your partner, right? In my world, I'd make dinners, and you'd wash the dishes, and we'd watch movies or bad TV. In yours? I have no freaking idea. Do you order takeout from Paris, and they teleport it here? Then the house elves come and clean it for you? If the internet is out, do you get the cast of Bridgerton to come re-enact the entire show for you in full costume? Who do I call to schedule that? Or do you just push a button and it all happens through billionaire magic?"

Phillip is nearly falling over from laughing so hard. He puts his hand on the couch to steady himself, and I pull out my phone. "Like this. You touched the couch, so you obviously need a new one. Who do I call for that?"

"You make me sound like the most wasteful person on the planet," he gets out through the laughter.

I just stare at him with an "are you serious" look. "Okay, maybe I've been a little wasteful in my life," he confesses. "But I don't order a new couch after touching it. And I don't have any house elves, though if you've found some, I might contact their agency…"

I gawk again, and this time Phillip picks me up and tosses me over his shoulder. I scramble to get a hold of something to keep me from falling and end up wrapping my hands around his face.

"What are you doing?" he asks. "I was trying to be sexy and carry you to my bedroom to show you the most important room. Now I feel like I'm rescuing a drowning victim who might just kill me in the process."

"Well, don't scare the shit out of me, and maybe I won't use you to save myself."

He laughs as he slowly lowers me to the ground, and I look up at him. His hair's insane, and there's a red mark across his cheek where my nail might have dug into him especially hard. "Sorry about acting like a spider monkey," I say, a little frustrated with myself. It would have been sexy to be carried over his shoulder and taken to the bedroom like Tarzan carrying Jane through the jungle.

"Well, I've learned my lesson. Move more slowly when being aggressively sexy." There's a sparkle in his eyes that reminds me he's still the Phillip that enjoyed sitting at my dining room table all night long. Even if he's rich now, he's still that man.

"Might be a smart decision, but now that I know what you were going for, I might not fight for my life if you did it again." I give him what I think is a sexy and seductive wink, but it might just look like I got something in my eye.

He grins and wraps his hands around my waist. It still all seems too fast as he tosses me onto his shoulder, but once I'm there with his hand on my ass, I definitely understand the appeal.

There's no professionalism about this, and he pushes my skirt up so he can run his hand over my ass while he walks. It sends a shiver through me. Like being bent over his desk today, I don't feel like I could get away, and it turns me on.

Maybe there's something to the whole cave man alpha male thing. It sounded like something stupid when I was younger, but maybe I'd just never met a man who could embody it.

"This is hot and all, but I can't see anything except your floor and ass," I say as he walks up the stairs. "And I thought I was getting the tour."

"It's a blindfolded tour. We're skipping the uninteresting parts."

Blindfolded tour? "You're a terrible tour guide."

"It's a good thing my second career option worked out better. You know, I think the first way I'm going to celebrate having my money again is by buying a ton of lingerie for you."

"Are you telling me there's something wrong with my underwear?" I say this while I'm laying across his back and staring at the floor. I'm getting a little lightheaded.

"Well, no. Just like there's nothing wrong with my saffron shirt. But there might be *better* options out there, too. Plus, I'd love to see you model it for me. I could drink Scotch and you could try on clothes. It'd be like we were in a movie. Then you could crawl across the floor…"

I slap his ass. "I am not crawling across your floor, buddy. Okay, maybe I might with the right incentives, but maybe you should let me stand up before I pass out. Your house is too big for this kind of guided tour."

He chuckles and sets me down. "Well, we're to the good part," he says as he turns me around. The room is luxurious, but once again, it feels more like a hotel room or maybe even a movie set. Dark gray walls are accented with black trim. Glossy white marble floors shine so strongly that I can almost see my reflection in them. The minimalist furniture is made of dark wood that doesn't stand out against the masculine feel of the room.

And nothing is out of place. Nothing like my bedroom in my apartment where random mail has found its way onto my dressers. Clothes that belong in the "kind of clean" pile sat on every surface. There might even be a cup or two out.

I turn around to look at Phillip. "Okay, I need to understand something."

He cocks his head. "What's wrong? I thought you'd like this room."

"Am I supposed to keep everything looking like this, or can I actually live here?"

He runs his hand through his hair and grins. I think he understands what I mean. "I'd like it if we didn't turn my house into a dumpster, but having a few things out of place won't drive me insane, if that's what you're asking."

"That might be a struggle, Phillip. You need to know that." I turn around and look at the room again. It's so big. And empty. My instinct is to fill it with things. "Okay, so the first thing I'm sure of is that I need two laundry hampers. One for dirty clothes and one for wearable but not clean clothes. Otherwise, that dresser right there will become a pile of clothes."

"I already knew that. I called the maid this morning for you." He walks across the room to a door off to the side and opens it. Inside is a walk-in closet the size of my old bedroom. Suits hang from half the racks while my handful of outfits hang from the other side. And in the center are two laundry baskets. Of course, they're not the classic plastic ones that normal people use. No, these are made of black wood that's been carved with decorative shapes. Inside them are mesh bags that can be pulled out and carried to the laundry room.

Phillip walks into the closet, and I follow him. "I bought you something, Addison," he says.

"I think you bought us both something," I say, thinking he means the laundry baskets. It's not. He walks to a wooden dresser that's so dark that it's almost black and picks up a gift-wrapped box before solemnly bringing it to me. At first, I think he bought me jewelry since that's what all the rich guys in movies do. I can't figure out what kind of jewelry would fit in a box like that. It's a square about the size of his fist and obviously professionally wrapped in gray and black like his room.

"What is it?" I ask, more than a little nervous. I did tell him I hated surprises.

"A shrunken head. Or maybe the world's smallest typewriter. It might even be a box of cookies that I ate half of. Or maybe it's none of those."

I glare at him, but I take the box when he offers it to me. "If it's a shrunken head, you get to put it on your side of the room. Just letting you know."

He grins as I set the box down on the dresser in front of me and unwrap it. Phillip's eyes follow my movement as the paper falls away and a plain white box appears.

"Good," I say, realizing that it's not jewelry. "For a second, I thought it was some kind of diamond coated jewelry."

"I considered buying you the French Crown Jewels, but didn't think you'd appreciate having to carry around a scepter. Guess I lucked out, huh?"

I chuckle, but then I question it. "Wait, could actually buy the French Crown Jewels? What exactly are Crown Jewels?"

"Just open the damn box, Addison!"

I sigh and undo the tape holding the top of the cardboard down. I don't know why it's such a big deal that he bought me a present, but it is. Neither one of us has ever bought the other anything. It marks a change in our relationship almost as big as me moving in with him.

But when I open the box and pull out the bubble wrapped item, I can't help but grin. It's a coffee mug.

The nervousness that I'd felt earlier evaporates as I rip the bubble wrap off and look at it. It's a pink mug with white letters. "Roses are red. You have really great tits. I want to read your book. So you'd better not quit!"

He laughs as soon as I do, and I can't be happier with his present. I mean, it's not a thrift store find, but can you really expect a billionaire to limit his coffee mug gifts to thrift stores?

"I don't know if I should be grumpy because you're pushing me to finish this book or take it as a compliment."

I set the mug down on the dresser as he wraps his arms around me. "Take it as me thinking about you and wanting to get you a present, while knowing that you'd be pissed if I bought you something expensive, like jewelry."

Standing on my tiptoes, I give him a kiss. "That's just how I'll take it. Just know that I have to get you a present now, and there's no telling what I'll end up finding for you. I might get you a very special tie since that's what every billionaire needs, right?"

His eyes open wide. "Maybe don't get me a tie? Please?"

I can't help the sneaky smile that crosses my lips. "You never know. They always have great ties at discount stores, and those are brand new, so there aren't even any stains on them."

The look of horror on his face is priceless. "Please, no?"

"Fine. Well, I'll come up with something good. Don't you worry. I saw a pair of nice dress shoes…"

It's too hard to keep it up, and I burst out laughing. Phillip still looks terrified. "You're just joking? You're not really planning to buy me shoes or a tie?"

I shake my head, but I have to take a few breaths to stop the laughter. "I know you're the big shot boss now, so you have to dress like it. You don't want me to buy a bunch of stuff that you don't want to wear, and I get it. Be warned, though, I will have to give you gifts. We can't have this be completely one-sided. Just because you're rich and I'm not doesn't mean I can't get you presents."

My words obviously have the intended effect because he visibly relaxes. "You know, I'd love presents. I can't think of the last time someone actually bought me something that I cared about, but I usually just buy whatever I want."

I give him a grin and wink. "Well, I guess I'll just have to find some things you didn't know you wanted."

"Like you?" The fear has completely evaporated, and he's grinning as wide as ever.

I fain shock and put my hand on my chest. "Even you couldn't afford me normally. It's a good thing that I'm on sale to the first customer at the rock bottom price of a good kiss. Mind you, it'd better be a fantastic kiss." I look around the closet, grinning just as wide as him. "Now where could I find a customer…"

Phillip doesn't even let me finish before he crushes my lips with his. I'd felt nervous all day. I'd felt even worse after work. Even after we'd gotten here, and there wasn't a monster ready to eat any poor people that walked through the door, I still had butterflies. It all just felt so foreign.

That's all gone, now. The feeling of his lips on mine brings me home and reminds me that regardless of where we are, this is still the man that I've fallen in love with.

Passion explodes from him, spoken in a kiss. There's nothing in the world that could make me nervous right now. Like the touch of his lips on mine is a spell that makes the rest of the world quiet while they're touching. Or maybe it's just that I can't care about anything else.

Phillip's hands pull me toward him, his tongue dancing with mine. Why did I ever pull away from him? Somehow, I knew he'd set me alight with every kiss, and I ran from it. Now, the running's done.

"I love you," he whispers.

"You'd better because I have a very special set of skills. I will find you…"

"…and you'll what?" he asks with a grin. "You'll buy me stained shirts, fantastic coffee mugs, and tell me love stories?"

I shrug. "I'm an enigma wrapped in a paradox, good sir. There's no telling what I'm capable of. Especially if you walked away from me."

"That's very true. But I won't walk away from you. I promise you, no matter what happens, I won't walk away."

I turn and grab my mug. "Good. It's settled then. We're keeping each other captive forever. How about you teach me how to make your fancy coffee, cell mate? Then I can try out my new mug?"

Phillip just grins and leads me back downstairs to the very fancy and expensive coffee maker. I watch as he goes through the motions, which aren't all that different from when I taught him to use my Mr. Coffee. Once again, we're coming full circle. There's only one thing missing to make this little circle complete.

He hands me my new mug filled to the brim with some kind of coffee I can't pronounce, and I set it on the counter.

And take off my shirt. He gawks at me, but I ignore him as I drop my bra on the ground and pick up the mug. "Meet you at the table," I say and walk away.

Phillip Loughton is a man I never imagined meeting. He's a man that no one would have expected I'd connect with so well. We're completely different. And the same.

If I'd met him at Loughton House, I never would have gotten to know him. I never would have considered talking to the ice-cold boss. But I didn't meet him at Loughton House.

I met him on a dark and stormy night at a shitty motel.

Forty-Two

PHILLIP

IT'S BEEN A BUSY WEEK BETWEEN CATCHING UP ON work and getting Addison all moved in. I feel like I'm burning the candle at both ends, but it's the best feeling in the world. There's something to be said about having a job that you can walk away from when five o'clock rolls around, but I've spent my life living for this company. I don't know if I could ever really stop thinking about it.

Now I'm back to doing all the things I feel like I was born to do, but I also have everything I never had before.

I may have been catching up for the past five days, but I've also been setting myself up for some freedom. I may not be able to disconnect completely with Loughton House at night or on the weekends now, but I'm working on making more time for myself and Addison. There are new upper management positions that will effectively do all the tedious parts of my job for me.

Father refused to allow it previously because both of us knew they wouldn't be as effective as me. They won't have the knowledge that only comes with a lifetime of running this company. I'm okay with that now, and Father doesn't have a choice in the matter if he wants me to stay.

My time and freedom are more important than perfect optimization. These new upper managers will still report to me. I'll still be involved in most major decisions and changes and releases. But I won't be doing it all by myself.

This morning, I expect my father to barge into my office and tell me to go to LA. My bag's already packed, and I'm ready for it. I agreed to go today, and I won't back out of that decision. I may have yearned for freedom, but my job and Loughton House's success are the reasons that I'll be able to give Addison anything she wants.

I'll go to LA or Beijing or wherever, but I won't do it exactly when and how my father wants me to. My entire life, if he said jump, I asked how high. Now, when he says jump, I want details, and I'll make my own decisions.

I've looked into this agency, though. It's a solid start-up, and I'd like them to bring me new prospects to look over. See, the thing with working with agents is everyone benefits when they bring a talented author to a good publishing house. I can blow a superstar book up like no one else, but I can't find them. Publishing houses aren't meant for that.

That's why we make connections with top-end agents, so they'll do the legwork for us. Addison is perfectly fine staying at the house by herself, and I think she's going to enjoy getting to explore.

I'm just wrapping up the expectations for the new VP of Agent Relations role when my father walks into my office and closes the door behind him. When he turns to look at me, there's something different. He's not standing tall like he normally is, as though the world could do its best to knock him down, but the world would fall before he did. Instead, he's almost slouching.

There are bags under his eyes, and he looks... small.

"I need to talk to you," he says with none of his normal strength behind the words.

I raise an eyebrow. My father has dealt with a lot of terrible situations. Even ones that would leave a normal man terrified or crying. He's never faltered, never lost his poise. Not even when my mother died.

"Take a seat," I say, a little unsure of how to deal with him.

He nods and sits down across from me. And sighs. What the hell is going on?

"You're ready," he says and reaches into his jacket pocket without looking at me. "I've spent the last fifty years building Loughton House from nothing." He pulls a rolled-up paper out and slides it across the table to me, still without actually meeting my gaze. "I have spent damn near every moment of my adult life worrying about this business. I've built this place with my own two hands."

He finally looks into my eyes and says, "But it's yours now. That's the contract transferring ownership from me to you. You can read it over, but it sections off a part of the family fortune to me and leaves the rest to you and your brother. The company is yours, though. When we argued on Monday..." He takes a deep breath, as though this process is exceptionally painful. "I left your office and opened a bottle of Scotch."

What? I've only seen my father drink once in my entire life, and that was the night my mother died. The night I stopped breaking promises.

I just listen to him as he continues. "Son, you've spent your life learning how to run Loughton House. You know every piece of the business better than anyone else. I probably could have retired years ago and left it in capable hands, but there was one thing I could never teach you: how to be unrelenting. And you showed me that on Monday."

He trails off, and I see a tear roll down his cheek as his voice shakes.

"You've got grit now, Phillip. When you bite down on something, nothing in the world will be able to make you let go, and that's what you need to run this place." He takes another deep breath and lets it out. "I'm proud of you."

Part of me has been looking for that praise since before I can remember, but the other part, the part that was willing to go to war with my father only four days ago, doesn't give a shit what he thinks.

"I'll take good care of her," I say. I know some men would give each other a hug. Others would say thank you. Some would even shed a tear themselves. I am not that man, and neither is my father. And our relationship is exactly what he created. Nothing more, nothing less.

The most I can say is exactly what he wanted to hear. "Thank you," he whispers and stands up. "You know, if you have questions, I'll always be happy to answer them."

I nod to him and give him the barest hint of a smile. "If I run into problems, I'll call you."

I won't, and he knows that, but that was the goal from the beginning, wasn't it? He has his legacy. A company that won't die with him. It will not retire or crumble or be forgotten. He has created something that will live beyond him, and I will be its caretaker, just as he always wanted.

And I will do it better than he can now.

The tear I saw earlier is gone, but the streak it left behind still glistens in the hard light of the office. He turns to walk away, and I look down at the papers that change everything. My father is not at the helm of Loughton House any longer.

I'm the one that will determine its success or failure from now on. I should be a little nervous or even excited, but I'm not. Nothing has changed.

I slide the papers to the edge of my desk and finish what I was doing. I have a plane to catch.

Forty-Three

ADDISON

The storm rolls through the city like an army. Rain-drops pelt the glass and steel like machine gun fire. Lightning splits the sky with explosions, bright light with rolling thunder. Tonight was supposed to be the night that Angela had dreamed of. Donovan had a ring for her. He was going to propose to her.

Instead, she's standing on a balcony looking at the city while the pouring rain hides her tears.

"I can't do this anymore," Donovan whispers through the gusts. "I can't compete with your business and dreams, and at the same time, I can't just sit in the shadows and wait for you to find time for me. I'm sorry, Angela. I love you, but I can't let you be my everything when I'm not yours."

He walks back into the restaurant, and Angela doesn't even turn around...

. . .

GOD, THIS IS THE HARDEST PART. THE DARK NIGHT of the Soul should break the reader, and I can feel the tears welling. I should be proud that I could give myself these emotions, at least.

I lean back in my chair and pick up my pencil. The steady whir of it rolling over my fingers is reassuring as I think of how Angela will respond to her true love's rejection.

"Nope. I need to take a break," I mutter when nothing comes to me. I've spent the weekend throwing myself into this book. It's so close to being done, but every time I sit down to write, it's like pulling teeth to put words on a page. My mind goes straight to Phillip being all the way across the country. He comes home today, though.

Plus, this place doesn't even feel natural yet. I've been here for a week, and I'm still discovering things. Sometimes I just walk around and open doors and cabinets to see what's inside. This place has a literal rain shower. The whole ceiling sprays water down so it's like you're getting rained on. It hasn't sunk in yet that this could be how I live forever.

I walk toward the kitchen and sigh. How am I supposed to get used to this? I'm not the girl who knows what to do with a billionaire's lifestyle. I tried to explain that to Phillip, but he just laughed. There are plenty of people out there that would get used to lighting money on fire quickly, but when I think of getting groceries, the first place I turn is the weekly ad.

There's a platinum credit card in my wallet with my name on it that has an unlimited spending limit. Phillip told me I could go out tomorrow and buy a car, and it wouldn't bother him.

But it would bother me.

When I step into the kitchen to make a sandwich, I stop short. "Andrew?"

Andrew Loughton, Phillip's youngest brother, looks up from the fridge where he's shoving groceries. He grins at my shock and stands up. "Phillip said that he was going to get home late, and that you'd need some groceries for dinner."

A frown crosses my face. He's supposed to be home in a couple of hours. "When did you talk to him?"

"About an hour ago. He said he texted you, but that he thought your phone might be dead."

I walk all the way into the kitchen to see what Phillip asked Andrew to get. I can't believe I let my phone die, but then again, I tend to forget a lot of things when I sit down to write. The same goes when I pick up an amazing book to read. I just kind of get lost.

Andrew goes back to loading the refrigerator with food. "When did my big brother start knowing what kind of food someone would need to cook with? I didn't think he'd ever used a stove in his life."

"You'd be right, but being poor will teach you how to cook," I respond. Chicken alfredo. Nothing special. He even skipped the mushrooms, though he threw in some fresh spices.

Andrew stands up with a grin on his face. "He really did change because of that, didn't he?"

"I think so, at least. I didn't really know him before he became a broke junior editor." It's strange talking to Andrew about Phillip. Andrew knows everything there is to know about him. He could tell me all the stories, and I'm itching to pick his brain, especially about gifts, since I can't figure out anything Phillip would like. But I don't know Andrew. I only met him the one time when we played charades.

Andrew watches me dig through the bags, and I can't help but recognize the way he's watching me. It must be genetic or something. Do all the Loughton men look at people like that? Like they're analyzing everything about them?

"I don't think it had much to do with being poor," he says. "And I think it had everything to do with you."

I look up at him. "What do you mean? Being poor changes everyone. All I did was give him a couch to sleep on."

Andrew chuckles. "Right. I'm sure he slept on the couch. But that's not what I'm talking about. I mean that he's different because he's more… human? I know my brother, and the way he's acted since I came back into town is unlike anything I've ever seen. He's fun, Addison, and I can't help but give you the credit for that."

"What do you mean 'more human'? The very first night I met him, he seemed pretty normal. I mean, he was kind of an ass, but most rich guys are. I think it just comes with the territory."

Andrew shakes his head. "No, he wasn't normal. The only reason he woke up in the morning was to work. He'd never have played charades that night if there wasn't some bookseller or author that we needed to woo. Even then, he'd probably have sent someone else."

He chuckles and leans against the counter. "And now he owns Loughton House, so let's all thank our lucky stars you got to him before that happened. He'd have fired the lot of us and had robots working for him. Or just forced us all to become robots. I'm not sure which would be worse."

He owns Loughton House? What the hell did I miss? And why haven't I heard anything about it?

"Wait. What? I thought your dad owned the company, and you two just worked for him. Did something change?"

Andrew's enjoying my confusion, and it shows. I'm glad that his snarky grin isn't as genetic as the way he watches people. "My big brother didn't tell you? Dad transferred control of Loughton House to Phillip on Friday. He retired and split the family fortune and gave Phillip control of the company. Now, instead of working for Dad, I work for Phillip. I'd always worried about what it'd be like when that happened, but now, I'm actually kind of excited."

How the hell did Phillip not tell me about this? How did he just blow it off like it's nothing? Maybe he was waiting to celebrate until he got back from his trip? Maybe he's nervous or scared of the extra responsibility? I don't know. I still feel like he should have told me.

"Well, I guess that's good, right? Your dad's kind of an asshole, isn't he?"

Andrew chuckles. "On the best days. But Addison, you're missing the point. I was more worried about Phillip being the boss than my dad. Dad knew everyone was an idiot compared to him, and no one would work as hard as him. He'd accepted that. Phillip never did. He was always pissed that he couldn't just run the entire company himself. This week, he created more positions for senior management to take the load off him. He's actively trying to do less work, even though I'm sure profits will fall because of it.

"My brother is trying to do things other than work, Addison, and that is a literal miracle. I didn't think it was possible before that night we played charades. Hell, he made a fool of himself on purpose. For fun."

That's a lot to take in. All of it. Phillip's talked about how he never felt like he could do anything except work, but the way Andrew makes it sound, he never wanted anything else. Andrew can tell that I'm struggling with the information, and so he stands up and grabs the bags that the groceries came in.

"Well, I guess I'd better get going. Tell my brother congrats for me, okay? I put a bottle of bubbly in the fridge for you two to celebrate with since I'm such a thoughtful guy."

I nod to him, but my thoughts are running wild. There's so much information, so many confusing little pieces to the man that I love. I don't know how to process all of them, especially with Andrew right here.

Why hasn't he told me about inheriting the company?

I don't know. I take a deep breath and let it out. It's stupid to worry about that. The only way I'll understand is by talking to Phillip, and any overthinking I do right now will only end up with me freaking out for no reason at all.

I barely even notice that Andrew's gone when I go to the refrigerator and start pulling things out for dinner. There's no reason to freak out. I'm sure that there's a perfectly reasonable explanation for why Phillip didn't tell me he's now officially the owner of Loughton House.

I'm sure. At least that's what I'm going to tell myself until I can talk to him.

Forty-Four

PHILLIP

ADDISON WASN'T HAPPY ABOUT ME BEING GONE ALL weekend, but we both knew that work would take up a lot more time now that I'm not just a junior editor. We've talked about it.

Me not getting home until almost midnight might have pushed things a bit too far, though. Her texts weren't exactly the normal, goofy Addison. Then she was asleep when I got home, so we didn't have a chance to talk about the weekend.

I don't know how to do this whole reassurance thing, and I'm exhausted. This weekend was shittier than I expected. Instead of meeting with an agency and talking them through what we're looking for, the agency dragged me all over town to meet with each agent individually. It was fucking stupid, and I'm tempted to just block their emails and phone numbers, so I never have to go through another weekend like that.

But their client base is far stronger than I'd expected. Which means I have to put up with it. Next time, I'm sending someone else, though. I am the owner of the company, after all.

Addison is sipping coffee across from me at my dining room table, and she's using the mug I bought her. That's a good sign, right? Fuck, I don't even know at this point.

"Anything interesting happen?" she finally asks.

I shrug. "I met a lot of agents and repeated myself probably a dozen times. Mostly, I think a good email would have sufficed. Or maybe a Zoom call."

She stares at me, and I get the feeling that I'm missing something. "Sorry I got home so late. I tried texting, but I guess your phone died?"

Addison's stare gets more intense as my words hang in the air. "I got the texts."

"Okay Addison, what did I say or do that has you acting like this? I've had a terrible weekend and am exhausted. Please, just talk about what's bothering you."

It's like I pulled the pin on a grenade. Two seconds pass while she stares at me, and then she explodes. "You're the new owner of Loughton House, and you didn't tell me? What other secrets are you keeping? Were you spending the weekend in LA with a bunch of agents who happened to be women? Without clothes? Did you even go to LA?"

I blink. "Oh that. Yes, my father gave me Loughton House on Friday. Why is that such a big deal, though? I'd already decided that I was going to do what I wanted, regardless of what he expected from me. I assume the rest of the questions are just you… being you?"

Addison looks shocked, like what I said was something a lunatic would say. "You just became a real-life billionaire. Not a guy whose family is rich. Nobody can take your money away now, and that's a freaking huge deal, Phillip. Plus, now you don't have to listen to your father yell at you like he did on Monday."

She doesn't understand. He couldn't yell at me anymore. On Monday, I won. If he'd pushed, I'd have walked away from the company. He couldn't take away my money either. Sure, he could have taken away the family's part or Andrew's part, but I negotiated my own piece of the earnings from Loughton House long ago.

"It didn't matter, Addison. I could work for Loughton House, or I could work for any of its competitors. I have plenty of money. Nothing changed except that now I don't have to worry about my father getting in my way. This was the only answer for my father, and I had a feeling that it'd happen. What else could he do? I'm the only person he trusts to take care of the only thing in the world he truly cares about."

Addison sits down on the chair again, the shock still very visible on her face. "It should be a big deal," she mutters. "It's a big deal to me. I wanted to celebrate with you, but you didn't even tell me."

"I'm sorry. It just slipped my mind, truthfully. It didn't matter and there's so much that does. I feel like taking that month off has created a mountain of extra work for me. Between finding people to fill the new positions I've created, catching up on the things that no one took care of, and dealing with the day-to-day operations of Loughton House, I'm running myself ragged. Especially since I'm doing everything I can to come home and get to spend at least a little time with you."

I can see that the last bit grates on her, but she doesn't lash out. Hopefully, she understands that I'm not upset about that. She's the reason I'm doing this. I'm trying to walk a razor's edge between running Loughton House the way it should be run and having an actual life with the woman I love. It's wearing on me, but it's going to be worth it.

She gives me a nod. "I trust you, Phillip. I know I kind of blow up sometimes, and I've got some serious fear when it comes to trusting people. Maybe in the future, you could just text me a quick, 'Hey babe, just letting you know my dad gave me the company, and I'm a billionaire now. How's your Friday? Anyway, back to work.' Just something. Especially when it's a big thing like that."

I grin. "Maybe I'll just text you that I want you bent over my desk. Then I can tell you my news in between your moans."

She almost blushes. "I like that idea a lot more. Maybe you could find some news to tell me today."

"That sounds perfect. It's been too long since I've been inside you."

She downs the rest of her coffee and hops out of her chair. "Good. My pussy isn't even sore right now, and that's a terrible feeling. Like you've forgotten me completely."

I chuckle and take another sip of coffee as she goes back to the bedroom to get dressed. I'm too busy today to spend lunch with her. There's so much work to do. But she's right. We've been slowly sliding further and further away from each other with each day now that I'm back in my old job. I don't even want to think of the extra workload my father dropped on my shoulders.

I need to hire more people, but that only makes me sigh even more. My world is falling down around me, and Addison doesn't even see it. To her, nothing's changed except I work in a different office.

There's no way to explain to her how much rides on my shoulders right now. She can't understand that the thing she wants to celebrate is the thing that could break me if I'm not careful. Balancing work would be hard enough, but learning how to weave time in with Addison may just be the straw that breaks the camel's back.

And that isn't something I can ever tell her.

Forty-Five

PHILLIP

"Profits are down this quarter, and we're expecting them to drop even more next quarter. We don't have enough strong authors, and the self-publishing industry is eating at our margins."

My financial director is clicking through a slide show as Andrew and I watch the charts that aren't surprising at all. They may not be surprising, but they're still terrible news. We've stayed in a growth trend even while the other major publishing houses are starting to freefall thanks to our ability to push winners to the moon. We just haven't had enough winners, though.

I turn to Andrew, interrupting the financial director's presentation. "Have you thought about picking up proven all-stars from the self-publishing sphere?"

Andrew shrugs. "They expect a lot, and they never want to go fully traditional publishing. Plus, there are so few that can dominate the lists that we need to do well on for success."

I frown. It's the same thing I've heard so many times in the past. They expect a lot because they know what they can do without us. If we can't give them something they don't have, then what purpose do we serve them?

"What about small fish that haven't become popular? Why don't we treat self-publishers like the slush pile? Hell, they've already got reviews so we can eliminate the truly bad. Sure, we can't really afford to pick up the chart-toppers, but we might find some diamonds in the rough. They probably won't even have an agent, so we'll be able to negotiate better deals."

Andrew frowns as he lets the thought percolate. "Dad would call you a fucking idiot," he says. Neither of us is paying any attention to the financial director, and he's already sitting down, quietly listening to our conversation.

"Father doesn't run this company anymore. I do. And I want your honest opinion. Do you think we could turn the enemy into a product?"

Andrew stretches out and puts his hands behind his head before he stares up at the ceiling. "It sounds like the perfect place to steal talent. No one else has done it, though. How would we go about it? We're not set up for direct acquisition. We run through agencies like everyone else."

I grin. "What if we bought an agency whose only job was to go through the slush pile of self-publishing?"

"That'd be the worst job in the world." I don't disagree with that at all.

"Good thing we're not the ones who would do it."

Andrew thinks about it for a few minutes. "I mean, that sounds fantastic."

Then the financial director pipes up. "Where would that money come from, though? Your revenue is falling, and it doesn't look like it'll be coming back up anytime soon. Where would you find the money to do all of this?"

Andrew glances at me and back at the financial director. "You know what Dad would say, don't you?"

"Cut costs before any expansion. That's the rule."

He nods. But what costs? Everything's running as tight as possible. I chew my lip and look at the financial director. "Any thoughts?"

He sits back in his chair, the presentation completely forgotten at this point. "There are some places with excess... I'll write up a list of possibilities."

"Have a preliminary list on my desk by the end of the day. This is the answer, guys. Short term, it'll be a pain, but in the end, I'm almost positive that this is our way out of the hole the entire industry is falling into."

I look back at Andrew, who's grinning but kind of looks terrified. "We need to focus on the big goal. A complete shift in trajectory toward blending a side of our business with self-published authors. We're going to kill the Beijing expansion."

"That was Dad's baby," Andrew says. "He was sure that was the answer."

"Dad was wrong. This is the way we're going to dig ourselves out of Dad's hole."

I stand up. "Come up with ideas on who we can get to run that side of things. I'll look into how we'll afford it. By the end of next week, I want things to start moving."

Andrew and the financial director nod to me, and I walk out of the conference room, more excited than I have in a long time. For a decade, my family has watched our growth shrink while other publishing houses have started to actually see contraction. No one's had answers to the changing industry.

We figured it out. I'm sure of it.

I sigh as I look at my phone, which was silenced during the meeting. We went over the expected time by thirty minutes.

And I missed lunch.

ADDISON ADELAIDE

Are we still on for our special lunch?

ADDISON ADELAIDE

Hello?

ADDISON ADELAIDE

Guess not.

ADDISON ADELAIDE

Is everything okay?

I can feel the frustration building inside me. Not at her, obviously. Just at how impossible this is. I've left the big decisions to my father for so long, and he's taken the safe route. Nothing new or innovative. Just tweaks and optimizations on the old systems.

I'm trying to step away from the workaholic that I was, but now that I'm running this shit show, it's on me to fix it, and that's going to take time. Time that I would rather spend with Addison with her bent over my desk. Or with her legs wrapped around me in bed.

Or even just watching an old movie.

PHILLIP LOUGHTON

> I'm sorry. A meeting ran over. Want to come up to my office now?

I hope that she'll still take me up on it, but I know she can't just wait around for my schedule to open up.

ADDISON ADELAIDE

Sorry. Eating with Victoria. Rain check?

PHILLIP LOUGHTON

> Definitely. Enjoy your lunch. I love you.

ADDISON ADELAIDE

Love you too.

. . .

Damn it. I sit down in my chair and take a deep breath. Why couldn't this have all happened after Addison and I'd had a few months to get settled in together? I can already feel the tenuousness of everything. We've spent nearly every moment together for a month. Now, I barely see her.

I look at the scratches across the otherwise unmarred desk that Addison made the first morning I was back in my office. Deeper than I'd have believed she could make, they're a constant reminder of why I'm doing all this.

Taking a deep breath, I steel my resolve. She's worth it. The weight of a multi-billion-dollar company is on my shoulders in the middle of a collapsing industry. My fingers trace the scratches, feeling the indentions, the way my desk is forever changed because of her.

If I can't find a way to get everything squared away, the cracks that are starting to show are just going to grow. And I cannot let that happen.

No matter what it takes.

Forty-Six

ADDISON

New employees were the answer. Angela sits at a table and watches the first two working to prep the bakery, terrified of the razor's edge she's walking. This bakery was her dream for so long, but now... Now, she's not so sure. Is running Sweet Temptations really what she wants from life? Now she knows what else she was missing.

Donovan.

The man who stole her heart and then refused to give an inch when she got lost in expanding her bakery. It took Angela a long time to understand why he walked away. She thought he was being selfish, that he'd been afraid of a strong, independent woman. But that's not it. He wants her to have her dreams, but he wants to come first. Just like before, when she'd gone to college for business and left him behind.

Her dreams had always come before him. Now she'd have to show him that things had changed. She wants him more than anything. Even more than being covered in flour and icing sugar. Even more than being able to claim that it was her hand that gave so many people joy when they ate her food.

She wanted to run Sweet Temptations to see people smile. Now, she has to show Donovan that his smiles were more important than anyone else's.

That's why she'd hired a manager to run Sweet Temptations. That's why she hired two more employees. Now, she'll run the business, but she won't have to work fourteen hours a day, six days a week. But what if the employees who are giving her the chance to be with Donovan ruin her reputation? What if they don't do as good of a job as her? That's just a risk she has to take because some things are more important than business.

Her eyes turn to the door as a man walks in. She's expecting the last employee the employment agency chose to come in for training. But this definitely isn't him.

The man with dark hair and eyes that seem to burn into her smiles as he hands her a sheet of paper. She glances down, completely confused. Why is Donovan here? And why is he handing her his resume?

> *"I heard you appreciated employees showing up early,"*
> *he says with a grin.*
>
> *"What?" Angela is lost. This doesn't make any*
> *sense.*
>
> *"I'm your newest employee. I tried to walk away,*
> *Angela. I really did. But I couldn't stand losing you a*
> *second time. I still won't let you put your dreams*
> *above me, but maybe if I'm part of those dreams, you*
> *can't forget about me…"*

I SMILE AS MY HEART PITTER-PATTERS A LITTLE TOO fast. I never thought that I'd be giving myself goosebumps when I was writing my novel. That always sounded like something that only the truly great writers did.

But it *is* actually good. Well, at least this part. I lean back in my chair and pick up my pencil to spin it. Another night sitting alone in Phillip's house while he's still at work. It's been almost two weeks since Russel Loughton handed the company to Phillip, and I think I've spent nearly every evening alone, including weekends.

I'd known that this was how Phillip's life was before me, but I thought he was going to change things. He says he still is, but it feels like it's taking forever. He spends all day at the office, and when he gets home, it's like he's a ghost of the man I fell in love with.

I hear the front door open, and I hit save on my manuscript before shutting the laptop. I glance at the wadded up crocheted laptop bag that sits on the edge of the desk I use in Phillip's office. It's a reminder of who I was before I met him. Before every piece of furniture in my life matched. Before I rode in a limo to work. Before I'd swam naked in a rooftop pool.

Back when my life still made sense.

I follow the path I walk every evening when I hear the door close. Down the hall, down the stairs, and into the foyer. I see the downtrodden eyes as Phillip hangs up his laptop bag in the closet. The way he slumps just a little more every day.

"Rough evening?" I ask, and he just nods and sighs. Without saying anything, he walks up to me and wraps his arms around me.

"I've missed you," he whispers, and it feels like he's about to crack. How'd the man that had seemed so strong and unbreakable only weeks ago start to feel like this?

His lips find mine, but there's no passion in the kiss. No fire. I expect his lips to move to my neck, to set my body alight like his kisses always do, but he just steps back, looking even more fragile.

"Dinner's still on warm," I say as I walk toward the kitchen. Phillip follows me, and when I make plates, he doesn't move to help.

I'd thought that he'd seemed off the past few days, but it hadn't been like this. He hadn't looked like he was falling apart. He was just tired. Now...

"I've only got a few more pages in my manuscript left," I say as I spoon the alfredo over the noodles. They've gotten a little sticky from being on the warmer for an hour. "It might actually be good."

Phillip smiles at me. "Of course, it's good. I've never doubted that. I can't wait to read it."

Even though the thought of him reading it still terrifies me, I give him a smile. He's someone I can trust. I've learned that even though he can be ruthless when he wants to be, he's never turned that side toward me.

"Tomorrow's Saturday. Maybe we could spend some time together. I could finish the last few pages up, and maybe I'll let you read the first chapter or two?"

Phillip sighs. "I have to work this weekend. But I could probably come home tomorrow evening and read some of it?" He tries to smile, but it cracks. "You know, Addison, I hate that we haven't had much time together. Hopefully, by the end of this coming week, I'll have more time. The positions I've posted have been filled, and I'm trying to get them trained up to take over those pieces of my schedule."

I try to be understanding. It's not his fault that he's having to work this hard, and I know that. I may be jealous of his time, but I'm not Donovan. This was who he was before he met me. He's trying to change things, too. And change is hard.

"I can be patient, Phillip. I can't wait until we can spend more time together, but I don't expect you to ignore Loughton House. Just promise me that you're working toward making more time for us, and I'll believe you. I love you."

His smile comes together a little better this time. Not quite as many cracks. "I promise I'm working to change it. I can't wait until we can spend every weekend together. It would be nice to make *you* dinner occasionally. I want it to be like it was when I was poor. Except, you know, with lots of money too."

I grin at him and try to ease some of his worries. "Then do what you're best at. Fix the business. Make your changes. If there's something I can do, please just let me know."

"I don't think you can help. Thanks for understanding, though. I've been really worried about whether this was going to affect us. It all just seems so fast."

I hand him his plate. "It is. But I learned how to roll with the punches a long time ago."

Holding the plate in one hand, he runs his hand over my lower back and says, "You're the light in my life. You know that, right?"

"Maybe I do. Maybe I don't. I certainly enjoy you telling me. Now, let's go eat this food before it gets cold. I'm starving and have had to smell it for an hour."

He just chuckles, and I follow him to the table. This is hard, but we can get through it. We can survive a bit of struggle at the beginning. I've always said that I'll work hard and sacrifice to get what I want. I'll deal with whatever hardships stand in the way of what I want.

And what I want is Phillip.

Forty-Seven

ADDISON

I STARE AT THE PICTURE ON MY PHONE FOR THE twenty-seventh time today. *The End*. I finished writing *Sweet Temptations* last night. I poured my heart and soul into that book, and I think it's the best thing I've ever written.

It's hard to focus on work, and Sera's noticed my inattention. She glances at me again as my chair squeaks. "Is the boss sending you dirty pictures?" she asks, just loud enough for me to hear. She knows how inappropriate our relationship is, and she's done her best to keep it relatively quiet. Though how we expect it to stay quiet when I ride in his limo every day isn't a question I want to think about.

"Nope," I say and pass her my phone.

"The end? Why are you looking at the end of someone's manuscript like a crackhead?"

I grin. "Because it's mine. And Phillip's going to edit it for me."

Her eyes go wide. "Holy shit. I didn't know you were writing a book. When were you going to let me know? I feel like this calls for a celebration or at least a quick drink. And when do I get to read it?"

I've only just begun to get used to the idea of showing it to Phillip. "Umm… I'm kind of nervous about anyone reading it…"

That's when Trish walks into our cubicle. Typical. "You wrote a book? Holy fuck, that's awesome." Before I even have a chance to feel the embarrassment creep in, she does a 180 and changes subjects. "But more importantly, check your email. If I'm going to get fucked this hard, I expect some aftercare. You can tell your boyfriend that I said that."

I frown, but I turn around in my chair and pull up my email. An email to the entire company from Phillip is sitting at the top of the list. The subject line reads, "Big changes for Loughton House".

Oh, it must be him announcing the new positions he's opened at the top of the food chain. But why would Trish be upset about that?

When I open the email, my heart sinks.

Loughton House, like all the other publishing houses, has consistently felt the strain of the digital age. Unlike our competitors, we've continued to grow regardless of the rising pressures, but this quarter marks the first time that our growth has slowed. We're at a turning point, and we can't ignore it any longer. Without change, Loughton House would be accepting a slow and painful death, and I refuse to allow that.

In order to gain a foothold in the shifting sands of the digital environment, we are creating a new division whose sole purpose is to make this transition into the future of publishing.

This is an exciting opportunity for the company, and it could push us into a new Golden Age. If you are interested in becoming a part of this division, there are openings posted already. We'd prefer to hire from within, but we will also look for outside hires. Interviews will begin next week as all of this will happen on a very fast timetable.

As with any growth, there is a cost. It pains me to say that in an effort to maintain our commitments and accommodate this growth, we will expect many employees to work a small amount of overtime consistently over the next six months as we transition. As everyone is salary, we will provide a bonus at the end of the year based on hours worked and projects completed as compensation. Details on the bonus structure will be forthcoming as things ramp up.

Thank you for your understanding.

Phillip Loughton, Owner of Loughton House Publishing

Fuck. I look up at Trish, who's furious. He's going to take advantage of the fact that everyone's salaried so he can increase their work without any extra pay.

"Can you fucking believe that?" she hisses. I glance at Sera, who's just as pissed. "If that son of a bitch tries to make me work weekends, I'll fucking quit. That's all there is to it."

Sera nods. "I've been with Loughton House for three years. I still don't make as much as newly hired cover designers at other companies. How can he expect me to work more without paying me?"

I feel torn. I know Phillip wouldn't have sent out that email if it wasn't necessary, but it still feels like a violation of the unspoken agreement between the employees and the company. We're all salaried, so we don't have any reason to dawdle on projects. Not so that we'll work on extra projects during our time off.

"There has to be a good reason for it," I say.

"Yeah, Loughton House is cheap and doesn't want to pay us for our work," Trish says. "The stingy bastards took my office and shoved me into a cubicle. They took away the snacks in the break room. They even started firing people for taking unauthorized long lunches. Now they're making me work more hours without a raise? Fuck the Loughtons."

"The email mentioned a bonus…"

Sera blinks at me. "Are you serious? I know that you and Phillip are a thing and all, but do you hear yourself? He's making us work overtime for half a year. For a freaking bonus."

What did you do, Phillip?

"I don't know," I say.

Trish leans against the cubicle wall. "Phil seems like a decent enough guy. Great singer. Funny. Also, a super dick for a boss. I think that's a hill I'm ready to die on." She grins. "I guess I've got a resume to polish up on company time."

"You're serious?" I ask. "You'd leave over this? What if this really is the only way to keep Loughton House alive?"

"If they expect me to work for free so they can survive, then it's a sinking ship to begin with. Why can't the Loughton family float the company's finances since they're the ones who'll be making all the extra money? This isn't my company, and they shouldn't expect me to donate to the 'Make the Loughtons Richer' fund."

She's not wrong. Damn it, Phillip. Why are you doing this? "Don't leave until I talk to Phillip. Please?"

Trish sighs. "Fine. I have to talk to John, anyway. But you can tell the boss that I'm not going to just accept this like I have with every other stupid way they've cut costs."

I nod. I don't blame her at all, but there has to be a reason for the changes. Phillip is running the company now. Not Russell. And Phillip knows what it's like to be one of us. He's experienced being poor and living on a shoestring budget. He gets it.

At least, I think he does.

Forty-Eight

PHILLIP

So. Many. Ranting. Emails. I knew that email would cause a lot of frustration. Maybe even some anger. I guess I underestimated the effect it would have because I've spent the past six hours dealing with the hundreds of angry emails. Trying to calm people down so they don't leave isn't my favorite part of the job.

No matter what the response was, this is the best solution. I'm sure of it. I've spent the last week trying to decide what route to take to manage this transition, and Andrew and I have gone through every feasible option. Downsizing our typical business. Holds on bonuses. Even bringing in new hires with less experience. They all had their pros and cons, but this way, everyone gets to experience the new department, and nobody loses anything.

It's just a little extra work. They're salaried, so that's part of the contract, and it's not even that much extra. Four or five hours a week, most of it from home. Plus, we're going to give them bonuses based on those hours, which isn't necessary at all.

But since we've never expected them to work overtime consistently, they act like we're taking advantage of them. They're the ones that signed the contracts. I don't want them to quit, but it's a little outrageous that they're so fired up over a few extra hours.

Leaning back in my chair, I look out at the city. I've given so much to this company. Probably more than I should. I want to go home to Addison, to spend my time enjoying the woman that I crave. She needs a chance to experience the world, to see why she should put up with these stupid hours.

But I can't. Not yet.

I'm close, though. People are in their new positions. The plans are decided. Now, all I'm waiting for is some execution, but I won't have to oversee every little decision at this point. It'll be back to detailed reports and checking over people.

And going home at five o'clock. And spending my weekends with Addison.

I just have to get through the next few days. That's all.

My body is exhausted. My head hurts like I've been slamming it into the wall all day. At least I got through half of Addison's book while I was waiting on the end of day reports.

And it's pretty fantastic. I think?

I'm not thinking straight at this point, and when I walk in the door, Addison is coming down the stairs. Even after a hell of a day, seeing her reminds me why I'm pushing so hard. I get to have my cake and eat it, too. I get Addison. I get time. I get a life. And I get to run the business that I was born to run.

All I have to do is survive the rest of the week. That's all.

"You look beautiful," I say as she stops in the foyer's doorway.

I hang up my laptop bag and glance at her. She hasn't said anything since I walked in the door. No hug. No kiss. What's going on?

"You sent an email today…" she says. Her voice is quiet and uncertain. I can't help but cringe at her words. Wasn't I supposed to be done with criticism for the day?

I take a deep breath and let it out. "Can I have a beer and some food before we talk about that? I've spent all day dealing with that email. I'm not trying to ignore your question, but I think it'd be better for both of us if I had some food first."

She chews her cheek for a second, as though she isn't sure she's okay with that request. But then she nods and heads toward the kitchen. I follow her, glad that she didn't push the topic yet. "I made herb crusted tilapia with a side of cilantro and citrus rice. It's nice getting to play with weird ingredients," she says with a smile.

"You can play with any ingredients you want if you're making food. I still think that your food is better than any chef's."

"Flattery will get you everywhere, Phillip. I'm glad you've embraced it." Addison's trying to be happy, to ignore the thing that's been eating at her, and I appreciate the effort. I hadn't expected the responses to that email, but after getting all of them, I should have known that she'd have questions.

She's not just my live-in girlfriend or the girl that I'm madly in love with. She's also an employee.

"Well, sit down and I'll get you a beer. The tilapia may be a little dry since it's been in the oven on the warm setting, but that's the price of a boyfriend who doesn't have any idea when he's getting home."

I chuckle and sit down at the table, glad to be home, even if I'm dreading the conversation that's going to happen after dinner. Living with Addison is still a little strange. It was one thing when I was living in Addison's apartment, and she cooked, but now we're at my house. The house that had almost no life before she moved in.

Now, instead of empty cabinets, she's filled them with groceries, her ridiculous mugs, and more than one set of dishes. There are pots and pans she brought over from her apartment which don't fit at all. None of them match, and half of them have dents in them. There are weird crocheted oven mitts hanging from haphazard screws she's stuck in the walls in seemingly random places.

I'd have been furious to have had my space ruined by her crazy before I lived with her, but now... Well, now it only brings me joy. I don't want to buy her new oven mitts that match the countertops. There's no need for fine china or crystal glasses. I want all the things that make this space hers. Because I didn't fall in love with a body or even a personality. I fell in love with all the things that make her so special.

And that includes inappropriate chipped mugs from a thrift store and handmade oven mitts she got from her Nana.

Addison brings me a beer and starts making plates for us. She hums a song I don't know as she scoops fish and rice onto plates. She slathers a slice of French bread with butter for each of us. I could have paid a chef to make this same thing, but it wouldn't bring me so much happiness.

Because food is a part of her.

"Yeah, the fish is a little dry. Which is disappointing, but it is what it is. Maybe you could text me when you're getting close to finishing up at the office so I can start cooking then."

The aroma of crispy chives, thyme, parsley, and a hint of basil fills the air. Bits of parmesan stick the breading and herbs to the fish, and I can't help but grin. "You definitely missed your calling. This looks and smells incredible."

"That means that you either didn't read my book, or it's terrible. I'm kind of hoping it's the first, but I'm guessing it's the second."

Of course, she's going to bring up the other thing that will be a difficult discussion. Not because the book is bad, but because she's so sensitive about it. Hell, reading it was one of the highlights of my day.

She stares at me and sighs when I don't respond to her comment. "Fine. Eat the damn fish. But then we're going to talk about a lot of things."

"I'll be happy to," I say as graciously as possible. All I really want to do is eat this fish and drink this beer, though.

I wait for her to cut into her tilapia before I move my silverware. It's a silent nod to the fact that I'm grateful for her efforts. I've gone most of my life without home-cooked meals, and I never want her to think that I take them for granted.

The first bite makes me sigh. "You're wrong, Addison. This is perfect."

She almost seems surprised at my praise. "Thank you," she says sheepishly. "You know," she says after a moment, "I was wondering if your mom made dinner for your family. You never talk about her, but I always imagine her cooking big dinners for you and your brothers."

I shake my head. "No, my father had a personal chef come cook dinners for us every night. I think my mother could cook, but she never did. Now that you mention it, I don't know why she wouldn't. From what I remember, she always had time."

Addison frowns. "Would your father have cared if she worked hard to make food? I wouldn't cook if you didn't care. I'd just let you buy it."

Now that she says it, I remember her cooking one time for a birthday. "No. He didn't. I don't think he even ate dinner with us very much. He was always working."

Addison shrugs. "That's probably why."

We eat in silence, and I think back on my childhood again. The nights I didn't even see Father. How everything revolved around his schedule. We had plenty of money, but we never traveled. We never did anything except a few trips to parks or that little vacant lot down the street.

I think we made the best of things, and we were happy, but we should have been happier. It should have been the best childhood imaginable. Instead, we were nearly prisoners. I'm not even talking about myself. My brothers were just as trapped. They just didn't have the same expectations put on them.

I slide my plate forward and lean back in my chair when my food's gone. "You really are an amazing woman," I say, feeling so much better now that I have a full stomach and I'm staring at Addison.

She grins and takes one more bite of her fish before doing the same. "Now, can we talk about something? I've been going crazy all day waiting to talk to you."

I nod. "Which topic first?"

"The work thing. Everyone's pissed, Phillip. Not just a few people. Everyone. Why didn't you just hire more people? The entire office thinks that you're just being stingy and expecting them to work for free. They're talking about leaving and going to other publishing houses."

I sigh. This is the same thing that I've dealt with all day, and the words come easily. "Everyone's contracts state they should expect to work up to fifty hours per week without any extra pay. We're in a bind, and we need people to work a little more for a while. Plus, we're giving bonuses because of it. I know that it's more work than they're used to, but we need our veteran employees to work on these other projects. Not new employees."

"But you want them to be excited about the new projects, right? Why not just keep track of their hours spent and pay them extra on their paychecks like they were hourly workers?"

I shake my head. "That would increase the cost of an already enormous expansion. If we did that, we'd have to make serious cuts in other areas, most of which would piss people off even more."

Addison frowns. The look on her face tells me she's not sure if she should say what she's thinking. "Phillip, can't Loughton House handle a loss for six months while you expand? Isn't that a normal thing in business? I mean, I'm not you, and I haven't spent my life managing a multi-billion-dollar business, but that was my assumption about how expansions work."

Andrew and I briefly discussed that possibility, but it was almost immediately pushed aside. I take a sip of my beer and wish we were talking about her book instead. "In almost sixty years, Loughton House has never had a single month with a loss. My father made sure that we made money every single month. Would you want to work for six months without getting paid?"

She squints. "But you make a paycheck too. Loughton House is a company, right? Profits don't go straight into your bank account. You wouldn't be working for free."

My jaw tightens as I feel the frustration welling up inside me. "Yes, I earn a paycheck just like you, but it's nothing compared to bonuses that are based on company profits. I'd say that ninety percent of my income is in bonuses. Six months without a profit would mean that I'd make roughly half what I would normally make in a year."

Addison sighs and doesn't look happy with my response. I don't understand. She doesn't think the employees should have to fulfill the requirements in their contract, but I should basically work for free for six months?

"What is it? Why are you looking at me like I'm an idiot?" I finally ask.

She chuckles and shrugs, but it's not a goofy, fun-loving chuckle. It's that terrible kind that makes you wonder what you're missing. "I just don't understand, Phillip. You're a freaking billionaire. What does a year of pay even matter to someone like you?"

"Millions of dollars. That's why it matters."

She stands up and shrugs. "It's your company, Phillip. Do what you want, I guess. I just… I thought you'd be different. That's all."

She turns and walks away from me, leaving me seething. How can she suggest that I just not get paid for six months? How can she, a person who's spent her life counting every penny, think that my pennies don't matter? Much less, millions of dollars.

I watch her walk away, and I don't have words for how I feel. Most business owners would have squeezed even more out of them, but I haven't. I've spent my life trying to do the right thing for all of them. No one was mistreated. Now this? My company is trying to make me into a bad guy because I need them to work a little harder.

I could handle that, though. They've always thought of me as terrifying, as the man who could make or break careers. But Addison? I've never been that in her eyes. There's never been a single moment where she looked at me with the same fear, or even worse, looking at me like I'm disappointing her. Thinking that she's seeing me that way cuts me more than anything I've ever experienced.

But I'm not doing anything wrong. I'm not taking advantage of anyone. The only thing I'm doing is trying to keep my company afloat when the entire industry is failing.

She doesn't see that, though.

Forty-Nine

ADDISON

I STARE AT THE COMPUTER SCREEN, UNABLE TO DO MY job. I keep flashing back to how Phillip felt last night at dinner. Felt really is the only word that makes sense. It's not that he said anything wrong or even had a tone. He just *felt* like he was pissed.

And I trust those feelings.

He tried talking to me about random things. We watched a movie I completely ignored. Then we fell asleep on opposite sides of the bed. I have never felt so alone in bed with another person.

I glance at my phone when a text message comes through.

PHILLIP LOUGHTON

I emailed you my edits. I can't eat lunch with you today.

Of course, he can't. He hasn't been able to eat lunch with me in what seems like forever. I told myself that I would be patient, that I knew things would be hard at first when he went back to his old position. Then his father dropped the rest of the company on his shoulders, and there are all the recent changes he's instituting. He's got a lot on his plate.

He just doesn't feel like himself these days. There's that word again. Feels. He does such a good job hiding what's going on in that head of his. Then again, it might just be because I see him so rarely.

I open my personal email on my phone and open my manuscript. It's covered in comments. When did he have time to do this? Did he really edit my entire manuscript in two days? Is that what he's been doing the whole time?

I read through the comments, and by the end of page two, I feel like I'm about to cry. He ripped it apart. Damn near every paragraph has serious commentary.

There's no way I can go through this right now. Not with how low I feel. I was sure this book was good. Angela and Donovan were amazing, but this… This does not feel like I wrote a good book.

I stand up, and Sera turns around in her seat. "You getting some pre-lunch coffee? Because I could definitely use some."

I shake my head. "I'm going to take the rest of the day off," I say.

She frowns. I've never taken any time off, much less leave before lunch. "I just need an afternoon off."

"Are you feeling sick?"

I shake my head again. "Nope. I just need some space away from this place for an afternoon." My eyes go toward the elevator that leads to the top floor, where Phillip is probably in the middle of a heated discussion about the future of the company.

Sera hesitates, but then she says, "Need some company? I don't think I've taken a day off since I started here. I must have a whole quarter worth of sick days saved up."

It's tempting, but I don't think I'm ready to talk about the way I'm feeling. Plus, Phillip keeps saying that everything's about to get better. Maybe I'm just being emotional. Patience has never really been one of my strong suits.

"No, I think I'd prefer to be alone. Thanks though."

She nods and turns back to the computer. "Feel better, Addison," she says. "Whatever it is, it's probably not as bad as you think it is."

"I'm sure it's not," I say as I walk out of the cubicle. I head toward the lead editor's office, and I overhear a woman whispering inside of a cubicle.

"Yeah, I heard that the real reason for that email is because a bunch of the new people are getting laid off. Just like two years ago when they opened that London branch."

That sends a shock through me. Could they really be laying people off, too? Would Phillip hide that from me? Would I be one of the ones who got laid off? I mean, I haven't been with Loughton House for very long. Or would Phillip keep me from getting let go?

No. I can't think about any of that right now. I can't let rumors push me into darker territory than I'm already in. I take a deep breath and try to let out as much stress as I can.

Just tell James Pritchard that I'm feeling bad and need to take the afternoon off. Get some distance. Breathe some fresh air. See something other than a computer screen…

Fifty

PHILLIP

I'm done. All the plans are set, and I managed it a day early. Tomorrow, I get to go home at a reasonable time.

I can't believe my financial director decided it was a good idea to chat about cutting the workforce by ten percent in front of the staff. I should fire him for that. Or worse, make him answer the seventy-two thousand emails I've had about it.

On that note, when the hell did everyone start thinking that I was so personable that they could just email me when they hear a rumor? Is that a very terrible byproduct of me working as an editor for a month?

I can't stop smiling, though. Everything's finally going to get better. I open the door to the house, expecting Addison to be at the top of the stairs like normal. But she's not.

She hasn't responded to my edits, so I assume she's still upstairs in the office looking them over. The strange thing is that I don't smell any food. Usually, even if I'm home far later, I can smell dinner as soon as I walk in.

Tonight, it's almost like she hasn't cooked at all. Then I remember I was supposed to text her. *Damn it.* Well, at least I'll get fresh food tonight. I just might have to wait a while.

I put my laptop bag over the hook in the closet like normal and walk up the stairs, trying my best to be quiet. I don't know why I'm trying to be sneaky. Maybe it's because I'm so freaking happy, or maybe I'm just so exhausted that I'm acting like a child.

As I approach the office, I hear Addison's voice, and she sounds more exhausted than I am. I know that the distance between us has worn on her, but it's all done now. At least as done as it can be.

"Mom, how many times do I have to tell you? An extra dollar an hour isn't worth changing jobs."

There's a pause, and I wait outside the door. The last time I heard her talking to her mom, she seemed happy. Now, it sounds like her mother is more exhausting than work is.

"Yes, a secretary job is a great change. But why didn't you keep working at Woodson's while you were going through the hiring process? It took me almost three weeks to get through mine at Loughton House. You can't survive without a paycheck for three weeks. Then there's the delay before your first one. Mom, you've put yourself in a bad place again."

I clench my jaw, trying my best not to rush to Addison's rescue. Her mother's asking her for money again. She told me about that before, but I didn't understand how often it happened.

"Fine. I can send you some money, but it won't be enough." There's a pause. "Absolutely not. His money is his, and mine is mine. I'll lend you mine, but if it's not enough, you're just going to have to deal with the mess on your own this time."

Her mother was asking if she could borrow some of mine. I wish she'd have asked because I'd be happy to pay whatever it took to keep her from worrying or being stressed.

I know Addison is the last person who would ever ask me for help, though. Our entire relationship has been proof that she refuses to be her mother. It's been ingrained in her to never ask for help from anyone, and especially today, the last thing I should do is offer to help.

"Look, I'll send you five hundred dollars. It's literally all the money I have. There's nothing else I can do. And Mom, this needs to be the last time you call asking about money. I have too much going on right now to worry about keeping a savings account for you. You're my mom, and I love you, but I cannot take care of your financial mistakes anymore."

There's a pause, and I hear a sniffle. Then a louder one. God, I can't believe her mother made her feel like that.

I take a deep breath, readying myself to comfort her, and I walk into the office. "How are you doing?" I ask with a smile.

I expected the tears, but when she looks up at me and doesn't even give me a halfhearted smile, I feel myself shrinking. Every other day, she's smiled at me, glad that I was home, but today, it's like my presence doesn't give her any more hope or happiness. Like I'm just another burden.

"What's wrong?" I ask as I cross the room, doing my best not to let her sadness bring me down. I don't need to make this about my emotions. The best thing I can do is just be infectiously happy like I felt before I got home.

"Nothing," she says. Her voice is soft and shallow, like she's just retreating into herself. It's unlike anything I've ever seen before.

I wrap my arms around her and pull her to me as I squat in front of her. "Addison, please talk to me. I *promise* that I'm here for you. Whatever it is, I'll help to make it better."

The emphasis on promise is almost instinctual. My word has been my bond ever since I was eight and found out just what a promise could mean. She understands that emphasis, and when she looks up at me, I can see a spark of hope where there was none earlier.

"I don't want to publish my book anymore."

That isn't what I'd expected. I'd thought all of Addison's emotions were based on that talk with her mother. What does her book have to do with anything?

"Why? It was wonderful, and I can't wait for other people to read it, too."

She shakes her head, and more tears roll down her cheeks. What's going on?

"No. I don't think I want to be a writer anymore. It's too much. Everything is too much."

I pull Addison closer to me, forcing her body against mine, and she loses any hold on her emotions. Sobs come out as her nails dig into my back. "I thought I could do all of this. I thought I had everything under control. Working with you and living with you. Writing. Being in New York all alone. I don't think I can, though. Everything's so crossed and tangled that I barely even know who I am anymore."

My jaw clenches at our relationship being one of the things that's making her feel like this. There's absolutely nothing wrong with us.

She looks up at me. "Trish is leaving Loughton House. Victoria's thinking about it. They blame you. Not Loughton House. Not their manager. They blame you, and I can't help but think they're right. My friends are leaving, and there's nothing I can do. I can't even tell them they're right to leave because that would be saying that I don't support you."

My jaw locks up so hard that I'm sure Addison can hear my teeth grinding together. "They're leaving because they don't want to work a few extra hours of overtime?"

She shakes her head. "They're leaving because it's better for them at other companies. They'll make more money. There's no overtime." Another sob escapes her lips, and she shakes a little. "And I think they should leave, too. Loughton House doesn't care if they stay or go. You've never cared about the employees."

I don't know how to take that comment other than with anger. I growl, "I've always cared. From the very beginning, I cared more about the employees than anyone else in management. More than anyone at any other company. You can say a lot of things, but you can't say that I don't care."

"Then why are you doing the same thing your father did?" she whispers. For a moment, I can see fear in her eyes. The same fear as everyone in the office. It stops the rage that's building inside me. But it doesn't stop the anger. The seething, twisting emotion that I've held back my entire life.

From my father. From the employees. From everything in the world that's done its best to control me.

"I am not my father," I say as I pull away from Addison. "Everything I'm doing is to fix his mistakes. I am breaking myself to put everyone else first. The employees. The company. Even you. I am not my father, Addison, and don't you ever say that again."

The tears stop. I can see the shift in her almost instantly. She felt fragile a moment ago, as though a strong wind would have shattered her, but now she's no different from the night I met her at the motel. An unbreakable woman who's fought for every inch of success she's ever had.

And she's pissed.

"You will not talk to me like that, Phillip Loughton," she says, her voice low and dangerous. "I am not some businessman you're able to intimidate. Maybe at work you're my superior, but not here. You are acting just like your father would, whether you believe me or not. How could anyone expect anything different since you're basically a carbon copy of him?"

I try to interrupt, but she doesn't let me. She just keeps saying words that infuriate me, that make me want to throw things and scream. "Your father took every nicety away from his employees. He didn't pay them as much as they were worth. Loughton House is the most successful publishing house because of the people doing the work. Not because you're better at cutting costs.

"And once again, you're expecting them to sacrifice so that you can keep making money when you don't need to make a dime for the rest of your life. You could donate ninety percent of your money and still have more money than the rest of us will earn in our entire lifetime. Don't tell me you deserve anything. You want to expand *your* company, then *you* should be the one to make sacrifices. Not your employees."

It goes against everything in me. Thirty years of training and spending every moment working balk at the idea of doing any of it for free.

"Well Addison, if we're comparing each other to our parents, maybe I am like my father. And maybe you're like your mother. You ignore all the experiences you've ever had that are staring you in the face. Your mother may ignore her past mistakes when she sees a shiny dollar on the other side of the fence, but at least she's not afraid. At least she doesn't let fear of success make her run."

"What the hell are you talking about? I'm nothing like my mother." The way she spits those words lets me know I struck a nerve, and I revel in the fact that she's experiencing the same pain that she made me feel.

I smirk. "You've refused help every step of the way to becoming a published author. Now that your book is finally written and I've edited it, you're saying you don't want to be an author. Because why? It's hard? Because I'm trying to help you be more successful? I'll tell you why. It's because you're fucking scared, Addison. You're scared of doing anything other than being a dedicated worker bee. Just like your mother is terrified of making a dollar less per hour. You both live your lives terrified. At least she's willing to chase that extra dollar. You… You'd sit in that cubicle forever as a junior editor, making barely enough to eat when you have a multi-million dollar book sitting on your computer. That's the dumbest thing I've ever heard."

Addison stares at me for a few seconds as my words roll through her. "You know what? Maybe you're right. Maybe I am like my mother. As you said, though, I'd rather be my mother than your father."

She closes her laptop and shoves it into the balled-up laptop bag. The blue and tan crocheted pattern I remember from that very first night together. The one I made fun of.

I'm still furious. Still absolutely pissed that she could think that I'm anything like my father. All I've done for as long as I can remember is treat everyone as well as I can without hurting Loughton House.

But I know this is wrong. I know she shouldn't be packing her things or leaving. We're right together. We make sense even when the world is pure fucking chaos.

"Stop," I mutter. It's hard to make myself think straight, to wade through the emotional shitstorm in my head and make a good decision when I'm still this furious.

For a half-second, she stops. Holding the strap of her laptop bag over her shoulder, she glares at me. Not long enough for me to understand how to fix things or even to calm down. Just long enough that I know she's not ignoring me.

"Fuck you, Phillip. Fuck you and your company. I don't need any of it, and you can take this as my official resignation. Maybe I am scared of success. Maybe I'm afraid of a lot of things, but I can cross one of them off my list. I'm not afraid of you. I hope you live a long, long life, Phillip. I hope Loughton House never fails so that you never get to be anything other than the machine your father made you into."

She storms out of the room, and I can't do anything. I know I should. In any other instance, I'd know what to do. Catch her. Apologize to her. Scream from the rooftops that I love her. Something. Anything. But I don't do anything except stand there and shake.

I have never been so absolutely broken in my life.

I love Addison Adelaide, and she's leaving me.

Fifty-One

ADDISON

"Fuck that son of a bitch," Trish says from beside me. The appletinis in our hands are cold, but my insides feel colder. Everything feels colder right now.

Someone's singing a terrible rendition of Britney Spears, and I don't care. Victoria's polishing up her resume, and Sera's working overtime, so Trish and I are sitting at the bar together. Alone.

"And don't worry about anything, Addison. I've got more friends in publishing than you'd believe. I've already had three offers, and I'll have you hooked up with a new job by the end of the week."

I just nod. I'm strangely unworried about the money. For the first time in my life, the fact that I'm unemployed as of this morning doesn't seem to matter at all. It should. I should be terrified since I just sent my mom the last bit of savings I'd put together.

But I just can't let myself care about that.

It's the solitude that presses against me, that makes me terrified. That and the knowledge that Phillip wasn't wrong. I should be at home sending my resume out to every place that's hiring, but every time I sit down at the computer, I can't help but pull up the edited manuscript that Phillip covered in red marks.

It was that or sit with Trish at a karaoke bar.

She doesn't seem to be in a singing mood, though, so we've been sipping appletinis. "Thank you," I say softly, wishing the drink was a weird raspberry and coffee beer and that the chair was a dining room chair in front of an ornate table. Food that's slightly dried out from the warming oven in front of me.

And Phillip across from me, smiling like always.

That ship has sailed, though.

"When you and John fight, do you scream at each other? Do you say things you regret?"

Trish cocks her head. "Have you met me? Of course I do. John doesn't very often, but that's what fights are for. It's for saying all that shit that's been building up. It's getting it all out and both of you understanding that none of it is as bad as you're making it sound. Then you fuck like you hate each other, and after that, it's all better."

"What? I can't imagine a more toxic way to deal with your emotions."

Trish grins. "Maybe me and John just like hatefucking a little more than normal? But really, fights are going to happen. It's the talk afterward that matters. Honesty once neither one of you is mad anymore. And you can't be mad after screaming and fucking like that. I don't know if you should be listening to me since I'm not a therapist or anything, and as my husband says, I'm not exactly a wonderful role model. But it works for us."

I guess that makes some sense. It still seems a little insane, but I guess that's Trish for you. We watch as the next person gets on stage and starts singing *Bohemian Rhapsody*, a song that I've realized always makes the entire crowd light up. This time, Trish and I don't join in the group singing.

"I don't know what to do, Trish," I say. "I loved… no, I think I still love him. But he's just like his father and doesn't realize it. If he acts like this right now, while we're still new at this whole relationship thing, what will it be like when he gets comfortable? Will he just forget about me? He's talked about his father so many times, and I can't remember a single good thing he's said about the man."

Trish shrugs. "He was right on one thing," she says. "I don't know about him as a boyfriend or husband. He seems like a nice enough guy, but if he really is just forgetting about you, if he's putting work ahead of you, then fuck that guy. If it's temporary, then maybe you're overreacting? I don't know. Like I said, that's between you two. But you should publish that book."

I arch an eyebrow and look at her. "You haven't even read it. Why would you say that?"

"I've read the stuff you've done in editing, and it's all solid, especially your hooks. You say you've read romance books your whole life. Phillip Loughton, the literal King of Publishing, says you should publish it. It'll do great. You're surrounded by people who know how to make a book sell, and you have more contacts in the publishing industry than nearly any other unknown author. If you throw it in the dumpster, you really are running from success because you're already done with the hard part. You wrote a book. Polish it up, and turn that effort into a big fat paycheck."

I frown. Maybe they're right. I did write the book, and I think it's actually really good. I don't even know why I said that I didn't want to publish it. Probably because I was so stressed about me and Phillip.

"Okay. Maybe I will."

"Good. When you're done editing it, don't you dare throw it into some agent's slush pile. Let me call a few people and find you an agent."

I frown. I'd pushed back when Phillip had said something similar. But something he said bites at me, demanding my attention. "At least your mother isn't afraid to go after it."

Is it really so wrong to let a friend help me? I mean, no agent or publisher would sign me if they were going to lose money, right? Plus, it's different when an editor friend is trying to help me instead of someone who owns a publishing house. She may get me in contact with someone, but the rest is up to me.

"I'd appreciate that," I say.

"Excellent." She grins as *Bohemian Rhapsody* ends. "Want to duet some Aerosmith with me?"

"Yeah, but only *Dude Looks Like a Lady*. I need something fast."

"That's two of us."

I didn't know why I wanted to come out with Trish, but now I know. I needed to get out of my thoughts. I needed to hear someone who wasn't invested in my relationship, someone who could see the forest instead of just the trees.

She's right. It's time for me to publish this book. I'll figure out what to do about Phillip, but regardless, I can't work under him.

Plus, if Trish and Phillip are right, I may not even need a job for much longer...

Fifty-Two

PHILLIP

THE CITY SPLAYS OUT BELOW ME IN A MYRIAD OF colors. Oranges, reds, and golds shine off the steel and glass in the sunset as I sit in my office. Just like that day at the Brooklyn Bridge Park.

I don't have a reason to be here. All my work is done, but I don't want to go home. I don't want to see the emptiness where there was life only three days ago. A Styrofoam takeout container instead of a home cooked meal. Silence instead of laughter.

I don't want to accept that my life is exactly the same as it was before I met Addison. I don't want to be forced to see that nothing has changed.

The pen in my fingers moves, a twirling motion that I'd seen Addison do so many times while she was working on her book in my office. It rolls over my fingers awkwardly and then falls. The clink of the metal against the marble tile is the only sound in the room, and even that tiny sound seems to echo in the silence, but then it's gone.

"Is this what Father felt like when Mother died?" I whisper to no one. He had children, but other than me, he'd never spent any time with them.

How did I push her away? Did I really think that me being right was more important than her feelings? Even if Loughton House crumbled, is pushing Addison away worth saving it?

And is pushing her away any different from walking away? I promised her I'd never do that. I'd never walk away.

It's like I've been transported to the one night in my life I saw my father drink. The night my mother died.

He sat in his chair and stared at the wall as he drank glass after glass of Scotch. Nothing else mattered to him. Just that wall and the Scotch. I'd put my brothers to bed and read them a story. I'd been the adult that night even though I was only eight.

Then again, I'd been an adult since I could walk in my brothers' eyes.

When I went back into the dining room and sat down next to my father like I did so often, I didn't say anything. The tears had dried on my cheeks. Father wasn't crying, so I wouldn't either. I would be a man who could be strong when other people needed me. And my father needed me tonight.

"You had no right to leave," he whispered. I never found out whether or not he knew I was there. What I knew was that it wasn't time to say anything back.

"You promised me you'd never leave. We promised each other, and I've never broken my promise. I've never backed out of it, no matter how hard it was. No matter how much I wanted to play with you, with my children. I was strong so that you'd never leave."

And for the first time in my life, I saw a tear fall down Father's cheek. I saw the strongest man in the world cry. "I was strong so you'd stay with me. But you broke that promise, Margaret. You left me all alone, and I don't know what to do. I don't know how to live like this."

He poured himself another drink, and another tear followed the last. I never made a sound as I watched my father's heart break. "You betrayed me, Margaret, but I still love you. I'll love you forever, and I swear that I'll never break my promise. Our children will never want for anything. But I don't know how I'll ever survive without you. I'll do my best, but I'm nothing without you."

Then the tears had truly fallen. The only time in my life that my father cried was when my mother had died. I sat with him for more than an hour as he wept. Silent and motionless. He had talked more, but the more he drank, the less sense he'd made. Then, when the bottle of Scotch was empty, he stood up and walked to his room, leaving me all alone in the dining room.

That was the night I vowed to myself never to break a promise. In my entire life, a broken promise is the only thing that ever made my father cry.

I take a deep breath as the memory flows through me as it has so many times in my life.

I had been willing to walk away from Loughton House when Father was still running it. But now, it's in my hands. Now, I can't shake the weight that lies on my shoulders.

I'd been able to hold the weight when I saw the light at the end of the tunnel. When Addison was right there, supporting me. But now? Do I even care if my father's creation dies a slow death?

I hope you live a long, long life, Phillip. I hope Loughton House never fails so that you never get to be anything other than the machine your father made you into. Her words have echoed in my mind since she walked out of my life. Since I pushed her away. *Since I broke my promise.*

The same rage that filled me when Addison compared me to my father explodes inside me. I broke a promise to the only person I've ever loved.

I'm not my father. I'm worse.

I pick up my laptop and throw it across the room. It smashes against the marble walls in an explosion of silicon and plastic. I take a deep breath. And the door opens.

"What the fuck is going on in here?" Andrew says from the doorway.

"I walked away," I say in barely more than a whisper.

"What are you talking about?" He pauses and sighs. "Addison?"

"Yes," I say and can feel my body shaking as I try to control myself. The chair is next if I can't.

"Damn it. What happened?" He seems pissed, but I barely recognize it. The pain is too much. It's like the emotions are drowning me, and I can't get any air.

Training is all that keeps me from lashing out at the world around me.

"Phillip?" he says with worry in his voice as he plops his feet onto the tile and sits up straight. "Man, are you okay?"

I shake my head, still overwhelmed with emotions that have no outlet. "I don't know what to do," I say.

"Why did you leave? You two seemed so happy? She made you more… human."

I look at him and try to focus on the conversation. I give in to the emotions, let them rage through me, and hope that somehow Andrew can help me because I don't know how to handle them on my own.

"She told me I was a carbon copy of Father, and I told her she was an idiot for not publishing her book."

Andrew frowns. "That doesn't make any sense. You were making time for her and everything, nothing like Dad."

"She didn't understand how close I was," I say. I have to take a breath as another red-hot pain sears through me when I remember the conversation. "But she was pissed that I was making the same business decisions that Father would. She was pissed about the email I sent because her friends were pissed."

Andrew leans back, his expression turning thoughtful. "So, don't be like Father? Make a different decision?"

"We made the right decision, Andrew. We talked through every option, and the one we chose was the best one. It did the least damage."

He arches his eyebrow. "You're telling me that Addison didn't have any suggestions? I've gotten into a lot of fights with women. They never get into a pissing match if they don't have a better option. Or at least an option they think is better."

"She had an idea…" The one that triggered my instincts harder than anything she's ever said. "She said we should pay for the expansion out of our own pockets. Or rather, out of my pocket."

Andrew shrugs. "It'd be manageable. I mean, it's probably not the smartest business decision, but if we're right, and this expansion turns Loughton House back into a growth company, then spending fifty million out of pocket wouldn't really hurt very much. Which is more important? Fifty million or Addison?"

The lightbulb clicks. "Fuck," I whisper. I am an idiot.

Andrew nods. "I've seen that expression on your face before. I guess I'll get out of here while you get to work."

He's right. All the emotions that were raging inside me have mutated into a single thing. There's still pain in my chest, but it's not debilitating. No, it's pure motivation.

That single revelation has my mind seeing everything in a different light. Moments ago, I was focusing on how I'd failed. Now I'm focused on how I can keep my promise.

I want to to do to publishing what Google did to search engines. I want it to change everything.

And I probably won't make a dime by doing it.

Fifty-Three

ADDISON

Two weeks have flown by. A new job working next to Trish at Murray Press as an editor. Not a junior editor. I don't know how Trish did it, but she convinced my new boss that I was worth a thirty percent pay raise and a bump in title.

The work environment is better here. People smile more. No one worries about someone like Phillip walking through the cubicles and firing them. The senior employees all have their own offices. They have freaking cookies in the breakroom along with the coffee.

But it's not Loughton House. It's not the dream I had when I was ten. I guess that sometimes dreams need to take a backseat to the real world. Of course, that was always the backup dream. My actual dream was to become a world-famous author, and I'm two big steps closer.

I worked through all the edits that Phillip did on my manuscript, a parting gift from the man that I thought I was destined to be with. Then Trish went through it, too.

The real surprise happened yesterday. I spent an hour on the phone with my new agent, Brett Austin. I don't have any idea how Trish knows him, but literally hours after she sent my manuscript to him, he was on the phone with me, far more excited than I'd have expected.

The only problem? His agency is restructuring over the next month, so he can't do anything with the manuscript until then.

That's fine with me, though. Hell, I never really expected to get signed to an agent, so this is already beyond my wildest dreams. I have enough on my plate trying to navigate a brand-new job that it's better to not have to worry about what's happening with *Sweet Temptations*.

I stare at the wall while I sit at my dining room table. There's nothing left to do. For two weeks, I've thrown myself into work. I've done everything I could to hide from my own thoughts. Or, more accurately, the one thought that plays on repeat.

The fight Phillip and I had before I stormed out of his house.

I still haven't figured out if I was right to leave. He's sweet and funny, and he makes me feel a whole different side of myself. Especially in the bedroom.

Maybe I overreacted because we were fighting. Instead of storming off, maybe I should have stayed and given myself time to cool off. I should have even had one of those honest chats like Trish talked about.

But he's still the man his father trained him to be.

He's still the man that prioritizes his own wealth over the people under him. He pushed Trish out of Loughton House, and Victoria's on the fence on whether or not she's going to stay. That was the problem I had then, but it's not what I'm stuck on anymore.

If he's following his father's lead on business, is he really going to be all that different when it comes to our relationship? Could I see myself marrying a man who might raise a child like he was raised?

The thought sickens me.

I open my phone and go to the text message he sent me three days ago. The only contact I've had with him since I walked out of his house.

PHILLIP LOUGHTON

I'm sorry. I've spent a lot of time thinking about what you said. I was wrong.

I left him on read, but I don't know if that's what I want to do. There's a sense of floundering because every time I think of him, it's like the soul wound aches all over again. I want to be with Phillip, but I cannot be with the man he's shown every indication of becoming.

Every day after he went back to his old job, it felt like he was going right back to the way everyone talked about him. Cold. Ruthless. The perfect businessman.

And the worst partner I could ever imagine.

His father.

Then there was the fight. Everything about that conversation made me rethink where I stood and where he stood. I've never been able to read him when he goes cold. He's too good at hiding his thoughts from me. He lashed out at me, not about the thing that we were arguing about, but at me. It wasn't like he was trying to defend himself. His words were meant to hurt me, not have a heated discussion.

They cut me like a knife, and the wound still hasn't healed.

As I stare at the words on the screen, contemplating whether I should respond for the millionth time, a text comes through.

SERA WYLDER

You still coming to the party? I really need a buffer.

A buffer? Who's going to be there? Sera's getting a promotion to lead art designer, a well-deserved reward for how badass she is. It's come after the previous lead designer quit during the exodus from Loughton House.

ADDISON ADELAIDE

Yeah. I wouldn't miss it. Six tonight, right?

Yep.

Once again, I don't really want to go out with my friends, but I know I need to. I may have left Loughton House, but I don't want to leave them. They're the kind of people that I've never had before. People that bring life to my soul. I think back to how much Trish has helped me without expecting anything in return.

I'd be crawling back to my mom's house, tail between my legs, if she hadn't done that. Sera and Victoria would have done the same if Trish hadn't been so quick about it.

I sigh and flip back to the text from Phillip. His picture is sitting at the top of the text message. He's got a goofy grin on his face, and he's wearing that two dollar "saffron-stained" red shirt that I made him buy. God, he's handsome when he looks like that. Like a silly teenager who doesn't know how to make his own coffee or how to boil water.

No matter how "hot" he is in a ten-thousand-dollar suit, he'll never be as sexy as when he's relaxed and playful.

I shut off the phone's screen, not wanting to see the man I've walked away from. The smart thing would be to distance myself from him. To ignore him and go back to my normal life. Become an author. Achieve my dreams.

Forget the man that showed me what it meant to smile every morning. Forget the man that showed me what it was to be happy.

Fifty-Four

PHILLIP

BALLOONS, CAKE, AND A BUNCH OF EMPLOYEES surround me as I eye the door. Sera's company party is probably the last place I want to be, but it was the only way I was sure that I could see Addison. We don't have many company parties, but Andrew insisted on this one, and I didn't offer any pushback because I knew that she'd be here.

It's an absolutely terrible idea for me to have come, but like so many things in my life these past two months, I don't think there's a better option. She told me a long time ago that she hated surprises, and this is definitely going to be a surprise. How else am I supposed to see her? Just show up on her doorstep and bang on the door until she answers? This is at least better than that.

Andrew is talking to Sera with a grin on his face. Who knew that they'd had a secret fling the first year she got hired? It makes me feel a little better about dating and promptly falling in love with Addison two weeks after she got hired.

My eyes go back to the doorway as I wait for her. People walk into the Atrium's conference room, grinning and laughing.

They're dressed in business casual, most of them wearing the same things they'd wear to work. Simple button-down shirts, slacks, a few dresses, and black skirts.

And then she walks in, a dress that only she'd own. God, she's fucking beautiful. When she's at work, she looks good in professional outfits, but the real beauty comes out when she's wearing the things that fit her. Like this one. A light blue dress that reminds me of a fifty's housewife. Tiny little white polka dots cover it. Does it fit "business casual"? Maybe. Does it stick out like a sore thumb? Definitely. Do I fucking love that she wore it? More than she'd ever understand.

Part of me wants to jump out of my seat and rush over to her, but for the first time since I can remember, I'm actually a little terrified. I've turned the world upside down for her, and she doesn't even know it. Regardless of how she responds to me, I know that I'd do it again.

I needed Addison to yell at me, to show me just how much I fucked up when I inherited Loughton House. I needed to change it because I am not my father.

But I don't know what I'm going to do if she pushes me away again. Well, that's not true. I do actually know. When I was tiny, probably five or six, my mother told me something that stuck with me even though I had no intention of ever getting married. "Don't look for the perfect woman. Become the man that the perfect woman would want, and she'll find you."

I know there's only one woman that I want, and I will do whatever it takes to be the man that she could love like she did a month ago. Even if it means that I give this all up. I've even talked to Andrew about doing just that.

Addison walks across the room to where Sera is talking to Andrew, and Sera nearly screeches. She says something about the dress Addison's wearing, and they hug each other.

It's hard to look away from her. Until I hear a voice from behind me that I can't ignore. "You're doing all of this for her?"

I turn around and see my father sitting behind me at the table wearing the same suit that he wore at every important meeting of his life. He looks older now, like the wrinkles around his eyes have grown in the past month. Like his shoulders slump just a little more now.

"Yes."

He nods and gives me the barest hint of a smile. "I know how that feels, son. I... I know that you probably hate me, but I hope you'll listen to me for a few minutes."

I want to scream at him. I can't help but blame my father for so many things. It feels like I've been at war with him since that weekend I spent at that stupid motel. But I see something in his eyes that I haven't seen in a very long time. Sadness. Pain.

"What is it?" I can't keep the growl out of my voice. I may be willing to listen to him, but I can't stop the anger from rising inside me.

He nods. "I'm proud of you, Phillip. Not because of your business choices. Not because you're better than me at running Loughton House. I'm proud that you're willing to do all of this for her."

I frown, the anger dissipating somewhat. "What are you talking about? You've never said a single word about love in your entire life."

And for the third time in my life, I see a tear roll down his cheek. His lips quiver as he begins talking. "I know everyone sees Loughton House as mine, but it wasn't ever for me. I built Loughton House for your mother. Everything I've done, everything I am, is to fulfill a promise I made to her before you were ever born."

What? I've never heard anything about this.

His gaze grows a little unfocused as he says, "I met your mother when she was seventeen and working at a terrible little diner. She was barely surviving, living on food the diner was about to throw out. I was in college, trying to understand my place in the world, and I met this pretty girl who managed to smile even when she looked like she was about to collapse.

"I fell in love with her, but when I asked her to marry me, she told me she wouldn't marry me unless I could promise that our children would never be poor. Ever. Not even for a moment. She didn't want her babies or grandbabies to struggle like she had her entire life. She made me promise that no matter what happened, no one in our family would ever have to go hungry for even a day."

Father takes a deep breath, and it comes out ragged. "I loved her more than anything. And I made that promise. From that day forward, I did everything in my power to make sure that no one would ever be hungry. I couldn't make sure that Loughton House would keep my grandchildren fed unless I taught someone to run it. So, I made the hard choice to force you to learn how to run it, whether you wanted to or not."

"But what about Mason?" I say instinctively. This has to be a lie. A fabrication meant only to keep me from hating him. He has nothing in his life anymore, and now he's realizing that no one wants him. He's spent his life controlling us.

"I was wrong. I've already asked Andrew to let Mason know that he's welcome to come back. That I want him to come back. I'll split my portion of the family money with him. I… I lost sight of the purpose of it all. When your mother died, I got lost. I let myself become someone I never wanted to be, because it was easier than being alone. And I failed her by disowning Mason. I failed you by forgetting that you were still a child. All three of you still needed love, but I… I didn't have love in me when she was gone. And I'm sorry."

I steel my jaw. It's not a lie. I've seen every side of my father. I know him better than he knows himself.

And I remember the night he drank a bottle of Scotch and cursed my mother's name right before declaring his undying love for her.

"Why are you telling me this now?" I ask, and my eyes drift toward Addison, who's laughing with Sera after having wedged herself between them.

"I don't know. I guess I had to take a step back before I could see what I'd done. I'm not asking for forgiveness, Phillip. It's important that you know that. I don't regret throwing myself into Loughton House, into building it into an empire that could do exactly what I'd promised. My grandchildren will never want for anything.

"I gave my life to fulfilling the promise I made to your mother. I sacrificed my relationship with you and your brothers, and I don't regret it at all because the few years I had with her are worth it all. I need you to know that you're doing the right thing with Addison."

He puts his hand out and rests it on mine. It's a shock. I can't remember a single time that he hugged me or showed me an affectionate touch.

"Phillip, love is the only thing that matters in life. More than business. More than family. More than anything. Don't let anyone or anything keep you from her."

I'm speechless as Russel Loughton gives me a nod and stands up. He's the man who built an empire with his own hands to keep a promise to my mother. He's the man that taught me how to be the best in the world at what I do. And for the first time in my life, I feel like I finally understand him.

"Father?" I say as he turns away, stopping him. "You say you did all of this for her, but what about us? Didn't you care about how we felt? How it would affect us?"

He seems to age in front of me, his shoulders slumping even more, his always stiff posture failing for the first time. "I did. She promised that she'd make sure you were happy. I never realized that when she was gone, it was up to me to do both. I'm sorry that I failed you."

Then he walks away from the table, and I'm left shaken. He *failed us*? My father has never said anything like that before. He's never admitted fault. Ever.

Could he really have done everything for my mother? Could he have spent his life trying to fulfill a promise to her?

I look back to Addison, who's finally noticed me. She's staring at me, and I can't tell what she's thinking. Is that anger in her expression? Is it hope?

I don't know, but I can't just sit here. I have to talk to her, and even though I feel shaken to my core, I came here with a purpose. To convince the woman I love that I'm not the man she thinks I am.

The weight of my own failure weighs heavily on me as I cross the conference room. Employees mill about, each of them glancing at me out of habit as I pass them. I don't even notice them. Whispers follow me as I move through the crowd like a dull wave of excitement.

Everyone knows about Addison and me.

"What are you doing here?" she asks as I approach her.

"I hoped that you'd talk to me." I try to remain calm, try to ignore the inner storm of emotions that flow through me. "I wanted to apologize."

She shakes her head. "Did you just ignore the fact that I didn't respond to your message?"

I give her a broken grin. "Well, I heard that breakups in person were better, so an apology would probably be better as well."

"Phillip, I've moved on. I quit Loughton House, and you know it."

I shrug. "It doesn't matter where you work, Addison. Hell, give them the secret sauce to success while you're there, and it won't matter one bit. I didn't fall in love with my junior editor. I fell in love with you, and I don't want to lose you. No matter what it takes."

My father's words flow through my mind, and I know they ring true. With everything I've done, everything I've changed trying to prove that I'm willing to be the man she fell in love with.

She shakes her head. "I love you. I can't deny that. Well, no. Actually, I don't love *you*. I love the guy who needed a couch to sleep on. The guy who took me to see the Brooklyn Bridge in the sunset. The guy who understood me. He wasn't caught up in a thousand other things. He wanted to be anything but his father."

"I'm that man, Addison. I got a little lost, is all. Nothing has changed."

She shakes her head again. "No. Plenty has changed. This is still your father's company, and you're running it just like he did. Putting the bottom line before your employees. Focusing on production numbers."

With lips drawn tight, she continues, "Phillip, if you're going to run Loughton House like your father, will you live the life your father did? Will you treat me like he treated your mother? Will you raise children like he did?"

Now it all makes sense. Her over-the-top reaction to our fight. Her reluctance to even talk to me about it. She doesn't want to end up like my mother, even though my mother had the life she wanted.

And now that I think about it, I remember the way my father looked at her. I remember the way she smiled so softly every time he touched her. She was happy. She had everything she wanted, including the man she'd fallen in love with.

"How do I prove that I'm not him, Addison? I've already changed my work schedule. There won't be many trips. I won't work as long. All those things had already been put into the works when we had our fight. Things take time is all."

She shrugs. "I don't know, Phillip. But I don't trust you. I know that you've never lied to me, but I also know that the way we lived is not the way I want my life to be. You'll always put your company ahead of me. You'll always put it before any children we have. You're married to your company already, and I won't be your second wife."

"Isn't every man married to his job? Doesn't a welder have to go to work even if it's his kid's birthday? Doesn't a programmer have to work overtime during crunch time even if his wife wants to go on a date? How is my job any different?"

"A programmer doesn't work seven days a week for fifteen hours a day, Phillip. For weeks or even months at a time. Didn't your father do just that for your entire life?"

Those changes have already been made. I mean, there will always be nights I have to work late, but that's just part of owning a company. "I don't want to be the man I was before I met you, Addison. Let me show you I won't be."

She sighs. "No. I almost let you pull me into that life once. I won't do it again because you'll go back to that life. You'll always go back to the man whose life belongs to Loughton House."

Before I can say anything to argue, she says, "I'm sorry for the things I said in our fight. I want you to know that. I hope you find a way out of the chains that tie you to Loughton House. Find some freedom even while you run the company because you were the most wonderful man I could have ever dreamed of when you were free. But you're not free anymore, and that's a terrible thing."

She turns away from me, but not before I notice tears welling up. "Goodbye Phillip," she says as she walks away from me.

I'm left staring at her. I've worked so hard to create a work-life balance. Everything's been restructured. What else could I do? How else could I change my world for Addison?

I'm willing to do what it takes. I just don't know how. My instinct is anger, but it fades almost immediately as Addison walks out the door. Anger made her leave. It certainly won't help me now.

No, now is the time for me to do what I'm best at. Find the solution to an impossible problem.

And for the first time since Addison walked out my door, I feel like things make sense. I understand why she walked away, why she refused to come back. Now I just have to prove that I won't be my father and she'll never have to compete with Loughton House for my attention.

An impossible problem that I am absolutely ready to tackle.

Fifty-Five

ADDISON

It hurt so much when I walked away from Phillip the first time, but this was worse. Seeing him again, seeing the need in his eyes when we talked… It nearly broke me. I nearly gave in, and I still question whether I should just call him and beg him to take me back.

Because I do love him. I loved that man that spent a month living with me.

I just can't live the life that I was heading toward. Sure, he probably could come home at five or six every evening. He almost certainly could take a day or two off every week, and maybe he could take a couple of weeks off for vacation.

But what will happen in a year? What about when he gets a report about losses or needs to do another expansion? Will he be able to make time for me when his instincts are to live in his office and tackle problem after problem?

No, he'll keep going back to that life no matter what happens. I can't live that way, in a constant battle for the man I love with a mistress that he'll never leave.

I wrap Nana's afghan around me, the same one that Phillip slept with that first night he stayed with me. Full of memories, it's always been like a safety blanket for me, but now it's attached to him, too. That's the way it feels with everything in my life, and it's why I have to do this tonight.

I pull up the text message that I've gone back to so many times. Phillip's apology. With shaking fingers, I press down on it and, with a deep breath, hit the delete button. I can't keep thinking about him. I can't keep questioning my decisions.

My life is going in all the right directions, and Phillip Loughton isn't one of them. He'll do nothing but turn a wonderful future into me waiting on the man I love to get home for a few minutes before we go to sleep. Eating food that's been in the warmer for hours. Experiencing nothing except waiting for him.

I don't try to stop the tears that begin streaming down my face. I don't try to stop the pain or anger at losing what could have been the perfect relationship. Hell, I welcome them. I embrace the agony. That's why I'm wearing that silk shirt he left me in at the Neptune Motel. That's why I'm inhaling that dark scent that's never left it.

And then I block his number.

Tonight is the end of us. Nothing will change. Nothing will pull me away from the life I've always wanted, and regardless of how much it hurts, I need to experience all of this. I need to remember the good times and the bad. There will be tears, but there will also be laughter.

I refill the "You make me forget batteries" mug with wine and sprite. I may be sitting alone in my apartment, but tonight is a funeral.

The wine helps me to remember. The night we shared at the Neptune Motel. The way he stared at my tits through my soaked shirt. The bed we shared where I wished he would grope me.

Every little memory we made over the course of two months comes pouring through me like a river that can't be stopped. Sometimes I laugh, and sometimes I cry. The wine and sprite turns into wine as I purposefully relive the moments that made me fall in love with Phillip Loughton.

My apartment is silent as I stare at the wall in front of me while ghosts of the past dance through my mind.

Then it's done. The memory of tonight is the last. The last terrible moment of a relationship that I thought would last forever. That nothing could break. A man that was perfect in every way. A man I thought loved me more than anything.

There's nothing I can do to change him, though. Or myself, for that matter. I've lived my life having another person's decisions decide my fate. I love my mom for all her flaws, but I've spent so much of my life feeling powerless because of her decisions. I can't do it again. Maybe if I were different, I could be happy in that kind of relationship. Maybe I could be like his mother, but I can't.

I pour the last cup of wine into my mug and pull the afghan tighter against me, my fingers slipping into the holes in the yarn. Like it's triggering something inside me, a memory from my childhood rolls through me.

I was sitting on Nana's couch while she crocheted like so many afternoons when my mom was at work. We'd just finished an old romance movie, and Nana said, "Addy, you listen to me. There's no such thing as a perfect man. They're all going to have their little holes, but that's what makes them special. You'll never fix those holes, Addy. Trust me on this."

She turned to me and held her crochet hook at me. Her arm shook just a little as you'd expect a white-haired, seventy-year-old woman to do. "I was married to Grandpa George for forty-five years, and I loved that man to the moon and back. But he never learned how to take those damned muddy boots off at the door. Never. I yelled and I screamed more times than I can count. Finally, after your mama had already grown up and moved away, I gave up. I just woke up in the morning and swept the same path from the door to the bedroom every day before he even got out of bed. It became a part of my life, like making a pot of coffee or cooking dinner."

She smiled then and let her hand drop. "Then we didn't fight any more about those muddy boots. For more than twenty years, we didn't fight about much. I'd accepted that nothing would change that old man, and I stopped trying to change him. Then Grandpa George got the cancer, and there weren't no more muddy boots to worry about. You know what? I sure do miss sweeping up that mud cause that was part of the man I loved. Don't ever forget that, Addy. You can't love a man without loving the holes in him."

I lean back in my chair, remembering that moment as though it had just happened. Just as fresh as any of the memories I've mourned tonight, and just as painful.

Because I can't love Phillip's holes. I can't be the woman that changes for the man she loves. "I'm sorry, Nana," I whisper to the ghosts of the past that seem to swirl around me tonight. "I can't do it. I can't be like you."

There aren't any responses, though. No whispers of acceptance. "I love him, but I can't love his holes."

There's an ache in my chest that I'm not sure will ever heal. But I can't let my life center on Phillip's business. I cannot be his second wife.

The pain doesn't go away, but the tears do. I cannot be Nana because Phillip's holes aren't muddy boots. They're bigger than that. They're the kind of holes that you fall through and are forgotten in. I love him, but I cannot love his holes.

Tomorrow, I will wake up, and I will be the woman who came to New York City ready to tackle the world. I have a great job and an agent who swears I'll be published soon. I have good friends.

My life is better than it's ever been. Better than I'd ever really believed was possible.

And yet, at the edge of my thoughts, the doubts already begin to creep in. *Is there anything that could make me happier than that month with Phillip?*

Fifty-Six

"No. That's fucking insane." Andrew's sitting across from me at our conference table with a look of pure confusion.

"You're right. It is. Absolutely insane. And we're going to do it, anyway. Don't worry, you'll get to play with plenty of things soon enough, but right now, I'm still the one making the calls."

He leans back in the chair and looks up at the ceiling. "Dad would set you on fire if he were here. You know that, right?"

"I don't think he would," I say as I smile. Thinking back on that conversation with him at Sera's promotion celebration seems to happen a lot more lately. I don't think I'll ever forgive him for the way he treated us, but I think I understand him more now. Maybe even empathize with him.

"What about you, Mason? Do you have opinions?" I turn to look at him, a grin on his face as he listens to us.

"You know that I'm just here because I couldn't turn down the paycheck. I have no fucking idea what's going on, and even I think it's a little crazy. Then again, I've been living on a beach in the Mediterranean for the past decade, so even wearing this suit is a little crazy to me."

I met up with Mason the day after Sera's party. We haven't seen each other since Father disowned him, but it was like no time at all had passed. I convinced him to work for Loughton House that very night, and he's been spending his days scratching at his slacks since then.

Two weeks have passed since Addison walked away from me, and Loughton House has seen the biggest changes in its history in that time. But the changes are only beginning.

I'm going to do every possible thing to prove to Addison that I won't be the man my father was. And it all starts with Loughton House. If I'm to change who I am, then the company that I own has to change alongside me.

"Well, those are the plans. I need you two to get things moving, and once everything is finished up here, I'm going to need you to go to the London office and do the same thing. Rebuild it how you feel is in line with the new vision of Loughton House Publishing."

Andrew and Mason glance at each other. I feel like I'm being left out of something.

Andrew sighs. "I don't want to go to London for the same reason you don't."

I frown. "But you're single."

He shakes his head. "No, I'm not."

What the fuck? I sigh. "Alright. First, I'm not Father. You don't have to hide shit from me. Two, congrats. And three, why can't you bring her with you? I'm sure most women would love to take a trip to London. She can explore a new country while you disassemble and rebuild our office there."

Mason doesn't wait for Andrew to say anything. "It's because she works for you."

Sera. They had a thing, or at least I assume they did after that weirdness when we played charades. They're back together?

"Take her if she wants to go, and I assume she will. Hell, get her to help you out. There'll be plenty of design choices to make, and she's good."

Andrew grins, and Mason pushes his chair back so he can stand up. "Are we done?"

I glance at Andrew, and he nods. "Yeah, we're done. Do you have somewhere to be?"

"Anywhere but in here. I don't know how you two just sit around and talk all day. Don't you have any actual work to do? Or do you just enjoy doing it in the middle of the night? I'm pretty sure that's what your dream girl was complaining about, wasn't it?"

Andrew chuckles, but it's hard for me to take him seriously. He's been off playing on an island for years. What does he know about running Loughton House?

He nods to us and walks out of the room. I may not respect him in business, but I'm glad he's here. Everything feels more right now that we're all back together and running Loughton House.

"I know you and Mason haven't always seen eye-to-eye, but he's going to fit in well here. It's not like he's been lazing about on a beach."

I shrug. It doesn't really matter what he's been doing. He's a Loughton, and he deserves to be here. He'll pick it up as fast or faster than Andrew did. Mason has always been quicker than either of us. He just didn't work well with Father.

"I know he'll do fine," I say as I stand up.

Andrew doesn't leave his seat. Instead, he leans back and looks up at me. "You're doing a hell of a lot to win a girl back. You know that, right? Normal people wouldn't do this. I certainly wouldn't."

I give him a smirk. "Addison isn't just 'a girl'. She's the woman I'm going to spend the rest of my life with, and I'd burn Loughton House to the ground, if that's what it took. Lucky for you, I doubt that's what she wants."

The grin fades from Andrew's face as he realizes I mean exactly what I said. Father built this place for his wife. He gave every bit of time and energy to make sure he fulfilled his promise. I understand the way he felt now.

And I would absolutely light the match myself if that's what she wanted.

Fifty-Seven

ADDISON

It feels like a lifetime since I walked through these doors, even though it's been just over a month.

I only found out yesterday that my agent now officially works for Loughton House, and he got me a meeting with the acquisitions department here. Instinctively, I was over-the-moon at the thought of being published by them. That was the dream from the beginning, after all.

After I thought about it, though, I've decided that I'm going to have to turn this down, and I guess I'll have to find another agent. It doesn't hurt to hear their offer, though, since I can always use it to leverage other publishers.

Walking through the doors of my old employer and into the workspace I remember so well, I expect to see the cubicles that dominated the floors. I expect to hear quiet murmurs and the nearly imperceptible sound of music playing through headphones. Yet, none of those are here.

There are no quietly productive humans acting like a well-oiled machine, taking in raw manuscripts and turning them into wildly successful books. In fact, it's damn near silent.

"This way," Brett, my agent, says, as he leads me down a hallway between offices. Offices. With glass walls. Some with doors open and others with doors and blinds shut.

I glance inside one and see that there is a single desk with a single person there. Not four desks crammed inside a single cubicle to save space. There's no way that all the employees are here. They wouldn't fit.

What's happened to this place?

I try not to let myself get stuck on the changes. Of course, things have changed since I left. How many people left when I did? How many have left since then? I bet that all these people are working hundred-hour weeks to keep up the production that's expected.

I sigh, glad that I left when I did. Murray Press has strict rules on working hours. No one is ever supposed to work overtime even though we're salaried. There's a huge emphasis on work-life balance there.

Brett leads me into a conference room where three men I've never met sit. They're younger than I'd expected. No doubt, Phillip has the more inexperienced acquisitions team talking to an untried author with a single book to her name. This is almost certainly going to be a low-ball offer.

"Good afternoon, Miss Adelaide," the first one says. He looks happy, a spark in his eyes as he stands up to shake my hand. It's strange. When I started working for Loughton House, I was so nervous. Now, I'm expecting to turn down an offer from them, and I'm as calm as I've ever felt.

"My name's Charles Anderson, and this is Lewis Taylor," he says as he points to a dark-haired man in his late twenties sitting next to him. "And James Miller," he says as he points to a man with red hair, both on top of his head and in his thin beard. All of them are wearing suits that look reasonably expensive. They look professional. They're just young compared to the old men I'd expected.

"Thanks for having me," I say as I sit down next to Brett on the opposite side of the table.

Brett slides a contract to me and says, "Now, because I signed you before I started working for Loughton House, I'll refer you to a different agent after this meeting due to the conflict of interest. I needed to get you here, though, because *Sweet Temptations* is going to be the book that turns you into a bestselling author."

I frown. "What do you mean?" I'd expected to turn them down, but with the way Brett is talking, it almost seems like he's offering me a real contract. One that's too good to turn down.

Brett glances at Charles and the other two across the table, and Charles takes over the conversation. "Loughton House has created a new department for signing brand new authors. We're not able to give out as big of advances as other departments, but we're able to offer authors a lot higher percentage on their first books. After that, we'll re-evaluate things."

That's an odd way of doing business. I glance over the offer and see that Charles isn't lying. The percentage is far higher than I've seen in my research. "What's the catch?" I ask, having not read the rest of the contract yet.

"It's simple. This is a trial run. We want to minimize costs and have no desire to make any significant money on this book. But if you've written a winning book, like I think you have, then we get to renegotiate the contract for book two."

How did Phillip ever approve this plan? This isn't how anyone else does business. It's not like I'm a soccer mom from Indiana who's never dealt with the publishing industry. I know how things work, and this isn't it.

"That's not a catch, Charles. That's you publishing a book and hoping to make back the printing and marketing costs. There's a catch, though. Any time there's a deal that sounds too good to be true, it is."

Charles grins. "Read the contract. Get a lawyer and have them read it. I know it sounds too good to be true, but it's not. We're looking to expand faster than anyone in the industry ever has, and that means they're going to have some losses. But they'll also get some serious wins to offset them. Those winners are going to keep on winning, and we'll cut the losers."

I nod. It isn't real. Loughton House doesn't lose money. Ever. Arguing with Charles isn't going to do any good, though, so I might as well just do what he said. Read the contract and find how Phillip is taking advantage of new and ignorant authors.

"We love *Sweet Temptations*, Addison," Charles says. "And we're allocating significant resources to it, all of which are detailed in the contract. The advance is small, like I said, but if you sign with us, you're going to become a full-time author very soon if you keep writing like that."

It puts a smile on my face to hear them say that. I mean, it's still kind of hard to believe that complete strangers enjoyed my book this much. Angela and Donovan's love story made my heart melt even while I was writing it, but to hear other people talk about it, I feel like maybe I'm not the only one.

"I'll go through the contract, and I'll let you know by the end of the week," I say as I stand up.

They nod to me, and everyone else stands up as well. I follow them out, my mind on the fleeting hope that the contract is actually as fantastic as Brett and Charles are making it out to be. My head is down as the thoughts run through my mind. When I look up, I see the one man I'd been hoping to avoid: Phillip.

He's not even looking at me. There's a smile on his face as he walks toward Charles. The rest of the group keeps walking, and I hesitate. Do I want to see him? Do I want to talk to him?

I know the answer should be no. That's the smart answer, the reasonable answer, the "don't be an idiot, Addison" answer. That doesn't mean it's what I want.

Because I've never fallen out of love with the man. Even after the funeral, no matter what I've done, my thoughts have turned toward him.

My steps stutter. Phillip's eyes are locked on Charles, and I try not to look at him, try to let him pass me by without noticing me because although I want to talk to him, I can't. He'll suck me in just as fast as he did before.

"That's the third contract you've handed out today, right?" God, Phillip's voice washes over me like a heatwave, bringing back every memory. I mourned those memories, and I buried them in too many cups of box wine. I shouldn't remember the way he looked at me, the way he kissed me, the way he felt when I was moaning his name…

Charles glances at me, and I start to walk again, not wanting Phillip to notice me. "The first two were definite risks, but this one is the real deal, Mr. Loughton. We're going to push *Sweet Temptations* hard."

Phillip freezes and slowly turns toward me. My feet move faster, but not fast enough. "Addison?" he asks.

I turn to him and he's staring at me with those same piercing eyes. The same smoldering look that I've never been able to turn away from. "You published it?"

That's when it clicks. He knew. He's publishing my book because he wanted to talk to me. "You son of a bitch," I growl. "You promised you wouldn't touch my book. You wouldn't use your influence…"

"I didn't even know that you'd found an agent," he says, just as roughly. "I've never lied to you, and I won't now. How'd you even wind up here?"

414

He's right. He's never lied to me, and truthfully, I can't figure out how Phillip could have influenced Brett. Trish found him, and I doubt they worked together in some grand scheme. Whether he influenced things now, well… That's possible.

"I found an agent, and you bought him, so he's trying to get me to sign with you."

Charles is looking at us in complete confusion, and it cements the fact that Phillip didn't rig this. I earned the contract in my hand.

Phillip grins and shrugs. "Might need to give these two a raise since *Sweet Temptations* is going to make me a lot of money."

"Yours isn't the only offer on the table. I came into this meeting fully expecting to turn it down, since I don't have any desire to work with you."

He frowns. "Is there someone out there who's offering you more? Because I'll beat whatever it is."

I hesitate for a moment, and Phillip sighs. "You're willing to throw away your chance to be published just because it's with Loughton House? Because it's with me?"

"Yes. I'll do whatever I can, so I don't have to see you again."

I can see the pain in his eyes. I don't want to hurt him, but I need to get away from here. Every second I talk to him is another chance for him to suck me back in. And truthfully, I want to be sucked back in.

"I'm different now, Addison. Everything's different. Come with me, and I'll show you. I've turned my entire world upside down because I can't let you go. If you asked, I would set fire to Loughton House. I'd close the doors and burn the building down for you."

That takes me by surprise, and when he takes my hand, I don't pull away. "Why?" I can feel his hooks digging in already, but deep down, I want them to be there. If being with him could be like when we were living in my apartment, I'd go back to him in a heartbeat.

"Because I love you, Addison. I'll always love you. And I want to be the man you can be happy with." He leads me down the hallway that wasn't there when I worked here. "We don't have cubicles anymore. I asked the employees what they would like from their work environment, and the overwhelming winners were work-from-home and solitary offices. So I gave them the option."

I frown as I look around. "Wait, so you let people work from home? Where you can't keep track of them? Where you can't check up on them?"

He nods. "They still have deadlines they're supposed to meet. If they want to edit or make covers in their underwear at their house, they're free to do it. They send me status updates on a weekly basis, and if they fall behind, I suggest they come back into the office. It's still their choice, though.

"Other people chose to come in, and just like the work-from-home employees, they can come and go as they please. There are no watchdogs checking to see when they start or finish work. If they want to come in at ten in the morning and leave at four, that's fine by me as long as they're hitting their milestones."

He smiles at me. "But that's really the smallest change. We only had people work overtime to train the new hires. We gave everyone raises to help compensate for the temporary extra work, and now we have enough employees to cover all the projects. Everyone's left with more money for the same amount of work. In most cases, people are working fewer hours as well."

That's not what I'd expected at all. Phillip was adamant about the hours worked before. "How'd you pay for all of it? That probably cost a fortune."

He chuckles. "I paid for it. It's my project, and I'm taking the risk. It didn't cost as much as I'd expected, but I have high hopes for future profits to cover it. Addison, you were right."

He turns to me and takes my hands as our gaze meets. "About it all. From the way I was running the business to the way I was running my life. I didn't want to work like I had been. I never have. My father dropped the company in my lap, and I reverted to my old ways, but that won't happen again because I don't own the company anymore."

"What?!" Everything else has been surprising, but I could see him doing it and then reverting to the way things were before. It wouldn't change anything about the way he worked. But giving up the company? That's not something that his father would have done. Ever.

"I'm selling portions of the company to Andrew and Mason. Well, selling is kind of a stretch since the pricing is ridiculously low, but it's time that no single person has to be in charge of the whole thing. We'll run it together, and though I'm sure I'll still lead most things, the three of us will share the responsibility. None of us wants to become my father. None of us want to give up everything for a fucking business."

"But you won't make as much money, right?"

"Fuck the money. I want you. Addison, the only reason I don't just walk away from Loughton House is because I want you to have everything you could ever dream of. Even more than that, I want our children to have the best childhood they could dream of if we decide to have them. I know that may sound crazy, but leaving isn't something I could take back."

He faces me and takes my hands. Until now, I'd still been trying to back away from this. I'd been trying not to get sucked in to wanting the man that I fell so hard for.

Because he's never stopped being that man. He just didn't have time for me.

"Addison, you are the only thing that I won't give up. If you asked me to run away to a deserted island and never see another person again, I'd do it. I'd leave the company, my family, and my life. And I wouldn't regret a goddamned thing. As long as I have you, my world is complete. Without you, I have nothing. All the money in the world will never fill the hole in my heart that you left when I pushed you away."

"You didn't push me away," I mutter. I walked out.

I know exactly how he feels. I've been waking up and telling myself that my life is better without him, but I go through life like a ghost of the woman I used to be. My dreams are coming true, and I can't stop fantasizing about the days of playing house with Phillip.

"I wouldn't make you leave everything behind," I say with conviction.

He pulls me to him like he did so often before the explosions, before the fight. "I will never put you second, Addison. I want you to be mine forever, and I promise I will spend the rest of my life trying to make sure you're happier than you were the day before. Nothing and no one will ever compete with that goal. Do you understand me?"

When he looks down at me like that, when I see the absolute certainty in his eyes, I know he's telling the truth. "Addison, I promise that you are the most important person in the world. We may fight or argue because that's what happens sometimes, but I will move fucking mountains if that's what it takes to make you happy. I devoted myself to a company, and I became the best in the world in this industry in thirty years. Let me spend the next forty, fifty, or sixty devoting myself to being the best at making you smile."

"Yes," I whisper.

Instead of saying something, he leans in and presses his lips against mine. A hard, passionate kiss that rekindles the flame that has been dying inside me. His fingers run through my hair and tighten as his kiss deepens.

I remember this kind of kiss. The way it makes my body feel like it could float away, but he won't let me. Every fiber of my being is *alive* with it.

When he finally pulls away, I'm breathless, but Phillip seems more focused than I've ever seen him. "I love you, Addison. I will always love you."

"I never stopped loving you," I whisper back and know that it's the truth. There hasn't been a single day in a month that I haven't wished he was with me. I may have been following my dreams, but they don't mean anything without him beside me.

I smile up at him and say, "I'm publishing the book. You were right about that, Phillip. You were right about a lot of things, and I was just afraid."

"You don't ever have to be afraid," he whispers as his fingers brush against my cheek. "I won't let anything bad happen to you. Together, nothing can hurt either of us."

My arms wrap around his waist, and I press my cheek to his shoulder. "I didn't like being away from you."

"I hated it. Let's not do that again," he whispers in my ear, and I sigh. It's like coming home after being gone for a month. How did I ever walk away from him before?

"Never."

"You know, I think it's time you started working on another book. Maybe one set on a beach somewhere?"

I look up at him. "Why?"

"Because you'll need inspiration, and I think we both need a good reason to spend a month together, and playing on a beach together sounds like a dream come true."

A chuckle escapes my lips. He's always been the best at making me laugh. "Only if we go to all the tourist traps so I can find a new mug."

"Your wish is my command, my lady."

I can see the sparkle in his eyes, the life that had faded so much by the time we had that fight. It's how I know that this is what he truly wants. If he looked as weary as he did running Loughton House by himself, I wouldn't feel like I do.

He's as alive as he was when he rescued me from a torture room, as happy as he was when he was sleeping on my couch in a pair of too-tight athletic shorts.

I didn't know how to live with Phillip before. I was nervous about living in his house, about trying to be part of his billionaire lifestyle. But I'm not nervous now. I'm not afraid of walking that path with him.

Because it doesn't matter what kind of life we have. As long as I have the man I love, and he has me, then nothing the world throws at us will be too much.

Like he said, as long as I have him, my world is complete. Everything else is just icing on the cake.

And I'm going to enjoy every taste.

"You owe me a raincheck," I whisper, my breath teasing his neck.

He frowns, not remembering what I'm talking about, and the corner of my lip curls up. "You promised me a very special lunch date, and I'm taking you up on it right now."

Fifty-Eight

ADDISON

I DIDN'T THINK THAT PUBLISHING A BOOK WOULD BE so much work. Or involve so much travel.

Sweet Temptations has dominated the charts for the past two weeks, and I've spent every one of those days on a plane going somewhere to talk about it. Finally, two weeks after release, I get to come home.

The limo pulls away from the four thousand square feet in the heart of Manhattan, and I can't help but think that it all still feels so unreal. A year ago, I wouldn't have imagined living somewhere like this. The most I'd hoped for was an apartment that fit my books and mug collection. Maybe a few feet of closet space.

Now… Well, now things are different.

I slide the key in the door, and when I walk into the foyer, Phillip is already there. In an apron, and only an apron.

He winks at me. "I made your favorite," he says.

"I don't know what that is," I say, confused.

In a terrible fake Italian accent, he says, "Big fat sausage." Then, with a big grin, he flips the apron up and flashes me. I can't help but giggle. This is the first time I've seen Phillip in two weeks, and this is how he's decided to greet me.

"I love you." The weariness from traveling fades as I say those words. I wave to his crotch and say, "And I love you, too." When I see him smile, I ask, "Did you actually make dinner?"

He grins. "You've missed two weeks of home-cooked meals, and I couldn't think of a better way to remind my love of what she's missing at home."

"I missed a lot more than your cooking," I say as I set the suitcase down next to the closet. "You, for example."

As I walk over to him, I wrap my arms around his waist and press my cheek against his chest.

He instantly pulls away. "Ow!" he says.

I let go and frown at him. I hurt him? With a hug?

"I… I need to apologize for something I said back when I lived with you." He unties the apron and lets it fall to the floor, so he's standing naked in front of me. I don't quite understand why he did that, but I'm not complaining. "Well, I was making chicken carbonara and wanted to be naked when you got home, but when I was cooking bacon…"

That's when I see the angry red dots on his chest that have been covered in ointment. "You got bacon burns on your tits, didn't you?" I ask, unable to hold back the giggles.

"Yes. And let me tell you, bacon burns on your nipples are the worst."

"Are you okay?" I'm having a hard time not giggling even more. "I can't believe you didn't wear at least the apron. I thought you were paying attention."

He chuckles and turns toward the kitchen. "Oh, I was paying attention. Just not to anything other than your ass. Now, come eat before it gets cold."

As he walks into the kitchen completely naked, I run up behind him and grab his ass. "Hey now, you're not even going to give me a kiss? You haven't seen me in two weeks, and you care more about dinner than about kissing me?"

Phillip whirls around and puts both hands on my cheeks, holding me in place as he presses his lips to mine. There are kisses, and there are kisses that make your legs shake.

And there is no lack of quivering in me as he shows me just how much he's missed me. If I didn't know better, he'd been stressed about me being gone this entire time.

"Nothing's more important than you," he whispers.

"I was just playing," I whisper back, still trying to catch my breath.

His thumb runs over my cheek as he pulls his hands away, and I catch him breathing heavily, too.

My hand moves over his abs. "Show me to my dinner, boss. I just hope that your big fat sausage will be ready after I eat the carbonara. I've been craving it for too long."

He chuckles, and in that terrible Italian accent, he says, "It's always ready for you. Once, twice, even three times a day."

I like Phillip like this. It's six o'clock on a Friday, and he's laughing and smiling after making dinner for me. This is what I'd wanted when the two of us were playing house in my apartment for that month.

All my dreams have come true. I'm a wildly successful debut author. The man I love with all my heart is doing what he loves at work, yet he still has time to make dinner for me. He still gets to spend weekends with me.

"Go make plates. I'm starving and that smells wonderful." I can't help but stare at him as he walks toward the cabinets. He may just be the perfect man, but truthfully, I don't think I'd be happy if my life was all about him. I had that when I first moved in with him.

Now, it's not about him. It's about us. Both of us supporting each other, both of us experiencing life together. That's the real dream.

A partner in crime. A soulmate. My other half.

No matter what happens, we won't be separated. We may fight and argue, but no disagreement will ever break us apart anymore than I could split into two. That's what really changed. We were two halves, and now we've both become whole.

Phillip is mine, and I am his. And together, we're going to be happier than I could have ever imagined.

Epilogue

ADDISON

Snow is falling in the city as I hang the last ornaments on the tree. Sure, I probably should have gotten them up earlier, but I'm in the middle of writing my second book, and it's hard to walk away when I'm invested in another entire world.

The doorbell rings, and I jump. Every nerve in my body is on edge, and before I can run to the door, Phillip grabs my hand. "Calm down," he whispers, a grin on his face. "It's going to be fine."

"I know it is. But she's never visited me anywhere before. She certainly hasn't ever met a boyfriend. Now, let me go so she doesn't turn into an icicle on our stoop."

No matter what Phillip says, I'm not going to calm down until I see her. She's been the only constant in my life. Ever since Nana died, she's been the one person who I knew would never abandon me. Even if she's frustrating sometimes, she's my mom, and I want her to be proud of me.

When I open the door, she's got a smile on her face that could light up the whole block. "Addy, I've missed you so much," she says as she gives me a hug. I've missed her too.

"Come inside and get out of the cold. I made cookies and can make some coffee. I hope you like espresso."

She follows me inside, and I try to lead her to the kitchen, but she stops and just stares. "Addy, this is yours?" she says with a voice full of wonder.

I shrug. "It's Phillip's, but I've lived here for quite a while, and I don't think he's going to kick me out anytime soon."

"It's wonderful. Nothing at all like back home. I bet you've even got a big TV, don't you?"

I chuckle. "Fine, I'll give you the tour, and then we can have the cookies and coffee."

I lead her into the living room where Phillip is putting tinsel on the tree. He gives us a smile and I say, "This is Phillip Loughton, my boyfriend. Phillip, this is my mother, Lynn Adelaide."

He puts out a hand and says, "Nice to meet you, Lynn. Welcome to our home."

She takes his hand and gives it a quick shake. "Thanks for having me. You have a beautiful home." It's strange seeing my mom trying to be so proper. I'm sure that will wear off quickly enough since she's staying for a week.

"I'm taking her on the tour. Any way you could make a few cups of coffee for us?" Phillip nods and drops the tinsel back into the box it came in.

As soon as he walks out of the room, Mom whispers, "That man dodged every stick on the ugly tree when he was born, didn't he? I bet he could make some pretty babies."

Babies? That's the first topic she goes to? "Babies aren't really on our radar right now. I think we're trying to do the whole relationship process in order. You know, date, then get married, then consider babies."

"Smart," she says. "I got a little mixed up when I was playing with men. Didn't work out as well for me." She gives me a grin and says, "It looks like you two are happy."

I nod. "We are."

"Then that's what matters." She takes another look around the living room, which is bigger than the house I grew up in. "The house is a definite bonus, though. Do you know if he's got any openings?"

"Mom! You said you were happy with your job!"

She grins at me. "I am. Mostly. But if a job with your boyfriend buys a place like this, I might be willing to make a change."

I just shake my head as Phillip comes back in with the cookies and coffees. I take my cup and a cookie and look out the window at the snow that's falling even harder now. There's no question that it's Christmas Eve.

Turning back to my mom, she's settling down on the couch, a smile on her face, and I can't help but think that this is the best Christmas that I can remember.

"We're doing presents?" Mom asks.

"Yes, we are definitely doing presents," I say as I pick up two gifts wrapped in gold and red from under the tree.

She grins and says, "Good thing I brought something for you." Digging in her purse, she pulls out a small box that looks like it could be jewelry, and I frown. That'd be very unlike her.

I trade gifts with mom, and I turn around to see Phillip picking up a box that's about the size of his fist wrapped in shiny blue paper. "You have to open this one last," he says.

I look down at the box and recognize the shape and size of it. Definitely another mug. I don't know why he's making such a big deal about it, though.

"Okay. Here's yours. Merry Christmas, Phillip," I say as I hand him the box. I can't help but grin thinking about what's inside it.

We all sit down and kind of stare at each other for a moment before Phillip says, "I guess I'll open mine first."

Mom and I both turn to look at him as he unwraps the box. I'm having a hard time not giggling as the paper comes off and shows the little brown box it was shipped in.

"What is it?" he asks as he picks at the tape keeping the box closed. "It's really light. If I didn't know any better, I'd say it's a…" He opens the box and sees the tie that I spent months hunting for.

Blue and pink flowers cover the gray polyester. It's absolutely hideous, and as Phillip pulls it out of the box, he looks like he's seen a ghost. I can't help but poke him even harder. "Oh Phillip, that's going to look so good with your charcoal suit. I picked it out special for that suit."

"Umm… yeah, it matches." He unrolls it to look at just how terribly it will clash with the suit and then he sees the cherry on top. Or should I say "saffron" stain on top?

A big splotchy yellow stain covers the bottom tip of the tie, and Phillip seems to sink into the couch next to me for a moment before he frowns. "You picked this tie on purpose…"

I can't keep the laughter in anymore. "Come on, it'll match that red shirt."

"You little shit," he says as the disgust fades and he laughs.

My mom is sitting on the love seat, completely confused. Phillip doesn't leave her hanging, though. "When I first moved in with Addison, she convinced me to buy a shirt that had a yellow stain on it, and we've joked about it since then. This tie… matches it."

I add, "That's not his real present. He can buy his own ties. And on that note, your real present will have to come after we're done with presents here. We have to go visit it."

That makes him frown, but he doesn't question it.

"You next," Mom says to me, and I pick up the little box that could hold a bracelet if my mom was a different person.

"I didn't know what to get you now that you're famous, but then I remembered…" I open the box and see that there's a pen inside it. At first, I think that she's bought me a nice pen because I'm an author, and I guess every author needs fancy pens.

But then I pull it out of the box, and the whole thing lights up, and I almost drop it. "I remembered how you used to spin your pen when you sat at your desk and wrote. It was really cute when you learned to do it. I think you were probably five when you wrote your first story about a princess who fell in love with the dragon that kidnapped her."

I remember that story, and I blush a little. "You got me a light up pen to spin?" I ask.

"I doubt you use a lot of pens these days. Nobody does. But you've spun a pen when you were thinking ever since that first story, and I doubt that's going to change."

I don't know why, but the idea tickles the part of me that still thinks the princess should fall in love with the dragon instead of the stupid prince. "Thanks Mom. I love it," I say.

She gives me a smile, and I say, "But now it's your turn. Open up your present!"

Phillip and I bickered about this present for too long. I'm so excited to see her reaction.

She looks down again at the package in front of her that probably looks like a very large but thin book. With a shrug, she tears the paper, and I glance at Phillip. He's smiling. This is the first time he's ever met my mom, and this just goes to show how much he loves me.

"What is this?" she asks as she pulls out a stack of papers.

"A job offer," Phillip says.

Her head whips around so fast, I worry she's going to hurt herself. "A job offer?"

He nods. "Addison and I would like you to move to New York so she can see you more often, and that would require you to have a job. So I'm making you an offer at Loughton House. It's an actual position with real responsibilities, but it should pay more than most of the jobs you could find back home."

She flips through the pages with a frown on her face, and then the little piece of metal falls out into her lap. "A key?" she says, even more confused.

"That's to my old apartment, Mom. It's hard to find an affordable apartment in the city close enough to Loughton House. I've been paying for that apartment since I got here, so I can let you take over the lease after you get your first check from Loughton House."

"But Addison, I don't know how to live here. I've lived in that old house in Kansas since before you were born. I don't know how to ride subways or shop in a city like this."

I give her a smile. "Well, it's a good thing that I have some extra time on my hands to get you more acquainted with city life. Mom, I've missed you. And there's not a better company to work for than Loughton House. This way, you can be nearby, and you get a good job, too. We can actually spend time together this way."

And I see tears welling up in her eyes. "Addy, you're the best daughter I could ever have had. Yes, I'll move to New York and have a grand adventure."

Then Phillip chimes in. "Plus, if we have children, they'll need their grandmother here."

It's my turn to whip my head around and stare at Phillip. Children are not something that we've talked about. He just grins at me before he says, "It's your turn, Addison. Open up your present."

I can't stop looking at him, confusion all over my face as my fingers tear the wrapping off the box. What's making him think about kids? When I glance down at it, I'm sure that it's a mug. Normally, I'd be excited, but this talk of children is kind of hard to ignore.

I open the box, and it's a mug, just like I thought. White with Christmas trees on it, I lift it up to read what it says.

And nearly drop it.

"Will you marry me?" Bright red letters across the front in a cutesy font. When I look back at Phillip, he's getting down on one knee.

"Oh shit," I whisper.

He reaches into his pocket, a wide smile on his face, and he pulls out the little box. "Addison Adelaide, you transformed my life into a chaotic adventure. Every day is better than the last, and I can't imagine my life without you. Will you make me the happiest man in the world by marrying me?"

"And I thought a tie was a good gift," I mutter. He just grins. "Yes. Yes, a thousand times. I'd marry you every day if you'd let me."

He opens the little box, and inside it is a ring I'd never have expected to see. It's a simple gold ring with touches of filigree on the edges, but nothing fancy. And it looks old. Definitely not the ring a billionaire would propose with.

Did he get me a thrift store ring?

"This was my mother's ring, and though you can say a lot of things about my father, there was nothing but love between the two of them. I hope I can make you as happy as he made her."

He pulls the ring out of the box, and I put my hand out. As he slides the ring over my finger, it feels like everything in the world is right. I never thought that a ring would matter to me. It's just a little piece of gold and crystal.

But it's more than that. Today, it's more than that. It's the thing that connects us. More than words, this means that it's real.

"I love it," I whisper. Our gaze meets for a few moments, and I know that this is one of those perfect moments.

"Well, kiss the man!" my mom says from the love seat, and I can't help but laugh. Phillip laughs too, and I bend down to kiss him. That happiness is almost tangible as our lips meet. My life is perfect.

We are perfect.

When he stands up and pulls away, I say, "Now it's time for your real present."

Mom follows us as we walk down the sidewalk of Manhattan. A few blocks away from where Phillip's father has lived for almost forty years. "Why are we here?" Phillip asks.

"I had a chat with your father a month ago," I confess.

He turns to me, and I feel a little awkward with my mom listening, but it needs to be said. "You're a very hard man to buy gifts for, you know that, don't you?"

"I told you that from the very beginning."

I give him a smile. "Well, I sat down and talked to your father about what you enjoyed doing when you were growing up."

We take a corner and in front of us is an empty lot between two brownstones. Just a patch of green in a world of gray. And in the middle of it is a bench. In the corner, there's a statue of a woman and three little boys around her.

"The one thing you and your brothers all loved was coming here with your mother," I say. "He said that you used to sneak out and come here when you were a teenager."

He turns to me, shock in his eyes. "This is my Christmas present?"

"He bought this lot when you were born. He knew little boys needed grass to play in, and there weren't any parks close by. A week ago, he sold it to me."

And for the first time, I see tears well up in Phillip's eyes. "Thank you," he whispers.

I wrap my arms around him. "I love you," he whispers. "You were right. You knew what to give me, even though I didn't know it. This is the best Christmas present I could ever get."

I look up at him and say, "I'm glad." He holds me in his arms, squeezing me tight. "I was thinking, maybe when we're married, we could think about having a few kids of our own."

And it's like I'm seeing a different man. The fiery look that he's always given me is transforming into something softer. "You mean that?" he asks.

I nod. "I never thought I'd like having kids, but after talking to your father, I think I'm sold."

"I can't believe you actually talked to him."

"He's the guy you based your life on for a long time. I knew that if there was anyone in the world that would understand you, it'd be him. And he's not as scary now that he's retired. Would you believe he was playing poker on the internet?"

Phillip blinks in shock. "Look Addison, I can handle a lot of bombs in one day, but let's stop talking about the way my father's spending his retirement. I cannot think about the man who never had time for anything wasting his time playing internet poker. My brain is going to break."

I laugh, and he bends down to kiss me. "I love you, Addison," he whispers. "And thank you for the best day I can remember. And, you know, marrying me."

"I love you, too. I can't wait to get married. You can even wear your new tie."

He tries to look serious, but then he laughs. This is what Christmas should be. Spending time with the people you care about. Seeing their eyes light up. And knowing that everyone there is absolutely loved.

Because I've never felt so loved. "Come on, let's go home. The roast will be done, and then we can have an excellent Christmas dinner."

"Are Trish and John still coming?" he asks.

I nod as we walk back to where Mom's standing and smiling. "Andrew won't be here until after dinner. His and Sera's flight got delayed on the way back from London. Mason's not coming. He said he was going back to that little island in the Mediterranean for Christmas."

"Victoria's bringing a date. She's gone on a full four dates with this one, and he still hasn't shown his crazy, so we're betting on when it'll happen."

Phillip chuckles and wraps his arm around my waist. "Did you ever imagine life would turn out like this?" I say.

He shakes his head. "Never. I thought I'd be working Christmases until I died. Now… Well, now I understand what a good Christmas is."

A good Christmas is any I spend with Phillip is what I've decided. Just like every other day.

Because any time I'm with him, my life is complete.

Who knew that a series of unfortunate events surrounding the Neptune Inn could be the start of my very own romance? Maybe starting a romance with "It was a dark and stormy night…" wouldn't be such a bad decision…

Free Bonus Epilogue

Subscribe to Sylvia's newsletter to find out more about her upcoming books, deals, and why exactly she tends to write about trouble-making cats.

As a thank you, you'll get exclusive access to two bonus chapters about a little trip down memory lane. Specifically, what happens when Phillip and Addison go back to The Neptune Inn and finally get to experience The Snake Tour of America…

https://dl.bookfunnel.com/rr7yml7ybi

About the Author

Sylvia Hart Sylvia Hart fell in love with romance books at a young age (along with Richard Gere). She is decidedly against the daily wearing of corsets (bedroom wear is a totally different story), so she's decided to settle for a billionaire instead of a prince.

But not just any billionaire will do. This girl needs one that looks good in a suit and in the sheets.

Since she hasn't found said billionaire, she's decided to write about them. Cold and brooding or fiery and fierce, she's willing to explore the possibilities. But, behind every silk tie, there will always be a heart of gold. Even if he doesn't realize it from the beginning.

Join her newsletter and find out about new books first:

https://www.subscribepage.com/sh_signup1